People of the Wolf

WOLF DREAMER

In the Dreaming, he and Wolf walked side by side. Hunger did not stalk his limbs or make his head light. He walked strong, Wolf at his heels.

"There!" Wolf indicated with his nose. "You see? There to the south?" The Big Ice sparkled before them, a forbidding wall of cold and blue ice under mountains of snow. As they neared the wall, a wide, braided river spilled out of a crack in the ice.

"This is the way, man of the People," the beast's voice echoed from the walls. "I will show you the way to salvation . . ."

Moved by the promise of this awesome vision, a lone, courageous dreamer led his people on an epic journey to discover a lush, unspoiled continent for themselves and their descendants. This is a true story of those first Americans. This is the monumental saga of the

PEOPLE OF THE WOLF

Driven by the power of a dream, a handful of men and women fought to forge a path to a new land of promise and plenty . . .

Runs In Light—The young hunter who sacrificed love and power to follow a mystical vision, and came to be called the Wolf Dreamer.

Dancing Fox—The courageous young woman who endured humiliation at the hands of an aged shaman and an arrogant warrior to follow the Wolf Dreamer and lead her people to an awesome destiny.

Raven Hunter—Dark twin to the Wolf Dreamer, who defied his vision and led the People on a path of bloodshed and vengeance.

Heron—The fiercely independent medicine woman who took the Wolf Dreamer as her disciple, and taught him the secrets of her own awesome powers.

Ice Fire—War Chief of the Mammoth Clan, ancient enemy of the People, whose long-buried secret would forever alter the destiny of the Wolf Dreamer and his people.

Tor Books Presents
Kathleen O'Neal Gear and W. Michael Gear

Long Ride Home, W. Michael Gear
People of the Fire, Kathleen O'Neal Gear and
W. Michael Gear*
People of the Wolf, Kathleen O'Neal Gear and
W. Michael Gear
Sand in the Wind, Kathleen O'Neal Gear

*Forthcoming

W. Michael Gear and Kathleen O'Neal Gear

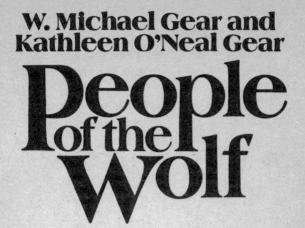

People of the Wolf

TOR®

A TOM DOHERTY ASSOCIATES BOOK
NEW YORK

PEOPLE OF THE WOLF

Copyright © 1990 by W. Michael Gear and Kathleen O'Neal Gear

A Tor Book
Published by Tom Doherty Associates, Inc.
49 West 24th Street
New York, N.Y. 10010

Cover art by Royo

ISBN: 0-812-50737-1

First edition: July 1990

Printed in the United States of America

0 9

TO RICHARD S. WHEELER
WHO HELPED MAKE
THE DREAM COME TRUE.

LAURENTIDE ICE SHEET

CORDILLERAN ICE SHEET

ATLANTIC

PACIFIC

The Route of
Migration of
the People of the Wolf

ACKNOWLEDGMENTS

In writing *People of the Wolf* we tapped a great number of resources to buttress our own professional understanding of early PaleoIndian culture. In addition to journal articles, professional reports, and reference books, we offer special thanks to the following: Stephen D. Chomko, Ph.D., Interagency Archeological Services, National Park Service, for sharing his expertise in recent developments in PaleoIndian studies; Ray C. Leicht, Ph.D., Wyoming State Archeologist, and former Alaska State Archeologist, Bureau of Land Management, for his help in reconstructing Pleistocene climatology and providing resources in arctic archaeology; George Frison, Ph.D., Department of Anthropology, University of Wyoming, for his observations on mammoth hunting in *The Colby Site*; Gary E. Kessler, Ph.D., Professor of Philosophy and Religious Studies, California State College, Bakersfield, for his invaluable lessons in mysticism and Native American religions; Katherine Cook, for her constant support and willingness to read and reread manuscripts; additionally, our professional colleagues have provided invaluable classroom discussions, conference papers, excavation reports, and, of course, so many stimulating arguments around field-camp fires where dirt archaeology takes place. You know who you are.

Additionally, a special debt of gratitude is owed our editor, Michael Seidman, whose interest in archaeology and Native American mysticism actually generated this series; to Tom Doherty who backed the project; to Tappan King who wrote in big pencil; to Wanda June Alexander for pushing so hard; and to all the talented staff at Tor Books.

Introduction

The pickup bucked and heaved as it bounced over the scraggy greasewood. Red dust whirled and puffed under the knobby all-terrain tires. In four-wheel drive, it growled and clawed its way up an eroded terrace, lining out to lurch and sway over blue-green sagebrush as it headed for the yellow equipment parked below the bluff on the other side of the flat.

The driver pulled up amidst the sweet smell of crushed sage and the bitter tint of alkali dust. Two cats, a backhoe, and a pipeline trenching machine, along with a handful of pickups, waited, engines stilled. Only the constant whisper of the wind competed with a low chatter of human voices.

The driver popped the wind-sprung door open and jumped out, stiffening his back and stretching after the long drive. Heads appeared from the pipeline trench, yellow hard hats bright against the windrowed dirt.

"You're here!" A foreman pulled himself up and stiff-armed out of the trench. " 'Bout time. You damned archaeologists are costing me money! We got to get this pipe laid by the tenth of December, and this delay's soaking up ten thousand dollars of the company's money a day."

The driver shook hands and nodded. "Yeah, well, let's see what we've got here. Old floodplain terrace like this, you won't find much. Besides, from the geomorphology, this terrace must be about fifteen thousand years old. That's the end of the Pleistocene. What you cut is probably intrusive. Some homesteader buried out here? Who knows?"

The driver reached in the truck, bending around the gearshift levers to pull out an old military ammo box and a scarred briefcase.

Together they threaded their way through the gnarled sagebrush to the trench to stare down at an area where the backhoe had peeled back the overburden. A one-man sifting screen stood propped over a conical pile of dirt.

"Dr. Cogs?" A young sunburned woman looked up.

"Hi, Anne, what'd you find?" The driver jumped down into the trench.

The young woman looked smugly at the catskinners and construction workers as she indicated a black plastic sheet over the square carved out of the backhoe trench.

"Just a solitary burial, Dr. Cogs." She wiped at a dirt-smeared face. "I was monitoring the trench through here. Thought this would be pretty dull. Then the trencher clipped an arm. Saw the distal portion of the radius and ulna in the backdirt. That's when I shut them down."

"Intrusive?" he asked, seeing the foreman cross his arms, face stiff.

"No way. She was here and got covered. Um, there's sorted gravels in the same strata she's in. If I was guessing, I'd say she drowned and got left behind in the flood."

"On a Pleistocene terrace?" he asked, reaching for the plastic.

Anne's serious response warned him. "That's right. Take a look."

Cogs, with Anne's help, lifted the protecting black plastic from the excavation. He paused, taking in the skeleton. From the pelvic bones, he could tell it had been a woman. One arm had flopped out in death. The severed bone glared garishly yellow white where the trencher bucket had taken it off.

He bent down over the skull. "Old. Only a couple of teeth in her head—and they're incisors. Can't hardly see a suture in her skull except for the squamosals. I'd say somewhere in her late sixties at least. Probably older. Look at the arthritis in her spine! Must have hurt like crazy.''

From his ammo box, he pulled a trowel and tested the gravel-laden silts the burial lay in. He chewed his lip and nodded. "All right, I agree.'' He looked up at the young archaeologist. "Caught in a flood? Sure, why not? Explains the preservation.''

"We don't find many PaleoIndian burials,'' Anne reminded.

"None from formations this old. I wonder . . .'' He began digging out around the rib cage, the trowel ringing across the gravel.

"I didn't want to take it down any further,'' Anne was saying. "Considering the age of the deposit, I thought . . . What's that?''

Cogs peeled back hard silt, using the tip of the trowel to expose something red orange. "You get any artifacts out of this?''

"One piece of weathered shell. Looked like it might have been clam. Can't say if it was associated.'' She bent closer as he reached for a paintbrush and whisked the loose dirt away, exposing a long, blood-red jasper projectile point.

"Jesus!'' he breathed. "Look at that!''

"What is it?'' The foreman and his crew jammed in to see.

"Clovis!'' Anne breathed. "A genuine Clovis burial.'' Troweling on her own, she began uncovering yet another point. "Beautiful workmanship. Look at this one, red-banded yellow chert. Exquisite!''

"That's a hallmark of Clovis.'' He studied the point as her deft hands uncovered it. "Incredible stonework.''

She nodded in elation. "That's the most beautiful point I've ever seen.''

Cogs frowned. "And an old woman carried them? Says something about the social structure. She must have been a leader of some kind. Of course after the Oregon points—''

"Hey, we gotta get this pipeline in!'' the foreman complained. "What's Clovis?''

"The first Americans. Oldest culture in North America,'' he answered, rubbing his forehead as he stared. "*Nobody's* ever found a burial like this before.''

"You're costing me ten grand a day for a damned old pile of bones? By God, I'm writing my congressman about this one. What the hell—"

Cogs breathed a disgruntled breath. "You're going to get your pipeline in."

"We are?" The man's voice had softened. He pushed his hat back on his head.

The archaeologist nodded. "We'll do some testing—um, put in some excavation squares to see if anything else is buried—but I don't think there's more here than just this one. You can see the evidence of the flooding in the pit walls." He shook his head. "Look at her right foot. See how the bone's all spurred? She broke her ankle once—years before she died. Must have hurt like sixty to walk on that. It'd never been set."

The foreman looked close. "Yeah, pretty nasty. How long for you to do that damned testing?"

"A couple of days."

"I wonder who she was. . . ."

Prologue

Fire crackled in the sheltered crevice, sparks whirling upward. Overhead, a matte black of soot had grown velvet, thick, softening the gritty surface of the rock. Along the lower walls, willow and thick dry grass broke the chill seeping from the floor. A double hanging of smoke-darkened caribou hide kept Wind Woman's arctic blasts from penetrating the cracks in the rock. In a ring around the edges, bleached skulls from Grandfather White Bear, Caribou, Wolf, and White Fox, eye sockets empty, stared at the flickering light. The clean white bone displayed odd colorful designs—symbols of shaman Power.

As the woman leaned tiredly forward, long tangles of thick black hair tumbled across her face, reflecting a bluish sheen in the fire's glow. Tenderly, she patted the decaying granite below her feet. In niches and crannies, fetishes lay bundled in drab browns of willow bark aged and tinged with smoke from sacred fires.

"I'm still here . . ." she murmured, "waiting. You didn't think I'd gone, did you?"

When no answer came, Heron settled back against the cold stone wall, grumbling irritably to herself. Once-bright designs, now faded from time and abrasion, etched the burnt sienna of her tailored hide clothing. Staring into the red shifting eye of the fire, she chanted softly, hands tracing ancient symbols of Spirit Power in the air before her. She plucked a handful of dried willow bark and dipped it in a skin water bag hung from a tripod to her right. Shaking the bark, she threw it onto the flames. Steam exploded, wood sizzling. Four times she repeated the process, warm wet smoke billowing upward to the draft hole high above.

"There," she whispered, eyes probing beyond the orange-tinged walls. "I've heard you calling. I'll find you."

Huddling over the flames, she closed her eyes, the traces of her legendary beauty barely obscured by time's hand. Through her straight nose, she inhaled four times, allowing peace and tranquillity to flow through her like morning mist in the valleys. The pungent odor of willow smoke filled her senses.

Four days she had fasted, singing, bathing in the warm waters that bubbled up from the earth, steaming in the frigid air beyond the shelter. She had sung, prayed, and purged her body of the ills of bad thoughts and wrong deeds.

But in the haze of smoky steam, still no vision appeared.

"Well . . ." she groaned. "This isn't working. I'd better try something else."

She hesitated, frightened, feeling the call. Slowly, she filled her lungs, exhaling, as she looked at the fox-hide bundle. "Yes," she whispered. "I fear your Power. Power is knowing . . . and death." Her tongue ran pinkly over tan lips.

The call came again, urgent, tugging her soul. Heron made her decision.

With trembling fingers, she lifted a second bundle from beside her and undid the layers of tanned fox hide, displaying four thin sections of precious mushroom. Each of these she passed four times through the warm willow smoke, once for each of the directions of the world. East for the coming of the Long Dark. North for the depth of the Long Dark. West for the rebirth of the world. And finally south for the Long Light and the life it brought.

Chanting, she forced her soul into the One, careful to keep from the nothingness that lay on the other side, beckoning, terrifying.

One by one, she purified the mushrooms and lifted them to her lips, slowly chewing. Bitterness stung her tongue. She swallowed and leaned back, palms propped on knees.

Before her, the smoke swirled like fog rolling in from the big salt water. Ghostly images twisted and turned, shimmering in a whirling dance.

Heron squinted her ancient brown eyes to focus in the haze. Minutes passed as she peered, forehead furrowed with the effort.

"Who . . ."

An image grew in the mist—breakers, smashing furiously against craggy black rocks. Spume hurled high to the gray skies. There, along the ebb and flow of the shore, a woman hunched, heedless of the power of the waves. With a stick, she pried mussels from the rock, dropping them into a hide sack. Overhead, gulls wheeled and dove. The woman scuttled to the side, avoiding a foamy wash of water as the surf rushed in. A crab darted away, disturbed by her movements. The woman—rich with the grace of full youth—leapt nimbly, cornering the crab, teasing it with the stick until she could artfully grasp it with long thin fingers and drop it into the bag.

Behind a towering bastion of black rock, a man crouched, watching. When the woman scurried along the retreating tide, filling her bag with the bounty of the sea, he followed.

A thick mammoth-hide belt bound his waist. From either side of a thin eagle's beak of a nose, gleaming black eyes stared. A cloak of white fox hide hung over his shoulders. Through the vision, Heron sensed the strength of his soul, throbbing, intense—a man of Power, of visions. "He Dreams—even now."

The scene shimmered, emotions billowing through the images: pain, loss of love, a longing from the very depths of his soul tangled about her. Heron reached for him, a chord from her own sorrow touched by his anguish. As she projected, something snapped, crackling along the edges of the vision like dry leaves. A feeling of parting trembled in the mists. Awed at what she'd done, Heron pulled back.

The woman on the beach stopped, head tilted, black hair blowing in the sea breeze. As a hare drawn to the gaze of a fox, she jerked around, eyes widening as the man approached, face anxious, arms spread as if to embrace her.

Fear contorted the woman's features. Desperately, she ran, seeking to dart past him, feet leaving white pocks in coarse gray sand.

He feinted and grabbed her, laughing rapturously as she screamed and beat at him with futile fists. With the hardened thews of the hunter, he threw her down, pinning her hands.

"Fight, girl! *Fight him!*" Heron spat frantically, knotting her fists.

Lost in his Dream, he avoided her thrashing legs, overpowering her until she lay under him, shivering with fear and panting. He worked her parka up over her long boots while she cried and twisted. The struggle was brief, the woman no match for the hunter's strength.

Heron shook her head as he took the woman on the sand, Power spinning out of balance in the vision.

Spent, the man stood, an absent look on his face. His fingers shook as he refastened the bindings of his long boots. Almost by chance, his eyes met Heron's as she peered through the mist. He stiffened, whispering under his breath. He looked back at the woman on the sand, horror melting his expression. Dazed, he shook his head, backing away.

As suddenly, he turned, staring into Heron's eyes with hot anger. A clenched fist raised. His handsome face twisted as he cried out, an impassioned plea in his voice, tears streaking his cheeks. Then he turned, running away, leaping rocks in his flight. His voice echoed hollowly, a howl in the fog.

Mist swirled as the vision faded into dusky obscurity.

The call came again, loud now, insistent. Heron rubbed a callused hand over her face. "It wasn't him. No . . . not him at all. Who then? Who . . ."

Reaching for willow bark, she threw a handful on the glowing coals, following the path of the call through the One.

Another vision grew in the billowing steam. The woman from the beach lay naked, her stomach child-swollen, navel protruding. Around her, other women watched, eyes gleaming in the light of a birch and willow fire. Sweat dampened the woman's brow and trickled down from between her breasts to stain the hide she rested on. She contorted, legs wide, as the other women leaned close, peering intently.

The woman gasped and cried out, breasts heaving as her water broke and pooled dark on the umber hides. One of the old ones nodded. The birth came with difficulty. The fetus emerged, red, blue, and streaked with the fluids of the womb. A striking woman bent down and bit the umbilical in two while others took the child, rubbing it dry with grasses. Heron's heart tightened with hurt as she recognized the beauty: *Broken Branch*. Clenching fists, she prayed fervently that Father Sun would curse her enemy to be buried at death, her soul locked beneath the dirt for all eternity.

Heron focused on the baby again. A shaft of sunlight filtering through a rent in the roof above danced on the child.

The woman, stomach still distended, writhed again, pushing, crying, legs twisting while two of the others held her ankles. A second child emerged, feet protruding. A crone moved to crouch over the mother, head cocked as she watched. The young woman wailed as gnarled hands reached, parting the tissues, and worked the child. The old one muttered and shook her head. Wincing, she pulled, turning the baby. The woman screamed jaggedly as the child came, gouts of blood following in a flood.

"Too much." Heron mouthed the words silently, knowing the signs. Something had torn inside. Bright blood welled over the infant as its head cleared the pelvis. Such a big child, he shrieked angrily into the new world, heedless of his mother's lifeblood where it trickled into his toothless mouth.

"Bad blood . . . bad," Heron murmured passionately, fear for the woman building in her breast.

Heron blinked as the mother's bleeding saturated the hides and her breathing stilled despite the healing songs of the old women. A slack look replaced the fevered glow in her eyes. Her legs kicked limply and stopped as her color drained with the endless crimson rush.

Boys, both of them. Hunters for the People. Careful hands stroked the second child, seeking unsuccessfully to wipe away the clinging gore, as the umbilical was bitten in two and the child placed by the first. From somewhere above, a black feather wafted down, settling beside the infant. As he squalled, his tiny fist grabbed it, twisting it in rage.

Heron studied them where they lay, side by side. One bawled angrily, blood-streaked, a raven feather in its tiny fist.

The other wiggled and kicked in the shaft of sunlight, eyes unfocused as if lost in a Dream. He blinked, wailing softly, and for a brief second, his eyes seemed to sharpen . . . seeking her beyond the mists of the vision.

"You? It was you who called?" Heron nodded, leaning back, tongue running over the gaps in her worn teeth. "Yes, you Dream, child. I see Power in your eyes. And now that I know you, I'll be waiting."

The vision broke, wisps of smoke carrying it up through the rock to the chill night beyond. Heron clenched her hands into fists, reeling from the effects of the mushroom. She staggered to her feet and wobbled past the caribou-hide hangings. Frigid night air gripped her, causing her to sink to her knees. The thick sulfur odor of the hot springs clogged her nose. She bent and vomited violently.

The voices of the mushrooms whispered in her blood, death hanging in their sultry tones as she struggled to keep the One, to allow the mushroom to fade in her veins.

As she blinked and rubbed her mouth, a wolf howled in the night, loud, piercing, tying itself to the vision.

Chapter 1

The Long Dark continued, unending, eating their souls.

Wind Woman whipped across the frozen drifts, whirling wreaths of snow into the arctic night. In her fury, she blasted the mammoth-hide shelters of the People with a gust that battered the frozen skins over the head of the one called Runs In Light.

Blinking awake, he listened to the howling gale. Around him, the others of the People huddled in their thick robes, deep asleep. Someone snored softly. Cold, so cold . . . An uncontrollable shiver made him wish they had more fat to burn in the fire hole, but it was gone. Seventeen Long Darks hadn't put much muscle on his skinny bones to start with—and famine had wasted the rest.

Even old Broken Branch muttered that she'd never seen a winter like this.

Carried on the wind, a faint whimpering came from behind the shelters. Some animal scratched for food scraps the People had long since chipped from the ice. Wolf?

Heart pounding with hope, Runs In Light traced chill-stiff fingers over his atlatl—the ornately carved throwing stick used by the People to catapult stone-tipped darts. He squirmed out from under frosty hides. Creeping tendrils of cold stroked the last warm places on his body as, bent low, he stepped silently over fur-wrapped sleepers. Even in the icy air, the stink of the shelter—occupied for months—came to his nose.

Buried under the hides, Laughing Sunshine's baby squeaked its hunger. A spear of sound, its pain reflected in Runs In Light's pinched expression.

"Where are you, Father Sun?" he demanded harshly, tightening his grip on the atlatl until his fingers ached. Then, like a seal through an ice hole, he wiggled under the crawl flap. Wind Woman rushed down from the black northwest, shoving him backward. He steadied himself against the shelter, squinting into the lighter darkness beyond. Snow crystals chittered mutedly on the packed ice.

Wolf's muffled sounds came again, claws scratching at something buried in the snow.

Runs In Light circled, following the lee of a drift, hoping Wind Woman would keep his scent from wolf's keen nose. On hands and knees, he crawled to the top of the drift and slithered over the crest on his belly. Dark against the stained snow, wolf struggled to dig Flies Like A Seagull's body from the clinging ice.

He bowed his head in sorrow.

He'd found his mother frozen in her robes a week before. Echoes of her stories would haunt his mind forever, voice warm as she told him the ways of the People. He smiled wistfully, remembering the light in her eyes as she chanted of the great Dreamers: of Heron and Sun Walker and other legendary heroes of the People. How soft and caring her hand had been as it resettled the furs around a younger and happier Runs In Light's cold face.

A bitter chill touched his soul as he saw a more recent visage of her toothless death rictus—her frost-grayed eyes.

So many had starved.

Too weak to do more than stumble out of the shelters, the People had carried Flies Like A Seagull's corpse only this far. Here, on the ice, they'd left her to stare at the skies, praying and singing her soul up to the Blessed Star People. Wind Woman had blown her stiff corpse over, snow drifting softly to bury her—until wolf came to chew her frozen flesh.

The urge to rush down over the drift, screaming his rage

and hurt, rose powerfully. He forced it back. Food, wolf was food.

Father Sun looks away when hunger forces hunter to stalk hunter. What had they done that He would punish them so?

Runs In Light took a deep breath, rising slowly to his knees, judging the distance.

Wolf stopped short, head coming up, pointed ears pricked. Willing himself to remain motionless, Runs In Light gauged the wind, waiting, hoping his hunger-robbed limbs wouldn't betray him this last time.

Wolf turned his head, sniffing, gaunt ribs working as he searched the wind, an uneasy presence leaving him wary.

Runs In Light cleared his thoughts, shifting his eyes slightly to the side. He breathed softly, relaxing, forcing gnawing twists of hunger from his consciousness. He himself had experienced that feeling of being watched, that subtle prickle of eyes upon him. For long moments he waited while wolf's nerves settled and the animal's gray nose dropped to gnaw the corpse again.

Runs In Light tensed—threw his weight into the atlatl— and watched the dart as it arced. True to the Spirit Power he'd breathed into the shaft, it caught wolf just behind the ribs.

The animal yipped—a startled leap carrying it straight up. Landing on all fours, wolf shot away into the night.

Hollow hunger voices echoed in his head as Runs In Light followed, the dark blotches of blood on the snow. He stopped, dropping to one knee. Weakly raising his atlatl, he pounded the stain to chip it loose. With a mittened hand he lifted a bit of red-splotched snow, sniffing. Gut blood, it carried the pungency of severed intestines. Burning blood, it would slow wolf, bring him to an eventual stop.

From blood smear to blood smear, he worked out the trail, growing uneasy as the distance stretched between him and camp. Wind Woman's breath shifted across the land, blowing snow to fill his tracks. The eyes of the Long Dark lay heavy and menacing upon him.

He gazed upward, murmuring to the spirits, "Leave me alone. I must find wolf. Don't eat my soul . . . don't. . . ." The drain on his soul abated, but the presence clung in the air, floating, waiting to see if his honor proved worthy.

In the lee of a drift, he studied the tracks. Wolf had stopped here and even lain down for a short while. A blacker patch of blood stained the snow.

Runs In Light's fingers trembled inside the heavy mittens as he used a stone dart point to carefully pry the frozen blood from the ice. Heedless of the wolf hair sticking to it, he chewed, grimacing at the gut-juice taste. Food. The first he'd enjoyed in four days.

Four days? The Dreamer's number. His mother had told him that. A day for each of the directions to bring the soul awake.

He stood, slowly scanning the landscape, whispering, "You're here, wolf. I feel your spirit close."

In the Long Dark, the white waste gleamed deep blue, shadows of purple creeping along the drifts. To the north, the land undulated, jagged peaks shining starkly in the light of the Star People above.

Eyes to the snow, he clutched his weapons: two darts, both as long as he was tall, and his atlatl, blessed by the blood of mammoth and Grandfather White Bear. He shuffled ahead, pace just fast enough to keep warm. Hunger stalked his rubbery legs as he stalked his prey.

Wind-sculpted snow wavered, shimmering in his tear-blurred eyes. How long since he'd slept? Two days?

"Dream Hunt?" he muttered hoarsely, wondering at the unreal sensations; hunger and fatigue played with his mind and senses. He staggered, dazed by his swirling balance.

"I must catch you, wolf."

The soul eaters of the Long Dark drifted closer, eerie whispers haunting his ears. He clamped his jaw tightly, crying, "The People need meat. Hear me, wolf? We're starving!"

An age-cracked voice murmured in Light's shifting memory, "Sun Father's losing his strength. Cloud Mother wraps herself around Blue Sky Man and sucks up his warmth." The old shaman, Crow Caller, had blinked, one eye black, the other white with blindness as he told the People of coming famine.

Seeing only snow, the aged leader had prophesied, "This year mammoth will die. Musk ox will die. Caribou will stay far south with buffalo. The People will wither."

And it was so. The melting time during the Long Light had barely lasted through one turning of Moon Woman's face. Then Cloud Mother had covered the skies. Constant rain and snow raged out of the north to kill the Long Light. Cold lay heavy on the land when the grasses, willows, and tundra plants should have grown tall to feed mammoth.

Crow Caller spent his time singing, praying for a Dream. The old shaman trapped Seagull once and twisted his neck four turns. The limp bird in his callused brown hands, he'd sliced through the down feathers with an obsidian blade to expose the guts. He'd peered, his one good eye gleaming, to see what news Seagull brought from so far out among the floating ice mountains on the great salt water to the north.

"Back," he had croaked. "We must go north . . . back the way we came."

The People had looked at each other anxiously, remembering the ones who pursued them, the ones they called the Others: mammoth hunters like themselves, but men who murdered and chased the People from the fertile hunting grounds to the north. Could the People go back? Could they face those fierce warriors?

Once—so the elders told—the People had lived on the other side of the huge mountains to the west. There, Father Sun had given them a wondrous land of rivers abounding in grassy plains rich in game. Then the Others had come, driving them from the land, pushing them north and east against the salt water. Father Sun, in his wisdom, had given them a new land at the mouth of the Big River where they could see the Big Ice extending out into the salt water. The Others had followed, pushing the People away from the lush hunting grounds at the mouth of the Big River, pushing them down this last long valley, ever to the south. Now the ground rose, the mountains hemming them from the west, the Big Ice encroaching from the east. What was left? And behind the Others continued to push, forcing the People ever higher into the rocky hills devoid of game.

So the elders debated while the People worried. Was there enough game in this high rocky country where little grass grew for mammoth and caribou? What would the People do?

And then the young hunter called One Who Cries had run into camp, calling to all that he'd found three dead mammoths. So they'd talked. Against Crow Caller's judgment, the People had gone farther south to butcher the giant beasts, eating their way into the carcasses while the Long Dark grew longer over their heads, chasing Father Sun to his southern home.

Crow Caller grumbled and growled, tormenting them, saying that hunger would be their punishment for disobeying Seagull's oracle.

"A mouthful of food is worth more than an earful of shaman's words," Runs In Light had told himself. And the People had stayed, splitting even mammoth's small bones for what marrow remained. They stretched the heavy hides over piled stones and propped them up with split mammoth long bone and curved tusks. But mammoth no longer came to Crow Caller's chanted prayers. Musk ox and caribou stayed far to the north near the great salt water.

Despite the protests of old Broken Branch, the People had eaten the dogs. First the pack dogs were turned into stew. Finally, in desperation, the bear dogs were dispatched and dropped into boiling bags—a sure sign the People were near catastrophe.

Men and women hunted, finding nothing but darkness and ice. Grandfather White Bear killed Throws Bones and dragged him away into the darkness to eat.

And the People starved.

Wind Woman tugged Runs In Light's furs, pushing him toward the land of the Big Ice and Father Sun's home: south— ever south. Even now, Wolf ran that direction—away from the shelters of the People and into the unknown where even Crow Caller feared to go.

"Crow Caller," he whispered, gut tightening. The cursed old shaman had taken Dancing Fox for a wife—knowing she despised him. But who could deny a shaman of Crow Caller's power?

It had been a winter of sorrow. Runs In Light had lost so much, his mother and even the woman who made his heart sing. He blinked, shaking his head. Dizziness swept over him; he fought for balance.

"A little longer," he muttered to the Soul Eaters of the Long Dark. "Just give me a little longer."

Hungry . . . too hungry. The People insisted the hunters be fed first. People without strong hunters died. Still, he had cheated—given his share to Laughing Sunshine. Her milk had dried up and her baby wailed pitifully. Yet if he could find wolf, she could feed it again.

Runs In Light gulped icy air, cold tingling through his shivering body. His mind slowed its wheeling. He continued his shuffling pursuit on leaden legs, knowing wolf lurked close, angry, unwilling to die peacefully.

His foot slipped on slanted ice. He fell hard, grunting, light-headed again. Pushing himself up, he dusted the snow away and looked to his weapons, resettling the long dart into the hook in the end of the atlatl.

Mind tumbling, for a moment he tried to remember why he'd left the safety of the shelters. "What was I . . . ? Ah . . . wolf." He concentrated on his prey, frightened by the lapse.

Again he bent to the tracks. For weeks the People had been living off mammoth's hide, cutting apart—section by section—the very roofs over their heads. By the hour they gnawed frozen skin, having no fire to boil it soft.

He stumbled, almost falling. As he struggled to stay erect, he saw movement from the corner of his eye. He spun sluggishly. Too late.

A cornice collapsed under wolf as he leapt, blood-weak, from the crest of a drift. Wolf crashed down, rolling out of control in a cascade of powdery snow, snarling his hatred and fear; he knocked Runs In Light sprawling.

He scrambled to his knees to face wolf.

"My brother," he sang softly, "let me kill you. The People starve. Bless your soul to our use. We are worthy of your—"

Wolf bounded forward. By instinct, Runs In Light rolled away as strong jaws snapped for his leg.

The beast panted hoarsely, frozen puffs hanging in the air. Head lowered, yellow eyes squinted, he bared his teeth.

Runs In Light stood, edging around. The bloody fletched dart shaft poked out of wolf's side, flopping loosely with each labored breath. Blood dripped from the torn wound and soaked wolf's coat, freezing in stringers.

Why do I feel no fear? Wolf faces me with hate in his eyes.

We are both hungry. Maybe starving makes men and wolves fools?

Wind Woman howled through the frozen darkness. A gentle dusting of snow glistened in the light of the Star People as it settled over them. Wolf's growl steamed out in a vaporous cloud.

"Wolf . . . I'm sorry. Father Sun has truly forgotten us when we must eat each other. Where has caribou gone? Where is mammoth?"

The beast's head lowered; for the first time, Runs In Light noticed the froth of red building on wolf's mouth. The tumble down the drift must have driven the dart deeper to wound a lung.

Wolf's limbs trembled in sudden weakness. The beast charged, but his feet lost their grace. He weaved, strained breath a tearing sound over the whimper of the wind. Clumsy, the animal stumbled, falling.

"Forgive me, brother," Runs In Light sang, arms lifted to the night sky. "I send your soul to the Star People. Your flesh will make my people strong. You are brave, brother wolf."

With all his power, he drove a long dart through wolf's shoulder, using it like a spear. Wolf yipped in pain, kicking violently as Runs In Light struggled on the end of the shaft. Then the big animal quieted, fierce yellow eyes staring vacantly at the snow.

Runs In Light sagged, looking up at the Star People overhead. "Thank you, wolf. Father Sun, are you listening?" he shouted resentfully. "Wolf has just given his life to save your people. *He* cared about us."

His hands shook as he sliced the gut cavity open, releasing a rising puff of steam. It swirled around, caressing his head in the warm odor of blood. He tore the heart loose and gratefully sucked the life-hot blood from it. With the razor-sharp points of his darts, he cut the thick heart muscle into strips and choked them down, almost enjoying the sudden cramps twisting his stomach. The acrid unpleasantness of wolf-taste filled him—Power in its own right.

Wolf's strength coursed through his body. A warm feeling spread along his limbs like ice melting at the dawn of the Long Light.

Softly singing a spirit song, Runs In Light turned to the high drift wolf had tumbled down and began pawing into the crusted snow. Within minutes, his skilled hands had hollowed out a shelter.

Looking to the night sky, he shouted, "Get away! I've shown honor! You have no claim on my soul. Go! Leave me alone!"

The malignant powers of the Long Dark pulled back, respecting him and his courage.

Praying Grandfather White Bear wouldn't find him, he pulled wolf's carcass up to block most of the entrance from Wind Woman's seeking fingers and curled into a ball, dropping into an exhausted sleep.

The long hunger mixed with fatigue, while the strength of wolf's blood warmed his stomach to run strong in his veins. The Dreaming swept in from the blackness of slumber, catching him off guard with its strength.

In the Dreaming, he and Wolf walked side by side. Father Sun no longer hid behind Cloud Mother. Here, in the Dreaming, hunger didn't ravage his limbs or make his head light. He walked strong, Wolf in a swinging gait at his heels.

"There!" Wolf indicated with his nose. "You see? There to the south?"

Runs In Light lifted a hand to shade his eyes from the searing glare of Father Sun's rays on packed snow. He looked, seeing what Wolf saw. The Big Ice sparkled before him, a forbidding wall of cold and blue ice under mountains of snow. Water ran from the huge wall, carrying gravel and rocks out into the light before freezing into odd shapes in the frigid air. The massive wall crackled, groaned, and squeaked before him.

No wonder Crow Caller feared it. Runs In Light swallowed as he and Wolf trotted closer.

As they neared the wall a wide braided river spilled out, glacial cobbles stacked and piled in the broad valley as the ice retreated from drainages and hills. They walked along the crystal waters, Runs In Light seeing salmon and char—red with the spawn—fighting their way up the river while grayling darted here and there.

"Through here," Wolf whispered. Together, they scrambled along a giant crack. Looking up, Runs In Light could see Blue Sky Man far above in a jagged line where the ice had been sundered. Then he walked in darkness. Black, eternal, the night closed around him. Only his fingers tracing Wolf's coat reassured him that his soul hadn't been forever buried.

After a time, a pinpoint of light twinkled, growing ever stronger. The walls spread wider, allowing more of Blue Sky Man's expanse to become visible. Fear slipped away like caribou's winter coat in spring. For a long time, they ran through blue shadow, gravel crunching and shifting under their padded feet, until at last, a ridge of water-smoothed boulders blocked the way.

Wolf jumped lightly from each, turning at the top to stare down over his shoulder. Wind Woman ruffled his long gray-white fur with her fingers.

"This is the way, man of the People," the beast's voice echoed from the walls. "I show you the way to salvation. I should've come here first. I wouldn't have needed to chew on Flies Like A Seagull and you wouldn't have shot me. Now, take my flesh. Eat it and grow strong so you can come this way . . . this way. . . ."

Wolf jumped from rock to rock, bushy tail catching the silver sunlight as he balanced and disappeared over the top of the ridge in a flying leap.

Runs In Light chewed his lip, sudden loneliness closing around him where he stood in the pale blue shadows of the ice-piled rocks. He followed, attacking the rock. Pulling himself slowly up, he flopped a knee to lever his straining body. Bracing off the polished surfaces of granite, he climbed higher, higher.

Father Sun bathed his face with light as he sweated his way—lungs heaving—to the top of the ridge. Half-blinded, he looked out and sucked in a sudden awed breath. Thick grasses waved under the caress of Wind Woman. Brown hair shining, Mammoth turned, raising his head, trunk curling up around ivory white tusks to sniff the air. Caribou snuffled, antlers nothing more than nubs under a new growth of velvet. Musk Ox pawed, dropping his nose to present horns in his age-old defensive posture. Far out into the grass, Wolf ran, greeting Fox, and Weasel, Crow, and others.

Runs In Light smiled, opening his arms so Father Sun could beat life into his veins. Below him, Grandfather Brown Bear rolled on his back in the grass, grabbing his toes before tumbling sideways to shake his silky coat in the brilliant light. Long-horned buffalo grazed, tails flipping nervously on their short-haired rumps. Moose stood in the wallows, moss hanging from antlers as he ducked his head to search for tender water plants.

"*This* is the land of the People," Runs In Light whispered. "This is where Father Sun lives. His home in the south. Wolf, bless you for showing me this way. I will bring the People here . . . and together, we will sing our thanks to you."

He turned, reluctant to leave such a land behind him. The climb down into the blue shadow behind the ridge sucked up his energy, leaving him cold and tired by the time he reached bottom.

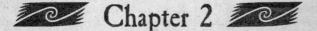

Chapter 2

A strong gust of wind battered the rock cairn, lancing through the frozen black rock. Ice Fire huddled in his double-layered caribou-hide parkas, arms crossed where he squatted in the protection of the rock pile.

Despite the wind-spawned ground blizzard that obscured the land in a white haze, he could see up through the wispy tendrils of snow, clearing his mind, letting his eyes catalog the myriad of stars. Snow rustled over the rock, sifting down around his long-booted feet in a fine powder.

Ice Fire, Most Respected Elder of the Mammoth People, ran his tongue over the remains of his teeth. The new gap was unfamiliar where the first upper left molar had fallen out. Only the right side of his mouth could still chew. He traced the ridges on the backs of his upper incisors and watched the stars.

"So many years," he whispered to the sky, "I've been alone. Why have you taken all I ever loved? Great Mystery above, what do you want from me?"

Only the ceaseless wind whistled and hissed. He listened, hoping for a voice, for a vision to form from the blowing snow rippling out of the endless plains, blotting out this terrible year.

He shuffled, an angle of rock cutting into his back as he looked to the north. The drawing unease still nagged at him. How long ago? Almost two tens of fingers since he'd first traveled there, following the call. Now it had begun again, only calling him south this time, leaving him sleepless, like this night. A subtle tugging, it worried the fringes of his thoughts, driving him to leave the warm mammoth-hide lodges of the White Tusk Clan to climb the heights and sit, and watch, and wonder while he waited.

The Enemy lay there. The Enemy whose land they now hunted. The Enemy who never fought—but abandoned their possessions and fled ever south. He sniffed. Where did a warrior find honor in such as them? How would the White Tusk Clan ever gain the distinction of cherishing and protecting the Sacred White Hide, his tribe's power totem, while war raged among the other clans in the far west?

"We must force these cowards to fight us."

Ice Fire rubbed an ice-encrusted mitten across his nose, leaning his head back to look up at the snow-misted stars. The Hide was the most valued sacred object of the Mammoth People. It had been taken long ago: the skin of a white mammoth calf, carefully tanned. The history of the clans, the symbolism of the directions, and the ways of earth and air and water and light had been delicately drawn around the Hide's symbolic heart area. The picture had been drawn with blood ritually poured from the heart of a freshly killed mammoth. Without the Hide, the people would starve; Mammoth would no longer hear them. They would die, blown away like so much down from a snow goose's breast.

Weary, Ice Fire let himself relax, warm in his robes, comfortable but for the cramp in his aging knees and the rock gouging his back.

As always on lonely nights such as this, the memory of the woman on the beach returned to haunt him. Such a beauty.

He'd been so sure she'd called him to that lonely place—part of the vision, of the Dream of pain left by the death of his wife. Perhaps she had. In the vision, she'd given herself to him, led him to love her, to lose himself in the embrace of her soul. Then the Watcher had interfered, changed it all. The vision had been jerked away—leaving him to stare in horror at what he'd done. Power had been misused. Future and past sundered. What might have been good had changed into something terrible. The Watcher had been there, her presence as tangible as hunger or thirst . . . or pain.

He'd run then, appalled at what he'd done to the woman he'd sought to love. In vain, he'd climbed the high places, seeking the Great Mystery's explanation, calling angrily into the night to confront the Watcher—all to no end.

"I am only your tool!" he hissed to the sky. "Why have you used me so, Great Mystery above? What am I to you, when I would only be a man? Why have you cursed me? Left me childless when all I wanted were sons?"

He closed his eyes, shaking his head. The wind lulled him, the snow settling in the crevices of his parka, lining the breath-frosted fur of his hood.

The pull of the new land strengthened, and in his exhaustion, he allowed himself to be drawn, southward, ever southward. Like smoke from a green dung fire, he drifted over the land, seeing, feeling, hearing the spirit and soul breathed up from the rock, dirt, and tundra steppe below. For a time he exalted in a total freedom, a light airy joy of broken bonds and unrestricted bliss.

Then a young man stood before him, blocking him. He rose from the rocky hills, feet braced, dressed in the manner of the Enemy, wearing a White Bear's hide, glowing eyes of a Dreamer.

"Move, man!" Ice Fire ordered. "You're in the way of the White Tusk Clan. In the way of my people."

"What do you seek?"

"What I was destined to find. The way for my people. The sons I would have borne."

The young man cocked his head. "You already have sons. Your destiny awaits—if you'll take it. Your sons are your destiny. Which will you choose? Light or Dark?" He lifted his hand.

The vision of a beautiful woman molded in the clouds, her hair blowing in the wind.

The tall youth spoke. "She is Light. Choose her and you and yours will pass this way." He lifted his hand, blowing across his open palm, and from it sprang a rainbow, arching across the sky, dimming even the colorful bands of Light that the Great Mystery played over the northern heavens. The young man pointed to a dark cloud. "Choose Darkness, and you will all die."

"I said, move! We'll crush you beneath us, despite your magic," Ice Fire gasped to hide his fear. "We won't tolerate this Dreaming, this magic of your kind. The Great Mystery will see to that. Our darts are stronger than your Dreams—your Watchers. Don't play with us, man of the Enemy. We'll break your people like a dry willow twig."

The young man smiled. "Is that what you seek? To destroy? That is your choice?"

"No," Ice Fire rasped, a desperate tingle of fright winding up his spine. "I seek my sons, the destiny of my people, possession of the Sacred Hide."

"And what would you give?" The youth's eyes twirled like lights in his head.

Ice Fire swallowed. "I . . . anything."

"Give me your son? I will pay you back in kind. A son for a son. A victory for defeat. Life for death."

"But I—"

"Do you agree? Will you trade what is yours for what is mine?"

Confused, Ice Fire opened his mouth. Involuntarily, he mumbled, "I would . . . if it—"

"Then it shall be." And the young man turned, shimmering, dropping to all fours, arms and legs multiplying until he'd become a red spider. Turning, the beast raced up the rainbow, slowing near the top. There, it turned, spreading its legs, spinning the colors of the rainbow across the heavens until they wove themselves into a web connecting the dewdrops of stars.

Ice Fire jerked awake, squinting into the darkness, windblown snow still streaming by in endless wreaths. He winced, legs numb from sitting so long. Gasping, he stood, feeling the sting of blood revitalizing his numbed limbs.

As he looked up at the snow-glazed stars, he found the shape of the spider there, hanging, waiting, watching.

"Then it shall be," he whispered, still seeing the vision. A pain settled under his heart. "A son for a son?" The old lines of misery resettled around his mouth. "I have no son to begin with. Great Mystery? Am I your toy again? To be thrown about like a fish-bone doll? Have you no other man to soak in sorrow?"

Limping from the blood tingles in his leg, Ice Fire climbed out of the cairn, hobbling slowly down the hill to the conical mammoth-hide shelters dotting the plain below.

Far to the south, Runs In Light blinked frosty lashes, wondering at the strange elder of the Others, the man he'd talked so blithely to in his Dream.

Where had his words come from? What did it mean? He wouldn't speak so to an elder. A frown etched his brow. And this business of peoples . . . and sons?

He shuffled in the blackness, hearing his parka scuff on snow, startled for a moment until he remembered where he was . . . the Dream Hunt. Curiously, he reached out, feeling the reassuring touch of Wolf's hide.

So many Dreams. Frightened, he stared into the darkness. "I'll go south with you, Wolf. But, man of the Others, who are you? Why did you seek me? How can I, Runs In Light, trade you a son?"

Chapter 3

Dancing Fox pulled the last scraps of leather tightly around Laughing Sunshine's dead baby, covering the tiny colorless face for the last time. She exhaled slowly. She was a beautiful woman with an oval face, high cheekbones, and flashing black eyes as wide and round as an owl's. She gritted her teeth in a mixture of anger and hurt as she fumbled stiffly to shove a bone awl through frozen leather.

"Curse this—"

"What?" Sunshine asked shakily.

"I was talking to the hide. It's frozen so solid I can hear the ice crystals crunching as the awl wiggles through them."

"Hurry, please," said Laughing Sunshine, "I can't bear this."

Laying the baby in her lap, Dancing Fox quickly pulled her hand up into her sleeve and used the hide cuff as a cushion beneath her fist as she forced the awl through the leather. A dull crackling sounded as the hide gave way. Placing the awl in her teeth, she worked the last segment of sinew through the hole and drew it tight, sealing the tiny face in the hide sack.

So many dead. Has the Long Dark eaten all our souls? Have light and life left the whole world? She rubbed her gaunt belly, fearing Crow Caller's seed might have taken root in her womb. Her bleeding hadn't come in the last two moons—but then hunger did that to a woman.

Across from her, Laughing Sunshine moaned to herself, rocking back and forth on her heels, a grimace tightening her triangular face and beaked nose. With a flake of stone she'd struck off one of Singing Wolf's cores, she cut at the skin of her gaunt cheeks until blood ran hotly. Then she turned the sharp edge on her hair, cutting it short to the collar, letting long black strands fall onto the frozen, stained ground.

"Sunshine?" Dancing Fox called softly, tying the death knot on the baby's sack. The child's haunted blue face hung heavy in her mind, like oil smoke on a cold morning. She held the sack out for the mother to take, but Sunshine only shook her head bitterly.

Dancing Fox laid the baby in the crook of her left arm and with her right reached out to squeeze Sunshine's shoulder. "Stop this," she ordered softly. "You're using up strength you need to live."

"Maybe I don't want to live," Sunshine whimpered, dropping her bloodied face into her hands. "All my children have died this Long Dark. I—"

"Hush! Of course you want to live. There can be other babies. You aren't so old you can't—"

"Doesn't anyone Dream anymore?" Sunshine wailed hysterically, slamming her fists repeatedly into the frozen floor. The dull thudding stabbed bitterly at Fox's heart. "What's happened to us? What are we doing here, starving to death? Has Father Sun abandoned us to the spirits of the Long Dark?"

"It may be," Dancing Fox said bitterly. "But I plan to go on living just to spite Him. And I'm going to drag you along with me. Now stop torturing yourself. We have duties to perform."

Sunshine wiped her eyes, whispering, "Is your heart as empty as your belly, Fox? What has Crow Caller done—"

"Done?" she asked reflectively, pain smoldering in her breast at the mention of her husband's name. She lowered her eyes to scowl at the floor. "He's made me stronger."

"You mean half-human. You used to be kind and—"

"Kindness is for the living," she said, pushing the door flap open. Cold splashed into the shelter, wind flapping their fur hoods. "The dead don't need it anymore."

Sunshine cocked her head curiously. "But my little girl's spirit can still hear—"

"There aren't any spirits."

"You . . . Of course, there are. What do you think makes—"

Fox shook her head vehemently. "No, there aren't. I've been praying to Father Sun and the Monster Children for two moons to—"

"Since you married Crow Caller?"

Fox let the flap drop closed and nodded tightly. "They haven't answered a single prayer."

Sunshine blinked away her tears, swallowing hard. "Maybe his Power prevents them from hearing you."

"Maybe."

"So they might still exist," she said pleadingly. "And my little girl can hear."

"Of course." Dancing Fox nodded, shame at her insensitivity reddening her cheeks. She fumbled with the death sack, stroking the covered head. What did she think she was doing, undermining her friend's last hope? "I didn't mean it," Sunshine. Of course she can hear."

"I know you didn't." Sunshine smiled consolingly, patting Fox's arm. "You're just hungry and tired—like the rest of us."

They exchanged a tender smile and crawled beneath the flap out into the faint gray light. Dancing Fox's legs quivered weakly as she got to her feet. Straining, she helped pull Laughing Sunshine up.

Crow Caller stood a short distance away, his withered features contorted with irritation. His aged flesh hung in sagging wrinkles. On one side of his hawk nose glittered a deadly black eye—the other stared white-blind, lifeless. His thin-lipped mouth held no humor—no feeling for another tragedy of death. Lifting his hands, he immediately began singing, ancient voice wavering up and down the scale as he sang the death song by rote, calling the Blessed Star People to accept this baby among them—even if it had no name.

Of course they hadn't named it. The People wouldn't name a baby until it passed five Long Darks to prove it would live. Until that time, a baby was an animal anyway. It didn't turn human until it learned to talk, and think, and began to become one of the People. That's when a human soul would come—during a Dream—and find a home in a child.

Singing Wolf, Laughing Sunshine's husband, strode forward to embrace his wife and take the child from Fox's arms. He laid the baby in Sunshine's reluctant hands. One by one the People lifted the frozen flaps of their shelters and stumbled awkwardly to their feet. Some swayed, dizzy from hunger.

The People were tall and straight, their skin browned in the snowy glare. Squint lines had been etched tight around their eyes and mouths, a legacy of sun, wind, and storm. Wide lips meant for laughter had grown thin, futility gleaming behind pain-sharpened eyes. Wind Woman's fingers caught their tailored furs, old grease stains shining blackly in the grayness. Against the subdued light, they looked soft and rounded in their mounds of hides, a people as worn as the polished glacial cobbles they camped on.

In a solemn line, they walked, all singing, following Sunshine as she plodded unsteadily around the ice-packed shelters to the drifts beyond. She started up a slope, kicking footholds in the white crust. Stumbling, she nearly dropped her child. Hugging it to her breast, she took a deep breath, and continued.

Following haltingly in her footsteps, the People crossed to the other side. Here and there the dead lay visible, parts of their bodies twisting gruesomely from the snow. The old had died first. In the early days they had quietly wandered out into the vast wind-ripped wilderness to die alone, as was their right. Later, as strength failed, the elderly had frozen in their robes, refusing to eat.

Sunshine placed the baby on the top of the drift, dropping to her knees, sobbing her anguish. Around and below her, the People sang, voices raised in the song of death, hoping to send the nameless infant to the Star People.

Crow Caller raised his hands, turning to look at them. "It was only a girl!" he shouted. "Let's get this over with quickly so we can get back to the shelters."

Sunshine's cries halted abruptly as she turned her swollen eyes to stare imploringly at the old shaman.

Dancing Fox lifted a brow, anger searing her breast when she saw the devastated look in Sunshine's eyes. "Shut up, husband," she murmured in a low voice that shook. "Any child is precious."

"Are you so anxious to have me fill you that you'll take any result? Keep your mouth—"

"Hardly."

He jerked around to glare at her. "Brave, eh? I ought to curse your womb so you'll never give birth."

"Would you?" she responded spitefully. "I'd be grateful."

A low murmuring eddied through the gathering, people frowning at Fox's defiance. A young woman didn't speak so to an elder—especially if he was her husband. As Fox glanced at the condemning eyes, a tingling invaded her stomach. She'd tried all her life to obey the rules. Why could she never quite manage?

Crow Caller lifted his chin slowly, rage gleaming in his one black eye. He stabbed a mittened hand toward her. "You see? Evidence that women are less than nothing—dirt useful only for growing a man's seed."

"It's true," the youth, Eagle Cries, wailed from the back of the gathering. "Everyone knows it. Let's hurry and get back to the shelters!"

"Listen—" Crow Caller began.

"You fools," a fragile old voice interrupted, resounding from the last shelter. "Who do you think wiped your butts when you were babes? Who wiped your tears when you were frightened? Eh, your fathers?"

People turned, watching pensively as Broken Branch, the oldest member of the band, struggled from beneath the heavy hide flap to hobble forward. Brittle gray hair stuck out at odd angles from beneath her arctic fox hood. The nostrils of her preposterously sharp nose flared; her ancient brown eyes squinted in what everyone recognized as utter disdain. The People faded back, clearing a path for her.

When she reached the top of the hill, she gazed down at the crowd menacingly, pinning each man with an evil stare. A few puffed out their chests defiantly, most dropped their gazes to show respect.

She waved a hand as though dismissing all of them. "What are you doing arguing when a member of our clan is dead?" Wind Woman accented her words by gusting ferociously over the drifts. People grabbed each other to steady themselves. "You ought to be thinking about how we can keep anyone else from dying!"

"Yes," Crow Caller spat, eyeing her askance. "We must leave here. Death stalks each of us—"

"Don't agree with me, you old fake," Broken Branch accused.

Crow Caller's eyes lit with rage. "I have the greatest Spirit Power among the People!" he yelled, shaking a fist in her face.

"So you keep telling me."

Dancing Fox took a step backward as her husband bellowed like a wounded caribou bull. "Don't challenge me, you old witch! I'll curse your soul so it never reaches the Star People. I'll see you buried—locked in the ground forever—to rot in darkness."

The people backed away from Broken Branch.

"We're leaving here tomorrow!" Crow Caller nodded to himself.

"Leaving?" Singing Wolf asked, hand playing over his wife's unfeeling head. "I've hunted . . . and seen no game. If we starve to death sitting . . . won't we starve faster walking? Worse, in hunger, we've eaten our dogs. Everything must be carried on our backs."

"If we go . . ." One Who Cries added thoughtfully, "we'll leave a string of dead. You expect these old ones to keep up? And which way will we go?" He raised a hand to augment his flat-faced expression. "Where is mammoth? Where is caribou?"

"Maybe we were supposed to come here," Singing Wolf cried passionately over his wife's renewed sobbing. "You're the Dreamer. Do something. I'm tired of watching my children die. Go back? But behind are the Others. If we go back . . . they'll kill us. Maybe if we go further south, we'll—"

"We *can't* go south," Crow Caller rasped, his ancient face lined and sagging under the pull of hunger. With his one good eye, he searched their faces, disturbed by Broken Branch's flinty squint. "My father's father went there." His fur-lined parka hood flapped around his white-streaked black hair. "He found a wall of ice higher than men can climb. Higher than seagull can fly. Eagle can fly that high . . . but nothing else. They hunted—"

"How do you know it's higher than a man can climb?" Broken Branch ran a sleeve across her running nose and taunted, "Eh? Did your grandfather try?"

A hush descended, Laughing Sunshine's wailing silenced by the challenge to the People's greatest shaman.

Crow Caller's face crimsoned. "He didn't have to. He could look at it and know—"

"He was a coward," said Broken Branch. "The People knew it then . . . and we see it in you now. You go back north if you want. Let those Others kill you." She waved a mittened hand to the gray horizon. "But I'm going south. Heron went out there someplace. Now there was a *real* Dreamer! She'd make—"

"What?" Crow Caller ridiculed. "You'd follow a witch? A wicked Spirit who sucks men's souls and blows them out into the Long Dark? Besides, she's just a legend. Like smoke blowing around your doddering mind."

"Bah! What do you know? *I knew her!*" the old woman spat. "She went south seeking Spirit Power to—"

"Then go!" Crow Caller shouted, nodding at the crowd. "This old hag deserves death. She's no good to the People. She's too old to hunt or fish. Her womb has gone as dead as her mind. *She can't even Dream anymore.*"

Murmurs swept the wastes, faces hardening. Unable to Dream? A sign the spirit world had abandoned a person. The old shaman straightened, gloating. Hesitant eyes flickered back and forth, watching, waiting.

Broken Branch lifted an eyebrow. "Well, that makes me more fortunate than you. At least I don't have to suffer false Dreams . . . Dreams that hurt the People. Or worse . . . make them up to keep people believing in a Power that died long ago."

Someone whispered, stepping back a pace.

Dancing Fox swallowed hard, seeing the spark of hate fill Crow Caller's black eye. His white one always made her think of death—like a corpse long hidden beneath the snow.

"*You* accuse *me* of making up Dreams?" the shaman shouted. "You—"

"Tell me about going north," Raven Hunter cried, spitting at the old woman in disdain. "Why should we go that way?"

"This land is ours!" the shaman shouted over the keening of Wind Woman. "Do we walk off and leave the bones of our fathers just because of some Others who—"

"I'm not afraid of the Others," Raven Hunter said calmly. "Think, people," he continued. "What's happened to us? The Others live in our best hunting grounds, on the path of the caribou. The farther south we go, the drier it is. The higher the ground and rockier. There's more wind. Lots of lakes we can't cross in the Long Light. We can't collect mussels on the beaches anymore. Why? Because the Others have driven us here! Will caribou come this far south? Will mammoth? Look at the sphagnum moss, the wormwood, the tussock grasses. See how short they are here? If we go farther south, will they go away entirely? If caribou and mammoth can't eat, neither do we.

"As I've killed Grandfather White Bear," said Raven Hunter, "I'll kill Others, too."

"You're a young idiot," Broken Branch snorted disgustedly. "Go sit down somewhere and don't bother anyone."

"Hush, old woman," Crow Caller croaked. "The People don't care what you have to say. Leave us!"

Broken Branch shook her head. "This is what we've come to under your leadership? Snapping among ourselves when we're praying for this baby's soul?" She gestured toward Laughing Sunshine.

"Go!"

But she stayed, eyes hard as obsidian. Behind her, old Talon nodded agreement.

Crow Caller surveyed the anxious faces in the gathering. Some looked down at the snow. Others watched him hopefully, remembering earlier warnings.

"I'm going to finish telling you about the south this old woman wants you to seek. My grandfather and his people hunted there," he cried harshly. "For days they found nothing but cold and rock and gravel and impassable lakes. Like us, they starved. They followed the ice wall for many days, eating their clothing to keep strong. Many, many died. They turned back to the north, thinking they might find mammoth, or even seal or fox.

"They walked until they came to the salt water. But there, too, the ice continued, stretching far out into the water. Desperate, they started back west for the Big River. They knew they'd find food there." He raised his voice, shrieking into the wind. "They found seal and shellfish and caribou. They lived and my father's father told my father, and he told me, '*Don't go south*. A wall of ice is there . . . death is there.' "

"Then we must go north," One Who Cries agreed. "Maybe we can cut west, follow along the mountains to—"

"Wind Woman will catch us," Gray Rock interrupted, mouthing her toothless gums. "Don't forget, this is the middle of the Long Dark. Wind Woman will laugh and call Cloud Mother. What chance will we have out there? Eh? You tell me. What chance in the middle of a storm? Wind Woman will freeze us as we walk. Our bones will—"

"What chance have we here?" Crow Caller asked. "Remember when I looked inside Seagull? I saw then that we needed to go north. I saw—"

"You saw nothing!" Broken Branch cried derisively, a fist pounding air. "You've seen nothing but darkness for years. And now you would lie to keep up the sham. Lie . . . and lead us all to our doom!"

From the corner of her eye, Dancing Fox saw Jumping Hare start suddenly, then run, weaving through the mass of dead bodies to fall on the ground, eyes widening.

"Look!" he shouted. "Blood. Here, by Flies Like A Seagull's foot."

Men shuffled forward. Dancing Fox ignored them, dropping beside Sunshine to comfort her in the turmoil. "Come on, I'll sing with you," she assured in a soothing voice. "You and I can sing the baby to the Star People by ourselves." She lifted her sweet voice in the haunting melody of death, Sunshine weakly echoing her words.

"Wolf tracks," One Who Cries grunted, stilling the women's eerie song. "Wolf jumped here." He lowered his head, studying the snow at an angle. "There, see? He landed and ran." On all fours he scrambled along, head bent to the crusted snow. "Aieee! Blood here, too! Wolf is hurt bad."

Raven Hunter looked around, searching faces. "Where is my brother, Runs In Light?"

Fox took a quick breath, heart pounding. "Runs In Light?" Patting Sunshine's arm, she struggled to her feet and slid down the drift toward the shelter.

Ice gleamed treacherously as she hurried. Even that exertion took her breath and left her legs trembling. At his shelter, she crawled under the flap, wide-eyed in the darkness under the mammoth hide. Some of the old people and a few of the weaker children looked absently back at her. Runs In Light's robes lay empty, his weapons gone.

Slipping back outside, she hurried up the slope, panting, "He's gone. He's taken his weapons and—"

"One wolf," Singing Wolf said through gritted teeth. He pulled off his mitten, placing the urine-soaked snow to his nose to sniff. "Hungry wolf. Like us . . . he's starving."

"And Runs In Light shot him!" One Who Cries sang out. "Perhaps Light didn't make a good wound—but it'll kill. I smell gut juice in this blood."

Like Wind Woman in the willows, a ripple of relief went through the People. Dancing Fox smiled, a lightness caressing her heart. Runs In Light would save them. Her pride at his—

A hard hand clamped her shoulder. Crow Caller bent her head back to glare into her eyes, hissing softly, "Happy, eh? Happy that Runs In Light has killed wolf?"

She twisted, but he held her tight. "Of course, I'm happy. You think I want to die?"

"One wolf? For all these hungry bellies?" The hand tightened until she winced. She couldn't help but stare into his white-blinded eye. As always, she shivered.

"The other . . . hunters . . . They haven't even got a wolf."

"You are *my* wife. But I see your eyes going to Runs In Light. I see your smiles for him. I know what's in your heart, woman." He jerked her shoulder so hard she cried out softly. "And I know what's in his."

"What difference does it make?" she pleaded. "I'm your wife. I can't—"

"Remember that," he said, shoving her away and calling loudly, "I'm leaving this place at the rising of Father Sun. I'm going north . . . then west around the mountains. That is the way—the way to mammoth! This I've seen in a Dream!" He whirled, trudging back for the shelter.

Broken Branch brought him up sharply when she yelled, "Who will follow? *Who'll follow a man of false Dreams?*"

Crow Caller straightened, then continued walking as though her words were nothing more than the howling of Wind Woman. Dancing Fox stared after him, heart stuttering a cadence of hatred.

"Leave him," Broken Branch whispered in her ear, unbidden. "I'll let you stay in my lodge."

"Then neither one of us would get any food, Grandmother."

"Light would never let you starve," she whispered. "His feelings for you haven't dimmed."

Dancing Fox felt a sob well in her throat. She swallowed hard to keep it from rising. "It doesn't matter anymore. Besides, Crow Caller controls my soul—and yours too."

"You mean those clippings of hair and smears of menstrual blood? Bah, those only work in the hands of man with Power. Don't worry about him. He's as harmless as a gutted wolf."

"So long as he has the backing of the People, Grandmother, he's not harmless. He can do whatever he wants to me and no one will dare—"

"Don't let him beat you to nothingness," Broken Branch grumbled. "That's worse than being an outcast." Turning away, she patted Laughing Sunshine's bowed head before tottering back to the warmth of the shelters. Old Talon bent to growl reprimands into Broken Branch's ear. The old woman cackled angrily, and waved Talon off as she bowled past.

Talon hesitated for a moment, took a step toward Fox, and stopped. Her lips twitched in her brown face before she sighed and turned for the shelters, following in Broken Branch's wake.

Dancing Fox shifted uncomfortably from foot to foot. She could never leave Crow Caller. He'd kill her—and the People would help him. From behind her, she heard Raven Hunter's soft condemning laughter and looked around sharply. He stroked his handsome face knowingly, as if his keen ears had caught every word Broken Branch had whispered.

"Take care," he murmured, striding to loom over her. "Your husband's Power may be gone, but no one believes it except Broken Branch. They'll tear you to pieces for shaming him."

"I don't need your advice."

He grinned, looking her up and down. "Not yet. But you will."

"Never!"

Smiling, he reached out and grabbed a tendril of her hair that fluttered in the wind. Caressing it, he whispered, "We'll see."

She jerked away, glowering. He held her eyes for a moment, probing deeply. "When you're trapped," he said in a conspiratorial voice, "remember . . . I'll be there."

"Get away from me!"

He cocked his head, laughing as he turned and trotted down the slope.

She squeezed her eyes closed.

Chapter 4

Dancing Fox huddled at the edge of the knot of people who stood at the corner of the big shelter. She stared out across the snow-blasted wastes, heart numb, watching three men buck the snow.

Runs In Light walked in front, Wind Woman flapping his worn caribou-skin parkas, the creases of his garments lined white where snow had caked and frozen. A whisper of awe rose as the last of the light caught his face.

Fox lifted a mittened hand to her mouth. *Look how he has painted his face!* Red lines of blood ran down around his cheeks, circling his mouth like a muzzle. In speckle-dried blood, the image of what might have been either a bear or wolf faced left on his forehead.

Her heart raced. *Look at the oddness gleaming behind his eyes—like a whale-oil fire in the night. He's seen something powerful. Maybe spirits do exist?*

"Hah—heeee!" Broken Branch shrilled, wild gray strands of hair whipping in Wind Woman's grasp. She raised a bony arm, knobby brown finger stabbing through the glacial air. "There . . . There's a Dreamer! See the light in his face? Spirit has walked there. Spirit has drawn marks of a powerful Dreaming!" She bobbed in excitement.

Dancing Fox stared fearfully at Crow Caller. He loomed black against the driven white. Tight jaw muscles jumped beneath his sunken cheeks.

"My brother?" Raven Hunter scoffed. "A Spirit Dreamer? More likely he conjures images of snowflakes in sunlight."

Fox squared her shoulders, feeling his gleaming black eyes trace the lines of her face. She looked away, hearing him as he approached to stand beside her. Teeth gritted, she kept her eyes on Runs In Light.

"My brother's mind is simple, woman," Raven Hunter whispered softly. "His thoughts are in a different world than yours or mine."

She swallowed and looked up into his hard face. "How would you know?"

"Your devious ideas lie on your face like tracks in fresh snow," Raven Hunter said, sarcastic humor and something else, something painful, in his eyes. "And it's not just me who sees them."

"I don't know what you're—"

"I think you do." Smiling, he walked away, lithe, a predator even in starvation. Curse him to be buried, did he have to be so sure of himself? Something, the way his eyes looked, made her wonder. Haughty or not, Raven Hunter rarely made mistakes. That was his genius, knowing how souls—human and animal—worked.

Two children broke from the knot, stumbling out to greet Jumping Hare and One Who Cries as they tramped nearer, bearing angular chunks of frozen wolf meat.

The only burden Runs In Light bore dangled gray from his shoulders: wolf's hide, head still attached, eyes crystal-frozen and dull.

"Runs In Light brings meat!" Jumping Hare cried. Then his voice thrummed higher, like walrus gut in the sun. "And he brings a Dream!"

They waited, tense, staring at the red-white slabs of meat on the hunter's shoulders, minds on the promise of life it bestowed. A Dream? A Spirit Dream?

Runs In Light stopped at the edge of their circle; he looked from face to face. Everything stilled except for Wind Woman, who playfully harassed their clothing, tickling their faces with loose strands of hair.

"Tell us," Broken Branch cackled eagerly into the silence.

"Wolf Dream," he said softly, face stony. "But not here in the cold. Let's go inside before Wind Woman takes all our warmth and blows it to the Long Dark."

"Cut up the meat!" Crow Caller snapped sourly. "Don't play games, boy. People are hungry."

"No," Runs In Light responded with eerie calmness. "Wolf gave the meat to me to take us south. He came in a Dream and showed me the way. His body will keep the People strong on the journey. Heart blood runs in my veins—it is the way."

"Bah! You? You're just a boy! You wouldn't know a Spirit Dream if it—"

"You *dare*! Look at him! Look and see Power! The

Dream's in his eyes.'' Broken Branch whirled, a crooked finger lancing dangerously up toward Crow Caller's face.

Fox caught her breath as Runs In Light's eyes swirled and shifted, reminding her of the way wolves' eyes gleamed beyond the butchering fires at night.

"We go north.'' Crow Caller's hand swung, pointing to where Father Sun brightened the far horizon. "I, too, have Dreamed . . . *boy*. Mammoth calls us back the way we came. Like I told you all last Long Light. Remember? Let's go back—''

"Then go.'' Runs In Light lifted his chin. "Spirit Power comes where it will. It's not a thing of men. Wolf gave me his Power. The Wolf Dream will take me—and those of the People who will follow—to the south. There in the Big Ice—''

"Lies death!'' Crow Caller's voice cracked.

As Runs In Light's eyes fell on him, the old shaman wet his lips and stepped backward, as though he feared the boy. Frosty breath plumed white in the feeble glare. Snow-shot wind stinging their faces, the People backed away.

"Death! You hear, *boy*?'' Crow Caller's white eye glowed baleful while his black one sparked like flint against granite. "Monsters climb in the ice. The souls of the lost dead sing from there.'' He turned, pointing to each of the People in turn. "When you get close to the Big Ice, you'll hear them . . . creaking and groaning, their bones cracking under the weight. They'll kill you! We have to go north.''

"You go north,'' Broken Branch shouted. "Maybe you and you alone are supposed to be killed by the Others.''

Hobbling to Runs In Light, she hooked taloned fingers in his worn skins. "See me, boy. Look at me. See . . . see . . . the Dream?'' She drew his face so close to hers that their condensed breath mingled in a white cloud to curl around their heads.

For a long second she stood stiffly, fingers tight around the back of his neck. Then she pulled him closer still, eyes almost touching.

"Ha-heee!'' she wheezed, letting him go and stumbling back, arms circling for balance. She sat down suddenly, crooning to herself as the People watched in frightened fascination.

"Fools, both of them," Raven Hunter grunted from behind.

"Grandmother?" Laughing Sunshine grabbed one of the crone's withered hands. "What's in Light's eyes?"

"Dream . . ." the old woman whispered. Slack-jawed, she stared absently at nothing. "Wolf's in his eyes. Wolf . . ."

One Who Cries shifted, turning uneasily to Crow Caller. "Is this true? You've led us many places . . . healed us when we were sick. Runs In Light says your vision is wrong. How do we know who's right?"

"He's a boy," Crow Caller said flatly. "He plays games with the survival of the People. Dreams take fasting and preparation. You don't—"

"He hasn't eaten for four days," Laughing Sunshine blurted. "He gave his food to me . . . for the baby." She pointed a trembling finger at the death drift.

"Aiieee . . ." Gray Rock, age-thin lips twisting in her wrinkled face, turned beady black eyes to Runs In Light. "Four days, eh? Spirit number. Like the way of Father Sun over the heart of Earth. Opposites crossed."

"He's a boy!" Crow Caller shouted, shaking a fist.

Runs In Light trembled as if the shaman's horny hand had slapped him. "Wolf came to me. He'll save those who go south. He showed me the break in the Big Ice where we can pass. Beyond is mammoth. Buffalo are there. Caribou grows new antlers in green grass."

Dancing Fox's mouth parted as she met Light's eyes. "I see the Dream," she whispered. "It's there. Reflected in his—"

"Get inside the shelter!" the old shaman ordered. "Go warm my robes. We go north tomorrow . . . and I want a good night's rest first."

"No," she said. Stunned by his anger, she looked up at him, uncomprehending, feet rooted to the spot. Rage burned fiercely in the old man's thin face. He drew back his hand to strike her.

She threw up her arms in defense, stumbling away, murmuring, "Don't touch me!"

"Go!" Crow Caller shouted.

As she scuttled toward the shelters, she glimpsed the

sharpness in Runs In Light's face as he stepped forward. Broken Branch placed a restraining hand on the youth's shoulder.

Crawling through the flap, she heard her husband's powerful voice: "Don't listen to this child! Mammoth lie just over there . . . to the north! I've seen our hunters surround them, driving darts deeply into bawling calves. The mothers whirl, trunks lifted to seek Wind Woman for our presence. But we're cunning! The calves flounder in the deep snow, their blood soaking our darts. The herd stampedes, running north, and we harvest—"

"*Liar!*" Broken Branch raged. "You see nothing. You make this up as you speak. There's no Dream in *your* eyes."

Fox cringed as the sharp slap carried through the shelter. Huddling in Crow Caller's robes, she pulled them over her head to block the continuing sound of flesh on flesh. Anger so violent filled her that she retched suddenly into the corner, her stomach twisting in pain.

She feared for the old woman, and for herself, for defying Crow Caller. As she had shamed him today, he would shame her tonight. She curled into a ball, wincing against the agony she knew would come.

Crow Caller drew his hand back to strike Broken Branch again. The old woman rocked away, crabbing over ice, muttering to herself. Cloud Mother crept through the grayness overhead, streaking the sky with ribbons of pink and orange.

"Leave her alone," Runs In Light said tightly, the vision of Dancing Fox's terrified face sharp in his mind. Wolf flowed rich and strong in his veins. Deep in his soul, a hatred rose for this old man who tortured his people.

"What? Words of valor from my brother?" Raven Hunter said, arms crossed as he watched.

"You would break the People's peace?" Crow Caller accused. "You? *You* would threaten me?"

"There's no peace when an old woman suffers. You've already broken the—"

"Don't tell *me*." Crow Caller pulled himself straight, chest thrown out. "I have the right to punish where—"

"No one has that right. Not even—"

"I'll kill you, boy. My Spirit Power is great!" Livid, the old shaman grinned, revealing yellowed and broken teeth.

Crouching low, his skinny arm snaked out of his sleeve, tracing magical signs in the air.

Runs In Light took a deep breath, nervously fingering his darts. "Wolf protects. I don't fear you." But he did. Once too often he'd seen the powerful effects of the old man's magic. Silently, he prayed to Wolf for courage.

Hushed whispers swirled behind him, feet sliding on snow to clear a space so the two shamans could face each other alone. Power sizzled on the frigid air.

"In four weeks," Crow Caller sang in a haunting melody with his head thrown back, "your stomach will ache from turning itself inside out . . . ." Soon the chant became incomprehensible. The old man raised his arms, and his voice trembled to the sky as he cavorted in an unknown dance.

Runs In Light squeezed his eyes shut. Crow Caller's Spirit Power chafed at the edges of his soul. "Wolf protects me. . . ." he repeated over and over, heart throbbing. "He won't let me die until I reach the land beyond the Big Ice." He touched the blood-wolf effigy on his forehead. "Wolf leads me south to the land of the Father Sun. I follow the Wolf Dream."

Crow Caller's Power seemed to ebb at the edges of his being. Runs In Light opened his eyes and smiled his relief at the old shaman where he danced.

Awed exclamations erupted behind him, at the demonstration of his Power. Broken Branch grabbed up her toes, rocking back and forth like Grandfather Brown Bear. A grin exposed her toothless black gums and pink tongue.

"Wolf Dream!" her gravelly voice cracked. "Ha-heee! I go south with Runs In Light. I go south with Wolf!"

Father Sun slid below the jagged horizon to the southwest, darkness accenting the hollowness of the People's cheeks and eyes. Dusk descended like opalescent veils of smoke. The wavering brilliant fires made by the Monster Children's war rose in rainbow patterns to light the northern sky. The Twins had fought from the beginning of time, one good, the other bad, locked in eternal combat.

"You go south to *death*! Hear me, Father Sun! I, Crow Caller, have your Dream. Feel my Power? I curse these . . . these traitors! Their souls will never reach the Blessed Star

People. Death!'' he shrieked, pirouetting, arms spread like an eagle to end in a low crouch facing Runs In Light.

"I follow Wolf. Anyone who eats the meat of Wolf follows my Dream." Turning, Runs In Light weaved through the crowd to duck beneath the shelter flap.

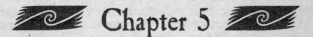 **Chapter 5**

Crimson light flickered over the hide walls of the shelter, accenting the fear and longing in people's eyes. They huddled silently around the low flames, letting the dark smoke warm them.

One Who Cries lifted the hafting of his new stone dart point to his teeth, finding the nub of sinew with his tongue. He clamped it tightly between worn incisors and pulled hard, feeling the knot go tight. With a critical eye, he examined the binding, grunting satisfaction at the set of the stone point in the split end of the dart shaft.

Singing Wolf poked at the smoldering chunk of mammoth dung in the fire pit. Along with dried moss, it made a meager source of heat. It had been a day of good luck; one of the children had found the fuel where the wind had stripped the snow away. The sadness of his baby's death still rested heavily in his eyes. The dung glowed red, smoke hanging thick and musty in the air.

One Who Cries sighted down the long shaft of his dart to the chunk of wolf meat in the middle of the floor. "Do I have to sit here all night and stare at that pile of meat?"

"What's stronger? Your stomach? Or your fear of what Crow Caller will do to you if you eat wolf?" Singing Wolf wondered aloud, hungry eyes on the thawing wolf quarters. The side of meat nearest the fire glowed eerily red. Singing Wolf swallowed hard, as if the watering in his mouth irritated him.

"Shamans!" One Who Cries muttered, twirling the dart

anxiously in his fingers. "Playing for Power while the People starve . . . I'm eating the meat." He started crawling across the floor.

"And going south with Runs In Light?" Singing Wolf lifted an eyebrow.

One Who Cries stopped short, hovering over the meat. Perplexed lines gouged his brow. He set his stubby teeth in his lower lip. His round face looked almost pudgy in the light cast by the fire. High broad cheeks emphasized his mashed-flat nose. Hunger ate at the perpetual merriment in his eyes.

Uncertain now, One Who Cries lifted a shoulder. "Raven Hunter says his brother's a fool. A fool can talk himself into believing things. You know Runs In Light, he's always seeing things. Maybe—"

"Raven Hunter, now there's a man with sense. How can two brothers be so different?"

"So, what do we do? Look at that meat." He stabbed a hand at it. "Why do spirits have to get mixed up with my stomach? Get mixed up with us at all with death all around."

"Because shamans are all crazy," Singing Wolf groaned.

"I'm going to eat it. You trust spirit meat?"

Singing Wolf scratched under his arm, eyes squinted thoughtfully. "Don't be an idiot. Of course not. Spirits are unpredictable." A pause. "Crow Caller didn't want to sing for my child. Didn't *want* to!" Behind him, Laughing Sunshine's eyes grew bright with tears. He clasped her hand firmly.

One Who Cries gave him a pained look. "You saw Light's eyes, huh? Did you see the Dream in them?"

He shrugged uncomfortably. "I don't know. There was something there, but . . ."

"But what?"

"Raven Hunter said—"

"I know what he said," One Who Cries grunted in disgust and rocked back on his heels, jaw vibrating with grinding teeth.

Singing Wolf shook his head, angrily jerking a burin from his pack. A graving tool with a sharp pointed end, he'd carefully crafted it for grooving wood, bone, or antler. From the ice-packed floor, he pulled a fragment of split mammoth rib—long since boiled for any marrow butter it might have held.

The lines above his eyes deepening, he began scratching figures into the cortical bone with the burin tip. Coolly he added, "Crow Caller cursed anyone who eats wolf."

"So? Both Crow Caller and Runs In Light are right about one thing. We've got to leave here—but we're not going to make it very far on empty bellies."

Green Water, One Who Cries' wife, crawled over, a wolf-hide blanket pulled tight around her shoulder. "Sitting here won't fill bellies either," she added in her well-modulated voice, an eyebrow raised. Not even hunger dulled the love in her eyes as she studied her husband. "No one has seen game . . . seen even sign. Will we have strength to even walk if we stay longer?"

One Who Cries glanced at his rehafted dart and took time to sing a spirit song under his breath to bless it before he slipped it into his caribou fawn-skin quiver. "I'm eating the meat."

"My child is dead," Singing Wolf added flatly, eyes going to where Laughing Sunshine sat watching him, quiet, pain in the set of her mouth. He looked back to the glistening meat. "All my children are gone."

The women stared, Laughing Sunshine's expression hollow-eyed as her husband studied her. The silence stretched.

Singing Wolf continued, "Is Laughing Sunshine next? Huh? Me? Am I next? Who starves next?"

One Who Cries lifted a shoulder helplessly, digging soot from the corner of one eye with a stubby finger. "Crow Caller says you . . . if you eat that meat."

"My child . . ." Singing Wolf repeated, "would have been a beauty, a bringer of life to the People." He paused. "Crow Caller wouldn't even sing for her. A worthless life, he said. Another death . . . and there lies meat. How many days have we gone out? How many times have we seen nothing but blowing snow?"

"Too many."

Singing Wolf expertly bent his fingers around the burin as it scritched on the flat bone he held.

"Throwing Bones went out and found Grandfather White Bear," Green Water reminded him evenly.

"And that's another thing," One Who Cries continued.

"Who ever heard of Grandfather White Bear this far south? Some spirit wants us out of here." One Who Cries sniffed at the cold and ran his thumb along the edge of the broken point he'd removed from the dart shaft. "I'll have to resharpen this. Good tool stone is getting scarce this far south. Maybe we'd find some obsidian on the other side of the Big Ice, huh? Or some fine quartzite? Maybe those lost dead of Crow Caller's will point the way? You think?"

Laughing Sunshine spoke softly. "How much bad could come of eating spirit meat?"

Singing Wolf sighed confusion. "If I have to choose between Spirit Dreams, I choose Runs In Light. He—"

"He's barely a man."

"Crow Caller's been right in the past," Green Water reminded them, fumbling with a fold in her hide robe.

"Two rights?" One Who Cries wondered. "Each going a different direction? There isn't enough of me to keep two Dreamers happy! I can't split down the middle!"

"But did you see the look in Runs In Light's eyes?"

"I think I'll starve before letting *my* stomach turn inside out. You remember that time Crow Caller cursed Seal Paw? All his teeth fell out." One Who Cries shuffled through his pouch, finding his fine-point antler tine and a thick square of rawhide with a hole cut for the thumb. In the red haze of the fire, he studied the damaged point and grunted. From long practice, he settled the stone in the leather where it would protect his hand. Squinting down his flat nose, he placed the antler tip against the edge of the tool and pressed, snapping a long pressure flake off the stone.

"Hey!" Singing Wolf growled. "Do that outside. I get those sharp little flakes stuck in my hands every time I sit down. They go all over . . . get in the food and stuff."

"So? We leave here tomorrow. You think wolf will mind when he snuffles around looking for something we missed? Unlike you, he can tell sharp stone from ice."

Green Water sighed irritably and bent her efforts to mending a long boot bottom, driving a bone awl through thick leather. She scowled at the men from the corner of her eye.

The click-snapping of the resharpening continued as Singing Wolf carved on the mammoth bone in his hand, turning it occasionally to study the image in the red glow. "Broken

Branch says Crow Caller's Power is gone. Crow Caller says Light is just a boy playing at being a shaman."

"Huh!" One Who Cries snorted. "Go north and we're right in the lodge doors of those Others. You know they killed most of Geyser's band—took a lot of the women and destroyed the camp. Those who lived and got away barely stayed ahead of them last Long Light. Those Others, they're bad men. Got sick spirits."

"Raven Hunter wants to kill them," Singing Wolf mused. "He thinks there's a way to drive them back. Get them to leave us alone. I wonder if maybe he isn't right? I wonder if we couldn't—"

"Raven Hunter wants status," One Who Cries snapped. His thoughts drifted to years before. Runs In Light and Raven Hunter were always fighting, the latter always winning. "Let him go die. There are better places for darts than my belly." He tested the knife edge against the callused pad of his thumb. "I'm going to eat the meat. Wolf wouldn't let Crow Caller torment us. That's not His way."

"Crow Caller is afraid of the south," Green Water added, eyes shifting back and forth between the men. Her gentle expression urged them to think. Green Water had that manner about her, strong yet sensitive, thoughtful, and composed.

"Yeah," Singing Wolf agreed, licking his lips. "What scares a man with Spirit Power like his?"

"Ghosts," One Who Cries said. He looked steadily at Singing Wolf, waggling the resharpened dart point as he talked. "If he has any Power."

"Runs In Light is unafraid."

"Uh-huh. Fools are like that."

The burin in Singing Wolf's fingers scritched hollowly on the bone. The flint caught the faint gleam of light from the fire as it turned in his strong fingers. "Now me, I wouldn't look cross-eyed at Crow Caller. Next time I needed to hide from Grandfather White Bear, Wind Woman would blow my stink right up his nose because Crow Caller killed my medicine."

"Don't worry. With your stink, Grandfather White Bear would probably run the other way anyhow."

Singing Wolf gave him a disgusted look. "Be serious. I don't care what Broken Branch says, that old man has Power.

And Runs In Light didn't even blink when Crow Caller called down his spirit magic. Didn't even blink!'' He looked over to where Laughing Sunshine hunched, eyes on the meat, sorrow creasing her expression.

He lowered his eyes, pursing his lips. The little bundle on the snowdrift weighed on his mind, too—heavy like an old bull's ivory tusk.

"So? What are you going to do?"

Laughing Sunshine interrupted, "When there is no game, no chance of finding food, what does anyone do? The question is to go south, or back the way we came. We don't know what can be found in the hills to the south. Maybe overwintered berries exposed by Wind Woman, if nothing else."

"And how long will those last? *What if Runs In Light is wrong?* What if his Dream was nothing more than a kid's imagination?" Singing Wolf asked harshly.

One Who Cries squinted at the floor. "Well, then, we can always come back. The Renewal meets in the same place every year. If Light is wrong and there's no hole in the ice, we can join up with Buffalo Back's clan at Renewal. He'll take us."

Singing Wolf swallowed and stopped his carving, looking down at the splinter of flint he held. "My child starved to death." He flipped the flat piece of bone in the air. One Who Cries caught it deftly and turned it to the light.

Singing Wolf looked quickly to Laughing Sunshine as he bent over the rear quarters of wolf that lay near the smoldering red eye of flame.

In the dull glow of the fire, One Who Cries stared at the bone while Green Water crawled to the meat. The best artist in the band, Singing Wolf had carved a four-legged beast with a long snout and pointed ears. The etching might have lacked distinction—it might have been a fox or dog. But it wasn't.

"Wolf meat?" One Who Cries grimaced. "That's like eating someone's old sweaty moccasins . . . but moccasins taste better!" Reluctantly, he crawled over next to Singing Wolf, using his new knife to cut long slices of rich dark meat from the haunch. With a weak smile, he handed slices to Laughing Sunshine and Green Water as they moved to join him.

* * *

The two old women sat close, the deep folds in their wrinkled faces glistening with smeared fat in the light of the fire. Long shadows stretched across the warm shelter to climb the opposite wall.

With skilled hands Broken Branch cracked the thighbone down the middle, exposing pink marrow. Using a long curled thumbnail, she neatly scooped the channel clear. Twisting the marrow in half, she handed a portion to Gray Rock.

"So much for spirit meat, eh?" Broken Branch grinned wickedly.

Gray Rock licked her fingers. "Curses scare me less than starvation."

"I always knew you were a smart old witch."

"No, you didn't. You've told me a hundred times—"

"Well, forget what I've told you before. I changed my mind."

Gray Rock smiled, chewing more of the fat. "Such a pity. You've finally come to your senses, and I won't have a chance to enjoy it."

"Come with us. Ha-heee, there's Power in the south! I feel it deep in my heart." Broken Branch used a bone sliver to pick at the spongy joint area, heedless of the sharp flakes in the whitish pink paste she spooned into her mouth. "One advantage of not having teeth," she mumbled with a grin. "There's nothing for the bone to stick in."

"Uh-huh," Gray Rock growled. "It'll just scour your old butt good and raw when it comes out the other end."

"At least it'll come out. Your problem is you plug up. Affects your disposition. Makes you cranky like you ain't had a man in a year or so."

Gray Rock waved her away with a desultory hand. "Who needs a man? All they do is moan and groan and you spend nine months packing their get—and that's the easy part."

"Come south with us," Broken Branch pleaded, looking up from beneath stubby gray lashes. "I need you. I'll be stuck with these kids. No one sane to talk to. Come. It'll be—"

"The farther south you go, the rougher the country gets. More piles of rock to climb over—and I'm not as nimble as I used to be." She bowed her head in thought, throwing tender glances at her friend. "Besides, I owe Crow Caller. He saved my life that time I got fevered."

"That was then. His Power's all gone now. Been gone for years."

"I don't know." Gray Rock pulled her legs under her, wincing at the pain in her swollen joints. "Remember when my last tooth rotted? Whole side of my face swelled up from the poison."

Broken Branch cackled, bobbing her head at the memory. "Your face looked like a blowed-up walrus bladder . . . all pooched out and skintight! Ha-heeee!"

"Yes, and you remember what Crow Caller did?"

"Don't glower at me like that, you old hag. Of course I do. How could I forget you howling like a wolf with his nose caught in a clamshell?" Broken Branch slapped her leg, chuckling dryly. "It took how many hunters to hold you down while old One Eye worked his healing? Five? Ten?"

"That's *not* the point!" Gray Rock bristled, wrinkles pulling tight as she hissed, "The point is, he saved my life."

"Bah!" Broken Branch smacked her lips. "He drilled a hole through your cheek with a big bone awl. I could've done that. And just as good!"

Gray Rock pouted before adding sullenly, "Still, he saved my life." She paused. "I'm going north."

Broken Branch carefully scooped the last of the marrow from the bone. She licked the shine of the fatty material from her fingers and the fractured bone before pocketing the fragments to boil later for whatever grease she could render.

"Well . . . go." She shook her finger at Gray Rock. "See what his Power brings you. You'll turn south soon enough—if one of them Others don't stick your guts with a dart."

Gray Rock worked her tongue over empty gums as she studied her friend. "Darts may be better than the ghosts of the Big Ice."

"What would they want with an old hag like you anyway? You'd be nothing but trouble for them—get in their way. Foul up their ghosting or something."

Gray Rock smiled weakly. "I told Jumping Hare to go with Runs In Light."

"You what? That's not right!" she gasped. "Your son should stay with you. Singing Wolf and that 'yes-no' One

Who Cries are going with Light. Crow Caller's band won't have enough hunters. If you're thinking that going south is really right, why don't—''

"Raven Hunter will be enough."

"Bah! He'll get you in trouble with those Others. Young idiot! All he wants is war. Something bad in his blood. I remember when he was born. Blood . . . bad blood.''

Gray Rock looked through the crack in the hide door to see how much time remained. Dawn light grayed the sky. "They're getting ready to go. I hear them." Almost as an afterthought, she asked, "Do you really think Heron went that way?''

"I know she did. I saw her leave."

"Most people think she's a myth, that she never really—''

"Only the old ones still remember.''

Gray Rock frowned uneasily. "The stories tell how wicked she was, how she consorted with the Powers of the Long Dark. Why'd she go? Did the clan drive her off?''

Broken Branch shook her head awkwardly. "No. She left on her own. Needed to be alone, she said.'' Guilt tinged the old woman's voice, guilt and remorse.

Gray Rock eyed her downcast face seriously. "What'd you do? Kill Heron's mother? That look on your—''

"Quit asking things that are none of your—''

"All right,'' Gray Rock said wearily. "I was just making talk.''

Broken Branch rose slowly to her feet, offering a hand to her crippled friend, who struggled vainly to rise. "You're walking to find another clan of the People? You can't even stand up!''

"Oh, shut up, you old bear bait,'' Gray Rock spat. But she took the hand, bones crackling and straining as she fought to stand. "Once I'm up, I do fine. Get me started and I don't stop. It's what all them oversized kids did to my hips that keeps me down!''

In an uncharacteristically gentle voice Broken Branch added, "Well, don't sit down, then. I won't be there to pick you up.''

Gray Rock nodded, hobbling to the flap and ducking under it. In the faint light, she looked back toward Crow Caller where he gathered the People going with him. "See you among the stars," she whispered, wrinkling her antique face in one last wink before she tottered off toward the old shaman.

Broken Branch watched her go, a familiar pain of loss smoldering around her heart.

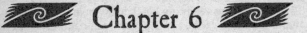 # Chapter 6

"Wolf Dreamer?"

Runs In Light turned, seeing Jumping Hare walking up behind him. They called him that now—at least the ones who accepted the Dream did. The others, well . . . Raven Hunter called him child. Nothing new in that. They'd been at each other's throats since they were boys—for reasons he'd never understood. Still, it hurt.

"I think everything's packed," Jumping Hare said. "People are ready. We don't have much time. The light is so short."

"I know." Runs In Light's eyes wouldn't stay away from where Crow Caller assembled his group. So many friends stood there including Dancing Fox. Pain constricted in a tight band around his heart. "I'm ready."

Following his gaze, Jumping Hare frowned. "You can't do anything. She's his. Her father gave her away to pay for healings. She owes him. It's just the way."

"I know. Only I feel this is my last chance. That if I don't go and take her from him—"

"It always seems that way. Me, I lived through it when my first love married another. Now, I've made a name. I'll find a wife at the next Renewal. You'll see. Wait until Renewal." Jumping Hare clapped him on the shoulder and turned away, walking back to duck into a shelter.

Runs In Light felt a growing urge to be alone. He trudged over the drift, out of sight of the camp. Fear tormented his gut, setting it to writhing like the tangle of bott-fly maggots he'd once cut from a dead caribou's throat. All his life, unfamiliar faces and voices had haunted his sleep, calling to him from some echoing cavern in his mind. One voice in particular rang out above the others, a woman's. He felt oddly as if he were going in search of her now. It frightened him. *Fantasy or reality? Am I taking my people on a Dream Walk . . . or leading them to their deaths?* Wolf *had* come to him; he knew that. Yet some unspoken doubt lurked, whispers of trickery or magic barely audible beneath his faith. Had that Dream-walking man of the Others cursed him? Sent him this manner of destruction?

Pulling the sinew strings of his hood tight, he gazed wearily out over the vast wilderness. Snow crawled like fog close to the ground, stirred by the glacial breeze. Ravens soared in the white glaring sky, sunlight flashing silver from their midnight wings.

"Wolf?" he called softly. The fur of his robe ruffled in the breeze. "Don't leave me alone out there. Help me—"

"Runs In Light?" a sweet voice said from behind him.

His stomach muscles went rigid. He knew her voice—would recognize it a thousand Long Darks from now in his Dreams among the Star People. He squeezed his eyes tightly closed, muttering, "You came to say good-bye?"

She stepped around to stand before him. He felt her presence, strong and warm, and opened his eyes. Despite the cadaverous thinness of her face, she looked beautiful, her waist-length black hair dancing around the edges of her hood.

He met her gaze. Her gentle expression remained unchanged, but something in her eyes seemed to grow still, as if balanced on a knife's edge, awaiting death's final heartbeat.

"You could come," he murmured lamely.

He thought she was going to respond, but after a sharp inhale, she halted. Grief and fear mixed in her eyes before she lowered them to stare uncomfortably at the creeping snow. "He'd kill me. He has . . . parts of my body. Things that give him my soul. Being with you, I could destroy you all. He could send a bad spirit out of the Long Dark."

"I'll take that chance. Come with me now, Dancing Fox. I can protect you. Wolf won't—"

"I ate some of wolf," she breathed.

"You—"

"Even if I can't come, I wanted to be part of your Dream. And I want you to know . . ." She looked up and he felt his heart rise into his throat.

She's made her choice. His guts fell, like intestines out of a belly-slit mammoth.

"Don't say it," he whispered harshly. "It won't do either one of us any good."

She took three quick steps forward, tears in her eyes, and before he knew it, wrapped her arms around his waist, pillowing her face against his chest. "Will you mark a trail for me? Maybe if I can—"

"I'll mark a trail." Futility swept him; Crow Caller would never let her get away. He crushed her frail body against him. Through the heavy layers of hide, he felt her uneven breathing.

Gently, she pushed back, staring feverishly past him to the top of the drift. "I must go. He'll be looking for me."

Reluctantly, he released her. She stepped backward, eyes going over him as if for the last time. She worked her fingers nervously in the tattered greasy mittens.

"If you can get away . . . come."

"I will." She nodded hurriedly, throwing him a final look as she raced over the drift.

He stared at her footprints for a long moment, before muttering to himself, "Stop being a fool. You know she can't." Shaking his head, he whispered, "And I'm not sure I really want her to. What if my Dream isn't . . ." He couldn't finish it.

He sucked in a deep breath and looked out over the waves of frozen snow. Streaks of dark brown reared where Wind Woman had scoured the ridge tops clear. Those rocky ridges would be his trail to the south, ever higher along the wind-worried—

"Touching."

Runs In Light whirled, seeing Raven Hunter rising to his feet. "Why, I thought for a moment she'd break, take a chance that Crow Caller's vengeance was weaker than her love for you."

"What do you want?" Runs In Light demanded.

"Why . . ." Raven Hunter spread his arms. "I'm saying

farewell, idiot brother. That's a family right, isn't it? To make a final act of charity and goodwill toward a brother.''

''Why?''

''I don't know myself,'' Raven Hunter said, cocking his head. ''You were always the strange one. I never understood why Seal Paw and Seagull fawned over you when I did so much better, learned tracking, could repeat the stories. But they always admired you.''

Runs In Light swallowed, an unease taking him. He staggered as if dizzy. Involuntary words choked his throat as the world hazed shimmery before his eyes.

''You . . . you and me, brother. We're the future. Don't do what you're planning. Or in the end, one of us will have to destroy the other.''

Raven Hunter's hard laugh broke the spell, shattering it like a sheet of ice dropped on jagged rock. ''Are you threatening me?''

''The fight will tear the world in two.''

''You'd best hope it never comes to that, brother.'' Raven Hunter smirked, leaning forward so his hard hot eyes bored into Runs In Light's. ''I'm stronger, meaner, and don't suffer your flaws of mercy and compassion. Threaten me? You're crazier than I thought you were!''

''I—I'm not crazy,'' he whispered uncertainly. ''It's in my head, the visions—''

''I won't forget your little warning, brother. Someday, you'll wish you hadn't threatened. Indeed, you will. I'll take something of yours for that and maybe even toss you a bone when I leave you behind. Hmm?''

He turned, laughing again as he climbed the drift, tramping over Dancing Fox's footprints, leaving them nothing more than gouged holes in the snow.

Drowning his fear in the Wolf Dream, Runs In Light closed his eyes and heard again the spirit's words, *''This is the way, man of the People. I show you. . . .''*

A prickle ran up his spine. He squinted at the circling ravens, then out across the undulating whiteness, eyes searching. ''I hear you, Wolf.''

Turning, he climbed over the top to where his own group gathered. Broken Branch waved to him, grinning.

From across camp, Crow Caller shouted, "Come on!" to his small band.

Runs In Light's eyes drifted over his own group. "So many?"

"Ha-heee! Wolf Dream!" Broken Branch chortled, waddling to the south, pack hanging down her back from a tump line that dented her ancient forehead. Her rickety legs pumped ferociously as she took the lead.

A bittersweet smile touched his lips. *They believe I can save them. Can I?* His eyes sought Dancing Fox where she gathered things together for her journey northward. Emptiness filled him.

A hard fist landed against his shoulder, making him stumble backward. "Quit that," Green Water reprimanded.

"What?"

"Looking like she's lost," she whispered. "Unless Grandfather White Bear gets her, you'll see her again."

He opened his mouth to ask how she knew but stopped himself. Instead, he narrowed his eyes and asked, "Are you having Dreams, too?"

"Yes, you young fool. You've got competition. Remember that." She winked at him, then grabbed his sleeve and flung him forward into a shambling trot.

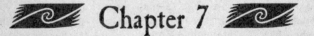 Chapter 7

Rising smoke from dung fires caught the first tints of morning as it twisted upward in the bare breeze. Cold blue shadows crept back, clinging against the drifts. Crow Caller's band hustled through camp, chattering about the trek north, watching Runs In Light lead his people southward.

Dancing Fox laced her parka tighter and secured the pack on her back, the tump line from which the pack hung biting into her forehead. She secretly followed Light with her eyes. When he reached the top of the ridge, he turned, looking back, sunlight gleaming from the wolf hide over his shoulders. He bent and placed a rock atop another.

The trail.

She straightened, stomach tingling in fear. Did she have the courage to defy—

"Take your eyes off him," Crow Caller demanded from behind her. "If you want your eyes to stay in your head."

She whirled to face him. "I didn't do anything!"

"And you'd better not." He grinned without humor and reached in his pocket to retrieve a small tan sack. She recognized it: his collection of hair and personal articles through which he controlled her soul. He swung it ominously before her wide eyes, glancing to Runs In Light, then back, withered face hardening. "Keep your thoughts on me, woman!"

Jerking away, she said shakily, "I'll think whatever thoughts I want, husband. You may control my soul but not my mind."

He gripped her arm tightly, shaking her so hard she thought her neck would snap. "You like punishment, eh?"

"No, I—"

"Well, you're heading for more!" He shoved her backward and strode haughtily away.

Dancing Fox secured her tump line again and followed slowly as he weaved through the tangle of people to the front of the procession. She kept her eyes down to avoid seeing the curious looks, the stolid expressions masking thoughts.

They climbed up to the wind-blasted ridge in single file, a weary people with nowhere to go. Ragged, hungry, their tattered caribou-hide clothing worn thin, they marched into the wind. Some looked over their shoulders, peering uneasily at Runs In Light's band where they threaded into the distance.

Dancing Fox shot one last look at Mammoth Camp, the place where her world had changed. Her love had gone cold when she'd been given to Crow Caller. Her father had thrown her to him for services rendered like an old blanket. When he'd died, she hadn't mourned.

So much of her life had been twisted like a hare from its hole. So many hopes and desires smashed and broken there under the white-patched brown hides of mammoth. Now she walked away; married, possessed by Crow Caller, who crawled onto her each night, spreading her legs, thrusting and going limp. Thank the Blessed Star People he was brief about it. Shame burned up her cheeks.

Behind, Mammoth Camp would slowly sink into the ground. The shelters would rot away, the bits of bone desiccating and splintering in the Long Light. The body wastes of the People would become fodder for beetles and bugs. The dead, their souls glistening above, would not only house insects, but feed the crows and gulls. Maybe a passing wolf would chew on them. The bones would be scattered, mice crawling through the hollow skulls. Some of the debris left behind would wash away, the rest would be slowly buried until nothing but tussock grasses, sedge, and wormwood remained.

"Only my pain will last forever," she whispered.

She winced at the burning that lanced through her with each step. She swung her legs wide to avoid chafing the places her husband had torn the night before. The bites on her breasts hurt where the caribou-fawn hair of her skins rubbed.

She cast a hard glance at Crow Caller's straight back where he marched at the lead. Hatred blocked her pain for a moment. *You want me to think of you, old man? Yes, I will.* She concentrated on filling her mind with so much hate, she could barely think at all. Her aches receded into nothingness. *I hate you,* she chanted silently over and over.

For hours they walked until they reached a rocky ridge they had to climb on hands and knees. Panting to the top, Fox stood for a moment surveying the land. Father Sun hung low on the distant horizon, wavering through clouds to dapple the white windswept wilderness in irregular patterns.

"Let's go," Crow Caller commanded as he passed her, slapping her arm.

She sighed and struggled down the slippery rocks onto a flat plain. Huge boulder outcrops dotted the expanse, drifts piled twenty feet high at their bases. Sunlight reflected so brilliantly from the snow, it almost blinded. She pulled her leather snow blinders from her pack and strung the slitted goggles over her head.

Raven Hunter roamed wide, his black shape like a fly on fat as he climbed each drift in search of mammoth or Grandfather White Bear. Broken Branch had warned them not to club their bear dogs to death, but hunger had overcome sense.

Now, without the dogs to warn them, they were in constant danger of predators. In this hunger-bleak Long Dark, not even their numbers would long deter a hungry bear.

A hollow chasm grew in Dancing Fox's chest, yawning wider with each step. Her ties with Runs In Light strained to the breaking point as she tramped farther and farther from him. At least when they'd been in camp together, she could talk to him occasionally—touch him guardedly. But now she'd have nothing, no solace from her husband's brutality.

For hours they trudged, Cloud Mother gradually pulling a roiling charcoal gray blanket over them. At first Wind Woman tugged gently at Fox's clothing, but by the time Father Sun had walked halfway across the southern heavens, howling gusts lashed her. Snow blew in chattering streams from the drifts, stinging her face like icy bone splinters.

Her hatred burned, thoughts drifting to Runs In Light and back to Crow Caller. *He owns my soul.*

I can protect you! Light's desperate voice promised in her memory.

She felt her tender breasts, knowing the bruises Crow Caller had left. The memory of his flesh against hers made her stomach heave.

Ahead, the old shaman bent into the wind, hawking to spit phlegm from his lungs.

"*I can't,*" she whispered, soul crying within. "I can't stay with you, old man. I can't stand the thought of your filthy mouth on me. Can't stand the thought of your wasted flesh rubbing mine. I'd rather die. . . ."

She looked around, heart like a rock in her chest. She bit her lip, thinking.

The storm raged down on them in hazy crystalline sheets, obscuring the plain, but still they strode on. When they were well out into the flats, Dancing Fox slowed her pace, falling back to the end of the procession. She fell out of line, squatting down as if to relieve herself. Her heart pounded sickeningly. People averted their eyes from her, as was proper.

She crouched there in the swirling snow, knees trembling. The band dimmed to a slithering ashen slash, finally disappearing into the squall. Only their rapidly filling tracks graved the snow.

Mustering her courage, she ran headlong for the lee of a

drift, pressing her back against it as she angled away from the People. She doubled back along an ice-packed ridge, throwing terrified glances over her shoulder. Would they be looking yet?

Shuddering, she turned her face into the frigid gale, praying, "Wind Woman, please, cover my trail. I must get away."

Faintly, as if the spirit carried it to her deliberately, she heard Crow Caller shouting. Fragments of curses shot through the storm, one word clear in its repetition, "Death . . . death."

Stumbling forward, she ran with all her heart, lungs heaving as she scrambled over another ridge and headed along the spiny backbone, hiding behind each upthrust rock to stop and listen. For a long time she ran, heedless of anything more than direction and her hunger-starved weakness.

"Wolf?" she whispered to the darkening gray of day. "Wolf, you promised your Power would be strong. Protect me."

She could find Light's trail, even in the brunt of the storm. Memories of his warm eyes and gentle touch soothed her.

She threaded down the ridge, hair darting wildly before her eyes, then skirted an eerily sculpted bank of ice; it stretched like a series of mammoths lumbering along in single file. Through the haze, she thought she glimpsed their old shelters, the black hides frosted with snow.

"Could I be this close so soon?" she murmured, brow furrowing in thought. It didn't make sense that she'd come so far, but time seemed to stop in the midst of a storm.

Her eyes darted along the ice wall, roving blue hollows and swirling mounds. Snow fell harder, draining color from the arctic landscape until nothing but white existed. Sliding slowly along the wall, her fumbling outstretched hand sank suddenly back into the bank.

"What . . ." she murmured unsteadily, bending cautiously down to peer into the small ice cave. Kneeling, she crawled inside out of the wind.

Her sanctuary stretched barely five by eight feet, the ceiling only a foot over her head. Duck-walking to the rear of the cave, she removed her pack, shoving it into a darkened corner, and sagged wearily against the wall.

"Wolf?" Her voice echoed from the irregular walls. "They'll be looking for me as soon as the storm dies down."

As she huddled, trembling from exhaustion, she closed her eyes, trying to feel her soul, to feel if Crow Caller had taken any part of it. But the lightness of hunger obscured any other feelings.

Whirling silver wreaths swept by beyond the mouth of the cave, Wind Woman's undulating shrieks piercing the day. Fox rested, mittened hands shoved deep in her pockets, watching.

Despite her fear, sleep came quickly, drifting warmly down her exhausted limbs, wrapping softly around her reeling brain. Runs In Light grew out of a shining column of light. He stood out from the darkness, weeping. Behind him, the Star People glistened brilliantly over a series of jagged ridges. Each tear that dripped from his chin froze before it hit the ground, landing with a soft clink. Was he crying for her? No, she felt it was something much deeper, a soul wound no one but he himself could heal. Still, her heart ached for him. She wanted to go to him, to—

"Ah yes. Dancing Fox. Here you are," a smooth voice cooed, intruding on the dream.

She gasped, starting as she opened her eyes. It all came back, Crow Caller, the flight, the storm . . . *fear*.

"Raven Hunter," she said in a quivering voice, tears welling. The old man must have sent him to find her. "What do you want?"

He laughed and sat down beside her, amused by the way she cowered, holding his own hands high in a gesture of truce. She watched him intently, expecting foul play—waiting her chance to scramble out into the storm.

"Then you're not lost, I take it?"

She kept quiet, closing her eyes, a yawning emptiness growing under her heart.

"Oh, come," he chided. "I'm not here to hurt you. Let's say it's curiosity." His straight nose and high cheekbones shone red with cold, his full lips curled in a grin. Only his black eyes burned dark and impenetrable.

"Curiosity?"

"Yes," he said lightly, pushing back his fur hood and shaking out his long hair. "I didn't expect to see you out here. It's not a day to—"

"Stop it," she commanded quietly. "You followed me. *He* sent you."

"No," he defended flatly. "I haven't been back to the band. The storm came on so quickly, I didn't have a chance. And when I saw you running back toward Mammoth Camp, I had to come see why."

She glared coldly at him.

Pulling off his mittens and opening his pack, he removed a fragment of mammoth dung and, with the butt of his atlatl, chipped a small hole in the floor. Laying the fuel into the pit, he lifted fire sticks from his pouch, spinning them deftly until the tinder began smoldering. Gently, he blew to encourage the fire, a crackling flame spearing light into the shelter. Holding long fingers over the frail warmth rising from the dung, he looked at her, an eyebrow cocked.

She glared back.

"I saw you running along the ridge top." He puffed condensed breath and smiled faintly. "Never run on high places if you're trying to escape. People can see your movements over amazing distances."

She dropped her eyes to stare at the crimson glow expanding in the fire pit. She'd assumed the snow blanketed her frantic efforts—and maybe it had, from the band. She'd forgotten about him. Silently, she cursed herself.

"What do you want?" she demanded brusquely.

"For the moment, to fill my belly." Removing a stringy lump of frozen meat from a bag in his pack, he skewered it with his long dart and propped it over the fire.

"And then?"

Slumping comfortably back against the wall, he sighed and pinned her with his eyes, remarking casually, "Depends." A pause. "So, you're chasing after my worthless brother."

"I . . ." Her throat bobbed with a difficult swallow. "He—"

"He's leaving a trail for you. Yes, I noticed. So did old One Eye, I think."

Though he said the words mildly, they struck her like a blow in the stomach. Could it be true? No, Crow Caller would have punished her immediately. It was his way. "You're a liar."

He laughed. "Am I? Light's actions were rather difficult

to miss, don't you think? I mean, that quaint ceremony on top of the ridge, and your eyes locked with his. Why, only a fool—''

"Then how did you catch it?" she asked, folding her arms and hugging herself.

He glanced at her from the corner of his eye, a ghost of a smile on his lips. "Don't tell me you're still in love with him? Why, I thought sure Crow Caller's caresses would have blotted him from your mind long ago."

"I'd rather have a bott fly lay its seed in me than that foul old—''

"Such devotion from a doting young wife."

"Old One Eye? Isn't that what I heard you call the most powerful man among the People? Such respect from a young hunter to his elder."

He chuckled. "Perhaps we understand each other."

She glowered, but inside she thought how honeyed his voice sounded, honeyed—and friendly. A dangerous sign. Raven Hunter only grew amiable when he thought he could gain something.

"Of course," Raven Hunter continued, "my idiot brother did ask you to marry him after your father had given you to Crow Caller. His timing is priceless, isn't it?"

"You're a sick man."

He widened his eyes as though surprised, pointing at himself. Then he whispered, "I'm also your only friend right now."

"Friend," she scoffed.

"I haven't dragged you back to your husband yet, have I?" He leaned forward to twist the shaft of his dart so the other side of the meat would cook. When he looked back, his queer black eyes glistened with speckles of crimson from the fire. "Aren't you wondering why?"

"The storm is too violent."

"I've found my way in storms far worse than this."

Her stomach muscles clenched tight, as though her body knew something her mind refused to believe. Instinctively, she huddled as far back in the corner as she could. "Why, then?"

He stretched out, crossing his long legs at the ankles. "I wanted to talk to you."

"Why?"

He smiled, shaking his head. "We've never had a chance to talk, just the two of us."

A ferocious gust of wind blasted into their shelter, snow frosting their faces and sizzling in the flames. Dancing Fox threw up her arms as a shield. Raven Hunter brushed at his robes, then softly blew on the dung again.

"Are you going to drag me back?" she asked, struggling to keep her voice even.

"I haven't decided yet."

"And when will you?"

"Are you in such a hurry?" He lifted his hands, mocking amazement. Then he turned to look at her, an earnest seriousness in his eyes. "But then, I've always admired that about you. You remember when your father gave you to Crow Caller back at the beginning of the Long Dark?"

"How could I forget?"

He looked out at the blowing snow, the world turning charcoal now as the Long Dark settled on the land. "I wish I could."

She shuffled her feet, the hunger knot in her stomach growling at the smell of meat. "What do you—"

"Remember when I came back?"

"You had Grandfather White Bear's hide. The one who killed and ate Throws Bones."

He nodded. "It was for you. For your father. I . . . I would have asked for you then." His lips trembled suddenly before he tightened them. "If . . . well, if you'd have had me."

Words froze in her throat. He couldn't be serious. There'd barely been three amiable sentences between them in her entire life.

"But you were already in Crow Caller's robes. Nothing remained to be said." He sniffed and leaned back. "Funny how things work out. Especially between my brother and me. You loved him. Our parents, Seagull and Seal Paw, they loved him. And why? Hmm? Everything he does is only half there. You know? Like he's only half in this world."

"Is that why you hate him so?"

Raven Hunter nodded. Softly, he said, "Yes." Then he laughed. "Only we'll see. Things have changed. Flies Like

A Seagull is gone. I have killed Grandfather White Bear. I am about to become the greatest man among the People."

"Bold of you."

"But true." He checked the meat and shifted to look into her eyes. "And I want you with me."

She bit her tongue, wary, heart thudding in her chest. The sincerity couldn't be mistaken. A shining Power was there. He'd meant every word.

"But Crow Caller. He'll—"

Raven Hunter shook his head slowly. "Not me, he won't. And I know what he's done to you. I've heard him at night. Heard your whimpers. I'll never hurt you like that."

Off balance, she swallowed hard, a curious breathlessness in her chest. "I . . . I don't understand. . . ."

"I want you for my woman, Dancing Fox. I've killed Grandfather White Bear for you. Crow Caller is a foolish old man. One I'll need, true. But foolish nevertheless. I can handle him."

"But his Spirit Power—"

"You don't seriously *believe* that, do you?"

"I—"

"Think about my offer. That's all I ask." He smiled, cocking his head. "I would make you very happy. Keep you fed. Make a place for you among the councils of the People. You could do no better."

"And if I decide not to?"

He sighed heavily. "I'll have you in the end. It will be more difficult for both of us, but I won't lose. Of course, I'll have to take you back to Crow Caller, but—"

"I'm not going."

"Oh, I think you are."

"No, I'm leaving as soon as the storm lets up."

"Consider . . ." He steepled his fingers, frowning seriously. "You have no one left. Your father was your last living relative except for some uncles and cousins in Buffalo Back's band. If I take you back, Crow Caller will denounce you, curse you horribly, and everyone will be afraid of his threats. You'd be an outcast, shunned. You'd be reduced to begging for scraps—whatever charity the People might have."

"Maybe."

"After that," he continued as if he hadn't heard, "a man

can take you any way he wants." He looked at her soberly. "Any man . . . any time."

"You'd do that to me?"

He filled his lungs and sighed. "I could. I probably would." He shook his head slowly. "It's a funny thing. Something I'm not sure I can explain well, but as much as I love you, I couldn't stand the thought of you in Light's bed."

"You hate him that much?"

"Oh, yes." He smiled wistfully.

"You'd destroy me? Ruin me rather than let me go to Runs In Light?"

"Actually, I'm saving you from a terrible fate." He turned the meat, now thawed and beginning to sizzle. "If you go to Light, you'll be so miserable you'll pray for Crow Caller to come back and get you."

"I doubt it."

"I know you do. Now. But like my foolish brother, I, too, see bits of things in my head. I've never told anyone. They're scattered, unconnected." He stared at her with a curious emptiness. "But I see how wretched you'd be trying to live with him and his delusions. He's mad, you know. Completely mad. Crazy as a maggot-infested caribou and just as possessed by things that eat at him."

"I don't care."

"Then you've made my decision for me. I'll be taking you back."

"I won't go."

"You think that has some bearing on the subject?"

Wetting her lips fearfully, she said, "Yes. You may kill me, Raven Hunter, but I'll fight you to—"

"Did no one teach you feminine shame when you were growing up?" he asked nonchalantly. Reaching to his dart, he removed the meat and blew on it to cool it, then sliced it in strips and handed her a piece.

She stared at the meat dangling in his fingers for a long moment, trying to convince herself not to take it, but when he started to withdraw it, she snatched it quickly and tucked it in her pocket—for later.

"Smart move. We'll have a long trip back to the People."

"You'll have to drag me the whole way."

The look he gave her froze her very heart.

A deep pain glinted in his black eyes. "I don't mean to hurt you this way, but I've seen, Dancing Fox. You understand? You'll think I'm ruining you, degrading you, but it's the right thing in the end."

Her eyes narrowed in fear. *He's insane. Dear Star People, I've got to get out of here.*

He smiled weakly. "I love you, you see. You're the only person in the world I truly love. What I'm about to—"

"Then prove you love me and let me go."

He shook his head miserably, then pursed his lips, brow lining with intensity. "Oh, I can't. It's because I love you more than you can understand—"

"Do you want me dead? Crow Caller won't cast me out! He hates me, he'll—"

"No." He shivered suddenly, as if possessed by a deep chill. "No, never that."

"Then—"

"I . . . I don't know why. I've just . . . just seen it. Dreamed it maybe, huh?" And he laughed sourly. "Like my bone-brained brother. Only this is real. It's like I'm only a leaf in the wind. I *have* to marry you or destroy you."

He said it so precisely, he set her heart to slamming dully against her ribs. He leisurely ate the thin strips of meat. He wiped his hands on his long boots and offered her another piece. "Eat," he said softly. "You'll need the strength if you're going to try and escape me."

She took it numbly, enjoying the warmth, chewing. She recognized the rank taste: wolf. So he'd eaten of it, too. She choked it down, afraid to do otherwise.

"What else have you Dreamed?" she asked, stalling, darting fear-bright eyes past him to the darkness beyond.

Handing her the last of the meat, he swallowed his mouthful and poked at the ash-covered piece of dung. "There's blood and death coming." He pointed northward with his chin. "I can't see it all, but I know my path has been fixed. Like a caribou bull in rut, I have to follow it."

"Even if it means ruining the woman you love?"

He nodded absently. "Even if it means ruining both of us. If I believed that mouse dung about Father Sun, I'd say I was his plaything. Made to do these things because they amused him."

She bolted, trying to jump past him for the snow-choked opening, but his powerful arms closed about her waist, dragging her back. His grip bound her tight, flipping her over. She kicked and struck at him as he wrestled her down. His legs pinned hers, hands tight on her wrists.

She stared up into his face, lit now as the disturbed dung fire flared up. She struggled, trying to avoid his eyes; they possessed her, drilled into her very soul.

He's so handsome . . . like Light.

His breath smelled sweetly of meat.

He lowered his head, his cheek brushing hers. His skin felt wondrously warm against hers, the touch gentle.

"Let me up." She seemed to fall into the soft blackness of his eyes. Her vision swirled. Exertion along with hunger . . . or the power of his soul searching hers?

"You won't be mine?" he asked, misery in his voice.

She shook her head slowly, eyes still locked with his. "Never."

He winced, pain tormenting his expression. "Then I'll have to do it the hard way."

She struggled as he undid the lacings of her parka and jerked it open, exposing her body to the light. His pained look deepened when he saw the bruises left by Crow Caller. "I told you I'd never hurt you," he whispered. His knee forced her legs apart.

She gritted her teeth, turning her head away, eyes clamped shut, waiting for the hurt. But he did something new. Unlike Crow Caller, he slid in, filling her easily. There was no pain.

Chapter 8

Wan gray afternoon light splashed the drifts, shadows stretching like long fingers to stroke the pinched faces of the People. Smoke curled from the mouth of a snow shelter. Someone had scavenged moss or dwarf birch from the drainages. The split bones of a winter-killed buffalo littered the ice, mixing with the scattered feathers of a hapless crow. Children hugged the white walls, bouncing as they curiously watched the two people approach. Crow Caller stood with his chin high, black eye flaring.

"Raven Hunter," Dancing Fox pleaded softly. "Don't do this. You know what he'll—"

"I already told you. I have to."

Crow Caller strode arrogantly out to meet them, withered face stretched tight in anticipation. He cocked his head at the rawhide straps that bound her hands. "What is this?" he asked unsteadily.

"I found her fleeing to Runs In Light," Raven Hunter said somberly as he shoved Dancing Fox to her husband's feet.

"I . . . I wasn't," she denied, gasping deep breaths, her fear so strong she felt like vomiting. People crowded around, eyes wide and worried. She searched their faces, silently begging help. Gray Rock started to reach out to her, but pulled back. She didn't dare.

The old shaman's jaw quivered in rage. He stabbed a gnarled finger at Fox, shouting, "You would shame your clan by abandoning me?"

"No, no, I got lost. The storm . . ." *Why do I lie? Why don't I just face him? Let him do his worst. Shame him worse than he shames me?*

Raven Hunter's face blanched, his expression that of a man forced into an unbearable situation. "Hardly. I found her running back over the path the People had just walked."

She grimaced, memories of the nights they'd shared filling her mind. "I was lost! I didn't know where I was! I couldn't—"

"She was on your own tracks, Crow Caller," Raven Hunter said, "following them back to Mammoth Camp."

"Liar!" Defiantly, she met his eyes, seeing the ironic sympathy there. He looked away.

"She can't help it," he added in a low voice. "She must protest. She has nothing left. But I . . . I ask you, Crow Caller. Take her back. She's not a bad woman, just confused and foolish—"

"I won't go back!" she cried. "I hate him!"

The People gasped, staring in fear at Crow Caller. The old

man's good eye blazed while the white one branded her with unseeing malice. The shaman flexed and unflexed his fists, then violently kicked her in the side where she lay. A small wretched cry of agony rose in her throat. Getting to her knees, she retched over and over, her empty stomach writhing in frenzied cramps.

She looked up at Raven Hunter, pleading soundlessly with him. And if she accused him of rape? No, it had gone too far. Who'd believe her? She bent her head.

"She tried to escape to my worthless brother," he said softly, as though it distressed him greatly to discuss it. "I brought her back to her rightful place beside her husband."

"Get up!" Crow Caller ordered, grabbing her chin and twisting her neck to stare into her tear-filled eyes. She tried to stumble to her feet, but weakness overcame her and she fell back to the ice.

"From this moment forward," her husband raged into the howling of Wind Woman, "I condemn this woman's spirit to spiral downward away from the Blessed Star People. When she dies, her body will be buried. Her soul will remain locked in the ground forever with the roots and mold and rot. She has shamed our clan!"

Fox saw old friends shake their heads and walk toward the shelters. Some of the young women stood awkwardly a moment, staring at her before they, too, shunned her. Only Gray Rock remained, hunched old and frail beneath her furs.

"Crow Caller," the old woman said timidly. "Don't hurt her. She's just young—"

"Get away from here!" he screamed, slashing the air with his arm. "Do you want me to curse your legs so they lose their strength and you can't keep up with the clan?"

Gray Rock cringed. "No, but you—"

"Then go!"

She cast a glance of regret and sorrow at Fox before turning to hobble away toward the shelter.

Crow Caller knelt, horny fingers gouging into her arm as he probed her eyes threateningly. "People will laugh behind my back. They'll say I wasn't man enough to keep my own wife home."

"So, live with the truth for once."

"Shut up!" he shouted, backhanding her so powerfully her head slapped loudly against the ice.

Dizzy and nauseated again, she lay limp, feeling the frigid breath of Wind Woman caress her face. She heard the scuff of ivory and stone on leather as the old shaman drew his knife from its sheath.

Better to die. Feel me calling you, Runs In Light? Beloved, I tried to reach you. Not your fault . . . don't blame yourself.

She opened her eyes in time to see Crow Caller's long obsidian blade glittering glassy in the pale light and held her breath as he wrapped his fingers in her hair. Her heart beat a throbbing cadence as she tried to swallow down a fear-knotted throat.

"Dreamer?" Raven Hunter said, grabbing the old man's hand and staying the knife. "She's disgraced you, made a mockery of your leadership among the People. But this is wrong."

"Hush!" Crow Caller's cheeks reddened, breathing quickening. "I'll kill her to erase the—"

"But death is so easy."

"It's no longer your affair!"

Raven Hunter shrugged, releasing the old man's quaking hand. "True. But think about it. If you let her live, you can shame her every day for the pain she's caused. That's a far more just punishment than ending her misery now."

His voice sounded so reasonable and controlled, but Dancing Fox swallowed at the desperation in his eyes. One of the long darts rested in his fingers, poised to strike.

The old shaman stiffened, blinking thoughtfully as he stared down at his wife. He wiped his mouth with his hand. "Make her an outcast?"

Raven Hunter nodded. "That way she'll survive only if people throw her scraps of food. Or on what she can scavenge, like a crow."

"Yes . . ."

Fox closed her eyes. *And you can torment me whenever you want.* "Husband," she said imploringly. "Kill me. I'm no use—"

"No one will share their scraps. We're all hungry," Crow Caller said thoughtfully, rubbing his wrinkled jaw as a slow smile crept over his face.

Raven Hunter smiled in return. "This way, her death will be a lingering one and—"

"Live, woman! And see what it gets you," the old man bellowed. Looming over her, he whispered malevolently, "In one turning of Moon Woman's face, *you'll wish I'd slit your throat.*"

She gazed absently at the distant peaks that glowed a dusty purple. Runs In Light would be there by now, going through the hole in the ice to paradise beyond. She imagined his face, the softness in his eyes when he looked at her—and her soul cried in silent misery.

"I'll tell the People," Crow Caller said. She heard his retreating footsteps.

After a few moments, Raven Hunter exhaled loudly, kneeling beside her. He lifted her chin, forcing her to face him. He reminded her so much of Light . . . except for the cold glitter in his eyes.

"I thought for a second I'd have to kill him. But it looks like we passed the test. Now we must—"

"What test?"

He frowned as though thinking her stupid. "Didn't I tell you? There'll be many on the path. But don't worry, I'll make sure you have enough food so you'll have the strength."

"Why?"

His face softened. "Because I love you. And you're important to the future of the . . ." He paused, cocking his head and staring absently at the cloud-strewn sky. "I don't know how exactly. But someday, I'll need you. Remember the life you owe me."

As she gazed into his crazed and glassy eyes, a tremor shook her.

"Don't worry," he said. As if quieting the hysterics of a child, Raven Hunter closed his hands around her trembling mittens. "I told you, I'll take care of you."

Somewhere out in the drifts, a wolf yipped, his mournful howling carrying on the wind.

Chapter 9

In the milky light of the evening sun, Wind Woman swirled the clouds into long stringers of gold and picked at the bones of the People. A thin gilding of frost lined their hoods. Dark circles beneath their hard eyes, the People squinted ahead to the endless tiers of stark ridges.

One Who Cries looked back at the staggering line of people, working their way up the long ridge. Broken Branch came at the end, placing her feet carefully on the snow-blown rock. Three of the little children paced in front of her. Ahead, farther up the ridge, the one they now called Wolf Dreamer plodded onward, darts over his shoulder, pushed by the lure of his Dream.

One Who Cries glanced at Jumping Hare. His young cousin looked as worn as the ancient landscape. Wiping crusted ice from the hood fur around his jaw, he squinted against the frigid blasts ripping the land. "Four weeks, Crow Caller said. Four weeks until we'd feel hunger."

Jumping Hare pursed his lips tightly. "We've caught what? Three rabbits since we left Mammoth Camp?"

"And that's been only a week," One Who Cries grumbled miserably, staring at Wolf Dreamer's back. "We should have gone back."

"One way's as good as another," Green Water whispered. "We could have starved just as easily in Mammoth Camp."

One Who Cries lowered his eyes and lifted one hide-wrapped foot in front of the other, keeping the slow pace, knowing from experience that the night would be upon them before they made the crest of the ridge. Shame burned in his breast. Had he lost faith in the Wolf Dream so quickly?

Step-by-step, they climbed, testing the footing with the deliberateness of hunger-weak muscles. No extra move wasted what precious energy remained in their tired limbs.

"Spirits," Jumping Hare muttered under his breath. "Runs In Light had to hear Wolf. Had to run out and get mixed up in Spirit Power."

"You still believe that?" Singing Wolf asked, condescendingly.

"You don't?"

"Wolf wouldn't torture us to death if we were following his Dream."

"Hush. We had to do something," Laughing Sunshine chided. "You don't notice the women complaining, carrying on. We save our breath and effort for walking. If men had sense, so would they."

A heavy silence fell. They glanced back and forth uncertainly. In the distance, Father Sun's face wavered silver through the blanket of clouds, crawling downward.

"Maybe it's a test of our faith." Green Water sighed.

One Who Cries looked up to the gray sky. "Starving isn't a bad way to die. There's worse. There's bad teeth that rot and swell a man's jaw with pus. There's the joint-pain where a man hobbles in agony, his joints grinding and burning. A fellow can always break his leg out away from help— be eaten by Grandfather Brown Bear. And remember old Walrus Tusk? His legs swelled up fit to bust his long boots. Then his water got bloody. And then there was—"

"Hush!" Green Water said in exasperation.

Ice Fire woke in the night. Around him, he could hear the soft breathing of his clan. Over his head, the vicious wind rippled the hide roof of the shelter. In the darkness, he could see condensed breath rising from the robes around him. He shifted his position beneath the soft piles of hides, frowning into the sea-scented darkness.

A curious dream; he'd been walking, seeking something in the south. Behind him came the White Tusk Clan, hungry, trusting, and through it all he'd wondered if he'd been betrayed by some Power in the night. Yet, as he led his band up the rocky hills, they could feel eyes upon them, someone watching from above. There, on the side of that windswept hill, he'd turned, casting a searching look to the cloudy skies.

And he'd seen her eyes, staring down: The Watcher!

As he resettled himself, he tried to shake the feeling of premonition. The haunting call echoed around the edges of his mind. He blinked, yawned, and rolled over, trying to sleep again. Hours later, he pushed back the robes, putting on his outside parka and heading for the cold trap and the doorway.

"Can't sleep again, Elder?"

"No, Red Flint, my old friend." He paused, feeling the chill of the deep blackness seeping up from where he held the door flap slightly ajar. "At times I wonder if I'm slowly losing my mind."

Red Flint stirred in his furs and reached out, prodding the ashes in the fire pit, exposing a red eye of coal. "So, you were going out to walk around the night like some homeless ghost again?"

Ice Fire lifted a shoulder as Red Flint pulled on his parka and bent over to blow on the coal, feeding a bit of dried moss to the tiny eye, coaxing a blaze with bits of willow stems and dried leaves.

"The light might wake someone up," Ice Fire said, gesturing to the sleeping bundles around them.

Red Flint grinned in the glow; humor pulled the lines of his flat face into comic patterns. "I doubt it. You kept them up too late retelling the story of the Sky Spider spinning the web that holds up the sun and the sky. No, they'll sleep."

Ice Fire settled himself on the foot of his friend's robes, crossing his legs carefully. He grunted acceptance and stared into the flickering yellow flames.

"You're not gonna die, are you? Sometimes men can't sleep before they die."

Ice Fire bowed his head and chuckled softly. "Not yet."

"Then what's bothering you?"

He reached a long-boned hand for a willow stem and slowly poked the blaze with a length as he thought. Where to begin? "I dreamed of an old woman—a witch. I . . ." He frowned. "I know her. At least, I've felt her before."

"You old dog, you! Been feeling women? You're not ready to die . . . except for maybe your taste? Now, I got this daughter, Moon Water. She's budded out. Make you a good—"

"Do you want to hear this?" he asked irritably.

"I'm sorry. You just seemed so . . . Well, I thought maybe teasing would help."

Ice Fire slapped a hand to his friend's knee and paused for

a time, staring at the flames. "You remember me telling you about the woman I caught by the sea years ago?"

"The Enemy woman," Red Flint nodded, eyes gleaming. "Yes."

"The witch was there. Watching."

"I thought you didn't see anyone."

"I didn't. But I know the feel of the witch's vision. Like the way a dart shaft fits in the hand. Familiar. You don't have to look down to know your dart. It's the texture, the balance, the weight. She has that feel, this witch."

Red Flint scratched the side of his weathered face. "You think she's calling you? Maybe witched you? We could have a Sing, try and drive her off. Maybe we can throw it all back at her, hurt her—"

"No." He lifted a hand. "It's something else. Some awakening of Power that's stirred her . . . and me. Something's happening."

Red Flint stared somberly into the fire. Golden flickers reflected in his narrowed eyes. "You know the other clans aren't doing well. Tiger Belly Clan lost a lot of ground last year. Hundreds of young men were killed fighting the Glacier People. To the west, the Round Hoof Clan was pushed away from the Great Lake. They've been chased clear into Buffalo Clan's area. Face it, we've been pushed out of all our old places."

"The whole world is changing and there aren't enough of us anymore to push our enemies back."

"Is that what the witch is telling you?"

Ice Fire coughed and rubbed the back of his neck. "That's part of it, but there's more. She draws me south for another reason."

"What?"

"It has something to do with that Dream Walk I made years ago, after my wife was killed. I traveled many days' journey over difficult country. For two weeks, I went without food. I remember sleeping on a rocky pinnacle. The rock grew up out of the ground, rising so high I could look down on the birds. To the south, I saw a huge wall of white, and beyond it, a free land, full of animals but empty of humans."

"But we have Enemy to the south," Red Flint pointed out.

"Now, but not then."

"Should we try to go to that land?"

"I'm not sure. The Dream was unclear and the next day I found the Enemy woman. We were to come together, she and I. I could . . . could feel the rightness of it. A healing, if you will. Her long hair swirled in the wind. Water crashed about her feet. In a Dream haze, I walked up to her and she smiled. We coupled passionately, she and I, there by the sea, and I planted my seed in her."

"But that part was real." Red Flint's bushy brows lowered.

"Yes . . . and no." Ice Fire winced and ran hard fingers over his face. "The vision broke as I got up and looked . . . looked into the Watcher's eyes. And the woman . . . I raped her. Left her broken and crying on the sand. She who I should have loved and cherished, I destroyed."

"And you think the witch who haunts your sleep caused this?"

"I'm not sure."

Red Flint shifted uncomfortably, retrieving a stick to prod the fire into crackling brilliance. "What happened next?"

"I turned and saw all the clans following in my tracks, chased by all kinds of enemies."

"That's how the Dream ended?"

Ice Fire blinked, shrugging lightly. "No. After seeing what happened on the beach that day, I ran. You know, getting away from the horror. That night I had nightmares . . . one after another. The woman in the Dream stood up and offered her hands to me. In one lay a piece of meat. In the other she held her dart."

"Life or death?"

"I read it so." He propped his chin on his palms. "Then I looked behind me and the sea was rushing in, trying to swallow us all. I took the meat and the woman smiled again, saying, 'You and I are one. We are one.' Then she took my hand and turned into a great bird, the Storm Bird, and flew with me, far to the south to the middle of the new land beyond the white wall."

Red Flint sucked at his teeth for a moment, thinking. "And that's why you've always forced us to move south, despite the dwindling game?"

"Not since I went on that quest have I felt the spirit move

so powerfully within me. Until now. It plagues me, keeps me from sleeping. I feel driven, as if the witch pushes me to bring all the clans south.''

Red Flint squinted at the firelight dancing across the ceiling. ''But the rest of the clans won't come. They say there's no warrior's honor there. The Enemy scatters before us like seagulls from a thrown rock.''

''I know.'' He turned to search his friend's concerned face. ''And what if I can't save our people before the sea comes to drown them?''

''Then our clan will push south without them. In all of this, there is one certainty; these gutless Enemy we face are few, and getting fewer. At least our clan can brush them out of the way like so many flies.''

Ice Fire rubbed his hands together, feeling the calluses on his palms. ''Perhaps. But I've dreamed of a young man. A tall, angry young man. I see him gathering his darts and bringing us death. He's a leader. The kind who can stir warriors. He . . .''

''Go on.''

''I may have to kill him.''

Red Flint stared, motionless. ''You've killed before. Why does that bother you so?''

Ice Fire turned anguished eyes on him. ''I'm not sure I can.''

''Why not?''

''I . . . I think he's my son.''

Chapter 10

Anxiously, Wolf Dreamer looked out over the rugged land. It undulated in sharp peaks. Wind Woman's harsh breath left them tottering on their feet. The emptiness provided no solace. In the crevasses, thick stands of willow and dwarf birch locked the snow, making hazardous traps into which he'd fallen more than once, floundering out with a dangerous waste of energy. Slick ice slopes had to be negotiated, treacherous footing always a peril. He could risk no fall, no broken bones. It would mean his death.

And the People were *his* responsibility.

Like the weight of a mammoth tusk on his shoulders, the burden bore down on him. The taste of Wolf's blood rested eternally on the back of his tongue, the fire of the Dream pushing him onward.

It had been real.

As tormented days passed, he fought to convince himself that Wolf hadn't played trickster with him. To joke so with the lives of the People lay outside his comprehension. Runs In Light stopped, leaning on his dart shafts, looking out at the piled rock where snow packed the rounded gray boulders.

"Another Dream Hunt?" he whispered, feeling the presence of the Soul Eaters of the Long Dark hovering close, held at bay for these few short hours of light. "I'm too tired." *If only I could rest, lie down in the snow, and let the Long Dark suck my life away into Wind Woman's chant. Death would be release.* He clenched his jaw, silently chastising himself. *Coward.*

He took a deep breath and drove himself over the crest of a ridge, forcing his crying body beyond its feeble limitations. Behind him they came, bellies hollow, the flesh of their faces sagging, accusation in their eyes. Most no longer believed in the hole in the ice.

"Wolf?" he pleaded hoarsely. *"Lead me."*

He looked back, seeing One Who Cries and Jumping Hare stop and begin cutting into the side of a tapered drift. With a sharpened bison scapula, they removed blocks of frozen snow, gouging out a shelter with the shoulder bone.

"Must we camp here?" he whispered.

He saw Broken Branch and the sight filled him with pity. She still waddled along, sallow-faced, the glow of the Dream in her eyes.

Clenching his fist, he walked away from the digging—away from the People.

Wind Woman blew twisting wraiths of snow over him in a veil. The crystals clattered in muted defiance across the empty land. Upward, ever upward, how far had they climbed into these craggy hills? Cold and desolate, this land around them could have been the chill spine of some monster of the ice. Wind-ravaged and worn, the blue-black rock loomed, massive in the darkening night.

"So many mouths, Wolf. So little food."

Out of sight of the camp, Runs In Light sank to his knees, mittens clutching the forever snow.

"Was my Dream false?" he cried to the gathering spirits of the Dark. Head bowed, he could feel them rustle restlessly around him, their fingers already pulling at his soul.

Moonlight tarnished the slopes, gleaming silver from the polished drifts. Yellow hollows flickered and shimmered where moss and birch fires illuminated shelter holes dug into the snow. Through wavering clouds, the Star People glistened, watching.

Dancing Fox crouched behind the shelter, listening to the turmoil inside. Weeping pierced the haunting death songs. Gray Rock had grown desperately weak, her frail old body unable to take the long torturous days of endless walking and climbing. A deep aching regret tormented Fox. She wanted to rush inside and hold the old woman in her arms, rocking her back and forth while she poured out words of love and gratitude.

But she was an outcast. She could not enter the lodge unless someone mercifully asked her to, and she feared Gray Rock was too far gone for that.

She shuddered there in the bitter cold, her breath a white mist in the air. Wind stung her face, carrying the pitiful mourning of wolves.

"Why don't you leave?" she whispered angrily to herself. But she both knew and hated the reasons. They were too far away from Runs In Light now and she feared the snowstorms had long since covered the trail he'd left for her. She could not touch the food reserves of the clan. If she ran away, it would be without food or weapons.

A hollowness throbbed below her heart. If only she could reach Runs In Light, he'd help her, comfort her. Knowing that only made her struggle for survival more unbearable.

The singing inside stopped suddenly.

Twining fingers tightly in her parka, she waited, fearing the worst. Feet crunched softly on snow behind her.

"She was a good woman," Raven Hunter said regretfully. "I'm sorry Jumping Hare isn't here."

Her back muscles crawled. "I wish I could—"

"You can't," he said sympathetically. "They fear your cursed soul would interfere with her rise to the Blessed Star People."

She looked up at him. His brooding eyes gleamed darkly in the reflected moonlight. "Why did you come out?"

He crouched beside her in the dark and she could feel his warmth on her face. "I had another glimpse in there."

"Of what?"

"We'll see the death of the People, you and I. Unless something is done."

"So?" she spat hatefully.

Wails rose sharply in the shelter to pierce the wind. Bitterly, she murmured, "She's dead."

She closed her eyes, trying not to think of the dead they'd left behind. Old Talon would be next. She already staggered on wobbly legs. Where would the deaths end?

"I placed some meat in your pack. It's not much. Some strips I salvaged from a winter-killed buffalo. What the wolves left, I cleaned up before the crows got it. I'll bring the bones in tomorrow. There's enough bone butter there to keep another couple of souls with their bodies for a while longer."

She ignored him, staring dry-eyed at the shelter, remembering the little scraps of food Gray Rock had left from her share of the band's scavenged meals. Such a welcome kindness. Gray Rock had been one of the few to share, to talk guardedly and wink occasional support.

"I'll miss Gray Rock," Fox whispered miserably. "She never forgot that I needed to hear a kind voice on occasion."

Raven Hunter sat silently, listening. She appreciated that, knowing she'd pay later when he crawled into her robes. Someone had begun to sob uncontrollably inside the shelter. Numbly, Dancing Fox stood. In a moment, Raven Hunter, too, got to his feet.

"I suppose you'll come by to force me again tonight?"

He shrugged. "You have no one to speak for you. I don't hurt you. With Gray Rock gone, who else but me will speak kindly to you? Besides, I leave you enough to get by. You eat better in disgrace than Crow Caller's pets in fine social standing.''

"I hate you, you know." She walked away.

"I'm not your enemy, Dancing Fox."

"Then what are you? My keeper? Why didn't you let me just go? Why drag me back here?"

He walked slowly, snow crunching under the soft layers of his long-booted feet. "Because I love you. I won't have you dying in the snow."

Anger swept her. "You don't love me!" She spat into the snow to emphasize her point. "I'm nothing more than amusement for you. And I can't do a maggot-cursed thing about it."

Her skin prickled at the sudden, crazed look in his eyes. He smiled sweetly. "But this way you're mine alone."

She took a step backward. "Yes, you've seen to that. You've tied me as firmly as if you'd bound me with a mammoth-gut thong like some prize bear dog."

He placed a hand on her shoulder, ignoring her flinch as he turned her to face him. In tones cutting as obsidian he remarked, "I'll tell you once again, I love you. One day, you'll understand."

"Take your hands off me."

He tightened the grip on her shoulder. "And I need you. I'm the hope of the People. I've seen it, you understand? I just . . . just can't see it all. But I have to keep the Others back or they'll bury the People."

"Your delusions will be the death of us all."

He sighed heavily, shoulders dropping. Head down, he added, "You can hate me all you want. I have to save the People. Just me . . . and a strange man. Face-to-face, he gives me something. Something that changes the People." He stretched out his arms. "I don't know what. Only that my son—"

She started, eyes widening. "Is that why you want me? For a son?"

"I don't know for cer—"

Her move caught him off guard, her ringing slap staggering him. He fingered his cheek. A slow smile crossed his lips in the subtle glow of the night. "The vision is incomplete, but

I've already seen some of the flashes come true. Like finding you in the snow that day. I'm betting my very life and the lives of our people, that the rest will come and I'll meet this strange man. He's like . . . like . . .''

"I've heard enough," she spat. "You're crazy!" She turned as Crow Caller led the way from the shelter, the others in his wake, singing as they carried the remains of Gray Rock to the top of the drift, singing her soul to the Blessed Star People.

He gripped her arm, eyes burning into hers in the darkness. "Remember," he said. "Even if I have to sacrifice both of us, I'll save the People."

He shoved her arm back at her, leaving her off balance and reeling as he went to sing for Gray Rock's soul.

Dancing Fox pulled her hair back where it tumbled from under her hood and forced a deep breath into her lungs. Teeth gritted, she walked wearily to her worn sleeping skins, finding several long strips of dehydrated meat stuffed in her pack. Mouth watering, despite the guilt, she attacked them, ignoring the rancid taste.

That night, Raven Hunter didn't come to her.

Chapter 11

"Let's go back!" Jumping Hare declared, looking from face to face. Around them, the snow walls of the ice cave gleamed orange in the firelight.

"To what?" asked One Who Cries.

Green Water placed the last length of knotted willow ripped from the unyielding snow on the glowing coals. She could see her husband's eyes on her, waiting for her words.

"Back?" she asked calmly. "We've crossed nothing but rock. Maybe better land lies ahead?"

"Maybe, but—"

"At least here we find leaves and sometimes a handful of

frozen berries. We didn't have that at Mammoth Camp. There could be game ahead."

Singing Wolf gritted his teeth, waving both arms hostilely. "But we're too weak to hunt. It takes strength to kill."

"We'll manage," One Who Cries assured him.

"But even the mice are burrowed under the snow," Jumping Hare muttered. "The rabbits are gone. The few ptarmigan we've seen fly too—"

"Raven Hunter warned us," Singing Wolf quarreled. "Runs In Light is just a boy."

"And we didn't listen."

Broken Branch, who'd been sitting quietly in the corner, suddenly leaned forward. "You young idiots," she said, sucking the remains of the wolf bone she continued to carry in her pouch. "What's the matter with you? You think *he's* a boy? Look at you!" She snaked a bony arm out of her hide sleeve to point at each of them in turn. Hollow eyes stared back. "Your stomachs knot up a little and you run to bury your heads in the snow."

"But, Grandmother," Jumping Hare said incredulously. "We're starv—"

"Bah! You're not worthy of Wolf's gift. Go on! Get out!" She sucked her bone loudly, glaring through wind-tangled strands of gray.

Jumping Hare closed his eyes, unwilling even now to chastise an elder. "We might have to, Grandmother. To survive."

"I think we all forget," Green Water cautioned, "this Long Dark is different. Worse than any in memory. The Others lie to the north and west, blocking retreat. Here, we're in a new country. At least the ridges are blown free of snow. In those flats in the north, we'd walk all the way on snowshoes."

"But we might find a camp of the People," Jumping Hare pointed out.

"Would they have enough to share?" Green Water raised a cautious eyebrow. "Or would our arrival doom them . . . as well as us?"

"Survival," Singing Wolf muttered. "We sit here trying to figure a way to save ourselves, and where is our great *Dreamer*?" He pointed to the opening in the snow cave. "He ran away because he couldn't stand to face us!"

An uneasy silence settled, the only sounds the crackling of the fire and Broken Branch sucking her bone.

"He's trying to call the animals," Green Water said finally.

"Hah! He's hunger crazy. It takes a man with Spirit Power to call the animals. And what animal would be here? In these rocks?"

"Maybe some mice or—"

"I saw him stumble and fall today. He's lost his Power! He's going to kill us all!"

One Who Cries exhaled heavily. "I don't think—"

"Maybe the spirits of the Long Dark have already sucked his soul from his body, hauled it out there into the dark to give them strength so they can suck up ours."

"You . . ." Broken Branch whispered, faded eyes glistening in the flickering light. Everyone held their breath at the hostile look on her withered face. "What have you ever done for the People? Eh? Nothing. You're a complainer, not a doer. You wait for others to take chances, then you prance around condemning them. You're worse than the spirits of the Long Dark, you suck up all our souls with your jealous whinings."

Singing Wolf's mouth gaped, bitter words on his tongue. "You crazy old—"

"Don't you backtalk me, boy. I'll skewer you with this bone." She lunged at him, striking his collar hard. He scuttled backward, slapping at her.

"Crazy old curlew of a woman! Crazy! Like that cursed Runs In Light!"

Broken Branch sidled toward him, bone pointing, eyes keen as she cocked her head. "Let me tell you something, *boy*. You've never proved who you are! That's why you always sucked up to Crow Caller. At least, you did until he didn't sing for your little girl out there in the snow that day. Eh?"

"I don't know what you're—"

"That's what did it." She tapped the bone on his knee. "That's what broke your faith in Crow Caller and sent you following the Wolf Dream. And before that? What broke your faith in Sheep Whistle, eh? Maybe the fact that he didn't make you hunt leader when you thought you deserved it?"

Singing Wolf dropped his eyes, staring at the compacted snow polished to ice.

"You're all emotion, boy. You better think about that. You're always sniveling, never taking time to consider what you're doing or where you're going. If anybody will kill the People, it's you and your kind."

Singing Wolf's jaws ground so loud everyone could hear in the deepening silence. Heads bowed uncomfortably around the cave.

"And you want to be a leader?" Broken Branch clucked derisively. "You've got the makings deep inside, but you've always been too much of a coward to do anything with them."

"Grandmother, he tries," Green Water said softly. "This is a hard time for all of us. Singing Wolf—"

"He doesn't try very hard. The boy's got to get out and test himself—take some chances. Then he'll stop insulting people who try harder than he does."

Green Water smiled weakly. "When we look about us and see so many empty places where familiar faces should be, all of our hearts are stung. It's hard to want more tests. Don't blame Singing Wolf. This Long Dark has been particularly hard on him."

Broken Branch gave Green Water a cool stare from the corner of her eye, then turned to Singing Wolf. He sat, head down, apparently cowed. "Is that right, boy? You've had it harder than the rest of us?"

In a sudden move, he crawled past the old woman and out the hole into the night.

Jumping Hare mumbled to One Who Cries, "Too much hunger. Makes the senses leave."

One Who Cries lowered his eyes. "None of us are all the way sane."

"Especially Runs In Light."

Broken Branch jabbed out suddenly with her bone, poking his arm. He yipped.

"What do you know of Dreaming? I saw it!" she growled, nodding, her battered hood creasing. "I saw it in his eyes."

One Who Cries, frowning at his cowering cousin, put a restraining hand on Broken Branch's shoulder. "He didn't mean it, Grandmother. He—"

"*Maybe* you saw it!" Jumping Hare defended. "Then again, maybe he's crazy like Raven Hunter said."

Broken Branch scowled, looking down at the hand on her

shoulder. "Let me go, you empty-headed fool . . . or you're next," she warned, waving her sharp bone. One Who Cries jerked his hand away as though burned. Glaring around the shelter, Broken Branch breathed, "We're not dead yet, are we?"

"No," Green Water softly agreed. "The Dream lives."

"Dream?" Singing Wolf called from beyond the crawl hole. "He's Dreamed us to death."

"No!" Broken Branch shifted, bony fingers knotting in the nearest parka. One Who Cries tensed as she tugged feebly. "Didn't you see? Didn't you see his eyes?" Her gaze unfocused and she leaned back, grip loosening. "It was real."

"I believe, Grandmother," he said.

Green Water reached over, patting her reassuringly. "I saw his eyes, Grandmother. He Dreamed."

Jumping Hare bit his lip, looking away.

Green Water stirred, blinking awake. Through her robes she felt the chill play across her flesh. Father Sun would be rising soon. She struggled to sit up, limbs shaking.

They hadn't moved for two days. People huddled in their robes, eyes sunken with famine. No one had the strength to walk.

Our final resting, she mouthed silently.

She glanced to Runs In Light's robes; he was still gone. Carefully, she crawled over sleeping people to the opening. Squeezing through, she peered at the landscape. Above, the Star People twinkled while the long twilight grayed the southeast. Moon Woman's half-light gleamed from brooding peaks. Ponderous glaciers crept down their flanks, majestic mountains glowing blue in the clear air. Wind Woman, for a brief moment, had stilled her restless roar. To the east, a broad valley opened, stretching to rocky highlands beyond. Even in the poor light, Green Water could make out the piled mounds of glacial rock.

Turning slightly, she saw him.

He crouched, head slumped backward unnaturally. Snow had drifted up around him.

Heart in her throat, Green Water shuffled over, shaking him by the shoulder. He didn't move. She shook him harder, tears welling. "Wake up! Runs In Light?" Fear etched her face as she looked at the thick frost lining his fur hood. Even normal breathing should have melted some. . . .

"No," she whispered. A yawning gulf opened within.

Settling on her heels, she clutched a mittenful of snow and slapped it into his face. "*Wolf Dreamer?* We can't come to this."

He remained stiff and silent.

Viciously, she slapped him again and again, screaming, "Don't you die! Don't you leave us to starve! *You led us here!*"

Still he didn't move.

"No . . . no . . ." she moaned, dropping her face in her hands.

"Tired."

The whisper sank through her anger. Green Water gasped, falling on her knees beside him to brush snow from his cheeks. "What?"

"*Tired.*"

"Get up!" She beat him with her fists. "Get up, now!"

In a frantic gesture, she jerked his arm, dragging him to his feet. Staggering along beneath his weight, she forced him to walk, hoping his body could still generate enough heat to keep him alive.

"You cursed fool! You'd stay outside to avoid our eyes? You could have died and then where would we all—"

"Food," he mumbled. "Found food. Got tired. Just needed to . . . rest."

Green Water stopped, staring at him as though fearing she hadn't heard right. "Food?"

Runs In Light nodded feebly. With his chin, he gestured. "There, beyond the rocks. It was so heavy. I couldn't drag it."

"Go and get warm," Green Water ordered, leading him to the shelter entrance and helping him inside.

Following the scuff marks he'd left in the snow, she trudged up over the ridge. Below the outcrop—blasted clean by Wind Woman's fury—a matted lump of brown lay wedged in the rock. Green Water recognized the thick hair and heavy hoof: musk ox. The better part of a hind quarter. No feast for so many, but enough, perhaps, to get them off this high rock and back to country where game roamed.

The wolves had been at it; slashes from their fangs scored the hide, ripping out long sections of hair. Carrion it might be, but in winter, in hunger, no one cared.

Reaching into her pouch, she pulled out a hafted knife. Trembling, she chiseled at the frozen flesh.

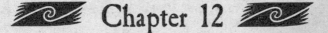 Chapter 12

Rejuvenated, One Who Cries, Singing Wolf, and Jumping Hare struggled to lift the hind quarter to the top of the rocks so the women could drag it down to camp.

"Sheeesh," Jumping Hare groaned, feet slipping down the icy ridge as he pushed on the slab of frozen meat. "How'd he get it this far?"

"The spirits must have given him strength," One Who Cries said through clenched teeth, pulling from the top.

"Spirits," Singing Wolf grunted. "Men just do crazy things when they're desperate."

"He said he followed wolf tracks."

"Who cares? You think we're saved?" Singing Wolf snorted. "Maybe we'll all have full bellies for one day from this slab. What then?"

Jumping Hare looked uneasy as he sank teeth into his lip. "Wolf Dreamer said there was more out on the plains."

Heaving one last time, they shoved the meat to the top of the hill and leaned back against the rocks, panting. One Who Cries eyed Singing Wolf uneasily. The man grew more difficult and hostile every day, inciting people to squabble with one another, shoving them to criticize Runs In Light behind his back. His manner had gone even more sour after Broken Branch's challenge that night. Singing Wolf acted like a man on the verge of coming apart. The Dreamer had stopped sitting around their nightly fires, fearing the whispered taunts.

"Let's go find the rest," One Who Cries said, shuffling down the Dreamer's back trail. Long dark brown hairs from the musk ox's hide marked the path. "Hope the scavengers haven't outscavenged us."

Singing Wolf grumbled, "We made the wrong choice. I knew better than to follow some crazy kid."

"Wait," One Who Cries said awkwardly, fleetingly meeting his cousin's hard eyes. "You'll see. Down on that plain, I'll bet we find—"

"Nothing! That's what we'll find. In another week we'll be starving again."

"You're in a good mood." Jumping Hare's sarcasm cut as bitter as the wind.

"I'm no fool. I know when I'm—"

"Stop it!" One Who Cries bellowed. "Wolf has provided for us. Quit trying to make everybody . . ."

Singing Wolf's condemning laughter stopped him. One Who Cries glowered, then trotted ahead faster, not wanting the trouble he knew lurked just beneath his anger. If only Broken Branch hadn't goaded his cousin.

"If Wolf was really leading us," Singing Wolf yelled, voice undulating on the glacial wind, "you think he'd bring us a pitiful winter kill? Huh? He'd call a whole herd of mammoth for us!"

One Who Cries didn't turn, wading through a patch of swirled snow to the top of a ridge. His heart pounded with anger. If things didn't start going better, he'd end up slamming a fist into Singing Wolf's big mouth.

"I think I'll take my woman and go back. Why don't you come with me?" Singing Wolf asked in sudden hope, racing forward to catch up. "We know what's behind us. We can—"

"Uh-huh." One Who Cries stepped over an outcrop of shale, surveying the gleaming country. "The Others."

"I'm not afraid—"

"I'm going to the plain," Jumping Hare murmured apologetically. "One musk ox died there. Maybe there's more."

As they descended the icy ridge, they saw the carcass. The wolves stood, marking the sight, watching with wary yellow eyes.

Singing Wolf ran screaming into their midst. "Get away. Go on!"

The animals scattered, whining and snarling their resentment.

"Why'd you do that?" One Who Cries shouted. "If you'd given us a chance, we might have shot one or two. Wolf's crummy meat. But it's meat."

Jumping Hare sighed, watching the wary animals now circling beyond dart range. "One of those wolves might have made the difference for some of the old people."

Singing Wolf opened his mouth, a hot retort on his lips. As if the reality had finally sunk in, he looked quickly away, shoulders slumping.

One Who Cries squinted at the remains. The ox had mired in deep snow, breaking through a hidden patch of larch. The wolves had taken their time. "No guts. Wolves got most of the fat. But it's life."

Jumping Hare licked his cracked lips. "People will call us stupid if we haul this all the way back to camp and then walk past this place on our way to some hole in the ice." He glanced sideways at his clan brothers. "We are going that way. Aren't we?"

One Who Cries filled his lungs with air, then exhaled. "I'm not climbing all those ridges back to Mammoth Camp."

"Good!" Jumping Hare blurted, flapping his arms gleefully. "I'll go get the rest of our people and bring them here." He turned quickly, running back along their trail.

One Who Cries glanced to Singing Wolf. His cousin looked away, guilt bright in his eyes.

One by one, Crow Caller's band began to fail. Two Whistles wandered off during the march. Slate Rock stumbled and fell, refusing to get up. Staggering on, they'd had no choice but to leave him. Crow Caller exhorted them, whipped them with words and blows, but the People had been pushed so far beyond their endurance they couldn't comply.

Dancing Fox plodded along, feeling how close she was to the edge, knowing that without Raven Hunter's extra donations, she, too, would have long since died from the cold or exhaustion. Determined, she held on, marching at the end, trying to keep the stragglers moving. Sometimes succeeding, other times failing.

Even Raven Hunter's face seemed empty. Only his indomitable spirit kept him roving before the band. His periodic offerings of rabbits, ptarmigan, and the scavenged remains of winter kills kept them going. Many on the edge of death, they still stumbled on.

In her dreams, Runs In Light watched, his eyes ever filled with tears. One Dream repeated over and over. Runs In Light stood high on a rocky hill. Below, Dancing Fox clambered over rough angular rocks, levering herself up, scrambling. The harder she climbed, the steeper the slope, the higher he seemed.

She called to him, reaching up, trying to touch the rock on which he stood. Again and again she tried, jumping, leaping fruitlessly. Yet he stood, face impassive, unaware of her as she tried so desperately to get his attention.

Finally, as she screamed her misery, he would turn, the Dream in his eyes, and walk slowly away in a shaft of light, leaving her in the empty darkness.

"Should have gone with Runs In Light," Talon mumbled weakly where she hobbled in front of Dancing Fox. "Should have. Wolf Dream. Broken Branch saw it. She knew a Dreamer when she saw one."

A chill lay around Dancing Fox's heart. "Yes," she whispered. "She knew."

Talon looked back for a moment, the stigma of a cursed woman forgotten. "Deep down, I knew Crow Caller's Power was gone. And he leads us anyway."

"He's a fool," Dancing Fox said. "And worse, he's killed people who trusted him—just to save face."

"Well," Talon gasped, breath puffing whitely before her, "he's killed me, too. I'm tired, girl. Tired and cold. I feel it in my joints. I shiver a lot now when I'm not moving. You know what that means? No fire in the body anymore. No fire, girl."

"You can make it," Dancing Fox insisted. "Here, lean against me."

The old woman shook her head, coming to a stop. "No," she said in a long exhale. "I'm just plain tired. You understand? I've gone over the edge."

Dancing Fox stopped, heart thundering. "Here, take my hand. I'll help. You'll die if you fall behind. You won't make it to shelter after dark."

Talon chuckled dryly. "Take your hand? And have my soul soiled by yours?"

Dancing Fox withdrew her offered mitten, dropping her eyes. "I want you to live, that's all."

"I'm joking, girl. I don't care about *his* curses. His Power's gone. He can't hurt me or you."

They held each other's eyes for a moment, probing the other's soul.

"I'm sorry I spurned you," Talon whispered miserably. "I worried about what people would think of me. And now look." She gave a halfhearted wave. "Those I lived with stumble off and leave me. And who takes time to offer encouragement? A cursed woman thrown out by that idiot, Crow Caller."

"Come on." Dancing Fox smiled and put her arm around the old woman's bony shoulders. "Let's go. Raven Hunter will bring me something tonight. I'll share with you. Just keep trying for me, all right?"

"Crow Caller will try to bury us both, you know?" As an afterthought, she added, "If he lives that long."

"If . . ." Fox muttered, helping support the old woman, feeling the cold seeping up through her own legs, knowing how close she was to collapse.

"Sure," Talon grumbled. "With all of us hating him so much, it ought to kill him."

Silently, Fox hoped the old woman was right.

Snowshoes were unstrung from packs and tied with knots to long boots. Warily, the People walked out into the open. Keen eyes scanning the snow, searching for tracks left by caribou, musk ox, or a rare moose. To the side, fox trotted close enough to identify them before hastening away. As the Long Dark grew out of the north, they dug into the drifts for shelter.

Runs In Light chewed a thin strip of raw frozen meat. The warm taste of ox lay lightly on his tongue, saliva running in his mouth. So little. One hearty meal. Enough to keep them alive. Where was mammoth? A few of the beasts should have been sweeping the snow with their huge tusks. Where were the caribou?

But the Dream had been so vivid.

He reluctantly let his eyes drift over their shelter. Children already lay snuggled under robes in the corner, their mothers huddled together beside them. Men slouched bleakly against the irregular ice walls. No one met his eyes. They talked as if he wasn't there. All but Broken Branch, who ambled over, helping him scoop a place for his robes out of the snow.

"Am I an outcast, Grandmother?" he asked softly.

She sniffed in the darkness, a mittened hand resting lightly on his knee. "Wolf Dream, boy. It'll lead us."

"Will it?"

"Of course. Wolf's just seeing if we're worthy."

He bowed his head and long black hair tumbled down over his chest. Fumbling with the laces on his boots, he asked, "What if it was just hunger playing with my mind?"

"Hunger—or a knock in the head—it doesn't matter what brings the Dream . . . so long as it comes."

He glanced around the dimly lit shelter. "They won't look at me."

Her taloned fingers tightened on his knee. "So? You need their approval before you believe what Wolf told you?"

"I'm not cer—"

"If you do, you've no business being here. Get out there in the darkness and call Wolf again!"

She mumbled incoherently after that, waving her arms in irritation as she waddled away on stringy legs, a gleam of stubborn faith lighting her old eyes.

Crazy old woman. What did she know? He'd tried calling Wolf a hundred times, but no answer came. And the memory of the Power that had supported him when he faced Crow Caller grew dimmer every day, hanging in the back of his mind like a vanished wraith.

"Wolf Dream," the old woman whispered gruffly as she nodded off to exhausted sleep. "Wolf Dream."

Runs In Light curled into a fetal ball and pulled his robes over his head, letting the warm blackness soothe his inner fears.

He slung his pack over his shoulder the next morning and strode to where Jumping Hare and Singing Wolf talked animatedly. As he neared, their conversation died, their angry eyes accusing him.

"I . . ." He fumbled for words, smiling imploringly. "Is everything ready here?"

"Of course," Singing Wolf told him stiffly.

He nodded, avoiding people's stares as he walked to the end of the line to stand beside Broken Branch. Jumping Hare took the lead, swinging out on his snowshoes. That day, and the next, forever, he limited his world to placing one step ahead of the next, calling Wolf with every breath. In his memory the green meadows and glistening hides of the animals shone in that vast lushness.

Chapter 13

Dark clouds roiled on the horizon, the scent of a storm riding the chill wind. Fading sunlight lay in streaks of rusty gold across Talon's ancient face. The old woman shivered in Dancing Fox's arms, her whole body spasming.

"Stay alive," Fox pleaded. "Live, Grandmother. Live."

She pulled the worn caribou hide around them, but one hide was hardly enough to keep them warm despite the insulating layer of snow. They'd wandered down from the heights into the flats. Here, they found no places where the snow had been blown free of the surface. No exposed dung, no caribou or sphagnum moss, no willow or birch.

Lumps of snow marked places where the People huddled together. This was the end. They all knew it.

"You're a good girl, Fox," Talon whispered. "My legs are feeling warm. My feet feel like they're over coals. You know, comfortable."

Dancing Fox closed her eyes. "I'm glad."

"Freezing's not a bad way to go." Talon sighed. "It really isn't. A person just sleeps."

"Grandmother, you're not going to—"

"Yes, I am. I got a deep cold inside me. A killing cold.

Odd that killing cold makes you ache all over—then makes you warm."

"Hush, save your strength."

"I'm going to sleep warm. Warm," she breathed, a faint smile curling her chapped lips.

Dancing Fox gripped her tightly, hugging Talon to her chest. The bones beneath the old woman's emaciated flesh felt as brittle as dried twigs.

"At least," Talon whispered, mittens stiffly tracing the patterns of light dappling their robes, "I won't die alone."

In the distance, she saw Crow Caller trying feebly to stand. Snow puffed from his robes. He struggled, weaving aimlessly, then fell back to the snow and tumbled to his side to lie still.

Fox smiled.

"A trail," One Who Cries said without emotion. He bent down, looking at the slashed snow, seeing the way it had drifted in. Moving a couple of steps, he kicked at mammoth dung, winter dung, thick with sticks.

Runs In Light glanced at the anxious faces around him. One of the children had been found, frozen in her robes. Singing Wolf supported a little girl who stumbled uncontrollably.

Mammoth? How could weak humans expect to kill a mammoth? Especially a full-grown adult? But the sticks in the dung proved that somewhere, at least, forage existed in the snow. Where enough remained to feed mammoth, perhaps a hare could be trapped? Perhaps caribou? Not even that hope penetrated the lackluster eyes of the People.

"We can't go further," Laughing Sunshine called listlessly. "I can't do it."

Green Water padded over, looking carefully into Laughing Sunshine's eyes, pulling a hand from her mitten to feel Sunshine's cheeks. "We've got to stop for a while. She's going to fall on her face if we push further."

"Me, too," young Moss agreed where he stood on trembling legs.

One Who Cries flinched, eyes searching the gray landscape, looking to the low-hanging clouds, feeling the bite of

Wind Woman's fury. Flakes of snow rushed past, borne on the wind.

"Let's stop. Darkness is falling. Tomorrow, those who can stand will follow the mammoth's tracks."

Runs In Light watched, gnawing doubt leaving him empty. He bent his back, cutting at the packed snow, lifting the light blocks from the drift. If nothing else, his efforts might keep some of the People alive to starve later. His faith in the Dream had stretched as thin as a caribou hair. *Had it been real?* He no longer knew.

Green Water watched him through furtive eyes for a moment before walking slowly over to place a hand on his shoulder. "I don't know what you're thinking, but don't let Singing Wolf's words hurt you."

He shivered and blinked at her, feeling the horrible pang of doubt knotting in his chest. "Maybe he's right. I . . . I'm responsible. I led you here."

"You did your best, Wolf Dreamer. There's honor in that. No one can give more than—"

"My best?" he whispered dully, scooping snow as his eyes darted over the wind-sculpted landscape. "Is that enough? I see their thoughts in their eyes. I see what they—"

"They're just tired," she chided. "Don't judge them so harshly."

He looked around dubiously, scanning the blood red sky behind them. Drifts hemmed them in like walls. "Singing Wolf called me a false—"

"I know. But he's confused. He's facing something he doesn't understand. For the first time since he sucked a teat, he's feeling helpless to provide for his family."

He lowered his eyes at the warm understanding in her frail smile. "None of us are providing for our loved ones."

"It's a terrible reality for a man to face."

"A man?"

Green Water nodded. "I've always felt sorry for men. They take responsibility for so many things that aren't their fault. Like Singing Wolf when he looks at Laughing Sunshine with the death of his baby weighing on him. He fears Sunshine might leave him for another man . . . a better provider."

"That's crazy." Wolf Dreamer chewed his lip. "She loves him."

"But Singing Wolf doesn't see it. Men are just that way." She winked at him. "You should be glad you have us around to keep you out of trouble. Women stay sane in times like these. We have to."

He clenched a fistful of snow. "I'm still responsible."

She patted his shoulder. "Come, rest. I believe in you. Laughing Sunshine, Ocher, and Broken Branch, we all believe in you. We all know what you've done—and appreciate it."

He stared at her as she smiled warmly, then nodded and walked slowly to where they handed blocks of snow out of the excavations.

When they'd cut three cavities from the lee of the drift, he carefully faded back, feeling the trail. Last time, wolf tracks had led him to musk ox. Perhaps this time, Wolf would come. Or perhaps he'd stumble over another winter kill—for Green Water and the rest.

On unsure legs, he turned into the growing darkness, feeling his way on the uneven surface of the trail.

Black's yipping brought Heron wide-awake.

She sat up and rubbed stiff fists into her eyes. "Something different in that bark of yours," she called out.

Red coals glowed around the rock-heaped fire pit. Retrieving her darts, Heron rose and pulled on her parka. Again the yip came, barely audible over the howling of the wind. She shoved her feet into her boots, snugging the laces tight and binding her hair with a thong before pulling the hood closed about her face. Last, she took her snowshoes.

Before leaving, she settled a couple of faggots of wood on the fire and ducked through the flap. Snow whirled from the darkness—a twisting cascade as she turned her head, half-hesitant to undo the hood and free her ears. No, not good to get her head wet in this. The head lost too much heat unprotected.

Black barked again. She got a fix on the direction and hesitated. Even with her knowledge of the area, only a fool walked out in the wind-whipped storm. Still, something in Black's call, some wrongness, goaded her onward.

"Never heard you yap like that," she murmured in concern, feet crunching on new snow as she angled away from her home.

She whistled, hearing the faint responding howl. Bending, she tied her feet into the webbing of the snowshoes. Steadfast, dart nocked in her atlatl, she crunched up the slope, into the brunt of the wind. Her lips chilled, making whistling difficult. Snow packed on the front of her caribou parka, forcing her to walk head down to keep the storm from blinding her.

Black yelped excitedly in the distance.

Rested though she was, her aged legs complained, aching in the deep drifts. Time and again, she whistled, following the lead of Black's cry. For what seemed an eternity of night and Wind Woman's incessant harassment, Black's call grew louder.

He bounded out of the dark, whining, the bitch White on his heels, as always, unsure. Black leapt away. Stolidly, she followed.

She almost missed him. He lay half-buried, face cradled in his arms, protected from the force of the gale. The snow around him had been packed by Black's feet. The dog looked up, whining, tail swishing.

"There," she cooed. "Good boy. Just like I trained you, huh?"

She bent down, squinting at his clothing in the blackness. "One of the People. Here?" She blinked, an eerie sense of familiarity taunting her heart.

Frowning for what seemed an eternity, Heron finally pulled his snow-encrusted arm away, looking at his slack features. "Too late." She sighed. "Looks like he's froze."

Chapter 14

Heron kicked him in the ribs, hard, and got a groan.

"Come on," she growled. "Get up."

Lifting, she got him to his feet, slipping on the irregularity of the snow beneath. Mammoth trail. Must have been the old bull headed for the hot springs. The boy had followed the tracks.

"Black," she called, supporting the staggering man's weight. "Home, Black."

Obedient, the dog loped away, a charcoal splotch in the windswept night.

Forever they walked. Her breath tore at her lungs. He faltered, trying to keep erect. Even through the many layers of his clothing, she could feel his bones. Starved. One foot at a time, they progressed, Black racing back and forth, leading the way, nose to the piling snow.

An hour later, on the verge of collapse, they crested the ridge, the stranger falling to his knees, almost dragging her down. Huffing condensed clouds of breath, Heron grabbed his hood and slid him down the trail.

He shivered, the spasms violent.

"You gonna die after I've done all this work?" she grumbled. Pulling off her mittens, she undid his parka with stiffened fingers, the dogs nosing about, anxious, reading her disquiet.

The stiff leather came off with difficulty. Heron turned her face away at the odor of him. Sickness and stale sweat hung heavily about him. Teeth chattering, she yanked the last of his clothing off and stripped herself, dragging him over the rocks, heedless of his tender skin until she had him in the warm water of her hot springs.

In the darkness, steam swirled wildly in the wind, enveloping them in a blanket of moist warmth. She held him, feeling the strangeness of human flesh against hers. Keeping his head above water, she listened to his heart, to his breathing. He stirred.

"You're safe," she assured. "Now tell me what you're doing here?"

The boy muttered, voice thick, the words only half-formed. In the darkness, she could read his confused eyes. She knew this boy. *Something inside tensed.*

"Long ago . . ." she muttered. "You've finally come."

The next evening Heron ducked under the door flap, leaving the wide-eyed boy to stare at her back. He'd remained quiet, absorbed in his own thoughts. She hadn't wanted to push him yet, but would have to soon.

Stepping along the mist-slick rocks at the edge of the pool, she stopped suddenly. The old mammoth lumbered down the hillside and into the pool, soaking up water with his trunk and spraying it over his back.

"Back again, are you? Brought me a human, you know? Followed your trail."

An explosive exhale and a grunt were her only answers as he scented the air warily. He always came before a storm. Regular as the call of a plover, the huge animal plodded to the hot springs to suck up the mineral waters and wade in the steaming pool. She accepted that, understanding how joints ached prior to the storm. Her own, stiff now with pain, reacted the same way.

She waited, speaking softly to her two dogs who watched with pricked ears. She motioned with a flat hand, keeping them steady, silent.

While they had a truce of sorts—she and the old bull—they didn't crowd each other's territory. On a rock, she waited, keeping a cautious eye on the mammoth who stood up to his belly in rolling mist. He swayed his trunk, splashing slightly as though the odor of the mineral springs was distasteful to his sensitive nose.

In the lee of the rocks, the wind didn't touch her, though tiny flakes of snow drifted down from the sky to disappear as they landed on the warm rocks. Magically, from the mist, caribou appeared. Young "one antler" held his head irritably, shaking it, as the itch to shed tormented his lopsided head. Warily, the caribou drank, feeling Heron's serenity.

Black shifted uneasily. She signaled the dog to quiet.

White stifled a low whine, her eyes on the caribou, speculative.

The old mammoth grunted, lifting his trunk, stepping gingerly toward shore. A ponderous beast, his huge legs ran silver-crested waves toward the rocky beach, the swirling fog from the hot water almost obscuring him from her view. Amidst splashes, the patriarch of the herd gracefully placed his treelike feet; rock grated under the weight. Rivulets of runoff drained in threads from his coarse red-brown hair.

"Yes," Heron cooed. "You'd best get back to your cows. What have you got up there? Three now? And two calves to keep track of? Better beware, old man. The Long Light is growing. Other young sprouts will be coming, trying to drive you off and keep the old dames to themselves, eh?"

At her words, he turned, facing her, grunting again.

"Oh, go on with you." She waved him away. "What's one old woman to you?"

He lifted his trunk, working his mouth noisily, and turned into the storm, a moving mountain of hair and meat. His bulk faded into the darkness, becoming one with the haze.

Black shifted nervously, nose working as he watched the big animal vanish into the roiling mists.

The caribou eyed her warily. Heron waited until they'd drunk their fill of the water, splashing disdain at the taste with their noses. Uneasy, they moved off, licking black muzzles. They, too, had been enveloped by the steam before she stood, stripping in the icy air.

She picked her way over the rock, wading into the warm water until it reached her hips. Gracefully, she dove, letting the warmth tingle and eat into her skin. Bathed in radiant heat, she stroked across the pool, rising, spitting a mouthful of sulfurous water before standing on the other side.

Ah, how the heat helped. With callused fingers, she squeezed her hair dry and sighed, swirling the waters around her. Ice crystals formed in her hair as the breeze skimmed the surface, fraying the mists.

Black scrutinized her anxiously from the shore, stepping lightly along the rocks.

Heron lay floating as the dusk settled, feeling life in her old joints. Indeed, this was bliss. Such a treasure, this pool of hers. Above, higher in the rocks and hidden by mist, the geyser hissed and gushed, steam billowing down as hot water shot to the sky. The fount splattered the rocks in a melodic staccato.

Refreshed, Heron paddled to shore, stepping from the water. Her breath fogged before her as she shook water from her arms and legs, shivering. Gathering her clothing, she walked a dart's-throw to the mouth of her cave, feet tingling on the cold snow. Black followed, White trailing him, sniffing the wind.

She passed the caribou-hide door flaps and dropped another stick of birch onto the glowing coals, standing above them in the heat, letting her body dry before dressing. The boy sat across the fire, watching her hesitantly. He was a good-looking brat, perfect oval face with wide eyes and full lips. Tall, too, with broad shoulders.

Black paced nervously at the doorway, looking back over his shoulder.

"Hungry," Heron muttered.

Black's tail wagged and he sneezed, stretching his front legs playfully.

"Go! See what you can run down." She waved a hand, White and Black both nuzzling under the flap and into the coming night.

Heron wrung out her damp hair, spreading it over the dry heat of the fire. "You look like you'll live," she commented.

The boy bobbed his head slowly. "I will, but I'm worried about my people. When I left, the three shelters were all crowded. I don't know how many will be alive."

"Tomorrow, when it's light, we'll go get them." She sighed. "There goes my privacy."

He said nothing, eating slowly of her pemmican. The mixture of berries and fat would provide nourishment for his skinny frame.

She nodded, unable to take her eyes from his. "You grew up to be much more handsome than I'd imagined."

He looked up, frowning. "What?"

"Never mind. I'll explain later. First, tell me why you're here." She nudged the end of another stick into the crackling blaze. "I thought old Crow Caller's father had warned everyone away from this place."

"He did." He looked away, eyes pained, guilt in his expression. "I brought people here anyway."

"Wise choice." She fluffed her graying hair. She was unaccustomed to using her voice to speak to a human being. Her tones, once a smooth and sweet contralto, had gone gravelly over the long years.

He dropped his head in his hands. At the broken look, her heart went out to him. Some terrible burden weighed him down, betrayed by his anxious eyes.

"You want to tell me about it?"

He shrugged uncomfortably. "I . . . I Dreamed. We were hungry. Hunger does strange things to a person's mind."

"Of course it does strange things, but that doesn't have anything to do with Dreaming."

"How do you know?" he asked, a twinge of fear and hope in his voice.

"I know."

His face flushed as he ran a hand through his long hair. "Wolf . . . called me . . . I mean . . ."

Heron's heart quickened. She reached across and lifted his chin. "Look me in the eyes, boy. Tell me what Wolf told you."

He swallowed, jaw working under smooth skin in the grip of her hard fingers. "We were starving in the shelters. I heard Wolf scratching at my mother's corpse. I . . . I thought only of meat." Once started, the story flowed, hesitantly to be sure, but it all came out. She stopped him when he told of trying to call the animals, to find them that they might eat.

"And when you tried to call the animals? What then?"

He shook his head, hands extended to the fire. "I couldn't feel them, couldn't . . . I'm not a Dreamer. Look what I've done. Led my people to the ends of the world—"

"Your mind was clogged. You thought other things? You were desperate?"

He nodded, cowed.

Heron scowled. "Yet you say you stood up to Crow Caller, that the strength of Wolf was in you."

He shot a hard look, a glint of defiance in his eyes. "Yes. I *felt* that! It was there . . . then."

"Yes," she said contemplatively. "I can tell it was. But why isn't it now? Did no one teach you—"

"I don't know why!" he shouted in frustration.

"Who Dreams among the People now?"

"Crow Caller."

She lifted a brow. What had happened all those long years she'd been away? "I always felt a wrongness about him. He never Dreamed right . . . like only half Dreams. He changed visions. Never let himself be free. Takes freedom to Dream . . . solitude."

"Broken Branch said—"

"Broken Branch?" Heron gasped. "Is that traitorous witch still alive?"

The boy winced. "Last time I saw her."

Heron chuckled, slapping her thigh, then unpleasant memories came to the surface of her mind, hardening her heart. "I think maybe I'll curse her joints."

"You know her?"

She looked at him out of the corner of her eye. "I know her."

"I didn't think there was anyone in the world as old as her. She's been around since—"

"Well, don't get your hopes up. She may not be around much longer after I catch up to her."

He frowned. "I think she's my only friend right now. She believes in Dreaming, talks a lot about it."

"Does she? Used to be she called me crazy when I had Dreams. Said I had bad spirits in my gut."

Runs In Light held his breath, disbelieving. "You Dream?"

"I Dream."

"Is that why you hate Broken Branch so much? The things she said about your Dreaming?"

She paused, memories stirring again. "No . . . no, that's not it. Once, long ago, there was a man. A great hunter. He was known for hunting Grandfather Brown Bear. Taunted bears, made them chase him. He'd run past an ambush, circle back, drive a dart behind their shoulders just so. Killed a lot of bear that way. I loved that man. Would have stayed with him. Until Broken Branch—beauty that she was—wrapped her legs around him and turned his head. Besides, the Dreams—"

A sudden light of understanding dawned in his eyes, memories of stories told flickering; he breathed, "You—you're *Heron*?"

Through slitted eyes, she studied him, watching like the great white-headed eagle watches a fish. Carefully, she said, "Does she still bad-mouth me?"

"People said you were only a legend."

"Except Broken Branch, I'll wager."

He nodded, backing crablike toward the far corner of the shelter. She enjoyed the growing fear, the tension relining his mouth. Crazy kid, what did he think? That she'd witch him?

"You won't get far that way," she added mildly. "The only other way out is up there." She pointed at the soot-grimed smoke hole overhead. "Used it a time or two when Grandfather Brown Bear wasn't discouraged by fire or darts."

He stopped, wetting his lips nervously. "Crow Caller said—"

"And you listened? Not very bright, are you? Well, just to set your mind at rest, I don't eat babies."

Runs In Light didn't look reassured. "Broken Branch says you used to talk to animals, call them to you."

"Sure, every Dreamer does."

He swallowed convulsively, guilt creasing his gaunt face. "I can't."

"Well, you're young."

"Others said you talked to the spirits of the Long Dark and shared their Powers. That you can make dead men rise . . . or suck the soul from a live man and blow it out into the wind to wail forever."

"Mouse dung!" she spat, irritated. Cocking her head, she studied him. "I do what any Dreamer does. Only I do it better out here away from confusion and old women's spats and silly young lovers."

He didn't relax, eyes searching for the door, as if judging his chances. "Why are you out here all alone, then? If you don't do things the People would disapprove—"

"For the same reason you ought to be." She narrowed her eyes, seeing him flinch. "*For the Dream, boy!* Because being around people clouds your mind. Keeps your thoughts from being pure."

A trace of confusion shaded his eyes.

She nodded. "Oh, yes, I know you, Runs In Light. I saw

you the day you were born. The day you were *conceived*! You looked into my eyes. A Dreamer, even then. And your brother? What's his name?''

"Raven Hunter." It came as a pained whisper.

She nodded, the vision coming back. "Apt. He's still clutching black feathers? Still seeking blood? He was born that way, you know. In blood.''

"He went with Crow Caller's band to face the Others. He—''

"Death there," Heron muttered. "Too many of them." She looked up. "Oh, I've seen them coming. Things in the world are changing, boy. The ice is melting. Animals are moving, humans following. Let me tell you something.''

A little fearfully, he said, "What?''

"I used to cross to the salt water over those high mountains west of here. Used to sit out on a rock and watch the waves crash. You can see things in surf, you know. Good Dreaming there." She frowned, seeing it again in her mind. "Last time I was there was three years ago. Waves swirl up over my rock now.''

"So?''

"Means the water's rising, boy.''

They held each other's eyes for a long moment, before he ventured, stricken, "Will it cover all the land?''

"How would I know?''

"Didn't you Dream—''

"Great Mammoth, no! I just saw the difference when I went there.''

"Oh," he exhaled in relief.

"If I had Dreamed it, would you have gone and cast yourself in the waves to drown?''

"Might have.''

She chuckled, slapping him on the arm. "I like you, boy. You got respect for your elders.''

He smiled weakly.

"Anyway, getting back to the Others. Nobody can beat them.'' She made a gesture that caused him to start. "The People can do one of two things. They can fight . . . and die. Or they can join the Others, be absorbed by them like blood in fox hair.''

"Absorbed? But Sun Father gave us the land and animals."

"Nothing's forever, boy. Not mammoth, not you, not me, not even the People."

His eyes went glassy as though seeing something far away. "The man from the White Tusk Clan said—"

"What man?"

"He was tall with graying black hair. He walked to me and I blew a rainbow out." He swallowed hard as though expecting her to call him a liar. "I told him I'd trade him a son for a son. I . . . I asked him to choose between light and dark."

"You knew him?"

"No."

Heron stiffened, lips clamped into a white line. "His face, it was oval? His nose thin? Lips full?"

The boy's nod came slowly, warily.

Heron squinted into the distance, searching the past, seeing a lean-faced man as he raped a woman of the People there on the gray sand, the surf pounding in the background. A white hide rested on his shoulders.

"Do you . . . know him?"

Heron nodded, exhaling slowly. "Your father."

Runs In Light's eyes narrowed in bewilderment. "Seal Paw was my—"

"Seal Paw adopted you. No, the man in the Dream is your real father." Her smile twisted. "And you'd trade him a son for a son? Interesting. What does that mean?"

"I don't know."

A long silence passed.

"Perhaps." Heron pondered. "I'm missing something. A rainbow is the road of colors that leads to the Monster Children's world up north; it takes a Dreamer smack into the middle of their war. Is that what this is about? Good fighting evil?"

"Maybe."

"You're helpful, aren't you?"

He blinked in embarrassment. "I never understand my Dreams. They leave me . . . well . . ."

"We'll have to do something about that."

"What?"

"We'll talk about it later. Right now, tell me how the Dream made you feel. Did you think that the People would die at the hands of the Others? At the hands of your father?"

"Wolf told me how to . . ." He floundered, tilting his head uncertainly.

"How to what?"

Runs In Light shifted his gaze to the glowing coals of the fire. "There's a hole in the Big Ice."

"Wolf showed it to you?"

He nodded tautly. "He said if we went that way, the People would be saved."

Heron's brow furrowed deeply. She puffed a long exhale. "Then you'd better get going. I've seen the Others coming fast. You don't have much time."

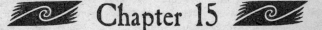 Chapter 15

One Who Cries crawled up to push the drifted snow out of the shelter tunnel. Bad choice that, there hadn't been time to dig a dipped entranceway to act as a cold trap. Wind sucked the snow past, the world a cloud of white. He pondered the possibilities of moving. He might be able to keep his direction by the wind. But what good would that do? They could walk over a cliff, flounder in a morass of soft-packed willows or larch. And where would they go? Worse, the children, the weakest, would fall behind . . . lost from the rest.

He slumped on the snow, staring blankly at the unending vortex of the storm. Cold leached up from the ice below. The storm might blow for days.

"It's over," he murmured.

With no strength to hunt, only another carcass could keep them alive, render up the life it had once held.

"Maybe we should have gone north," he whispered, looking to where Green Water slept. Her broad nose barely moved with the breath of life. "I'm sorry, wife. So sorry. I led you out here, following a fool."

He reached out to caress her hand, feeling the cold, knowing it wouldn't be such a bad death. Better than rotting from some sickness, wasting away. The wolves would get them in the end.

A sudden ironic thought dawned. He looked back to the windswept white plain, eyes searching for movement. "Was that it, Wolf? Did you fool the boy, lure him here to feed your fleshly brothers?"

He braced his forehead against his arm, laughing softly. "I guess I'm willing. Everybody has to provide for their own."

"Because we're all one, my husband," Green Water said, voice taking on the awed speech-giving tone of the elders around the blazing night fires of winter. "We were stars once. Father Sun threw us out of heaven. Muskrat saw us falling and dove into the sea, bringing up dirt so our landing would be soft. Then Father Sun blew life into us and other falling stars, making us brothers, all the same. We eat wolves; they eat us. It's all the same life."

"You're being awfully calm about this."

She shrugged weakly.

He crawled back to lie beside her, slipping an arm beneath her head and nuzzling her cheek with his own. "But who will pray us back up to the stars?"

Wind Woman howled outside, snow flitting in to frost their hides and sting their faces.

"Maybe Wolf will."

"I hope so."

His mittened hand clutching Green Water's, he closed his eyes and dozed. In the dream, he lived again, a young man. Green Water's shy smile and knowing eyes followed him as he strutted before her, a proud hunter, his first solo kill laid before the fire. Even then she'd seen through his laughter, seeing the man beneath. Green Water always knew. She always had everything ordered, each event planned for and accepted. Not even the death of their first child—starving so early that Long Dark—had disturbed her poise. Death came. She grieved, and accepted, planning for the future.

Such a woman . . . wasted on him.

Snow slid down on top of him. Had that much built up? He sighed, wondering if there was a purpose in climbing back up, pushing it away so they could breathe. Smothering would be a quicker death, a shorter suffering.

Someone's dog whined. But then, someone's dog was always whining. Dogs were that way. Either whining, or fighting, or eating up the food.

He shook his head, trying to clear the hunger haze. *Dog? They'd eaten the dogs!*

"Imagination," he grumbled, and looked up into a black dog face staring down the tunnel at him.

One Who Cries blinked, hearing with his own ears the sniffing of the animal. *Food!* He reached for his darts, feeling the trembling in his muscles. Cursed hunger robbed a man of . . .

"Get back, Black," a sharp voice called as One Who Cries shifted to free his darts. Green Water sat up, desperate hope in her eyes.

The black dog backed out in a new cascade of snow. One Who Cries mustered his strength to crawl up, only to be met by a hooded face looking in.

"Hungry in there?" an old woman asked. "Thought it was a nice storm. Not the kind to be wasted sitting home by the fire, so I threw a couple of guts full of fat and took a walk."

One Who Cries stared. "Are you a spirit trying to suck my soul into the Long Dark?"

"Hush," Green Water called, pulling him back to the side. The old woman wiggled in, the black dog leaning forward to fill the space, blocking the little light.

"Black!" the old woman growled. "Get out of here." She motioned and the dog backed hurriedly out.

"Where's Broken Branch?" the woman asked—a wicked light in her eye.

"Next shelter, I think. You know her?" One Who Cries asked.

She studied him for a second. "Know her? Twenty-five Long Darks ago, I promised I'd kill her if she ever came into my reach again. That's a long time to keep a promise."

One Who Cries looked sharply at Green Water.

* * *

Cold. Nothing else existed but the hunger knot in Dancing Fox's belly. Only Talon's weak raspy breath reminded her that she wasn't alone, that other humans existed, that the world had once held warmth, sunshine, and laughter.

Wind Woman ravaged the snow around them, rattling ice crystals off the worn caribou robe they snuggled under. So little body heat left to share, so little energy. Despite the hide they'd wrapped in, despite the double layers of hair-on parkas, the cold ate at them.

"Who will sing us to the Blessed Star People?" she wondered aloud.

"Maybe Mammoth, huh?" Talon murmured, not even moving her old gray head where it lay pillowed on Dancing Fox's shoulder.

"Four days we've lain here. I wonder if anyone but us is alive?"

"My greatest worry," Talon whispered, "is that you might have to pee again. You get up and I'm gonna freeze."

"I might have to. You're warmer if you don't keep that extra water. It sucks the heat out of you. Wastes what little's left."

"Ah, I know that. But I can't get up again, girl. Can't do it. Bare my butt to the blowing snow? No, it'll kill me. My thread's weak . . . weak. . . ."

Dancing Fox closed her eyes. "Thank you, Talon, for spending time with me. I don't think I could have made—"

"Bah," Talon hissed softly. "I wanted to be with you." Then she turned her ancient face up and stared at the ice walls. "Wish we'd both gone with Runs In Light. Wolf Dream. There's Power in that."

"I tried."

"I know." The old woman's head moved as she swallowed. "I . . . know."

Dancing Fox lifted the corner of the caribou hide, seeing the wraiths of snow rushing past. Here, on the ground, the whole world hazed white. Even in this little bit of day, she could see nothing. What a terrible way for her soul to leave its body.

"Runs In Light?" she called softly. "One day, perhaps among the stars, we'll find each other. I'll hold you then. Love you."

She closed her eyes, blinking back the tears, pain from the loss lancing her very heart.

"Still calling after my idiot brother?"

Even through dreams of death, Raven Hunter's voice penetrated. She willed his knowing tones away.

"Come on, my dearest Dancing Fox," the voice called again, insistent, real. "Raise your flap and eat this."

Talon shifted next to her as the caribou hide lifted, and despite the cold snow that blew in, she stared up into his handsome face.

"I found Sheep Whistle's camp a day from here." He handed her strips of meat. "They're setting up a shelter now. We'll have a fire going in a couple of minutes. Heat some fat up. It'll be hard, but I think we can save the ones still alive. Until then, stay warm."

"We'll live," she whispered. *Oh, Runs In Light, I'm going to live!*

"Good boy, that Raven Hunter," Talon whispered. "You could do a lot worse than him, Fox. A lot worse."

Dancing Fox winced, shuddering.

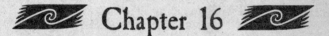 **Chapter 16**

Ash-colored rays streamed down through the ice cave's narrow opening, accenting the sallow cheeks of the People pressed close together inside. Clutching robes tightly around them, they spoke little, or not at all, despair a palpable thing—all hope fled.

"Grandmother?" Red Star, a five-year-old girl with wide brown eyes and a cadaverously thin face, called. She weakly tugged the hood over Broken Branch's head.

"Hmm?"

"Grandmother, I'm cold." She tightened her hold on the fish-bone doll clamped in a death grip against her cheek.

Broken Branch roused herself, rubbing fists into her eyes

before staring down at the child. Red Star looked up, blinking slowly, lashes crusted with ice. She lifted her arms, begging to be taken.

"Come on, child," Broken Branch murmured tenderly, picking the girl up and sitting her in her lap. She wrapped ice-stiff robes around them both and squeezed Red Star hard, kissing her forehead.

"Thank you." The child sighed, leaning tiredly against the old woman's chest. She took off one mitten to tuck a finger in her mouth, sucking softly. "I'm hungry."

"I know you are. But it won't be long now. Wolf Dreamer's coming back real soon. He'll get us out of this mess. He's probably out talking to Wolf right now."

Red Star frowned disbelievingly. "Are you lying to me because I'm little?"

"Of course not," Broken Branch protested with hurt pride. "He's coming back. You'll see."

"Maybe he's dead and can't."

"Who told you that?"

Red Star tilted her head awkwardly as though hesitant about telling. "Well . . ."

"Come on. Who can you tell if not me?" Broken Branch wheedled.

"Singing Wolf said maybe Grandfather White Bear ate him and we were all going to die for following him."

Broken Branch puckered her lips disdainfully. "Well, Singing Wolf's a fool. You listen to me. I've lived twice as long as he has and I know the way the world works. Wolf Dreamer's coming back."

Red Star's stomach rumbled and she dropped a tiny hand to pat it. "It's been growling and knotting up."

"Maybe one of the Monster Children came down and crawled in there, huh?"

Red Star laughed weakly, incredulous. "You know they never come out of the sky."

"Don't they?"

The girl shook her head. "No. That's why we don't have to be afraid of them. They're trapped in the rainbow lights, locked there for all time."

Broken Branch patted her frigid cheek, smiling. "You remember the old stories pretty good, don't you?"

"You told me I had to. 'Member?''

"Did I?''

"Uh-huh. When I was little. You told me you'd beat my butt if I forgot any of them."

"Good for me. It worked."

Red Star nuzzled her cheek against the old woman's furs, something else clearly on her mind. Broken Branch lifted a mittened hand to trace the furrows in the young forehead.

"What are these? You trying to look like me?"

The girl glanced up timidly, eyes dark and brooding inside her gray fur hood. "Grandmother, what's death like?"

A tight band constricted around her heart. She spewed an exhale and hugged the child fiercely. She'd wondered that herself a time or two. "Oh, it's not so bad. Unless some old—"

"But what if a bear comes and swallows me while I'm still alive?"

Broken Branch took the stone knife from her belt, twisting it so the obsidian blade glinted menacingly in the dim light. "If a bear did that, I'd slice his gut wide open to get you back."

"But, what would it feel like . . . if . . . if the bear ran away and you couldn't find me?"

"Well," Broken Branch whispered, contemplating the cold blue shadows clinging to the irregular patches in the ceiling. "It feels like going to sleep. You know how you kind of drift off. One minute you're awake and the next you're not?"

Red Star nodded. "It doesn't hurt real bad?"

"No, child, not for long."

"Maybe it just lasts a minute?"

"Oh, less than that even. You'd hardly know."

Red Star heaved a small breath of relief, sucking her finger again as she rubbed the painted muskrat fur of her doll's face against her itching nose. "I was worried about it."

"I could tell."

"Salmon Tail said it hurt for a long time, that you screamed and screamed until the Soul Eaters came to get you."

"He's only seven," she growled. "What does he know?"

"Throws Bones was his uncle. He said he could hear him groaning for days after the bear got him."

"Bah! Throws Bones was such a pain he probably gave

old Grandfather White Bear indigestion and *that's* what Salmon Tail heard.''

Red Star sighed patiently, as though she was thinking about it while she blinked at Broken Branch's hide-booted foot. ''What happens afterward?''

''You mean after death?'' The girl nodded. ''Well, when you wake up, you're flying among the stars, soaring just like Eagle. You get to—''

'' 'Cause I'm one of the Star People again?''

''Sure.''

She cocked her tiny head seriously. ''Grandmother, do you believe Wolf really came to Runs In Light and gave him a Dream?''

''There's not a doubt in my whole body, girl. I've seen Dreamers—real Dreamers. . . .'' Her voice faded as her thoughts drifted to bittersweet days twenty-five years before. ''Real Dreamers . . .''

Up the slanted tunnel to the opening, a sibilant rustling of furs sounded, dogs barking. Red Star jumped, a short cry of joy erupting from her bluish lips.

''It's him!'' she cried shrilly, scrambling up the tunnel. ''Runs In Light! Runs In Light!''

Broken Branch closed her eyes, offering a soft prayer of thanks to Wolf before dropping her head to her mittens.

''Hello,'' she heard Red Star say, as if she didn't know the person she spoke to.

''You hungry, little one?'' an unknown woman asked.

''Oh, yes, my stomach's been howling.''

''Well, here. You eat some of these and you'll be fine.''

''Thank you!'' Red Star moaned gratefully and slid back down the tunnel with a long stuffed rope of intestine.

What is it about that voice that stirs . . . With it came tremors of fear and regret, tears welling in Broken Branch's wrinkled old throat. She swallowed with difficulty.

''Broken Branch?'' the woman's gravelly voice demanded. ''You in there?''

''I'm in here,'' she answered in shock. ''Who—''

''Well, come out before I come in to get you.''

''Who are you?''

When no answer came, Broken Branch hesitantly threw off her robes and crawled on hands and knees up through the ice opening. A haze of white blew around a hooded figure, stabbing at her eyes, forcing her to squeeze them closed. She pushed up to stand on weak tottering legs, trying to make out the ancient face in the caribou hood. The vast expanse of white encircling them seemed to swirl in Wind Woman's grasp.

"I'll be a cursed . . ." the woman grunted. "That pointed nose of yours used to be beautiful. Now it looks as sharp and ugly as somebody's dart point. Makes me feel better."

"Who are you?" she demanded roughly this time. "Do I know you?"

"You old bitch. Of course you do. How could you forget someone whose heart you broke?"

Broken Branch gasped a deep wheezing breath as recognition dawned, her hands fluttering wildly about the woman's shoulders. Touching her to make certain she was real. Getting control of herself, she put a hand to her trembling lips and stared with trepidation. "Blessed Star People . . . *it's you.*"

"Of course it's me," Heron snapped. "How many other people's hearts have you broke?" Then, squinting in thought, she added, " 'Course, I guess I wouldn't know. Maybe you've stacked up quite a few by now."

Reaching out timidly, Broken Branch grabbed the hide strings of Heron's parka and clumsily pulled her forward before wrapping frail old arms around her and hugging her as though she were a vision that might disappear at any moment. "I thought you'd died long ago."

Heron raised her own arms, patting Broken Branch's back tenderly as she chided, "Couldn't let myself. I always figured I'd see you again."

Broken Branch shoved gently back to stare into the oval face of the Spirit Woman. Heron's graceful features were still finely etched, lips full and nose turned up. "You still want to kill me?"

Heron slowly filled her lungs and held the breath as she scowled for a long moment. "Not as bad as I used to."

"You just come to that conclusion because of my nose."

"Mostly. I still might curse your joints, though."

"You're too late. Somebody else already did. I can barely walk most of the winter."

"That right?"

Broken Branch nodded, bowing her head as guilt swelled in her breast. "You know, I never meant to hurt you. It was just that I—"

"Oh . . ." Heron shook her head sternly. "You did me a favor, really. I didn't have the courage to become a Dreamer by myself. Needed some deep wound to force me to let go of the People."

"I sure gave you that, didn't I?"

"You did."

"I never felt right about it after you left. There was always an empty place inside me."

"After, sure. But it never occurred to you when it counted!"

Broken Branch's eyes narrowed, jaw clenching. "Of course not. I didn't like you."

"Well, you weren't exactly lovable. That sharp tongue of yours waggled all the blasted time. Why, I—"

"Grandmother?" Red Star's young voice interrupted, a sweet timid face peeking out the opening to the cave. "Come and eat before this is all gone."

"I'll be there in a minute, child," she called over her shoulder.

Wind Woman playfully tousled the ties on her parka, setting them to flapping across her chest. She chanced another look at Heron. A slow smile crept over her former enemy's face, a twinkle in her eyes.

"Come on," the Dreamer said gruffly. "I got just the thing for your joints."

"What? You gonna do a spirit healing? *For me?*"

Heron shook her head. "No, I got something much more powerful."

"What could be more . . ."

Heron went into a fit of hysterics as Broken Branch's eyes jerked wide and her jaw gaped. "You're not gonna cut them off, are you?"

"I might," Heron said with a slight smile. Turning, she waved for Broken Branch to follow as she strode across the white windswept plain toward Runs In Light. People were crawling out of the ice cave to gather in weary joy around him. They were hugging him, and gratefully shouting that they'd never doubted him.

Broken Branch pursed her lips and lowered her eyes to stare at the wispy tendrils of snow creeping around her legs like ghostly fingers.

"Curse you," she whispered to herself, squinting at Heron's back. "You're the only Dreamer I ever believed had Power." Hearing the odd words, she quickly amended, "You and Runs In Light."

Over the whistling wind, she heard Heron's voice shouting: "Yeah, I found her. That old bitch never could leave well enough alone."

A faint chuckle escaped Broken Branch's withered throat. She inhaled a deep soothing breath, the first in days, and let her gaze drift over the joyful faces emerging from the snow caves. Around them, the icy plains gleamed with a pearlescent sheen. Drifting clouds seemed to glow brighter, their edges gilded with shimmering gold.

"Grandmother?" Red Star called. "I saved you some. But you'd better eat it fast before my stomach growls again."

She turned to see the girl weakly handing out a loop of stuffed intestine. Broken Branch knelt and took the blessed food. "Thank you, baby. You're a good girl."

Red Star cocked her head against the brilliant sun, squinting up. "Grandmother? Does this mean Light's Dream was real?"

"Of course, it does. Didn't I tell you he was coming back?"

"So, no bears are going to eat us? We're going to be all right now?"

Broken Branch took a bite of the delicately flavored meat and gazed back at Heron. The old Spirit Woman was waving her arms expressively, bullying everybody to get them organized. Her muffled words seemed to blend with Wind Woman's, becoming one plaintive and powerful voice in the wilderness.

"We're saved, baby," Broken Branch said. A few tears had frozen on her lower lashes, glimmering like crystals. She wiped them away with the back of her sleeve. "Our souls are in the hands of a master Dreamer now—the most powerful Dreamer our People have had since Father Sun himself walked the earth." She turned and patted Red Star's gaunt cheek. "Yes, don't you worry, baby. We're saved."

Chapter 17

The People rested and ate and rested through another stretch of darkness, reviving. When the storm finally abated, Heron led them off in the new snow, webbed snowshoes crunching while she followed Black, who drove his nose deep into the powder, sniffing for the trail.

By sunset, Green Water stood at the top of the ridge, staring in awe at Heron's shelter; it was a marvel. For a brief moment, Wind Woman stilled her constant howl to provide a glimpse of the little valley. White water bubbled from the ground through a rent in the rocks, cascading down to a deep aquamarine pool. Beyond, the water ran open and foggy as far as the eye could see. Tall stands of willow lay buried deep under the snow; nearby, depressions lined by living grass could be seen. Below them, the snow had melted away.

"How long have you been here?" she called timidly to the Spirit Woman.

"Awhile," Heron shouted from the front of the procession. "Now, to me, it looks like the ground broke here and all this hot water come up. A couple of years back . . . let's see. Well, maybe twenty or so, the ground shook. Scared me to death. Till then, that hot spring just dribbled. Afterward, it started shooting water up way high. Like something broke loose down there in the rock. Scares me what might happen if the ground breaks again. Don't get near that geyser. It'll cook you. I mean it. I boil meat in that."

Green Water shook her head. There'd been stories. Old Geyser—dead now—had talked of such things. Had he been here? Slowly, trying to take it all in, Green Water followed them down toward the smoking waters. Unsure, she remembered the stories told around the fires. Stories of how Heron had left the People. Stories of how she bartered with the spirits of the Long Dark. Hesitantly, she looked over her shoulder, staring out into the white wastes. Well, perhaps there were worse fates.

When they reached the edge of the steaming pool, Heron disappeared into a crack in the rocks and returned with a pile of caribou hides. "Here," she said, dropping them on the snowy ground. "I got more inside that you can use to make a shelter. While you do that, I'll put on some moss tea and get out some meat for dinner."

A tremor of relief went through the People. Hurriedly, they joined hands to make hasty lodges. Hours later, Heron returned and surveyed the shelters approvingly.

"Come and sit down now," the old woman instructed. "We've got things to talk about."

Gratefully the People gathered around the edges of the deep pool to drench in the warm mist. Heron had built a fire in front of her rock shelter and the flames licked upward, casting long shadows over the surrounding boulders and flickering amber across the greenish pool. She passed out sacks of meat and told people to help themselves to the bags of hot moss tea.

When everyone had settled down to eat contentedly, the Spirit Woman declared, "I can feed you all for a couple of weeks on what I've stored. But after that . . ."

Singing Wolf nodded, cupping a horn full of thick black tea. "How much game is here?"

Heron lifted a thin shoulder. "Enough. A small herd of caribou winters out in the basin down by the river. The wind sweeps it clean. They can get willow there, dig for moss and grass. Seems like every year more grass grows. Lot of changes since I came here . . . let's see . . . Well, no matter—back when Broken Branch there was still young enough to steal my man."

Broken Branch stiffened, stopping in midchew to narrow her eyes.

"As far as hunting goes," One Who Cries said, clearing his throat, "we can build a drive line. Green Water and Sunshine can work the wings, the extension of the lines, with the children between cairns to keep the animals moving. With Singing Wolf, Jumping Hare, and me, there are three men to run down the—"

"Four," Heron added, jerking her head toward Runs In Light, who sat silent, head down.

People grumbled among themselves. Now that their bellies were full, they'd started complaining again, calling Runs In Light a false Dreamer.

Heron lifted a brow, spitting, "You fools. He's seen more than you'll ever understand."

An awkward silence descended, the flames lighting tense faces.

"Grandmother." Runs In Light spoke. "Don't worry. I—"

"Hush, boy. You and I aren't done yet." She turned and looked at him, heedless of his embarrassment. "Don't know what you are yet, eh? Keep that attitude and you might never know."

"Wolf Dream," Broken Branch muttered, her eyes bright again.

Heron turned, head cocked. "You saw it?"

"It was in his eyes."

Heron nodded. "Much has changed since I've been gone? No Dreamers?"

Broken Branch waved miserably. "Crow Caller had it once. I think he killed it. Dreamed sour . . . like maggot-filled meat. These young ones, they've never seen a real Dreamer before. You need to come back, Heron. The People need you. There's no heart. No fire. The old ways, the true ways, they've gone like smoke in Wind Woman's breath."

Heron turned, pointing. *"He's the future."*

Wolf Dreamer shook his head in the silence. Ashen, he got to his feet and vanished into the night beyond.

After the long pause, Broken Branch shook her head. "I don't know. His spirit left him." She sighed. "It's no longer in his eyes."

"You're wrong." Heron grinned. "As usual."

Singing Wolf cleared his throat. "He's young. Like his brother, Raven Hunter, said, he's susceptible to delusions."

"Raven Hunter?" Heron whirled, a thin finger jabbing at Singing Wolf like a dart. "You'd listen to *him*?" Her eyes narrowed wickedly. "What's happened to you? Has that maggot-mouthed Crow Caller broken all of your Dreaming? *Curse you all. There is no life without Dreaming!"*

Singing Wolf's chin stuck out as he mumbled, "Runs In Light nearly Dreamed us to death."

"Idiots." Heron shook her head. "Do you think you're all just eating machines? Huh? That your only purpose here is to eat and make babies to do it all over again after you're gone? Curse you! No wonder the People are dying! *You have to Dream to LIVE!*"

"Yes!" Broken Branch cried, clasping her hands together. "See?" She pointed at Heron. "There's Power! There's a Dreamer! Hear how she speaks? Hear the Power? Ha-heeee! Wolf brought us here. Wolf Dream!"

"What of the boy, Wolf Dreamer?" Heron crossed her arms, eyes on Singing Wolf where he looked away, shame creeping up his face.

"He's feeling guilty." Broken Branch waved it away. "We lost one little girl, though the rest of us are here."

Heron fingered her chin. "Did Crow Caller tell you Dreams came easy? Did he?"

No one ventured an answer, but their crimped faces told her what she wanted to know. "Well, they don't. Dreams don't come without pain . . . yes, and even death. Remember that."

She shook herself, gray-shot hair spilling loose about her shoulders. "You, Singing Wolf?"

He looked at her with wary indignation in his eyes. "What?"

"You think you're a hunter?"

"I'm the best—"

"No, you're not. I'm going to take you on a real hunt. *A Dream Hunt.* I'll *call* the caribou. I know the place. A drive line is already there. They hear me and listen. They'll help the People if I ask."

Singing Wolf glanced around uncomfortably. "You mean we're not going to go stalk them? To drive—"

"No. I'm going to go Dream them in. Don't disturb me." She turned and walked out into the growing darkness, following Wolf Dreamer's path.

Singing Wolf chewed his lip, confusion on his face. He raised his eyes to Broken Branch as she waddled past, heading out into the dark.

She stopped to scowl at him. "Didn't I tell you to keep your mouth shut?"

He dropped his eyes.

Runs In Light heard the soft tread. He bit back the frustration. "I'm not the one."

"No?" Heron's voice carried a subtle power.

"No."

A hand rested on his shoulder. "Tell me again of what you saw."

"I . . . I passed through a hole in the ice with Wolf. We climbed rocks. There on the other side, a green valley opened as far as the eye could see. Caribou, elk, moose, mammoth, all kinds of animals were there. Then I had the Dream with the man. The Other *you* call my father."

"I knew you'd be a powerful Dreamer the first hour of your life."

He shook his head, doubt twisting his gut. "I'm no Dreamer."

The edge of hostility in her voice caught him by surprise. "You won't be if you keep that up. I guarantee that," she spat over her shoulder.

Runs In Light sighed with relief as her steps receded.

After a few moments of silence, Broken Branch's voice came from the darkness to his side. "What did she tell you?"

He blinked to make out her dark silhouette. "That I'm a Dreamer."

"Hardly news."

He shook his head. "I don't understand all this. That, and the man in my Dream."

"Man?"

He nodded. "Heron says Seal Paw wasn't my father."

"What else does she say?"

He heard the stiffness in her voice, felt the growing tension. He bit his lip. Tell her?

"That my mother was raped. That I was born first and lay in a shaft of light. That Raven Hunter was born next. That he came out covered with blood. That it ran into his mouth as he was placed beside me. That a raven feather floated down and he grasped it."

"Hah-heeee," she gasped, placing a hand to her mouth. "Yes. Yes, I was there. I bit your cord in two myself. Where . . . where did your mother . . ."

"On the beach, beside the salt water. Heron says she was collecting mussels."

Broken Branch slowly settled on a rock, eyes focused on the moon rising over the western horizon; it gilded the drifting clouds with silver. "Yes, I heard the rumors." She looked up. "A Dreaming. And she saw you?"

Runs In Light nodded heavily. "Says I looked into her eyes."

"Hah-heeee, I knew it. Wolf Dreamer. Even then you were . . . different."

He got up and paced angrily. "I don't want to be different! I want to be a hunter! That's all!"

"What else did she tell you? About the People?"

"That we would be killed by the Others . . . or taken in among them. Soaked up like blood in fox fur."

Broken Branch covered her head. "You would turn from your people?"

"I'm not the one!" He struggled to keep his voice down. "I went the wrong way! Crow Caller was right."

"We're not dead yet," Broken Branch mumbled to herself. She looked up. "If not you . . . then who?"

He looked up at the geyser, hearing its roar, seeing the water flying high, sparkling white in the moonlight. "I don't know!" he shouted plaintively, squeezing his head between his hands. "I don't—"

"There's no one else."

"How do you know?"

"Who could it be?"

"I don't know! If the Other in my Dreams is my father, then maybe this Dreaming is in our blood!"

"What does that—"

"Maybe the savior is Raven Hunter!"

Broken Branch sat deathly still, eyes squinted in thought.

Chapter 18

The caribou came, a black line out of the gray. From where he waited, Runs In Light watched, awed. Just like the old stories, they walked deliberately into the wide-spread wings of the drive line.

To his right, Heron sat in a blind, chanting and singing. To his left, Singing Wolf looked uneasily at the caribou coming steadily toward them. Then his eyes shifted to Heron's blind, awed.

A strange warmth built in Runs In Light's chest, a feeling of rightness—of Power. On the wings of the drive line, the women crouched, their darts nocked in the hooks of their atlatls. A total silence descended, broken only by the haunting chant from Heron's blind.

Heart racing, Runs In Light watched the animals; ever closer they came, breath puffing up from their black noses, white beards waving, flanks gray against the snow. So many?

"Only kill thirty," Heron had warned, the glow of the Dream bright in her eyes. "That's what I've promised. Only thirty. Be quick, be merciful. They must not suffer."

"Only thirty," he whispered under his breath.

The lead cow was even with him now. She pulled up, head high, two streams of breath blowing from her nose before she stepped lightly forward, cocking her head at him.

Runs In Light picked up the chant, adding his admiration of her stately beauty, how he would sing her soul to the Blessed Star People.

"You will live through me," he promised. "Your life is our life. Share with us, brothers and sisters of the stars." A warm feeling spread in his breast as she stepped closer, one hoof held in the air, waiting.

In that moment, their eyes met and a soft harmony possessed him, as if his soul drifted to touch hers. He reveled in it, a unity with all life, a weaving, dancing wholeness.

Awed, his heart bursting with love, he explained his need. "Please, Mother. The People need you. Hear our cries? I'm sorry to have to ask."

She stepped forward again, the Power of the Dreaming reaching her. He heard the snow crunch under her splay-toed feet, the huge hooves sinking down until the dewclaws locked in the ice. With her, he breathed the uneasy air. Her concern became his. They moved forward into the killing pen— together—the old cow turning sideways.

Gripped by the Power flowing through his veins, Runs In Light stood, rock steady, every nerve humming. He cast, seeing the dart sink deeply into the cow's side, feeling the point angling forward into her vitals. She stood as he nocked his second dart and pivoted, throwing with all his might, sending the dart home in the side of a young bull. The bone patches left by recently shed antlers gleamed white against the black of his fur.

The cow dropped to her knees, frothy blood at her mouth. Runs In Light continued to sing, soul-sharing the pain with the caribou. Tears filled his eyes, streaking his tanned cheeks. Vaguely, he could sense Singing Wolf on his feet, casting his darts. From the sides, the women ran forward, sending their darts true as the caribou milled. Green Water's arm whipped forward, burying a dart in a bull's shoulder. Laughing Sunshine rushed, her weight impelling the stone head of her lance into a young cow. Another and another went down.

"Enough!" Heron cried, standing, breaking the trance. Caribou turned on their heels, dashing through the ranks of the women, dark feet throwing spurts of snow into the air.

A wounded caribou hobbled to one side, circling to stand meekly before Heron. The old woman settled her dart, balancing the weapon, casting true. The young cow turned, reeling, and pitched on her side to kick futilely.

Only the rasping breath of dying beasts broke the silence. Runs In Light gasped a deep breath, unaware of how he'd become so winded. Across the space, Heron's eyes locked with his, probing.

"Did you know you did it?" she called. The words echoed in his mind.

He shook his head. "What?"

"You sang them the rest of the way in. *You did.*"

Runs In Light eased down on a rock to stare dumbly at the bloody snow, the feel of the cow's pain still deep in his breast.

"I'm sorry, Mother," he said in a wounded voice, gazing at the dead animal.

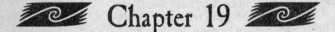 **Chapter 19**

The Long Dark waned.

The spirits that haunted the eddies of Wind Woman's breath whimpered to the north while warmer winds circled up from the southwest, leaving the snow sodden and heavy. To the west, the mountains gleamed dazzlingly white on the few days when the sun shone in the sky. Water trickled from the knife-edged ridges. To the north, the huge braided river poured in torrents, white water shooting high as it bashed from rock to rock.

Time after time, the People hunted the caribou and—best of all—the small herds of musk oxen who foraged in the foothills. Musk ox's flesh had always been a favorite, rich, sweet, heavy with fat—even in this terrible year.

"Leave the mammoth alone," Heron warned, seeing the old bull entering the lower portion of the pool to soak his joints. "Sure, he's got cows and calves up there—but I know them. I won't Dream them in."

Nevertheless, the People grew strong, rendering the carcasses of the kills, boiling fat from the bodies—poor though it might be after so much endless cold. Faces filled, limbs grew strong and hale.

One Who Cries laughed and sang, finding an outcrop of fine-grained quartzite from which to craft his long dart points. The finest flint knapper among the People, he studied the head-sized boulders, judging the stone with a practiced eye before driving off thick wedges of the rock. These primary flakes he quickly thinned with practiced strokes of his hammerstone.

"Good stuff!" he called to Singing Wolf. "Look, look how well the stone flakes, broad and flat with good control."

"Such little things make you happy." Singing Wolf shook his head.

"Uh-huh." And he couldn't deny the truth of that. He pulled his caribou antler from the pack, feeling the use-smoothed texture of the tool. He used it as a baton to shape a preform—a basic blank flaked off both sides into a thin lenticular shape. One Who Cries sang spirit songs as the baton snapped long thin flakes from the preform. One by one, he made a supply of preforms, most of which went into his pack for future use. From the lenticular shape, he could produce a variety of styles of tool including scrapers, knives, burins and gravers, or dart points as the need arose.

"Nice to see you working again." Singing Wolf settled himself to watch.

One Who Cries whistled loudly, feeling his soul swell. "A person's spirit goes into the stone, you know. There's wonder in that. Good tool stone, like this quartzite, or a fine chert, well, it takes soul better."

Having achieved the basic shape, One Who Cries used his antler and leather to carefully thin the point. He ground the sharp edges down with sandstone, preparing a platform—a purchase surface—for the antler tine. Doing so allowed him more control as he snapped long thin flakes from the point. When he finished, he had produced a parallel-sided point with a needle-sharp tip that just covered the breadth of his hand. He gave the base of the point a final grinding with the sandstone to keep the keen edges from severing the binding sinew when he hafted it to a foreshaft.

"Now there," he whispered in awe, "is a real beauty."

"And here's the shaft that will hold it." Singing Wolf raised a section of birch sapling to the sky, sighting along it for irregularities. Having collected three dozen, he laid them aside to prepare his tools. He re-formed thin sections of a waste flake from the pile at One Who Cries' feet, using an antler tine to create a steep-angled cutting edge along one margin of the stone. With that, he carefully peeled the bark from the shafts, smoothing the knots, using a bone-shaft wrench to straighten the rods over a low fire. The best of the specimens he split to hold One Who Cries' expertly crafted points.

"You know, for a while there, I thought we'd never have

the chance to do this again." One Who Cries stared at the wood, thoughtfully slipping his dart point into the groove.

"Wolf Dream, huh?"

One Who Cries grinned. "We're not dead yet, cousin."

Green Water, Laughing Sunshine, and the other women spent the growing days measuring hides carefully against the bodies of the People, sewing the closely tailored garments to fit. In a careful stitch, they closed the seams, leaving the hair inside to provide insulation and circulation to carry away deadly sweat.

"Now, you've got to do this right," Green Water explained to Red Star.

"These are just outer parkas?" Her eyes grew big.

"That's right. Undergarments, the ones that fit next to the skin, we'll have to wait and make from caribou fawn. But for these heavy cold-weather parkas, we have to use winter hides. See? The hair has to be tight. If we killed any later in the season, the hair would slip, fall out."

"So we have two parkas," Red Star observed soberly. "The outer parka goes with the hair out . . . and the under parka from the fawn hide goes hair in!"

Green Water reached over to ruffle her hair. "You're going to make the best of all, huh?"

"Yes!" Red Star giggled. "They're like shelters for each person. That's why they hang down almost to the knees, it makes a tent around you and the long boots come way up high inside."

"You won't freeze," Laughing Sunshine called, inspecting the parka she'd just finished. In all, the complete suit weighed just over ten pounds and could keep a human from freezing— even in the deepest biting cold of the Long Dark when a man's spit froze before it hit the ground.

"I'll be the best!" Red Star promised. "You'll see."

Green Water smiled, eyes closed to feel the sun on her face. "Yes, we'll see. Thanks to Wolf Dreamer."

Broken Branch waddled around, enjoying moments of delight as she floated in the hot pool or picked at the curious yellow crust that formed where the water lapped at the rocks.

From the rocks—exposed by the retreating drifts—moss, lichen, and overwintered leaves were gathered to make the strong black tea. As the thick brambles of blueberry, bear-berry, and cranberry melted out, fat berries remained, pre-served through the Long Dark, sweet and succulent as their juices melted in the mouth.

The children ran, laughed, and played, splashing in the warm waters, eyes twinkling.

Standing a hundred yards from Heron's cave, One Who Cries, Jumping Hare, and Singing Wolf watched the water from the hot pool rise in twining wreaths, casting occasional glances to where Runs In Light stood talking to the old Dreamer. Heron's cackle rent the air like a knife.

One Who Cries stood tall, filling his lungs with crisp spring-scented air as he studied flights of ravens coming up from the south. A flock of scavenger gulls wheeled to the west. "Caribou," he mumbled. "There must be a herd coming."

"Then the cursed flies will be here shortly." Jumping Hare looked westward, pursing his thin lips as though regretting what he had to say next. "And the clans will be gathering in a turning of the moon or so."

"For the Renewal, you mean?"

"Yes."

"You're going?"

Jumping Hare lowered his gaze, awkwardly scuffing the toe of his long boot against a rock. "I've reached the mar-rying age. The only place I can look for a wife is at the Renewal, where all the clans come together."

"True."

"We've made mistakes, but we have to go on living."

One Who Cries puffed out his cheeks and spewed a long exhale. "Mistakes? We're alive."

Ignoring the comment, Jumping Hare added, "And I want to know if my mother lived."

"She's a strong woman."

"You know Runs In Light will stay here," Singing Wolf said from the side where he watched the young man talking in low tones to Heron. "The old woman won't go back. I don't . . . Well, Runs In Light doesn't know he'll stay yet, but he will."

One Who Cries cocked his head. "You've become an ex-pert on Runs In Light? I thought you couldn't stand him."

Singing Wolf's expression didn't change. "Remember up in the hills when Broken Branch landed on me with both feet? That wasn't anything to what Heron told me a couple of days after we got here."

"What did she say?"

"She . . . she's smart. Knows a lot about people and how they work. She told me . . . I . . . could be a great leader if I learned what made things happen. She said I could be one of the best leaders the People ever had if I'd give myself the chance, keep my mouth shut, and think about things before I acted."

"I think she's right. You've always been smart—just too emotional."

Singing Wolf pursed his lips. "Laughing Sunshine and I have talked. She thinks maybe the time has come for me to think instead of yell first."

One Who Cries grinned. "Then you will become a leader, my friend. And next time we're starving, I won't feel like driving a dart into you."

"Did you feel like that?"

"Oh, yes. The day we found the musk ox."

Singing Wolf dropped his head, staring forlornly at the new spring grasses. "I can understand why. I wasn't very good company. Always complaining."

"Too bad you can't make the point bases thinner." Jumping Hare wound damp sinew around a point he'd conned away from One Who Cries. A frown lined his forehead. "I wonder . . . The Wolf Dream. You suppose—"

"I don't suppose anything about spirits," One Who Cries said, rubbing his mashed nose. "But I know this: Runs In Light found musk ox on the march and kept us alive. He brought Heron to us when all of us would have starved. Remember her words? Dreams don't come easy." Eyes roaming off to the east, he added, "But nothing does out here."

"Heron says the Big Ice is five days' walk away."

"And she knows of no hole," One Who Cries mumbled somberly, meeting his cousins' eyes.

"Spirit Dreams make people crazy," Jumping Hare said. "Me . . . I think it was all in Runs In Light's head. I think he—"

"Runs In Light doesn't make things up," One Who Cries protested.

"I didn't say that!" Jumping Hare cast an irritated glance at Runs In Light. "I think *he* believed it at first. But if there ever was a Wolf Dream, it's dead now."

"Just because he can't understand it anymore doesn't mean it was false," he countered, though he, too, had wondered if the boy ever really saw Wolf.

Jumping Hare shrugged. "What about the gathering of the clans? What about my mother? Why go farther south when there's food right here? Out there, in the ice, I won't find a wife to warm my robes."

One Who Cries' heart pounded in guilt. "If we go back, we'll brand Runs In Light a fake . . . forever. He'll never live it down. People won't forget."

"*He* dreamed it. Not us," Jumping Hare snapped, slapping a hand on the rock. "A man can't be responsible for another's Dream. It's his trouble. He can deal with it in his own way."

"He blames himself because we didn't walk in a shaft of Father Sun's light all the way beyond the Big Ice," One Who Cries grumbled. "I hate to see him suffer."

"All right," Jumping Hare said, slapping a hand against his thigh. "You don't want to see him suffer. Fine. Neither do I, but I want to go dance the Renewal, see the girls, find out if my mother lived. Face it, there's nothing out here. No magic path to the south and unlimited game. This is the end of the world! Everything we have is back with the People. And we've got responsibilities, the Dance of Thanks, the Renewal rituals—"

"How do you *know* there's no magic path? We never looked for Runs In Light's hole. Along the river, that's what the vision showed," Singing Wolf pointed out, looking from one to the other.

"You go hunt. I'm not missing the Dance of Thanks. It's unthinkable," Jumping Hare said sharply.

"Unthinkable." One Who Cries reluctantly sighed agreement.

"Remember last year? We missed the Renewal, then the Long Light faded," Jumping Hare reminded them. "Maybe it was the fault of the People, huh?"

"Well, if we're going back," Singing Wolf added, "we'd better leave soon. If we wait, we'll have to cross the muskeg. You know what that's like when it gets all mucky above the frost line. Tussock grass twists and flips enough to break your ankle. We've got the spring storms to keep the ground frozen. A man can walk on frozen ground."

"And Runs In Light?"

Jumping Hare shrugged. "His decision is his. We can always come back here and see if he's—"

"Heron doesn't like company," One Who Cries pointed out. "You want her mad at us for coming here again?"

Singing Wolf picked up a rock, scratching a design in the dirt. He lifted a shoulder noncommittally.

"Not me," Jumping Hare declared, "I wouldn't want to make a woman with her Power mad."

Singing Wolf's jaw vibrated with grinding teeth. One Who Cries watched him closely, seeing in the background the scattered puffs of clouds winding southward.

"Something's happening. Can you feel it?" Singing Wolf looked from frown to frown.

"What do you mean?"

"I mean . . . I mean I feel drawn to the Big Ice, like maybe there really is a hole there."

"Do you?"

Singing Wolf stroked his thin face, nodding once.

Jumping Hare chewed his lip. The silence lengthened before he said, "Let's go to the Renewal. We could come back and camp in the foothills where Wind Woman blows the snow clean. We know there's game here. Then we could look."

"What about the Others?"

"They won't come here!" Jumping Hare cried incredulously. "Why would they? They—"

"Following the game, just like us," One Who Cries assured. "And even if they don't come this Long Dark, they will the next or the one after that."

A tremor of apprehension went from man to man. Jumping Hare's flat nose flared. "I can't believe—"

"Believe it. One Who Cries is right. If we found this place, the Others will, too."

Jumping Hare flapped his arms helplessly. "We've got to

go back to the Renewal. It's the way of the People. It's just the way, that's all.''

"The way . . ." One Who Cries echoed regretfully.

No more was said.

Chapter 20

Grassy hills rolled in green waves around Dancing Fox; scattered marshes glistened with dew. Bushes sprouted green leaves along the jagged drainages, the pungent scents of willow and wormwood wafting on the breeze.

Fox huddled in the blind she had painstakingly excavated from the slope of the hill. With rapt attention, she stilled the desire to move, to redistribute her weight so the circulation would restore feeling in her foot.

Movement.

She froze, hardly allowing herself to breathe. The head-high sedges obscured her vision of the side of the slope, but she could make out the blotch of gray brown. Creeping tendrils of horror traced around her heart. Not Grandfather Brown Bear! On this wondrously warm morning, he'd amble along, winter hungry, looking for anything edible.

The wind still blew in her face, hiding her scent from any potential prey.

Heart battering her breast, she waited, eyes glued to the brown. A head shook; a soft snuffling carried on the wind. Moose! How long since she'd seen a moose? Five years? Maybe more? And then it had been far to the west in lands long wrested from them by the Others.

Fear leached into excitement, overcoming hunger and fatigue. Her long fingers tightened on the slim wood of the dart shaft. From the feel, she knew the atlatl hook still rested in the notch. Maybe today. Maybe.

Dancing Fox refused to remember the week before when her cast had been too quick, the dart falling short to cut a long weal in a caribou's hide. Hitting at an angle, the dart had failed to penetrate and the animal bolted sideways in fear. Not this time. This time her throw must be perfect.

She waited, searching her memories for everything she could remember about moose. Not much. They usually didn't roam this northern high steppe. Mostly they stayed west of the mountains, farther south in the ancient lands where the grasses were thicker, bending around the open lands below the forests she'd heard of but never seen. The Others had taken much from the People.

The moose stepped closer, allowing her to pick up some details through the sedges. Perhaps the weather had driven a herd of the animals this far east? A long ear flipped back and forth as the animal lowered its head.

Step-by-step, she watched, energy charging her muscles, the numb cramp in her foot long forgotten.

Now? No, wait. Just a bit longer.

The moose raised its head, looking off to the north, ears flicking this way and that, wide nostrils flaring. A second animal—a calf—hovered at the edge of her sight, following the footsteps of the first.

Dancing Fox's throat had gone dry, the charge in her muscles almost unbearable as her heart hammered excitement. So much meat! So very much!

The cow moose trotted ahead a couple of steps, head up. She scented the breeze with her bulbous nose, trying to compensate for her poor eyesight. The calf moved up to the trickling spring Fox's blind overlooked, anxious, wary of ambush.

She'd chosen a perfect place here. Free water this early in the year came and went with the sun, and the melt, but this early, the little spring drew game like flies to a raw wound.

Wait, she told herself. Animals are always more relaxed after they drink. Be patient. The cow finally lowered her head to drink after the calf, then walked back, dropping its muzzle to the tussocks again. She moved ever closer.

Moose, despite sharp noses and acute hearing, were weak in the lungs. A good shot through the ribs would kill her. The information lined out in her jumpy mind. Such a huge animal, and only one weakness to exploit. Further, they had thick skins—if poor for clothing or making shelters.

As if by magic, the cow turned sideways, no more than

ten paces away, and began cropping the vegetation. From where she sat, Fox could almost count the white hairs that gave the hind legs a hoary appearance.

Now!

Dancing Fox rose smoothly, arm back, muscles rolling as she used the atlatl to catapult the dart forward, all her weight behind the thrust. The dart sailed true, striking just behind the floating ribs, angling forward.

The huge moose jumped, squealing as it kicked both feet out behind, bucking twice before hunching up. The calf bawled a hideous squeal.

Dancing Fox nocked a second dart, balancing, sending it flying as the cow raced away with a beating of hooves. The worried calf followed in her wake. In the action, the second cast just missed the calf.

"That's all right! You got the mother!" Talon called from above. "Nice shot that, struck deep. You killed her, Fox!"

She nodded, a feeling of satisfaction deep within as she heard the old woman making her way down the cobble terrace, rocks grating beneath her feet.

The cow had slowed to a walk far out among the lingering snowdrifts that etched the bases of the hills. She crested a rise and disappeared from sight.

Dancing Fox marked the place in her mind, walking forward to where she'd hit the animal, checking the tracks. A fresh pile of manure had been dumped where she'd hunched.

Talon ambled over the sedges and grinned, stooping to stare at the heart-shaped tracks. "You see," she said, "I told you this would be a great place to come. I remembered from when we camped here . . . what? Ten years ago? Long time. Never been so far south. My man came here. Wanted to hunt out this way, but it didn't look good. Vegetation got shorter the farther south we went."

"And Runs In Light is a lot farther south than this," Dancing Fox murmured, eyes searching the southern horizon where glacial hills grayed the land. "Well, Grandmother, are you ready for a walk? It shouldn't be far, she was going pretty slow last I saw her."

Talon worked her lips over her gums, setting out on the tracks, old eyes following the sign. "Blood here. Dark stuff. Liver blood. You hit her solid."

"You haven't lost any skills."

"Not a one, child." Talon chuckled dryly. "Just my muscles is gaunted up some."

They walked on, the sun slanting slowly to the west.

"She slowed here," Fox decided, looking at the tracks. A thick puddle of blood had formed. She looked up, measuring the height of the sun off the horizon with her hand. Three handsbreadths of light left? It might be close. The thought of losing the moose to wolves hurt something deep inside.

"She's not far," Talon added, pointing. "Look there. Frothy. That dripped out of her nose. She's dead as we speak."

"That or laid down."

"In which case, she's as good as dead. They lie down, they bleed out inside, stiffen up. We've got her."

They walked on, eyes to the tracks and ever-increasing blood as the cow had hobbled along, the calf crisscrossing behind her.

"You've made it longer than I thought you would." Talon eyed her askance.

Fox looked over, squinting against the westering light. "And I'll make it longer still."

"I'm a little surprised. I didn't expect you to be this strong. I thought you'd run back to the band in a week."

"Then why'd you come with me?"

Talon smiled wryly. "Oh, I don't know. I guess I wanted to see how you'd do. Been a long time since a woman left to be on her own. Been a couple of men every now and then who took off. But a woman? Heron was the last and that's been over twenty Long Lights ago."

Fox nodded slowly, wishing she had Heron's reputed Dreaming talents so she'd know if she'd made the right choice. Things were going to be a lot harder from now on. "I couldn't stay," she said simply.

"You don't like Raven Hunter, do you?"

She started to shake her head then stopped. "I . . . To tell you the truth, I don't know. I don't really hate him." She puffed derision through her nostrils. "Can you believe that? He dragged me back to Crow Caller to be humiliated. He used me just about every night he could until you moved into my robes. I . . . I don't know just *what* I think of him."

"So that's why you're out here?"

She nodded and finally smiled. "And for the first time in my life, Grandmother, I'm free!"

"You go back and you won't be."

Dancing Fox lifted a shoulder. "Runs In Light will be coming to the Renewal."

"If he lives."

She bit her lip, a coldness within. "Yes, if he lives."

"You going to try and marry him?"

"I don't know if he still wants me."

"Well, you can find out. But, remember, Raven Hunter will be there, too. Along with Crow Caller." Talon's withered brow furrowed deeper. "Why'd that old fake live when so many good ones froze?"

Dancing Fox shook her head. "Bad luck."

Talon studied her from the corner of her eye. "No one will hold it against you. A woman has the right to run off from a man who's abusing her. And Crow Caller was abusing you. Everyone knows that now."

Fox lifted her hands helplessly, feeling the cool of the evening rising out of the land like a vapor. The deepening slant of sunlight cast long black shadows across the tundra, glinting silver from the new leaves on the sedges and wormwood.

"Do you think I did the right thing?"

Talon sighed. "Don't ask me, child. I can't pass judgment. I'm here on borrowed time. You kept me alive out there in the snow. You got a claim on my soul while it's still with my body. But, to be honest, I'm curious and happy to follow my nose for the while. We get eaten by a bear, so be it. There's honor in that. You'll pray me to the Star People if I die and that's enough for me."

"It's enough for me now, too."

Talon eyed her seriously. "You won't get away with this for long, you know? Someday, some man'll get you. Plant some kid in that belly of yours and you'll need people around. That's the curse of women. Always got some man driving his shaft into you. Either they're scared stiff of your bleeding and don't want you around . . . or they're parting your legs and climbing on." She shook her head.

"Well, so long as Raven Hunter doesn't find me, I'm free

of both,'' Fox said hopefully, watching the disappearing curve of the sun as it slid beneath the horizon.

In the blue-shadow afterglow of sunset, Talon studied the gently rolling terrain, muttering under her breath. ''Where'd that moose go?''

''Down there.'' Dancing Fox pointed to where the ground had been ripped up. A thick pool of blood soaked into the gravelly soil. Tracks angled off for a hollow to the right.

''And there she is,'' Talon breathed, a frail finger pointing.

Fox squinted, seeing the long head, the lowered ears. The calf stood to one side, looking back and forth between them and its prostrate mother.

''I'd hoped she'd be dead. How long until we're out of light?''

''Not long. But . . . wait. Her head just dropped. Wait. Ha! She's not getting up again.'' Talon's old legs trembled from the long walk, but she set out down the hill anyway. ''We'll make us up a fire and have liver and heart tonight, girl! What a hunter you made! Runs In Light will jump for joy to marry you.''

Dancing Fox glowed with joy. Yes, Runs In Light would be proud of her. Knowing she would soon be in his arms, the thought of bearing children didn't seem so bad after all. She longed to feel his arms around her, holding her on the long winter nights.

Chapter 21

Runs In Light stood silhouetted on the ridge crest above Heron's valley, his waist-length black hair blowing in the wind. Dressed in summer fox skins, his muscles bulged in the golden daylight. Below, the People threaded their way in the mushy paths between the receding drifts. Pools of water lay silver in the slanting sun. He crossed his arms over his chest defensively, hoping to ease some of his pain. *There they go. I feel like an abandoned shell: empty and useless.*

Heron ambled leisurely along the ridge to stand beside him, a hand up to shield her eyes against the glare of Father Sun. Her clean hide dress smelled of sulfur from the hot springs. "Not going?"

"How could I?" he asked bitterly. "What would they have said? The Wolf Dream . . ."

"They lived," she reminded. "But I'm glad you're not going."

"Why?"

"You're not ready yet."

He frowned, turning to search her lined face, trying to read the glinting eyes. "How do you know?"

"We looked into each other's eyes once. Seventeen Long Lights ago. You sought me even then—*for a reason.*" She smiled, brown lips hiding her worn and missing teeth. "No, you don't recall . . . but you did."

"I don't understand."

"I know you don't." She probed his eyes deeply, as if searching his soul. "Whether you know it or not, Wolf Dreamer, you made your choice. You chose me . . . my way. I saw for certain the day you Dreamed the caribou in. Like me, the Power taunts you, stirs your mind, *forces you toward the blinding light inside.*"

Fear tingled across his chest, tight, prickling. "I'm not interested in Power. Power is for someone else who—"

"Who what?"

"Who's more worthy."

She chuckled softly, shaking her gray head. "Giving in to cowardice, are you?"

He stiffened, stung deeply. "If I'm giving in to anything, it's good sense. I've been fooling myself."

"You like the feel of Dreaming, don't you?"

"Of course," he admitted. The *feel* soothed him like a warm fire on a cold winter's night.

"But you don't like it enough to give up your soul for it? You want to dabble like a child playing with fire, hoping you never have to surrender your precious self to know the secrets of the flame."

"I'm Runs In Light. Bastard child of an Other," he protested hotly. "I'm not—"

"So what?" She cocked her withered head, arching an eyebrow.

Dread and a longing to return to the old days welled inside him. Silently he cried out, pleading for the safety he'd felt before his Dream Walk. Oh, he'd been hungry, but his soul had been whole and untormented. Now he felt as fragmented as a shattered dart point. "I'm not even really one of the People. I'm unworthy!"

"Why?"

"I don't fit anymore."

"Nobody ever feels like they fit. It's part of the curse of being human."

"I used to fit—before Wolf called me."

"And why don't you think you fit now?"

He shuffled his feet nervously, struggling to find himself beneath the malaise of Dream undercurrents. "I'm different now."

"Of course you are."

A lump swelled in his throat, making it difficult to talk. "Why am I?"

"Because you've touched the soul of the world. You've seen the Monster Children's fight up close, heard the thunderous silence of their clashing weapons, and seen the brilliant darkness of your own soul reflected in their eyes."

"Words," he said gruffly, but their truth pounded loudly inside him like a warning drum. "Just words."

"Yes, you're different. Runs In Light died when Wolf called him from Mammoth Camp."

Staring out across the rocky wilderness shimmering in the sun, he sucked in a halting breath. *I'm half-dead, she's right about that. Why can't I just live anymore? Where's Dancing Fox? What's happened to me? All I want is the woman I love, a safe camp, and to watch my children grow. Is that such a terrible thing?*

Heron hobbled over to stand in front of him, then grabbed one of the locks of his hair that fluttered in the wind and tugged hard to make him look down at her. "Don't you see what you're doing?"

"No."

"You're grasping frantically to pull the threads of Runs In Light back together, when you ought to be letting him go completely."

"I can't let him go!" he shouted bitterly. "*He's me!* That's all I am. I'm—"

"Bah! Quit being a fool. If that's all you were, you'd have never heard Wolf calling you."

Pressure built to a violent crescendo inside. "I don't know what you're talking about."

"Don't you?" Her scratchy old voice had gone gentle, comforting. "I know exactly how you're feeling, torn between this world and the Dream world. I've been there. Fortunately I had Broken Branch to make my decision for me. Years passed while I scrambled to learn how to open the doors in my soul. With me teaching you, you'll learn it in a tenth the time."

"I don't want your teachings."

A smile creased her face, understanding, sympathetic. "Going to be a dabbler all your life, eh?"

"Maybe."

"I warn you . . . you'll end up like Crow Caller, out of sorts, unable to leave the Power alone, lost between truth and falsehood."

"I don't care!" he shouted hoarsely, turning his back to her. "It's my choice."

"No argument there."

He heard her steps going away down the trail, returning to her hot springs, and he swallowed convulsively, heart hammering. Looking out, he could see the People, smaller now, slow-moving dots in the gleaming plain as they picked their way toward piles of glacial rock buried in sheaths of snow.

The urge to follow cried hollowly in his chest. That way led back to the familiar world, to the People and comfort of knowing where he stood in the community. That way led to laughter, warm fires in the night, the old stories. His last link to the security that had always been his was fading with their tracks in the snow.

Too much. I can't give that up!

Resolutely, he clutched his darts and snowshoes up from where he'd laid them, and ran, following the trail of the People. A handful of paces later, he pulled up, looking back at the ridge, back at Heron's. Fear tingled along his spine.

"No," he growled at himself, at the longing tugging him to turn around. "I'm not the one."

Again he took the trail, stilling the wrongness in his heart, but his steps had no spring to them.

Night caught him in the open, stringers of cloud blowing in from the far horizon to burn orange in the sunset. Alone, he bundled himself into a niche in the rock where Father Sun's heat would radiate through part of the night. Miserable, he tried to sleep.

His Dreams left him uneasy, images of the Dream Hunt, of the green valley bursting with game, of Wolf's rasping last breaths. They teased him, haunting, pulling like the open arms of a lover. A lingering taste of wolf meat went sour at the back of his tongue. In the Dream, Wolf stopped frolicking through the lush grasses and turned to him, lifting his nose high. "Spurning my promise?" he asked.

"No! No, I . . . there's someone better, someone who can—"

"I chose you."

"No!"

As if a clap of thunder had sounded, he came bolt awake in the blackness. Sweat poured down his chest, tickling along his skin. The gritty bite of the rock and the edges of chill ate through his damp long boots.

"I'm afraid!" he whispered, tears stinging his eyes. He slammed a fist into the rock beneath him. "So afraid. What's happening to me?"

The wind brought a pungent odor, cutting. He leaned back, resting on his elbows. In the night, a wolf howled, a chorus filling in, eerie, searching.

Chapter 22

A crisp breeze skimmed the chopping whitecapped waves that blew up the river, tousling the fringes on Ice Fire's sleeves. From his high rocky perch, he gazed out over the Big River to the jumbled shore on the other side. The hazy blue green of vegetation carpeted the rolling hills. Far to the east, he could see the rising white of the Big Ice. Behind him, the snow-mantled gray summits of the mighty mountains raked the clouds. The heart of the Long Light had come. Life filled the land.

Flocks of geese soared through the azure skies, their chevrons stretching endlessly to the south. Birds wheeled over the water, preying on the abundance of fish. A deep longing filled his chest as he followed their flight.

"You've been watching the snow geese for four days now," Red Flint remarked, coming up behind him.

Ice Fire didn't bother to turn. "Birds are wonderful things. Imagine what they see up there." He let his eyes dwell on the far southern horizon. The call lurked, subtle, urging.

"They're also noisy. They screech and honk and they're stupid. You can lay out grass-stuffed snow-goose hides and they'll fly right into your net."

Ice Fire cocked his head to study his friend through a slitted eye. "I hope you came up here to ruin my contemplations for a reason."

"You haven't eaten in two days. Moon Water is getting nervous about your health."

"Your daughter is always nervous about my health. You'd think I was twenty years younger and she had an eye for raising my children."

Red Flint spread his hands, a neutral expression on his face. "She doesn't need you twenty years younger."

Ice Fire turned back to watch the flying strands of geese where they winged south. "I had a wife once . . . and a vision after that. That's enough women for one lifetime."

Red Flint shifted, boots grating on the gravel. "I know." It came subdued. "I wasn't serious about Moon Water. But she would, you know. She's worshiped you since she was little and you threw her up in the air and told her stories."

He laughed at the memory of the squealing round-faced girl, her hair flying out as he tossed her high and caught her. "She should be looking for a young man."

"Enough of Moon Water. You've been preoccupied." Red Flint settled himself on the rock just below Ice Fire's point of vantage. "What is it, Most Respected Elder? What do you see out here? What should we know?"

Ice Fire laced his fingers around his knee, leaning back, eyes still on the southern distance. Even from here, he could see the hills rising. The big gravel-braided river shone a deep blue, white-tipped rapids foaming over submerged rocks. For days he'd prayed to the Great Mystery, begging for a vision, an explanation of the tension mounting to a violent crescendo inside his breast—but no answer had come.

"I can't tell yet. Only," he whispered, placing a weather-hardened hand to his heart, "I feel it here. The long wait is almost over, old friend."

"Is that good?"

Ice Fire smiled grimly. "No, but it's not bad either."

"Then what?"

"The Great Mystery's path is opening before us. Good or bad, who knows? What matters is that things will be different, and we'll be changed forever."

Red Flint listened, nodding slightly, a skeptical frown on his deeply lined face. "When you talk this way, I hear your words . . . but I'm never really sure I know what you mean."

Ice Fire smiled warmly. As he laid a gentle hand on his friend's arm, he said, "Neither am I, usually. And it wouldn't matter. We couldn't change anything even if we did."

Chapter 23

Desperately, calling out with fear, One Who Cries held on. His fingers slipped on the wood as the buffalo whirled, spinning with incredible speed. Thick muscles straining, fingers tearing out of their sockets, he fought to keep his hold. His heart pumped, and the world flipped and spun in a blur as his feet lost their grip.

His body slapped to the ground as the buffalo slipped on the ice. The dart shaft snapped in his hand, while the breath in his lungs blasted past his lips.

One Who Cries lay stunned, unable to move as his eyes widened in horror. The buffalo kicked itself to its feet, showering him with icy crystals. He looked into pain-glazed angry eyes as the buffalo thrashed its head, bloody snot slinging in an arc. Hot breath puffed in the cold air as the animal's muscles bunched in the shoulders and hips.

He's going to kill me! One Who Cries watched, unable to move, as the buffalo shot forward, head twisting to hook him with the long black horn.

He opened his mouth to scream.

No sound came.

The buffalo whipped around at the last moment, the mighty back feet splattering him with dirty snow and gravel. Another dart shaft stuck out at an odd angle, the buffalo's flank quivering as if to drive off a vicious bott fly.

"Hey! Whoooo!" someone screamed from the side. The buffalo backed away, wet hooves shining blackly as they danced before One Who Cries' nose. Another step back and . . .

The buffalo gave a startled jump as another dart slapped into its side. One Who Cries heard the huge animal grunt from the sting of sharp stone in its flank. Towering over him, a fuzzy black-brown mass, it swayed on its feet, breathing in grunting rasps.

One Who Cries swallowed, struggling to suck air into his spasming lungs. Turning his head, he could see blood drooling down between the animal's front legs. As he watched, the buffalo's beard lowered between its legs. The animal staggered to one side.

He gasped as his lungs caught, fighting for breath. He heard the buffalo's feet stamping the ground as the animal turned—reminded of his presence. The creature swayed, fighting for balance.

To the side, more desperate calls and screams echoed in the chill afternoon, trying to distract the animal.

One Who Cries struggled to rise through a haze of pain that lanced his body, blinking up at the huge beast, who was moving slowly because of the pain.

The buffalo, sides convulsing with each breath, wheezed. The huge head raised, the big body trembling as more darts hit home.

One Who Cries gripped his broken dart shaft, jabbing it up.

Hate-crazed eyes locked on his, the buffalo sighting down its long horn. One Who Cries thrust the splintered shaft into the mad beast's eye, making the animal flinch.

Yipping, One Who Cries rolled away, the huge horn driving deeply into the frozen soil, pinning his parka to the ground.

One Who Cries whimpered, waiting for the pain.

He squirmed, fear lending his ravaged body strength. Nothing happened.

"Now that's a sight."

One Who Cries looked up at the calm voice, seeing Jumping Hare peering down, shaking his head.

"Never seen anything like it," Singing Wolf added in mock awe before cocking his head and sucking his lips. "Looks like he's bleeding to death."

One Who Cries glared, wiping the dirt and blood from his face. He started to vault up—only to be reminded he was still pinned by the buffalo horn. The huge animal trembled slightly and relaxed as One Who Cries yipped again.

"It's the point." One Who Cries studied the dart he'd taken from the bison's side. "This is the first one I threw. See, caught the rib and shattered." He lifted a section of rib to show everyone where the lenticular point had embedded in bone and snapped off. Then he pointed to a blunted stone point which had fractured upon impact.

"See, you can't help it when you hit a rib. That's part of the job. But this one"—he picked up a second dart—"didn't hit any rib. I cast, it hit, and the buffalo turned." He twitched his lips as he looked at the blood-caked point still hafted to a forearm's length of splintered shaft.

He scratched his head. "I couldn't think what to do as those horns started hooking for me, so I grabbed the dart. Figured that was the safest. But it didn't go in all the way. Where the point is bound to the shaft, it's too thick. Makes a big knot so the point doesn't cut all the way into the animal."

"So?" Green Water lifted an eyebrow in question. "What are you going to do about it?"

"Get a lot of new clothes." Jumping Hare laughed, holding his nose as he indicated One Who Cries' filthy, torn parka. The smell of buffalo blood still hung cloyingly in the air.

One Who Cries growled and glared through slitted eyes. "I'm going to make a better point."

"The People have been making points like that forever," Singing Wolf told him hotly. "That's how points are made."

"Why?"

"Because that's how, that's why."

One Who Cries fingered his chin thoughtfully, looking at the point. "The problem's the hafting. Too thick."

"I told you," Jumping Hare reminded from the side. "Make the shaft thinner."

"Then it's too weak," One Who Cries argued. "Our darts already break too easily. Willow and dwarf birch are crummy—"

"You've got to use that much binding," Jumping Hare insisted. "If you don't, the point slips sideways when it hits."

"A thinner point?" One Who Cries turned it sideways to the fire, closing one eye to squint down the length of the ripple-flaked stone.

"That's not the way the People make points," Singing Wolf declared. "It's bad enough with Runs In Light stirring things up. Now you want to go changing the People's point?"

"Uh-huh," One Who Cries murmured, lost in thought as he fingered the stone.

* * *

"Going someplace?"

Runs In Light started, grasping his darts, looking owlishly up at the jagged gray rocks above.

"If I'd been Grandfather Brown Bear, I'd have had you for dinner." Broken Branch smacked toothless jaws. "And from the looks of you, a poor one at that. You call yourself a hunter? Walking along, eyes to the ground?"

He puffed relief, fear draining from his charged muscles. "What are you doing out here?"

"Me? What are *you* doing out here?" She cackled, sliding down the polished glacial rock. He didn't answer, instead reaching up to grip her hands in support. They felt birdlike in his. When she reached the ground, she stared up at him, brown eyes sharp.

"You're going back?" he asked, fearing her answer would be a part of the vision.

"My legs hurt. Heron's pool made me feel ten seasons younger. Besides, I've been to the Renewals. I've danced enough thanks that if Father Sun doesn't know how I feel by now, he never will. There's nothing there for me anymore."

He watched the gray strands of her hair being tugged by the wind.

"And you? Where are you heading?"

He hesitated, not really sure he knew: a leaf in a gale, pirouetting to some unknown Power's whim. "I'm . . ."

"I'd say you were following the tracks of the People," she said, eyeing him inquisitively. "Long walk that, longer than this old woman wants to make."

He dropped his eyes, hands knotting on the dart shafts until his knuckles stood out white.

"Given up, huh? Couldn't stand the thought of making your Dreaming powerful? Gonna go suck up to Crow Caller? Be a laughingstock?" She shook her head dismally. "Wolf should have chosen better."

"What I do, Grandmother, is my business."

"Suppose so." With her fingers, she shooed him away. "Then go on. Be about it. Me, I got important things to do. I haven't lived my life all away yet." And she hobbled off the way he'd come.

Runs In Light gritted his teeth, heart pounding sickeningly. He turned, running to catch up.

"Go on," she growled, making tracks, bent back swaying with each step. "Go grovel at Crow Caller's feet. Me, I'm fine. I been stumbling about these plains since before your mother sucked a full teat, and her mother before her."

"But I . . ."

"What? Speak up, boy. Wind Woman's been blasting my ears so long they're stopped up."

"I never knew my mother," he said lamely, just wanting to keep her talking, needing reinforcement for the decision that tore at the depths of his soul.

"You never . . . No, of course not! She died bringing that smirking brother of yours alive. Even then he was backward. Came out feetfirst. Flies Like A Seagull tried to turn him, but, well . . . You know. Things happen. He was trouble even then. He'll be more trouble now that he's older. Works that way. I always thought maybe you could temper his violent side, but I guess not."

"His violence was always more powerful than my—"

"Oh, I know it. So did old Seagull. She loved your gentleness, reminded her of her lost daughter. Did you know she'd lost a daughter before she got you?"

He shook his head impatiently.

"Yes, that girl was born funny. Part of her lower back was open. Spine all sticking out, no skin or bone over it. Ugly thing, that child. Never did have use of her legs. Died pretty quick, but not before Seagull came to love her. She was sure happy to get you two. Filled the need in her and she could put her milk to use." Broken Branch cackled suddenly, slapping her thigh. "She used to wince something fierce when that brother of yours clamped down on her. Grew teeth early. Guess he's still got 'em—and they're fangs, to be sure."

He nodded heartily to himself. "He's bit *me* a time or two."

She cackled again, smiling broadly. "He's bit everybody at least once."

"Broken Branch," he began uncomfortably. "Did you know then that Raven Hunter and I were only half-People?"

She shrugged, laying a hand on his shoulder. "Some of us

thought it, but your mother wouldn't say and we didn't really care anyway.''

"How could you not care?'' he pleaded incredulously. "They're our enemies!''

"Because the happiest days of all are days when babies come to the People. Keeps us and our ways alive. You belonged to us, not them. We wanted you.''

He inhaled a deep breath, battling with himself, shoving at the fears roiling through him, silently screaming in confusion.

She looked up at him from the corner of her eye. "How long has that been bothering you?''

He waved a hand negligently. "Since Heron told me.''

"Well, forget about it. When you reached five Long Darks and a human soul came to live in you, it was a soul of the People, not the soul of an Other.''

"But I still have the blood of the Others running in my veins.''

"Turn it into a trail between two worlds, then, if it worries you.''

"A trail between . . .'' The words echoed in his head: *trail . . . between . . . worlds . . .*

"Sure, someday we're going to have to face them. Put that blood of yours to use. Just like old Seagull did her milk.''

He stumbled, mind reeling. Images swelled; a web of blood shot out from his chest, spreading to the Others' camp, touching the tall man with silver hair, entangling him. The man turned abruptly, staring breathlessly at him.

"The red web,'' he gasped. "I see fragments—''

"What?'' Broken Branch said sharply.

The vision burst and he jerked his eyes wide, panting into the chill wind. "A web, it spreads out like—''

"What does it mean?''

"I don't know. It just appeared.''

"How are you ever going to find out what those visions mean?''

An empty chasm yawned in his chest. She was asking if he was ever going to take responsibility for the glimpses, look deeper to find the roots.

"You know *why* you don't know, don't you? I've seen Dreamers, dozens of them!''

"Why?"

Her jaw worked in her sagging cheeks. She nodded slightly, eyes mahogany orbs. "Your head's full of mush. All cluttered up like bott maggots in a caribou's back."

"And how do I unclutter it?" he demanded, irritated, whispers of the vision taunting from just below his awareness.

"Watch your tongue, youngster," she snapped. "We taught you better."

Chagrined, he dropped his eyes, feeling the flush of embarrassment.

"How'd you learn to hunt? Seal Paw took you out. You listened to the stories—watched the animals. You had teachers."

"Teachers . . ." He sighed, closing his eyes, feeling the threads of destiny pulling tight around him, so tight he couldn't breathe.

"Of course, teachers. Heron offered, didn't she?"

He nodded.

"She's the best. That fool Crow Caller? A sham, a mocker hanging on to his position by making things up. Oh, sure, he heals, but he doesn't cure. You get my meaning, boy? Like, take old Gray Rock. Remember when her tooth went bad? Any simpleton can punch a hole to drain pus."

"But the People still listen to him."

She sighed, gesturing irritably with a clawlike hand. "They've forgotten what real Dreamers are like. I'll tell you, boy, we don't have Dreamers anymore. Not like the old days. Maybe it's the world changing, but People forget . . . and the old ones who remember are fewer and fewer. These young sprouts—like Raven Hunter—they don't know how powerful Dreaming can be!"

"Powerful . . . more powerful than the Monster Children's War."

She sniffed and nodded. "You *do* know, eh? And you're *still* tagging along behind the band, going to sneak into the clan gatherings and make believe it'll all go away? It won't."

He hugged himself fiercely, as though he might disappear any instant into the void expanding in his breast. "I know. And it's tearing me apart."

She smacked her gums and rocked back and forth. "Well,

do something about it. You've only got two choices. Forget it all, go back, find a nice wife with a good disposition . . . and hope the Others don't stick your guts with a dart. Or follow the call Wolf gave you—*save the People*."

"And lose myself?"

"No, young idiot. Find yourself! It's high time you quit fooling around. You're like a fox with two rabbit holes, unsure which to watch. Choose. Now."

She braced her hands on her hips, watching through hard eyes. "It doesn't get any easier. Only harder. You put off, and put off, and next thing you know, you've got a wife and four kids and you've never taken responsibility for yourself in all your life—and you'll never be able to again."

His thoughts spiraled in confusion. The old woman watched, a keen light in her eyes. On the far horizon, a pack of wolves loped, running south. He grimaced after them, feeling the hurried beating of their hearts inside his own chest, seeing the world through their eyes for a moment. He tried to swallow, but it stuck in his throat like a swollen rawhide knot.

"Let's go, Grandmother." He said it slowly, feeling like his life had been uprooted, blown away in Wind Woman's chill breath.

She chuckled dryly and patted his shoulder as they started back down the trail.

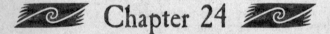

Chapter 24

Ice Fire shivered, sensing hands on his body, voices slowly penetrating the numbing haze in his mind.

"Wake up!" someone yelled in his ear. Red Flint. No one else had a scratchy voice like that.

He blinked his eyes open, seeing hides and feet and knees where they pressed into the soft ground.

"What happened?" His voice cracked and broke. Red Flint bent down to hear him.

Out of the blur of vision, he could see the sky, puffed with white clouds. The sun slanted down from an angle—early morning. The camp lay just behind him from the sound of women and children. Around him, scrubby wormwood clung to the thin gravelly soil. The southern horizon seemed to glow orange, like red filaments of . . . webbing. . . .

Red Flint spread his hands in mystification. "I don't know. You were walking out toward the hill again and you cried out. We all saw you spin around and stare into the sun. Then you screamed, raising your arms and batting at the air, like flies or something were swarming around you."

"Like you were batting away darts in battle," Walrus offered, frowning fearfully. "You know . . . *struggling.*"

Ice Fire tensed, the vision coming back. "Yes," he gasped, seeing the blood-red threads searching for him. "I remember."

"Tell us," Red Flint pleaded. "What did you see?"

"Red spindles, like strands of a web, spinning out from the south. The Enemy Dreamer was there, spinning the web—like some strange spider."

"Do they make magic against us?" Sheep's Tail demanded, clattering his darts against the ground.

"They'll wish they hadn't!" Horse Cry added vehemently. "They'll see! They'll see what Mammoth People do to those who—"

"No," Ice Fire croaked, fighting his way to sit up, still dazed as he cataloged the faces around him and braced himself on his arms. "It wasn't magic against us. I was afraid at first. Feared the web he'd spun. But in the end . . . yes, in the end it wrapped around me. Drawing me, drawing me south to the . . . to the . . ." He frowned, shaking his head.

"Was it the Watcher again? Did she do this to you?" Red Flint dropped to stare intently into his eyes.

"No, not the Watcher. I didn't feel her."

"What? Think. Remember, old friend," Red Flint pleaded.

Ice Fire looked up, shaking his head. "I can't . . . can't remember more. The vision broke then."

"South." Horse Cry looked around with a predatory smile. "To the Enemy."

Ice Fire looked at him, a curious premonition rising within. "Beware, Horse Cry, things are not to be as you imagine." *Not when Power wraps its threads around the lives and souls of men.*

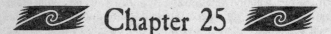 Chapter 25

Broken Branch and Runs In Light struggled together up Heron's ridge. The old Dreamer stood alone, watching them weave along the rocky path. Her eyes riveted on Runs In Light.

As they neared, she turned to Broken Branch. "Back? You like punishment, old woman?"

"Oh, shut your mouth," Broken Branch muttered, craning her thin neck to look up at the Dreamer. "Kill me if you want to, but do it when I'm lying in your hot springs soaking my aching bones."

Heron guffawed, eyes twinkling. "Go soak. I'll come kill you when I have time."

"Come to talk, first," Broken Branch said tenderly. "No one remembers the old ways like we do. I miss them."

Heron's smile turned soft, she lowered her eyes. "So do I."

"And teach this boy what to do with the images floating around his head." Broken Branch hooked a thumb at him. "He'll go crazy if he doesn't learn soon."

His heart fluttered madly as he met Heron's eyes. A flame burned there he didn't understand, but it made his gut go tight.

"You're no longer Runs In Light, you know that?"

"Yes," he rasped anxiously, "I know that now."

The next night, he sat awkwardly in front of Heron's fire, the shelter walls glowing softly around him. The skulls in the corners seemed to glare suspiciously at him—as though they doubted his resolve. He shifted uncomfortably, pulling up his knees and propping his chin on them. He'd been listening to the old Dreamer for over three hours, listening, but understanding little. On the other side of the fire, Broken Branch sat quietly, preparing freshly snared hare for dinner.

"Magic? The world's full of it. But it's not the kind you think." Heron pointed. "I can't make that rock move. I can't breathe life into the dead. There's rules that keep everything together. A Dreamer has to sink into the world—let it swallow him until he doesn't exist anymore." She cocked her head, eyeing him seriously. "You listening to me?"

"Yes."

"What do you think happens when you call the animals and they come?"

"They hear me calling and—"

"Wrong." Heron leaned forward to stare him hard in the eye. He swallowed nervously.

"Then what?"

"They don't hear you. They hear their own voices calling them to die."

"What do you mean?" he asked in confusion, restlessly prodding the fire with a long stick.

"I mean the basic rule of all magic, or all Dreaming, is that there's only *One Life*." In a swift violent motion, she stabbed another piece of wood into the fire. Sparks whirled upward.

Her eyes gleamed as she waited pensively, expecting him to respond, but his gut roiled so madly he could think of nothing to say. Finally, "Go on."

"You've seen a mother charge Grandfather White Bear with a rock when he's grabbed one of her children."

He nodded.

"Why does she do it?"

"To save her child."

Heron spat derisively into the fire. "Great Mammoth, no."

He squirmed. What was she getting at? He searched his own feelings and thoughts. "I don't . . . understand."

"She does it to save *herself*."

"But Grandfather White Bear has her child."

"Child is Self," she whispered cryptically. "People sometimes touch the One Life—feel inseparably linked to others, or places. That's what it's all about, never letting that link go." She spread her arms wide, pinning him with her glinting gaze. "That's why the caribou came. For a single moment, you touched the One, and when you called, begging them to give themselves, they heard their own voices and came. Offering the sacrifice so they themselves could live."

"If there's only One Life, then why doesn't everyone feel it. Why aren't we always in contact with it?"

She stared, hardly aware that Broken Branch sat quietly roasting meat. "Thoughts get in the way. People block their minds to the Dream, disbelieve, shut themselves off from the voice of the One. If they listen to themselves, they can hear it, but a person has to tear down the walls he's built in his mind before he's free to listen. Most people won't. It's too hard. Instead, they fill their minds with petty nonsense, gossip, thoughts of revenge."

"But creatures *are* different." Wolf Dreamer spread his hands. "Look at how we're shaped. Nothing else uses darts to hunt. Nothing else warms itself by fire."

Heron reached over, plucking an age-darkened skull from the wall. "This is human." She pulled another. "This is bear. Both have teeth, both have the same bones . . . just differently molded. Two eyes. See? One nose. You peel the hide off and bear looks just like man. The feet have the same bones. So, outside of the fur coat and the different shapes of bone, all animals share things. You have fingernails. A bear has claws. A caribou hooves. It's the pattern. All the same."

Broken Branch huffed, disturbing the tension. She pushed a strand of brittle gray from her withered face, whispering, "In the legends of the People, all creatures were stars once, each formed from the same star dust. Father Sun sent us tumbling to earth and breathed life into us. People were the worst of the lot. Father Sun forgot to give us a fur coat. The caribou let us use theirs when we eat them. A gift to a brother. We didn't get mammoth's trunk, but we got hands to do the same thing."

Wolf Dreamer blinked contemplatively. "I remember, Grandmother."

Heron shook a finger in his face. "Do you? What is it in you that remembers?"

He pointed quickly to his stomach. "My liver. I—"

"Bah!" she growled, slicing the air with a fist. "I know the People believe that but it's wrong. It's your brains that remember—and Dream."

"What makes you think brains do that?"

Heron leaned back, lips pursed. "You've seen a man hit in the head? What happens? He forgets things. When his arm is cut off, he doesn't forget. When his stomach is sick, he still thinks the same as he always did. Ah, but when he hurts the bone around his brains, he thinks differently. If the damage is bad enough, he doesn't think at all. Same with anything. Club a caribou in the head, and it dies. Shuts off the mind."

"I guess so."

"Don't guess," she told him. "See for yourself. Learn. Think on your own. Don't believe everything the People have always told you. Question!"

Broken Branch bristled. "You telling him I was wrong about Father Sun and the star dust?"

Heron blinked as though it hadn't occurred to her. "No. That's one of the few things you've ever been right on."

"You old witch. I ought to—"

"Why do you know all this?" Wolf Dreamer interrupted. Inside him, a horrifying anxiety built. What was he doing? If he learned what Heron sought to teach him, he'd lose the world he loved completely. "Why doesn't everyone?"

Heron chuckled at Broken Branch, then shrugged. "In the camps of the People, no one has time. Hides need to be tanned. Meat needs to be hunted. Moss has to be gathered. Children *always* need something, or are fighting, or are hurt, or are curious.

"A Dreamer has to clear his mind to be able to think and feel without worrying about who's squabbling with who. Without being interrupted by nonsense."

She rubbed her nose. "Here . . . before the People came . . . you could hear, feel, let the world wrap around you. The land breathes, the animals follow their ways. Seasons, cycles, it all goes around. Everything's inseparably locked together. Grass grows where mammoth dung falls. Seeds blow in the wind. Mammoth eats the grass and makes more dung. The People know this, but not what it means. And who can think about the One Life when three kids are howling for food and someone is telling jokes in the back of the shelter?''

"So, all I have to do is be alone?'' he asked skeptically. It sounded far too easy to be true.

She bowed her head and laughed. "All you have to do is set yourself free.''

"How do I do that?''

She grinned insolently. "First you have to learn to walk.''

"To walk?'' he asked, bewildered.

"Sure, then you learn to *Dance*.''

"Dance?''

"Uh-huh. Then you learn to stop the Dance so you can get a good look at the Dancer.''

He shook his head. "What in the world are you talking about?''

"The One Life. It's all a Dance and you have to feel its motions before you can understand it.''

"And you think I don't know how to walk yet?''

She sniffed lightly. "Wolf Dreamer, you can't even crawl.''

He twisted the fur on his parka hem, forming it into a sharp point as he thought.

"You'll teach me?''

"Are you ready to learn?''

An unaccustomed dryness parched his mouth. *Am I?* "Yes.''

"Come.'' She stood, joints cracking, and pushed the door flaps out of the way.

On the way out, he noted the bear skull, empty orbs staring at him darkly. He clenched his fists in determination. He'd learn.

She led him along the ridge to a high place above the hot springs. Below, the water splashed and bubbled, sizzling. In the blackness of night, she placed a robe on the rock. "Sit. Stay here until I come get you. The only thing you *must* do is still your mind . . . find the silence beneath all the sound.''

He squinted incredulously. "There's no silence here. It's all a mass of constant sounds.''

He saw her broken teeth flash in the dim light of the Star

People. She put hands on hips and gazed out over the rolling hills to the distant ridges. "You think there's a hole there?"

He followed her gaze, staring at the jagged peaks of ice. A soft pain twined through him. "Yes."

"You have to find the hole inside you before you'll find the one in the ice."

He squeezed his eyes shut a moment, clamping his jaw in disbelief. "This is all gibberish. The One Life, the Dance, the hole. What are you—"

"They're all the same. Everything *is* nothing." She cackled, hilarious.

He lifted a brow. "You've lost your mind."

Heron shoved his shoulder playfully. "Exactly! And you must, too. Come. Sit. Clear all words from your head. Not a thought. Not a single image in your mind. You have to lose your mind, be empty before you can be full. Sound easy?"

He nodded in the dark. "Of course. Just shut off the voice in my mind."

"I thought you'd say that." She turned and walked off, steps fading in the darkness. Softly he heard her add, "Remember, your only enemy will be yourself."

Wolf Dreamer rubbed his chin dubiously as he watched the steam rise from the geyser, glowing silver in the starlight.

"Well." He sighed. "Here goes." He closed his eyes and stilled all the words in his mind, concentrating on the sound of the hot springs. It was easy . . . for all of a half-dozen heartbeats.

Then words crept into his thoughts. Scenes remembered glowed to life in his mind. Slips of conversation oozed from nowhere. The sound of the springs disappeared in his struggle. Nothing helped. Around him, only the cold of the night and his discomfort on the rock agitated his constant battle to keep his mind clear.

Dancing Fox's face floated in his memories and he felt a tearing confusion, longing, desire to see her again. Hurt, he tried to force her away, his mind chattering to itself.

No sooner had he vanquished that vision than Seagull's voice began, the subtle tones of her speech welcome and comforting. Daydreams followed, all erupting out of the turmoil in his mind.

"Your only enemy will be yourself," Heron's words re-

minded, mocking his effort. His butt hurt. The first tendrils of hunger drifted through his stomach.

The long hours continued.

He caught himself musing at the sunrise, smiling at the red and blue bands drenching the sky. Desperately, he battled to still his thoughts about the day. His imagination wove patterns out of the steam lifting from the gurgling water. The gentle breeze filled with familiar voices.

His butt had gone numb. A loud rumble reminded him of his empty stomach.

It got worse.

He didn't remember rolling over on his side, but the flies brought him awake. Tiny gnats plagued him.

"Fine Dreamer you are," he chastised himself, feeling frustrated to the point of screaming. Viciously, he swatted an insect and wiped the remains on his pant leg.

The day wore on. Had Heron forgotten? Gone drifting off on her own, unaware of time? Maybe he ought to go look for her?

"I won't leave."

The sun heated the sky, a thirst growing as he began to perspire. The insects got worse, drawn by the odor of his sweat. A shimmering cloud, they hummed around him. The black flies and mosquitoes sought his flesh. Gnats rattled in his nose, bit at his waist and neck. In desperation, he rolled over and pulled his hood up to cover his head. Sweet oblivion . . .

A sharp kick to the ribs brought him scrambling up. To the west, a faint glow marked the vanishing path of Father Sun.

"Asleep?" Heron mused, looking down at his bite-swollen face. "You Dreamed?"

"Uh . . . yes. I was back in the—"

"Didn't you ever find the silence?"

"There's no silence here!" he insisted adamantly, glowering at her.

"Great Mammoth, you're worse off than I thought." She spun on her heel.

He got up unsteadily, dusting himself off, feeling like a gruesome failure. Crestfallen, he followed her.

Chapter 26

Dancing Fox and Talon sat together at the base of a tall basalt ridge. Broken rock spattered the slopes. Grass filled in the spaces between the tumbled boulders, weaving an irregular green and black patchwork. An eagle circled curiously through the cloudy sky over their heads, diving low on occasion to keep an eye on them.

"It's not very good." Dancing Fox held up the point she'd been working on, flake scars catching the light. The basalt outcrop contained a gritty rock that flaked poorly, unlike the colorful cherts and fine-grained quartzite tool stone One Who Cries cherished.

"So be it. It'll work. The point's the thing, Fox. Got to have that tip sharp so it cuts in. Now, the next thing is the binding. I remember what that worthless man of mine always said. 'Get the hafting too thick, and it hangs up, slows the dart.' Well, at least the old maggot bait could make good darts. But keep in mind, girl, when you haft it, too little binding and the point turns on impact instead of penetrating."

Dancing Fox frowned, sucking at the red slip of skin on her hand where she'd cut herself. It was the bane of all flint knapping; she'd driven a flake deep into the webbing between her thumb and forefinger. About her feet lay a litter of stone chips—including more than one of the long, thin points that she'd cracked during manufacture, striking too deeply into the stone. She lifted the point again and grinned.

"Now," Talon added softly, "you must breathe spirit into the point. That's the key—making it live so it knows it's supposed to drive deeply into the side of the animal, to seek its life. Use all your soul, girl. Sing!"

Dancing Fox nodded, slowly chanting, feeling the Power of her soul as it washed over the dart tip. She clutched the point in her bloody hand, willing herself into the black rock. A warm feeling filled her.

"Now do the binding and the shaft," Talon explained. "You have to get your Power into the whole thing. The point is only part of the whole. Without a strong straight shaft, the point can't kill. Without the point, the shaft is harmless. The binding makes them one. Then you have to run the grooves along the base and tie the feathers on. That's important . . . keeps the dart flying straight and stable in the air.''

''I never realized how much went into this.''

Talon rubbed her fleshy nose. ''Think of it like a man and woman. The binding is the marriage to make a whole out of the system. It joins the spheres of Power. Taps the spirits of the rock, the wood, the animal, and the bird. A union, that's Power. Male and female, understand?''

Dancing Fox stared sightlessly at the point. ''Like I would be with Runs In Light,'' she whispered.

''Still can't get him out of your head, huh?''

Dancing Fox pulled long strands of gleaming black hair back from her face, looking longingly to the south. ''No, Grandmother, I can't. He fills my dreams, making my nights lonely and empty. I hear his voice, feel his arms.''

''Well, it won't be long until Renewal. We'll find him there.''

Fox sighed heavily. ''I hope so.''

''You'd give up your freedom for him? After all this work you've done to learn how to survive on your own?''

Dancing Fox lifted her slim muscular shoulders. ''I'd rather survive with him helping me. Is that bad?''

Talon considered, tongue prodding the gaps in her teeth, eyes scanning the darkening sky. A few stars poked through the slate blanket overhead. ''To be honest, child, I don't know. Without children, there's no People. But once you've got a baby, you can't hunt like we've been doing. Men are free. They don't have to stay around and look after their brood. Women do.''

''Won't you take care of my child for me while I go out to hunt?''

Talon smiled. ''Of course I will. But I won't be around forever.''

Dancing Fox nodded thoughtfully. ''Well, even without help, there's hunting I can do with a baby. I can still run animals off a cliff like we did that buffalo. Or use a pit trap, like you showed me for the caribou. I can smoke out ground squirrels, club mice, rob eggs out of nests, and snare hares. I don't have to *stalk* the way a man does."

"And where's the baby going to be while you're doing this?"

"For small game, I can carry her on my back. For big game I might have to find a safe place away from the jump or surround, then come back and get her later."

"You *can* do it, that's true." She squinted hard, rearranging all the lines in her ancient face as she studied Dancing Fox. "But consider this. If you go out and get killed by a wounded buffalo while you're hunting alone, then what? You see, that's the real difference. If a man dies, his child is home safe, but if you die when your baby's with you, well . . ."

"So I'm stuck with having other people to care for my children while I hunt." She shook her head.

"Or you don't have children." Talon leaned forward, bending over her knees. "And then where would the People be?"

"All I want is to love Runs In Light, to be with him. Why do I have to give up my freedom?"

"Because Father Sun made men one way and women another. You tell me, what if Runs In Light walked over the hill just now? What then, huh? How long until you were under the robes with him?"

Dancing Fox lowered her eyes.

"Uh-huh, that's what I thought. That's the trouble, girl. Everything alive has a drive for coupling. It's deep, keeps us going. Man's worse than woman. Always got to stick his spear into you. But a woman—a young woman in love—that's just as bad. And that's how Father Sun made us."

"And it takes away freedom?"

"Can't help but take it away." Talon shrugged. "Thank goodness, though, that Father Sun was smart enough to give the burden of babies to us. Hard to say what would happen if he'd given those fool men the responsibility. People would have died off of stupidity clear back when Father Sun blew life into us after we fell from the stars."

Dancing Fox ran a finger absently along the dart tip. *Could I stand to be near him? Could I stand to see him every day without holding him close? Could I give up Runs In Light to live in exile out here by myself?* She swallowed hard, looking up to the sun. The time for Renewal grew closer. A slow ache built under her heart.

"For him," she whispered, "I could give this up."

Talon nodded, exhaling heavily. "I think maybe you're being foolish . . . but I understand."

A summer like none he could have imagined. Blue Sky Man glowed above, his ponderous belly only hidden by occasional clouds. The flies, mosquitoes, and gnats rolled across the green land in droves. Sprigs of willow and dwarf birch rose from the rocks, lining the yellow-caked sides of the stream. Broken Branch smiled in the sun, eagerly attacking the moss and plants with her digging stick, creating feast after feast for dinner. Blossoms, sweet and delicate, scented the slow breezes in a rich promise of bear berries. Sour dock and wild rhubarb greened above the verdant blaze of willow and alder.

Overhead, flights of snow geese, ducks, and chattering ravens passed in a whir of wings. Curlew called lonely from the ponds to the east. Eagles twisted and turned, spiraling against the endless blue.

Wolf Dreamer floated in the spring, blessing the stink of the geyser that kept the columns of bloodsucking black flies and mosquitoes at bay. The day before, he had marched to the big river with Heron. The tumult of the water had shaken him to his bones. Such Power, such violence, the very ground reverberated from the tormented sandy flood.

"Never seen it this high," she muttered, looking across the rush. "Never."

"Where does it all come from?"

She turned, features stony. "Your Big Ice, Wolf Dreamer."

So much? Only the salt water was so large—and almost tame compared to the river thrashing its way to the north.

He settled back, letting the warm water support him, and cleared his mind. Peace filled him. The battle had almost been won. Time after time, he'd forced himself, each attempt bringing longer and longer spans of silence. Heron had been patient.

"Not even a child learns to walk in a day," she'd reminded.

The feeling of water lapping at his sides, slapping in his

ears, soothed him. The voice of the water, he'd discovered, resembled human speech. Lulls punctuated the noise, lulls of pure silence.

By some sense, he felt her presence, raising his head to watch her disrobe. Even in her old age, Heron's beauty remained. Her breasts, though sagged with age, still held an allure as did her flat stomach, unspoiled by children. Firm legs and arms bespoke the graceful essence of woman.

And Dancing Fox? Would she have that look at Heron's age? He tried to picture her, the image of her bursting youth forming in his mind. She walked in his imagination, hips swinging, eyes sparkling promise as she made for him. His manhood hardened.

Her hair would shine blue black in the sun, tumbling down over her smooth shoulders. She dove seallike into the pool, water rippling from her brown back. Beside him, she came up, breasts bobbing. Her touch would be light on his skin as she reached for him. He would turn, stroke her, holding her close as her legs went around him. He could feel her as she opened herself, ready to . . .

"You have something in your mind?" Heron asked, popping the image, causing him to start. Water rushed into his nose, leaving him coughing and sneezing as he struggled to get his feet under him.

A wicked light gleamed in her eye. She looked at his hard maleness, protruding from the water. "Not this old woman. Too old . . . even for a handsome boy like you."

He gasped, rolling in the water to hide himself, shame running hot in his veins.

She laughed, diving under the water, forcing him to turn again to hide himself.

Her old eyes twinkled as her head broke the surface. He huddled there, chin barely above water. "I'm still a man," he challenged, anger covering embarrassment. "Dreaming doesn't take *that* away from you."

She wiped her face of the crystal beads of water and chuckled dryly. "Oh, you're a man all right. Seems they think of only one thing." Then: "But excuse an old woman. People coupling, that's part of the Dance."

He swirled the water with his hands, hoping the shimmering ripples obscured what the water revealed. Desire drained; he felt better.

"It wasn't you I was thinking of."

She moved to sit on a rock, the water lapping about her waist. "Ah, a young woman?" She looked out over the willows, partially shaded now by the stark white font of geyser steam. "Is she waiting for you?"

"She's not . . . Crow Caller took her as a wife." He splashed frustration. "She ate of the wolf, accepted the Dream . . . but she followed him. A wife doesn't . . ."

"Run off with another man," she finished. "But she could have."

"It would have brought dishonor. She would never—"

"More likely she *fears* Crow Caller. Fears what he would do to her." She wrung water from her hair, appraising his defiant glare. "What's this I see in your eyes? A bad case of young love?"

"Don't," he warned. The pain of losing Dancing Fox seared his chest.

She nodded, giving in. "I won't torment you about her. Her love is your burden."

"Burden?" he gasped incredulously. "More like solace."

"I think you'll see it differently in the near future."

"Didn't you ever long for a man? Didn't you love your Bear Hunter?" He regretted the words as he spoke them.

She watched him, impassive for several moments. "Yes, I did. Would have given anything for him. Thought about killing Broken Branch when she weaseled her way into his robes."

"Why didn't you go back? As . . . pretty as you are, any man would have come here with you."

She shook her head, sighing. "No, no man." Looking to the sky, she worked her lips. "Wolf Dreamer, you must know this. Dreaming—real Dreaming—doesn't leave room for a mate. When a man and woman are together, they take a part of each other. His or her problems become yours. Coupling produces children. No way around it. Children demand all your attention—and they deserve it. So much work goes into turning an infant from an animal into a human being. Children have no sense of time, they need attention *now*. You can't Dream when your child is hungry, or has a question, or gets cut on a chert flake.''

"That's why you're still here after all these years?''

"That's why. No man, no temptation. Just me and my thoughts and Dreams. I made that decision when Bear Hunter went to Broken Branch.'' She smiled wearily. "And I was young then, hurt. I didn't want to have to see him . . . and her.''

"And now she's here.''

Heron tilted her head. "It's been a long time. He's many Long Darks dead. Both Broken Branch and I have changed. And she's brought me a different man. One more important than a lover could ever have been.

"Oh, I could wonder about what-if's, but if you look hard enough, there's a purpose, a reason why everything happens. Maybe you were calling me . . . even then.''

He frowned, moving up to sit beside her. "You're sure it was me in your Dream?''

Her eyes left no mistake.

"But why would you Dream of me?''

She drew a full breath. "You're important to the People somehow. Maybe we'll all die if you don't find that hole in the ice.''

A tremor of anxiety touched him. He fumbled with the gritty surface of a rock. "What should I do about Dancing Fox? She fills my thoughts more every day. I can't concentra—''

"Your choice, Wolf Dreamer.'' The brown orbs of her eyes revealed nothing. "These gifts of yours, they're powerful. I see you changing. The man you were, the one she knew, doesn't exist anymore. Worse, you're growing so quickly into someone different, she'll hardly know you when she meets you again. Will she understand? More importantly, will you want to go back to what you were before the Dreaming?''

"You tell me. You've walked this path.''

"I have no answers for you, but I can tell you the Dreaming is like eating a spirit plant. Once started, you can't get enough. It fills you, drives you, guides you.''

"Constantly? Isn't there time for—''

"Constantly.''

He frowned, watching steam twirl over his head. "That's a heavy price to—"

"A terrible price."

He propped his chin on one knee, staring unblinking into her serious eyes. Wet strands of silver-shot hair draped over her breasts. A grim smile curled her lips. "Is the salvation of the People worth it?"

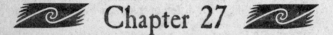 Chapter 27

Branches of dwarf birch and willow twined through the mist of the hot springs, stretching into the turquoise sky. The yellowish green crust on the boulders at the edge of the pool sparkled in the golden sunlight.

Wolf Dreamer shook aside the sweat-dampened ends of his long hair where they clung in curls to his forehead; his oval face glistened with sweat. He watched as Broken Branch used a hand-sized stone and flat rock to pound the dried corpses of ground squirrels into paste. She mixed the flesh with mashed berries, then slid handfuls into caribou intestine. After each handful, she poured hot fat into the ropy sack. Broken Branch rammed home the whole lumpy mass with a stick until the gut bulged.

He stood uncomfortably, thinking. They'd hunted, Dreamed the caribou in again. And this time, he thought he'd heard a single breath of the One voice they shared. But had he? Or had he simply imagined it? Heron's steps crunched over gravel behind him and he turned, smiling at her.

"Come," she said, heading for her shelter.

He followed, eyes losing focus in the narrow darkness. She threw a finely tanned hide at him, which he caught before it touched the ground.

"The flies are gone. The frost has sent them to hiding. How many days since you've eaten?"

"Three."

"Go high. At least a day from here. Remember the Dance. Dream."

He took the robe and turned, pausing to look back. "I called them all the way this time, didn't I?"

She studied him, thoughtful. "I did nothing. You called; they came. We killed enough for winter. We'll have fat for the cold times. Meat for strength."

"I thought . . ." He hesitated, afraid to mention it lest it be a false perception.

"What?"

"For a moment, I thought I heard a breath of the One."

"What did it sound like?"

"It didn't have a sound . . . really."

A wry smile lit her face. "Then maybe you did hear it. Is there a 'voice' we share with the animals that goes deeper than the world we think we hear around us?" A veiled look in her eye, she waved him away. "Go Dream. Listen for it."

Uneasy, he walked into the light, turning his steps west toward the ice-shrouded mountains. She always did that, left him wondering what was real . . . what was imaginary. Had they come to his call? Was there really only One voice for the One Life? Or had it been accident that they'd walked into his trap? What was real?

This year, the shelters looked shabby, worn, poorly repaired. Dancing Fox led the way down the slope slowly, aware that Talon hobbled painfully behind. The old woman wasn't as strong as she'd been before. Since the starving days when they'd left Buffalo Back's camp, some part of Talon's soul had been diminished. She hobbled along, little more than an ancient wraith in hide rags.

Before them, the camp stretched, nestled on the edge of the marshy flats, muskeg spreading out into the northern horizon in a green haze. The flies and mosquitoes would be miserable here this year. To the east, the Big River raced in a torrential flood, overfilling its banks to drown portions of muskeg. To the south, behind the camp, the rumpled gray hills rose to obscure the horizon until they merged with the mandibular teeth of the glacier-patched western mountains.

From the smattering of shelters on the terrace overlooking the muskeg, winding spirals of blue smoke rose toward the sky. The odors of cooking meat, wet dog, and camp trash already carried on the air. A rack of fish had been placed beside a shelter to dry; a young boy with a stick guarded it from the dogs. People sat around smoldering fires, hiding in the smudge while they talked and gestured.

"You don't have to wait for me," Talon called, voice thin and wavery. "Go. Go find your Runs In Light. I'll be along."

With a fleeting smile, Dancing Fox began to break into a run—and stopped short, a cold chill in her heart.

"Why did you stop?"

"Crow Caller. He'll be there. So will all the others who survived. The story of his casting me out will have gone around. No, Grandmother, I want you to walk in with me."

Talon studied her from the corner of her eye. "Not ready to go it alone, eh?"

Dancing Fox fought a flush of embarrassment. "I . . . Maybe. Still, no matter what I think, I owe it to you. We go together. It would be . . . more proper."

Why do I lie?

The dogs saw them first, running out yapping, growling, snarling, their hair stiff and menacing. Dancing Fox slapped them away with her darts. Children followed on the heels of the dogs, calling "Who comes? Who comes?"

"This is Talon," she called. "I'm Dancing Fox."

An older boy, evidently the leader, stopped short, kicking one of the big dogs out of the way, a deep frown on his forehead. He was tall and thin, his face long and eyes small. "Are you the wife Crow Caller cursed?"

Dancing Fox stiffened. "I am."

The boy's eyes narrowed. "You supposed to be around a Renewal? Your soul won't do anything? Cause sickness or the Others to find us?"

Talon brushed past her shoulder. "Who are you, young brat? Did no one teach you manners?" She charged him on her thin sticks of legs, the youth's eyes going wide as he scrambled back.

"I'm sorry!" he bawled. "Forgive, Grandmother. I didn't mean you. I was only . . . only—"

"Only acting like an animal!" Talon spat. "Oh, your parents will hear! I promise that. And so will the leader. This may have been a bad year, but that's no excuse for sniveling brats like you to lose your manners and act like maggots in the body of the People!''

The youth turned on his heel—eyes downcast in shame—and ran. The rest of his group stared wide-eyed and broke after a heartbeat, pounding away after him.

"Looks like my fame has spread far and wide." Dancing Fox sighed. "This may not be pleasant."

Talon turned to face her. "You knew that before we came here. But don't be so worried. After Crow Caller killed so many, people will think twice about his curse."

"We'll see."

They plodded forward, weaving through the array of hide lodges, seeing hundreds of new faces.

"Look over there," Talon said, pointing. "Isn't that One Who Cries and Singing Wolf?"

Fox held her breath, searching the faces of the people near the two men, searching for Runs In Light. "I don't see . . ."

"I don't see him either. But the fact that two of his cousins are here means he led them safely. They didn't die."

Pride welled in her chest, a broad smile lighting her face. "Yes, it does."

Talon clucked her lips, muttering incoherently under her breath. "Well, let's go find your hero. Maybe he'll let us move right into his lodge, eh? You figure he needs an old woman to sew for him? Cook? Maybe tell your brat kids the old stories?"

Dancing Fox grinned, patting the old woman's shoulder. "After Seagull's death, I'm sure he'd be grateful."

At One Who Cries' shelter, she called out politely. Green Water ducked through, waving at the horde of flies, a slow smile coming to her face. "Dancing Fox!"

"Green Water! You lived. The Wolf Dream . . . it was true."

Green Water's warm hug enfolded her first, Talon next. She stepped back, looking Fox up and down, her broad face beaming. "Yes, the Dream kept us alive. As to the hole in the Big Ice, who knows? But we found a haven from the Others."

Dancing Fox's eyes cast around hopefully. "And Runs In Light?"

"He's not here."

"Not . . ." Her heart stopped.

In her calm way, Green Water took her hand and motioned for them to enter the low tent. "He's stayed at old Heron's to learn to become a great Dreamer."

"Heron!" Talon gasped.

Green Water nodded. "Yes, she's more than a legend."

As she sat down on thick robes, Dancing Fox looked her confusion at Talon, seeing reservation in the old woman's eyes, some veiled secret. "Why would he stay with her? He's already a great Dreamer."

Green Water leaned forward, earnest eyes on hers. "He wants to be as great as Heron. Better even, maybe."

Talon slapped gnarled age-spotted hands on her knees. Her eyes met Fox's, challenging. "If that's the case, girl, he'll never have time for you."

"I don't—"

"Dreaming!" Talon hissed to herself, eyes focused someplace beyond the shelter. *"Real Dreaming!* The People need a Dreamer. Been so long since we had one. And now . . . who'd think it would be Runs In Light?"

"But I don't—"

Talon started, attention returning to the present. "No, of course you don't! Girl, if he's going to be a Dreamer, he's become a man possessed. Oh, he'll know you, and if he really cares for you, he might even be swayed from his Dreams. But know this, Fox. Even if you win him back for a while, draw him away, he'll never be all yours. Never."

A cold hand tightened on the bottom of her heart. "Why not?"

"Because the visions cage a Dreamer's soul and never let it go."

Chapter 28

Rocky ridges surrounded the small camp, boulders jutting high into the cold night air. Small bushes grew in the crevices, leaves silvered by starlight.

Five men, tall, long-legged, walked in graceful single file through the rocks. Hoods dangled over their shoulders, the blank eyes of wolves, foxes, and eagles staring from the hides wrapping their heads. Their eyes searched in the manner of hunters. Mammoth hide wrapped around their loins like thick belts. Long darts, fletched with eagle feathers, were clutched in bony hands.

They didn't see Raven Hunter or the rest of the young men hidden in the boulders. Fierce they might be, but they also walked arrogantly, heads high.

Heart thudding in his chest, every limb vibrant with excitement, Raven Hunter waited. Soon, now. Very soon. The first man had walked well within the trap. Wait. None must escape.

Despite his fear-dry mouth and the charged blood rushing in his veins, Raven Hunter floated on a crest of exaltation. Here, before him, walked the murderers of his people. Now, at last, he would strike back. By this act, the People would prove themselves, and under *his* leadership. Despite his youth, he would step into the circles of power and decision where he belonged. A feeling of invincibility and premonition burned in his breast.

"Shhh!" he hissed to Jumping Hare, whose foot slipped on loose rock.

The last Other walked within range.

Raven Hunter bunched his muscles, rising, his cast sure from years of practice. The dart pierced the man's chest. He spun, gasping "no!" then quivered, dropping his atlatl, a look of incomprehension on his face as he tumbled to the ground.

A frightened murmuring eddied through the Others. Men raced, tripping over each other, raising weapons.

"There they are!" one shouted, pointing up into the rocks.

Raven Hunter nocked another dart, driving it deeply into the chest of the second-to-last man, his aim true. On all sides, Jumping Hare, Strikes Lightning, Three Falls, and Eagle Cries bounded to their feet, darts flashing in the air.

It ended quickly, leaving Others writhing on the ground. Blood smeared frantic hands as they groaned and gasped, clutching the shafts protruding from their bodies. Raven Hunter jumped lightly down the rocks. Two! He'd killed two! Brutally, he wrenched his dart from the body of the first, delighted with the gouts of coagulating blood that followed.

"Don't! Don't!" the man whispered. His eyes pinned Raven Hunter's, growing still and sightless as foaming blood welled on his lips.

"Filthy murderer!" Raven Hunter growled, then spat in the Other's face before turning to the second, lancing him through the heart.

Around him, the rest of his victorious party clambered down slowly, eyes wide, shocked at what they'd done. Moving from man to man, Raven Hunter dispatched them with calculated jabs of his bloody dart.

Jumping Hare shook his head slowly, staring at the man his dart had killed.

Raven Hunter eyed his cousin curiously. "They aren't so terrible in death, eh? No longer will they run us from our ancestral lands—lands given to us by Father Sun! A new day has dawned, *We are the People!*"

Strikes Lightning smiled proudly. "The People," he repeated. Then in relief and joy, he jumped high into the air, a yip of delight clearing his throat.

One by one, they caught the fire as Raven Hunter walked about, clapping each on the back, praising courage and cunning.

"And to think we ran? *Ran*, from such as *these*?" He raised a fist and shook it in the air. "No more, eh, my friends? No, indeed! Together, we shall drive these men back!" He bellowed a shriek of victory to the skies. "We won't let them chase us like frightened caribou from the land where our fathers' bones rest in peace!"

Eagle Cries pursed his lips tightly, nodding. "No more."

"Follow me!" Raven Hunter urged conspiratorially. "Follow and we'll drive these Others from *our* land!"

Softly, Eagle Cries began the chant, "Raven Hunter. Raven Hunter! *Raven Hunter.*" Then it was picked up by the others, growing louder until it boomed from the surrounding rocks.

Ice Fire let his soul sway to the chant of the White Tusk Clan's singers. The elder, Red Flint, led the younger men in the ancient songs that would placate the souls of the animals, call them back into reach of the Mammoth People's weapons in the future.

In the endless light of the solstice, summer had reached its peak. The sun hung like a growing golden ball in the sky, the gift of the Great Mystery. The shelters of the White Tusk Clan spread around, built higher in this season of moderate winds. Ice Fire could smell the odor of roasting buffalo and caribou. The memory of fawn backstrap, cut from the side of the spine, hung at the back of his tongue, a savory feast of wondrous delight.

Young women surrounded the dancers, clapping their hands, smiles on their happy faces. Dogs nosed about, seeking scraps, the males hoisting their legs on tent corners, lifting lips in the eternal pecking order of the pack. A constant babble of happy voices rose and fell with Red Flint's singing.

The shelters reflected prosperity. The children were firm-limbed, with full faces. Clothing—newly made—graced strong arms and legs. Spires of flies hovered around the drying racks surrounding the ceremonial camp of the White Tusk Clan. Best of all, no widows watched from the outskirts, no short hair could be seen. Despite the horrors of the Dark, this long summer had graced them—a gift from the Great Mystery who'd all but forgotten them in the horrible winter.

Before Ice Fire, the young men leapt and danced, their feet stamping in rhythm with the wavering chants. He closed his eyes, drawing deeply of the smoke of the willow. A sacred plant, the willow; its odor soothed, purified the soul. In the annual clan festivals, the willow made them all whole.

Ice Fire opened his eyes again to stare into the fire, feeling the harmony of life around him. Flames licked and twisted, shafts of yellow light rising, sparks whirling. He stilled his mind, enjoying the peace of this evening.

In the coals, he watched the patterns flow and change by the second. Entranced, he watched the eddies of wind over the burning eye, feeling the Power before he was really aware of it. Out of the curls of light, a face formed, staring back at him.

"Who are you?" he asked, the Clan Dance fading out around him, only the chant carrying him forward.

"You ask, Father?"

Ice Fire knotted a fist at his breast. "Who . . ."

"I threw you a rainbow once. Wasn't that enough?"

"Father? You call me Father?"

"The man who raped my mother. Now you come for the rest of us? Go away. Leave our lands that Father Sun blessed for us. Give us—" He cried out suddenly.

A pain lanced through Ice Fire's breast, a sharp sting like the cool keen edge of a dart piercing him.

"Death," the face in the fire whispered. "My brother has killed the Others. See them? See their bodies lying bleeding and broken?"

A vision formed in the back of Ice Fire's mind. Five crumpled figures, flies thick in the clotted wounds, their eggs lining the torn flesh in ivory piles.

"Hoop Thrower, Five Stars, Mouse Tail . . ." One by one, Ice Fire named them, the vision shimmering in the back of his mind. He stared at the face in the fire, swallowing hard. "You . . . you have done this?"

"My brother, Raven Hunter . . . your son . . . did this. I am Wolf Dreamer . . . born of your seed, man of the Others. You have reaped the actions of your lust. What you planted has grown in the rocky soil of the People. Pain, death, and misery walk with Raven Hunter."

Ice Fire shook his head. "We'll kill you. It's now a matter of honor. Mine are a fierce people. Yours are soft, bleating like wounded caribou calves. My warriors won't let you run any longer, they'll hunt you down for this."

"See the way you have made, Father. Your son, born of blood, comes. Your son, born of light, leaves. Which will you choose?"

"Choose? What do you mean? Wolf Dreamer, what is your message?" He stood, leaning forward. "What?"

"Death . . . or life. Is there any other message, Father?" And the flames crackled, a shower of sparks spiraling into the night in a crimson swirl.

"Wolf Dreamer? *Wolf Dreamer?*" Only the flames flickered, the slender branches of willow hissing, their sacred smoke rolling over him like a blanket.

Ice Fire looked about, blinking, the Power of the vision fading from his taut body.

"Old friend?" Red Flint's voice sounded uneasy, hesitant in the silence.

Ice Fire rubbed his masklike face, feeling the warm hand of the Singer on his shoulder. He turned to look, seeing the dancers where they watched, casting wary glances at him and each other.

"What . . . what happened?"

Red Flint met his gaze, deep worry behind his brown eyes. "You stood, shouting into the fire. Like you were talking to someone there. I came quickly, and saw nothing but glowing coals in the fire pit."

Ice Fire shivered suddenly, the image of the dead hunters in the back of his mind, the very humming of the flies roaring in his ears. "Death. He said death was coming. My son is coming. And he was born of blood."

Slowly Ice Fire walked through the still dancers, hardly aware that they stared at him, faces ashen.

 Chapter 29

Bonfires made from piles of alder and willow crackled high, sending wreaths of sparks to glow orange-red against the mauve heavens. The people danced, singing praise to the souls of the animals who had sustained them through the year, finishing the last of the four-day ceremony that brought each of the seasons. With all their hearts, they danced the Renewal of the world, calling their joy to the Blessed Star People. Now they would feast, the huge fires flaring in order that the spirits above might see their rejoicing and bounty and bring them more in the coming year.

In the reddish glow of the midnight sun, shelters of mammoth hide, caribou, and musk ox cast eerie shadows onto the trampled tussock grass. Wind Woman, her breath muted by the Long Light, played lightly across the camps of the clans, bearing the odors of roasting meat and the sounds of laughter and joy at another season passed.

"So few," Raven Hunter whispered, anger rearing.

"Not in memory has a Long Dark called so many," Strikes Lightning reminded him. "Nor has a summer been this warm. Not in any man's memory."

The warriors threaded their way, passing shelters, aloof, eyes ahead as they approached the main fire.

Together—a knot of resistance—they waited while the Sacred Dance slowed, ending in a final shout to reach the Blessed Star People above.

Crow Caller appeared out of the gathering, fire flickering over his withered face. Dressed in summer hides, he strode haughtily, hands raised. "The People live!" he called.

The songs quieted gradually, eyes turning to the old shaman.

Crow Caller smiled. "We offer thanks to the Blessed Star People. The souls of the animals hear us and rejoice. Their strength lives within us. We are made whole by their sacrifice. From above, they look down and see our joy, our thanks."

A shout rose from the People, half-thankful, half-hopeful. Now was the time to feast! They began to disperse toward the cooking fires, voices increasing in volume again.

"There is more!" Raven Hunter strode into the eerie crimson firelight, sensing the reticence of his followers, feeling them come forward despite their reservations.

Crow Caller turned, his blind white eye oddly lit in the flames.

"While you danced," Raven Hunter began, "I went away. Four went with me." He stared from face to face, watching the wide curious eyes. "We return victorious!"

Only the hiss of the fire broke the stillness as he held up the dart he'd torn from the Other's chest. People cocked their heads, waiting.

Raising his hands, Raven Hunter displayed the deadly projectile, black with dried blood. "Here, my people, is victory."

Crow Caller eased forward, black eye sharp. "You killed an animal! You know no one kills during the ceremony of Thanks. How could you—"

"Not one of our four-legged brothers." Raven Hunter smiled cynically. "I commit no sacrilege."

From the uneasy crowd, a voice called, "Then what?" Whispers of disdain and curiosity rose.

"Together"—Raven Hunter gestured to his group—"we, men of the People, have killed Others." In the sudden babble, he roared, "Others who killed the People of Geyser's band. Killed our relatives as they pushed them from the land of our ancestors—pushed them from the big herds!"

"No!" an old man cried, stepping forward. "We don't kill! It's not our way. We're peace—"

"We can't run anymore!" Raven Hunter bellowed, shaking his bloody dart. "This land is ours. *Ours!* Where else can we go? Into the Big Ice? Into the salt water? We're cornered!"

"They'll come to kill us!" The old man turned to the brooding crowd. "This is not the way of the People. We do not kill men! It is Raven Hunter who has brought their wrath down on us. What will we—"

Strikes Lightning pushed forward. "They killed my father, Geyser. I . . . *I* ran from them last season! You hear, Grandfather? I'm tired of running. Listen, all of you. They can be beaten, pushed back to the place they came from! Hear Raven Hunter, he has found a way."

"This isn't our way!"

"Cowards!" Raven Hunter accused, stilling the old man's words in his throat. "Have we no right to keep our land? To protect our women and children?"

"But the Others—"

"You think they'll leave us alone if we leave them alone?"

"Why not?" the old man challenged. "We don't threaten them."

Raven Hunter clenched his teeth, rage stirring his voice to boom over the assembly. "Did they leave Geyser's people alone? Huh?" His arm shot out to the tall man beside him. "Ask Strikes Lightning. *They murdered his entire family.*"

The old man shuffled his feet nervously. "I'm sorry for the boy, but Geyser must have done something to the Others to make them angry enough to kill—"

"Nothing!" Strikes Lightning insisted bitterly. "We did nothing!"

Raven Hunter let the silence hang heavy for a moment before shouting, "Nothing except compete for the herds!"

"Then we must teach them we mean them no harm. We'll share the animals."

"You'd have us open our arms to murderers? Accept them? Teach them of Father Sun and the Blessed Star People? Show them how to live like people?" Raven Hunter paused, running his grimy sleeve across his mouth as he stared into the somber, silent gathering. "They want nothing from us but our blood!"

His charge echoed across the grassy plain.

Several of the young men grunted affirmation. The old ones muttered uneasily under their breaths. An old woman covered her face with a fox hide, rocking back and forth, moaning.

Mouse pushed her way through the crowd, coming to stand by Strikes Lightning, her husband. "My boy is dead," she called unsteadily. "What use is the Other who killed him? He's not of the People . . . or the People's way! I am *proud* that my husband killed this Other! Hear me! How many must weep? How many of you will fall to their darts this coming year? Think on that before you mutter behind your hands."

"She's right!" Raven Hunter roared, a knotted fist to the sky. "Did Father Sun put us here for the sport of these Others? You've seen Grandfather Brown Bear play with a salmon, fling it around for his enjoyment, toss it, pounce upon it, and leave it to rot because his belly was full. I for one, will not be toyed with by the Others.

"From now on, be it known, *I will fight and kill to keep the land of my fathers!*" He thrust the dart deeply into the ground, a blood-black totem. Angrily, he crossed his arms, staring back at them, feet braced. The light of the bonfire flickered over his angry features, glinting in his black eyes.

The young men nodded, a growing murmur of voices in the crowd. Their tones rang with righteous anger. The young women looked to them, teeth flashing proudly in the firelight.

Only the older people glanced nervously back and forth, whispering hesitantly.

Crow Caller raised callused hands, palms out to still them. Face tight, he looked around. "This . . . this I would not have had happen." He turned, meeting Raven Hunter's eyes. "But something must be done."

"Not war with the Others," the old man in the crowd wailed. "What next? More raids? No, this is not the way!"

"Neither is death!" Raven Hunter lifted his chin, calling out powerfully as he extended a finger, "There lies the Big Ice, just to the east of us. More ice chokes the high mountains. No game in the ice, Grandfather—only starvation. And we know that to the south lie hills, piled rocks, dry land, and finally more ice! Think of what we've let the Others take from us! The bounty of the salt water—the game of the grassy plains. Only by driving the Others back can we find a way to live in peace."

Singing Wolf walked out from the line of the dancers. "Runs In Light said there was a way through the Big Ice to a land bursting with game and—"

"And you're here," Raven Hunter pointed out smugly. "So much for the Wolf Dream."

Singing Wolf shook his head, sighing. "I . . . I don't know. We didn't die." He turned, gaining courage. "You hear? We didn't die!"

"And where is my brother?"

"He stayed with old Heron." Singing Wolf's mouth hardened in the silence.

"Stayed with a witch." Raven Hunter laughed derisively. "He's probably conjuring evil spirits to kill us all for shunning him and his false Dreams!"

Singing Wolf's brows lowered. "He's a good boy! He'd never—"

"Then why isn't he here telling us of the way through the ice?"

"I don't know," Singing Wolf murmured humbly.

"Our fate is in our own hands, the hands of young men with straight darts!"

"And the Others?" another old man demanded, gesturing. "You think they'll just let us kill them? You think they won't kill us back?"

Raven Hunter shook his head. "Jumping Hare? How many of us died yesterday?"

Jumping Hare shifted, clearly bothered. "None."

"How many darts were loosed at us?"

"None."

"Oh, someone may die," Raven Hunter continued. "I may die!" He paced slowly back and forth before his bloody dart. "But I won't die like a trapped caribou, to be clubbed to death at will. Have the People lost their honor?"

Strikes Lightning sidled up beside Raven Hunter, narrow face gleaming orange in the firelight. "If we just sit by and let the Others kill us, there'll be no one left to sing our souls to the Blessed Star People! Father Sun will force our souls to spiral downward in darkness."

"Eternal darkness, because we were cowards," Raven Hunter added ominously.

A ripple of assent stirred the People. The old people, and some of the mothers with children in tow, looked uneasily back and forth. The children watched, wide-eyed, the tots sucking thumbs while they held to the hands of their brothers and sisters.

At the fringes, Raven Hunter could see Dancing Fox, her beautiful face somber. Even in this moment of greatest peril, he smiled at her, seeing her lower her eyes. *So, she'd returned. Later . . .*

"That's the future, my People." Raven Hunter stroked the blood-encrusted dart. "We must save ourselves. For four days, I will fast. Then, on the fifth, I will go and drive more of the Others from our lands. I'll take any who will go with me." He surveyed the faces of the young men. "But if no one else has the courage, I'll go alone!"

He caught sight of Dancing Fox as she slipped carefully to the rear, winding quickly away.

He turned, following slowly into the darkness. Behind him a babble of voices erupted. Like a man gambling with caribou toe-bone dice, he'd made his best cast.

"It's not good, this." Green Water shook her head, ducking into the blackness of her tent. "Raven Hunter's done it this time."

"I just want to hunt," One Who Cries protested, ducking to follow her. "That's not so much to ask, eh?"

"And the Others? They're . . . Hey! There's a foot in my robes!"

"A foot?"

"It's Dancing Fox," a soft voice whispered. "Please, I had to go somewhere."

Green Water caught One Who Cries shifting uneasily. "Had to—"

"Raven Hunter," Dancing Fox whispered desperately. "He'll be looking for me. He'll want to . . . to . . ."

"I don't care what he wants," One Who Cries began. "You can't just crawl into my—"

"Shut up," Green Water growled. "Raven Hunter wants to couple with her. It's not too much for a woman to ask shelter from a man like that."

"Wants to couple . . ." One Who Cries' voice drifted off.

"I'll leave," Dancing Fox murmured. "I didn't mean to cause—"

"Hush," Green Water ordered firmly. "These robes are plenty big enough for all of us."

"No, that's all right. Crow Caller cursed me anyway. It's not right that I should taint your souls with mine. I didn't think first."

"Crow Caller! He couldn't curse a maggot into becoming a fly." One Who Cries laughed.

"The robes are big enough," Green Water repeated. "I agree with my husband. We've seen Dreamers. Crow Caller is a fake."

"He threw me out. Cursed me," Dancing Fox reminded.

"I heard what he did to you. And I know why it happened in the first place. He beat you!"

"Hey!" One Who Cries started. "Doesn't a husband have a right to his wife any time he wants her?"

"You come at *me* like a bull mammoth in rut, and see how long it takes for *your* robes to be piled in the snow!"

"I'd never—"

"Of course not," Green Water relented softly. "That's the point."

"I'd better go," Dancing Fox insisted.

"You stay." One Who Cries pushed her down easily. "Like Green Water says, the robes are big enough."

"And *you* be careful," Green Water added dryly, punching One Who Cries sharply in the ribs.

"Ouch! Why'd you go do that?"

"Just a warning. The last thing you'd want to do is embarrass yourself by trying to stick that little thing in Dancing Fox." Green Water slid under the thin summer hide.

"Little thing? *Little! OUCH!*"

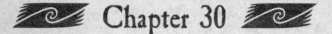

Chapter 30

"So, there you are."

Dancing Fox stiffened, hearing Raven Hunter's cool voice. She braced herself on the digging stick she used to pry starchy arctic potato roots from the mucky soil. In her bag, sour dock and fat roots bulged. Before her, the lumpy hills piled toward the mountains to the west. They looked so clear in the heady light. As if she could just reach up and touch the perpetually snowy peaks. About her, grasses and tussocks undulated in green—a stark contrast to the weathered gray of the colluvial rock washed down from the slope.

She turned. He stood tall, arms crossed, head cocked as he watched. The breeze tugged at his long hair, lying loose about his shoulders in a shining blue-black mantle. His too-perfect face reflected curiosity, challenge, a gentleness behind his heavy-lidded dark eyes.

"I looked for you the last night of the Dance."

"I thought you were up praying for a vision."

The smile curled his lips. "I've seen." He filled his lungs, expanding his chest. "This year, we'll be successful. This year, we'll push them back to the north. Breathing room for the People . . . for a while."

She watched him, feeling cornered. Green Water and

Laughing Sunshine, she knew, were just over the small hill-ock. All she need do was cry out.

"What do you want?"

A curious look of surprise flickered across his smooth face. "Why, to save the People from the Others. To—"

"With me," she clarified coldly.

He laughed. "Ah, but you've already become mine. Who else will have you? My silly brother is off to be a Dreamer. Fool!" He made a gesture of futility. "Used to tell me about his visions. About Father Sun living far to the south and strange animals. Red-brown caribou with butts the color of tanned leather. About a smaller deer, buff and white, that sheds its horns and can outrun Wind Woman. He went on about a little dog-wolf. Brown, he said, with a bushy tail and nose like fox. Quick, he said. Smarter than wolf." He barked a laugh. "Smarter than wolf? I'll bet his beloved spirit loves that!"

"I wouldn't discount his Dreams," she added stiffly.

"Oh?" He walked arrogantly toward her. "And why not? Tell me, Fox. I value your counsel. You'll be my wife one day."

She looked up at him, aware of how close he'd come. The faint odor of his body traced delicately in her nose. Almost fearful, she met his eyes, felt the magnetism of his person-ality. Were he not so handsome . . . no, unthinkable! Not him. Memories came back of the Long Dark, of Raven Hun-ter's body sliding under her robes.

"No, I won't," she whispered, struggling to keep her voice even.

The deep pools of his eyes stirred, drawing at her soul. A light shiver played along her spine as those eyes softened, beckoning her.

"You're going to be a leader of the People, Fox." The gentle tones of his voice soothed, caressed. A tingle warmed inside her. "But only if you're with me."

"A leader?"

He nodded seriously. "A great leader. That's why I've done what I've done. Talon taught you well out there, didn't she? Oh, I watched you kill the moose. Well done. A perfect throw."

"How?" she asked, suddenly recoiling a step.

"I followed you all through the growing of the Long Light. I watched, and I admired. I'll admit, at times I was tempted to ambush you, enjoy the temptations of your body."

"Y-you followed us? All that time you . . ."

"But of course. I wouldn't want the woman I cherished to come to any harm . . . not after you loved me so on the march from Mammoth Camp."

She shivered.

"I never hurt you," he reminded her. "I love you more than anything on this earth. Except perhaps our People."

Reeling, she turned and looked away, feeling him close, feeling his arms go around her, warm, protective. His fingers traced the firm line of her jaw, striking fire along her flesh.

"I . . . I'll never love you! Never. You forced me . . . used me for your pleasure like some . . . some . . . You brought me back to Crow Caller, threw me at his feet—humiliated me before the People. No, I ran to escape you."

"I know." He said it so sincerely.

She pushed violently away, fists knotted at her sides. "You know?" she demanded, rage building at her memories. "What do *you* know? What do you know of Crow Caller's caress, of my despair? How can you know what it felt like that day Talon and I sneaked away from Sheep Whistle's camp?"

"The visions." A mounting sadness grew in his eyes. "I told you, I'd never harm you. But I've seen. Seen your Power, Fox. Not now, not any time soon, but one day, your word will be law. In the vision you'll be the strength of the People and I—"

"And you mock Runs In Light's Dreams?" she cried, shaking her head.

"Did he ever have visions of you?"

She fumbled with her dirty fingers, eyes downcast. "No, he Dreamed—"

"*I* have visions of you. We're tied, you and I. I've seen you changed—made powerful. And it's my duty to force you onto the right path. Help you grow into what you'll need to be."

Bitterly she snapped, "I'll be what I want, not what your twisted imagination would make me!"

He shook his head slowly, a fragile set to his lips. "As I

love you, I would spare you. But I can't. Like me, you have your place. Eventually, we'll be together, powerful, the fate of the People in our hands. Then you'll love me and understand what I've done for you.''

Her retort died on her lips at the queer look in his hot eyes. "You're mad."

His odd eyes never left hers. "Maybe. Remember that I've sworn I love you. My wrath is for the Others who would drive us away. For you, I have only tenderness and I cry at the thought of what you will face. When you come to me—"

"I'll *never* come to you!" she spat. "I'll embrace an Other before I—"

He reeled, brow furrowed. "No! Never say that! You . . . you're mine! Mine, you hear? Why do you think I fight? That you would fall to the hands of an Other? It's to keep you clean . . . pure for my seed, that together, you and I, the greatest of the People can found a new line of—"

She scuttled backward. "Mad," she whispered as he looked at her, shaking his head.

"No," he pleaded. "You don't see it! I do. I see the child in your womb. *My child!*" A trembling smile touched his lips, eyes growing watery. He reached out a gentle hand to touch her. "I've seen our son!"

"No!" she screamed. On fleet feet, she whirled, leaving the hide sack behind her, bolting over the hill. Only when Green Water grabbed her in strong arms and held her did she finally stop shuddering.

"What?"

"Raven Hunter," she tried to explain, the horror too great. "He's mad, insane."

"Hush, it's all right. He won't bother you." Green Water hugged her again.

Dancing Fox jerked around, looking fearfully over her shoulder, searching, but seeing nothing more than waving sedges, wormwood, and the occasional grasses of the smooth hillside.

"Why is it always us?" One Who Cries lifted his hands, eyes on a knot of people arguing loudly a dart's throw away. The elders waggled scolding fingers and snapped at the smoldering young men who fingered their darts and shook their stubborn heads. Arguments filled the camp. Raven Hunter's actions had brought it all to a boil.

In the shelters on the terrace, a deep-seated tension had invaded the skin lodges. Women worked hides, eyes veiling worry as their men bickered. The children no longer ran among the dogs laughing and teasing. The stick and running games had fallen silent.

One Who Cries shook his head, studying his dwindling supply of quartzite point blanks. He chose one, looking carefully at the stone, practiced eye seeking any flaw, any irregularity. Stubby teeth sunk in his lower lip, he squinted at the point before rubbing the edge along his grooved sandstone, preparing the platform.

"First Runs In Light and his Dream!" he muttered over the rasping of the stone. "Now Raven Hunter wants to hunt the Others instead of mammoth and caribou! We always have trouble now."

Singing Wolf looked up from where he carved a segment of mammoth ivory, shaping it carefully into an atlatl hook. Laughing Sunshine patched his moccasins nearby, the new life in her belly barely visible.

"It's as Heron said," he muttered. "The world's changing. Nothing's the same anymore."

"Raven Hunter and Runs In Light have split the People right down the middle."

Green Water lifted her chin, thoughtful. "Which half should we go with? Runs In Light kept us safe—led us to Heron. We can't forget that." With a rounded cobble, she kneaded a mixture of brains and urine into the hide she worked. The caribou fawn skin would make undergarments, soft, warm and light. Already the bulge of a child rounded her abdomen.

From the side, Dancing Fox worked at stitching new fawn-skin undergarments together. Her hair swung in a black wave as she listened.

"I think we should have stayed with him," One Who Cries agreed. "I could have missed all this."

"You say that a lot now," Green Water mentioned easily. "What?"

"We *should* have . . . we *should* have. . . ." She smiled warmly at him, enjoying his scowl.

"Why do you think," Singing Wolf asked curiously, "that Crow Caller has said nothing?"

One Who Cries shrugged. "It's as if he's *waiting* for something."

Dancing Fox sniffed loudly.

"You know what Heron said about him. You heard Broken Branch." Laughing Sunshine turned the long boots in her hand. "Says he doesn't Dream. And Heron would know. Maybe he's waiting to see which way the wind's blowing so he can *make up* a Dream."

"Heron believes Runs In Light's Dream," One Who Cries muttered. He nodded to himself as he ran his thumb down the edges of the tool he crafted and picked up his baton.

"But people say she's wicked, a witch," Laughing Sunshine whispered.

"She didn't do anything bad to us. She fed us, kept us alive. No, she's all right. And she Dreams. She really Dreams. Remember the way she called the caribou?"

"Remember the way Runs In Light called the caribou?"

"Yes." One Who Cries whacked his baton along the edge he'd prepared, driving flat thinning flakes from the tool. "Good tool stone up there. Haven't found anything like it down here."

Dancing Fox crowded closer to watch, absorbed by his work.

"Hey!" Singing Wolf complained. "Quit that! Those flakes of stone go all over the place. Next thing you know, I'll sit down and have one stuck in my butt!"

One Who Cries looked around in disgust. "Man can't knap out a good point to save his soul around you. But just wait, huh? Soon as I'm finished, you'll want this point. You'll be trying to trade one of your little pictures for it."

"I can't help it if you make the best dart points of all the People. Especially that new thin one you created. What am I supposed to do? Let my family starve? Besides, these pictures I trade are powerful, give you luck."

"Then quit hollering about the flakes! You can't make a point without—"

"I want that point," Dancing Fox said boldly, studying the stone. "I'll trade two fine fox hides for it. Good hides, the kind for lining parka hoods or insulating mittens."

"It's yours." One Who Cries beamed his pleasure at Singing Wolf, who muttered something under his breath and bent to his ivory.

"Make me a detachable foreshaft—and maybe I'll trade you a couple of points," One Who Cries mentioned slyly.

"Detachable darts?" Singing Wolf waved it away. "You're out of your mind."

"Something I thought of after that buffalo almost got me." One Who Cries frowned. "Just think about it, huh?"

"You don't think we should follow Raven Hunter?" Laughing Sunshine asked, steering the conversation back to the matter that worried them all.

Singing Wolf scratched his chin. "Odd things are happening. What if he was right? What if Geyser's people should have turned and fought back? I wish I knew more. I just don't know."

"Fighting isn't our way," One Who Cries protested. "I remember a tale Flies Like A Seagull used to tell. About a long-gone time when we warred with Others. That's why the People came here, to get away from all that. She said it was better to leave than to have all that raiding. She said people looked over their shoulders all the time and nothing ever got done. There was no time to hunt. That's why Father Sun brought us here. Gave us rules so we didn't kill each other."

"Maybe Father Sun brought the Others here? You know, sort of a test?"

"Maybe." Singing Wolf paused, looking thoughtfully into the distance. "Maybe Runs In Light was his way of telling us there's another way."

"Runs In Light! Runs In Light! Enough of him."

"No one died but one little girl. My wife and I lived." Singing Wolf shook his head. "Brought us to Heron. A Dreamer. A real Dreamer. Not someone like Crow Caller."

"Crow Caller," Fox murmured in a low savage voice, closing her eyes.

"What he did to you was wrong," Singing Wolf agreed softly.

"Don't forget that Raven Hunter helped."

"And you think he's mad?"

She nodded quickly. "Something's tormenting his mind. He says Dreams. But I don't know."

One Who Cries sighed, looking at Fox with a thoughtful set to his wide mouth. "Seems like it always comes back to those two brothers, huh? Trouble in both of them."

"At least Runs In Light hasn't suggested you go off to get a dart driven into your belly," Green Water answered with a lifted eyebrow. "A leader should keep the health of the People foremost in his mind. I can't help but believe we'd be better off just avoiding the Others."

"Runs In Light doesn't want us to fight," Laughing Sunshine agreed, "he just wants us to go get eaten by the ghosts in the Big Ice." She pulled the knot tight with her teeth, inspecting the new boots she'd made.

"Raven Hunter comes back tomorrow. Most of the young men are planning on going with him. All ready to stick darts into the Others." Singing Wolf lifted his ivory, scratching furiously with the burin in his hand. "If it had to happen, it's a good time. Lots of meat now. The Renewal's about to break up. Won't have to make the fall hunt for a while yet."

"I'm not going," One Who Cries decided, looking to Green Water, seeing the relief there. "I have a family here. Young one on the way."

Singing Wolf looked at his wife. "Maybe . . . maybe I'll go."

Laughing Sunshine straightened, a horrified look in her eyes. "No, not you."

"I want to see. Maybe someone like me ought to be there. As a witness to what happens."

"No," she whispered again, reaching out to take his hand.

Singing Wolf looked soberly into his wife's eyes. "Maybe it's time I started doing what Broken Branch and Heron said. That's why we keep elders around. To make us learn. And I need to know, to see both sides. Someone with sense should come back and tell the People what really happened. I don't trust Raven Hunter."

He looked up at One Who Cries as a long silence lengthened. "If I don't come back, will you pray my soul to the Blessed Star People?"

Laughing Sunshine clamped her jaw tightly, looking away in dread.

"We'll pray you to the Blessed Star People." One Who

Cries nodded, gravity in his eyes. "But, look, there's no good in—"

"You'll take Laughing Sunshine? Make her a wife along with Green Water? Raise my child?"

One Who Cries bit off his next protest, nodded, and exhaled. "I will. You and I, we've been together a long time, eh? Hunted mammoth, saved each other's lives. I'll do this thing for you as you would for me. I'll take Laughing Sunshine as my wife. Your child will be as my own blood."

Singing Wolf looked down at his hands. "Maybe I can learn the truth of these brothers. One must be right."

Laughing Sunshine chewed her lip, eyes bright with worry. Dancing Fox moved to grip her hand, squeezing it reassuringly.

"And maybe," Sunshine moaned, "find out if Heron was right about you."

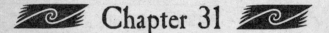 Chapter 31

Singing Wolf crouched warily in the gray morning mist, looking over the rim of the rocky terrace at the camp of the Others spread across the sandy plain below. A broad river skirted the lodges, its soft roar loud in the predawn silence. He turned slightly, glancing at Raven Hunter. A keen light filled the warrior's eyes. He stabbed his dart at the waking Others as if they would magically fall over. Two children—up before the adults—flitted around the lodges, laughter pricking the cold breeze.

A haunting hollowness throbbed in Singing Wolf's chest. *They'd kill children?*

Below, a tall man ducked out of the lodge, yawning to the horizon. The east glimmered in waves of red and orange.

"Ready?" Raven Hunter whispered, bracing himself to leap, to charge down the bluff.

Young men nodded impulsively, wetting dry lips. Singing Wolf's heart shriveled.

"Let's go!"

Raven Hunter shrieked a war cry and leapt over the bluff, racing down into the Others' camp. The People's warriors boiled out behind him, screaming their wrath.

Singing Wolf followed Strikes Lightning into a dark lodge, watching in horror as the man raised his dart, using it like a spear to puncture the throats of huddled old people and newborn babies.

Unable to move, he allowed himself to be shoved brutally aside as Strikes Lightning ran from the lodge to duck into another. Singing Wolf's stomach rose into his throat as he stared at the carnage. Sightless eyes stared back, the coppery smell of blood bathing him in horror.

"Come on!" Strikes Lightning screamed at him.

He backed unsteadily out into the cold morning, swallowing convulsively. He caught movement from his right just as an Other thrust a dart at him from behind a meat rack, ripping his forearm. Instinctively, Singing Wolf jumped away and let his own dart fly, piercing the man's neck. A garbled bark of fear and hatred rang out as the man fell.

Singing Wolf ran wildly through the village, jumping over dead bodies, shoving aside terrified women and children who struggled to flee. Wailing gashed the morning.

He spied Raven Hunter and stumbled in that direction, panting hoarsely. Their leader had caught a lodge still sleeping, skewering foggy-eyed men as they scrambled for weapons. It seemed that everyone in the world was screaming and crying.

A tiny boy, barely three, crawled madly from beneath the lodge cover, tears streaking his dirty face. Raven Hunter shouted, "Get him! He'll grow up to kill us!"

Strikes Lightning hurried, grabbing the boy by his hind foot and dragging him backward. The little one fought valiantly, bawling in terror, slamming his fists into his captor's face and arms. Strikes Lightning grabbed a large rock and raised it high over the boy's tiny head.

"No!" Singing Wolf shrieked, tears filling his eyes as he watched the rock hurtle downward, smashing the boy's head.

Strikes Lightning got to his feet, casting a look of utter disdain at Singing Wolf before he trotted away.

Survivors fled west, heedlessly abandoning their weapons, dragging the elders, carrying their children, stumbling away.

"Follow them!" Raven Hunter commanded, and several young men of the People lunged in pursuit of those fleeing over the hills. A gasping Other lay pitiously before Raven Hunter, a dart protruding from his gut. Raven Hunter brutally jerked the dart loose and knelt, smiling in mock sympathy. "I won't kill you," he cooed.

"I'll die anyway," the man gasped, rolling agonizingly to his side. He had a triangular face with a large bulbous nose.

"Yes, but this way will be long and painful."

The Other smiled, hatred gleaming in his eyes. "You'd better run far and fast, Enemy man. Ice Fire will search the mists of time until he finds your hiding place. Then we'll wipe your filth from the face of the world."

Raven Hunter laughed and stood, glaring down. "Ice Fire. Who's that? Some false shaman?"

"The greatest shaman in the world. He's seen your coming."

Raven Hunter snorted derisively. "Then why didn't he warn you so you could escape?"

The Other kicked out with his legs, slamming them into Raven Hunter and knocking him off his feet.

Raven Hunter scrambled up, dodging to kick the man hard in the side. Intestines spilled out through the gash in the man's abdomen. "We'll see how brave you are three days from now when the blood runs like a black river through your veins."

Singing Wolf held his breath, respect for the Other surfacing. This man knew what a horrible death he faced, yet he fought with his last strength. The wound would fester in a matter of hours, the gut juices boiling up like green slime, attracting the flies and animals. The odor would draw the scavengers who wait for death—or worse, Grandfather Brown Bear. But even if he managed, his death would be one of incomprehensible pain.

Raven Hunter spat in the man's eyes before turning arrogantly away. Waving to his followers, he growled, "Come. We have to make sure no one in the lodges survives."

Singing Wolf watched them stride from shelter to shelter.

A baby squealed somewhere; the cry stilled suddenly and eternally.

He walked weakly to where the dying Other lay. The man curled into a ball, pushing futilely at the ropes of intestine that lay on the ground, trying to tuck them back into his torn stomach.

"I'll kill you. If you want me to," Singing Wolf murmured in a strained voice.

The Other looked up, squinting in confusion. "Why? Why would you?"

"Because of your courage."

The Other frowned, then lowered his head, nodding tiredly. "We didn't think you knew of warrior's honor."

"How do your people . . ." Singing Wolf fumbled for the words. "Is there a special way that sends you to Father Sun? To whatever your . . ."

"Yes. The Great Mystery." The man blinked back tears, pointing a trembling finger to his chest. "Take my heart. Give it to the river. She'll carry it to the ocean. The Sea Spirit will come and . . . take me home."

Singing Wolf knelt and tore back the man's hides to bare his flesh. The Other's breast rose and fell rapidly, his whole body shuddering.

"Hurry," the man muttered. "Before your friends return."

Singing Wolf cast a quick glance over his shoulder. *Friends? Were these cousins even human anymore?* Raven Hunter's contemptuous laughter wafted on the breeze, the whimpers of a woman mixing hauntingly with it.

"Hurry."

Their eyes held for a desperate moment, and Singing Wolf sensed the man's distrust and fear. He raised his dart, watching the Other close his eyes tightly. Then he plunged the dart down, ripping the flesh of the chest and pulling it back to reveal the still-beating heart. A soft cry welled up his own throat as he slashed the arteries, blood splattering his face and clothing. He carefully cut the heart sac and drew the precious contents out, holding it hot, wet, and quivering in his hands.

The Other's face slackened peacefully, eyes staring into eternity. Singing Wolf stood on feeble legs and strode quickly to the river, wading into the chilling water up to his knees. Waves lapped around him.

Laying the heart in the water, he watched it sink, saying softly, "Take him home, Sea Spirit. He died bravely."

He watched the heart blood swirl on the surface, mixing with the green of the water until it disappeared, then he reached up to clasp the leather over his own heart, holding it tightly as tears welled.

They headed north, driving down the Big River, pushing the Others before them. Raven Hunter swaggered arrogantly now, smiling his pride at those he felt deserved his approval, glowering at the cowards like Singing Wolf, who stumbled relentlessly behind, killing only to save his own life, pleading with the warriors to remember the ways of the People.

They camped one night in the bottoms, the ever-lengthening night making such camps necessary. At the same time, they had tired from the long trail. As night lengthened, none could forget the Long Dark that rested just over the eastern horizon. More and more, Singing Wolf looked back over his shoulder, to the south, longing for home.

This night they camped in a narrow cove of a valley, the shoulders of the hills rising to either side to provide shelter from the winds. Below them to the east, the Big River rumbled and roared, white water marking its path despite the darkness.

Singing Wolf—who no longer shared Raven Hunter's favor—built a small fire to one side, burning old leaves and dry dung as he dried willow twigs for a hotter fire later. Overhead, the Blessed Star People stared down at his tiny eye of fire. Soberly, he wondered what they thought—if they closed their eyes at the sight of the People and the trail of blood they left behind. He reflected on that as he looked around at the other small fires where men huddled laughing, gesturing in the flickering light as they told of their war triumphs.

"Why do you defy me?" Raven Hunter asked, coming to squat before Singing Wolf's fire. His vigorous young face caught the reflection of the flames, glowing eerily red as his black eyes probed Singing Wolf's.

"What have we become, Raven Hunter? I've seen you do things which will haunt my sleep forever. Bashing babies, lancing old men and women to watch their guts roll out of their bodies. I've seen you reach, grab their intestines and pull while they shrieked. Why? What purpose does that serve?''

Raven Hunter nodded soberly, lines forming on his brow. "I understand your hesitation . . . and I truly feel disgusted at what I do. But there are so many Others. I have seen. Here." He pointed to his head. "I have seen." His earnest eyes studied Singing Wolf's. "Do you understand? Visions have come to me."

"No, I don't understand." Singing Wolf frowned, poking at the fire before him. "What use is torture? Atrocity, no matter how many—"

"If I make them fear, they'll leave us alone. That's why I leave their bodies looking so grotesque. If we chill their hearts, Singing Wolf, they'll avoid us, leave our land."

"There must be another way."

Raven Hunter settled himself, drawing his knees up to his chest. Sincerely he asked, "How? We have to kill these people, make them cry and scream . . ." He tapped his chest. "Here. It makes my very heart crawl and my soul shrieks in my dreams. These Others, they're not so different from us. They do many things the same way. But they've pushed us back, taken the sea, taken the grassy plains to the west, pushed us for generations until we've nothing left. You've heard the stories—about how once we had all the land west of the Ice Mountains. There was an abundance of game there. Our ancestors hunted all through that territory.

"And now? The farther south we go up the Big River, the drier the land is, the colder. You've seen that yourself. You've been farther south than any of the rest of us. From your own lips, you say the Big Ice narrows, blocks the Big River—the high mountains rise to the west. Endless ice to the east."

"Yes . . ."

Raven Hunter nodded sympathetically. "And what's left for us?"

"But to cause anything to suffer is—"

"Necessary." His face worked with the effort. "Consider. People make themselves share things. When you kill an animal, lance a mammoth in the gut and follow it for days, you feel its pain, don't you?"

Singing Wolf nodded. "Any hunter feels the pain of the animal he kills."

"That's our only weapon against the Others. Don't you see? Make them imagine themselves as the bloody corpses we leave on the ground. Make them see through our eyes. Make them feel that pain."

"Just as we feel it ourselves?" Singing Wolf considered.

"You're beginning to understand. When you look at an infant, its skull crushed, it twists your soul if you think your own child might look like that, doesn't it? Think what it does to theirs." The black eyes pinned him, the power of his certainty humming in the air.

"Your soul screams in your dreams?"

Raven Hunter's impassioned eyes didn't waver. "Their screams fill my sleep. It's . . . it's torture."

"Then why?" Singing Wolf demanded. "Why do you do it to yourself?"

Raven Hunter's eyes seemed to expand, his very soul exposed and twisting in the light of the low fire. "Because I love the People. I bear this burden, not because I want to be a monster . . . but to save the People. I have nothing more precious to give than myself."

The encompassing eyes seemed to suck him up—not the eyes of a monster, but of a man in hideous misery. Honest, open, Raven Hunter's soul pulsated.

A cold chill shook Singing Wolf. He looked around at the dark camp. Bodies wrapped in hides were only lumps in the crushed tussocks. Before him, the fire lay dead, a few tiny embers gleaming.

Raven Hunter put a hand on Singing Wolf's shoulder, patting softly. "War is hideous. But we *must* fight." He stood and stepped lightly over sleepers, going to his own robes.

Singing Wolf shook his head, staring off into the darkness.

Just after nightfall three days later, they peered through a series of jagged boulders at an unsuspecting camp of Others. Women roasted fish around a half-dozen low fires, laughing quietly, patting the children who played a game nearby. Men sat in a distant circle, talking in hushed tones, eyes vigilantly scanning the growing darkness. Rapids on the river glimmered silver in the moonlight.

"Nock your darts," Raven Hunter instructed, and men rushed to comply.

Singing Wolf gripped his atlatl fiercely, one finger roaming the grooves along the shaft. He'd cut a line for each man that died, so that now his weapon undulated like the bones of the spine. Strikes Lightning had died first, a dart catching him in the leg, severing the big artery that ran along the thighbone. Singing Wolf hadn't been able to find it in his heart to weep. A day later, Two Darts was lanced in the gut. He failed slowly, an oozing pus forming in the wound to fever him. Carried by other young men, he babbled and died horribly amid fearful dreams. Moss Stalker, Loon Voice, Blows With Snow, and many others fell. Some perished in the heat of the fray, others later, from infected wounds.

Raven Hunter's stature grew, the young men listening carefully, bowing to his expanding Power. Singing Wolf felt haunted—a foreboding eating at him. Where was truth? The memory of the pain and horror in Raven Hunter's eyes stayed with him. The logic of the butchery had proved so right. At one camp, they needed only to appear and the Others ran, horrified, into the darkness. It worked, the terror of the People proved as effective as their darts.

I should leave! Run home to Laughing Sunshine, Singing Wolf told himself repeatedly. But some horrible fascination kept him there, watching as though his very life depended upon the outcome. He peered at the warriors crouching around him. A hardness lay in the eyes of the People that he'd never seen.

Something is happening to us. What? Life is changing. See the set of the young men's mouths? See the way they look over their shoulders, wary, lean, and dangerous. The women they take, they take by force. They've grown brutal. Where is the laughter, the old humor we used to share?

"Ready?" Raven Hunter whispered eagerly. Nods went round through the boulders. "Now!"

At his command, men swept around the rocks, screaming viciously, striking down anyone they passed. Singing Wolf ran behind, weaving through the clashing crowd. A woman scuttled from a lodge to his left. He gasped, recognizing his cousin who'd been abducted so many years ago.

"Blueberry? Blueberry!" he called, and lurched to block her flight.

Wide-eyed with fear, she huddled down before him, trembling as she cuddled her baby protectively. "Don't kill my baby," she pleaded. "He'll make you a good son. Don't—"

"I'm your cousin, Singing Wolf. Son of Two Stones and Brown Duck. Your cousin. Remember?"

She looked up, frightened, the baby, upset, attempting to nurse at the hides covering her breast.

"The People," she murmured, barely audible. He bent to hear her low-voiced words. "The People have come for me?" Swallowing hard, she burst into tears and threw an arm around his neck.

"Yes, we've come for you," he assured quietly, patting her back.

As the last of the Others ran from their village, he held her close, keeping her from harm as other young women were rounded up by hungry-eyed warriors. They would have many new brides in the camps this year.

Around the campfires that night, Raven Hunter cornered Blueberry, smiling warmly to ease her fears. "When were you captured?"

Blueberry looked at him askance, fear in her eyes. "It's been six Long Darks since I was taken. A young man— Sheep's Tail—caught me and my sister, Onion, digging roots. He made us go west. Onion ran once and he killed her with one long dart throw. I was scared. I didn't run."

Raven Hunter nodded thoughtfully. "Then you've been with the Others long enough to know them. Tell us about them. How powerful are they?"

"Powerful. They call themselves the Mammoth People, but they're like a single snowflake compared to the blizzard of the Glacier People."

Raven Hunter frowned. "The Glacier People? Who are they?"

"The Mammoth People are being pushed up from the south and the west by the Glacier People who follow the game. The animals are moving north because the land many days to the far west is hot, drying out, and they can no longer survive there. Between the White Tusk Clan and the Glacier People are the Round Hoof Clan, the Buffalo Clan, and finally, the Tiger Belly Clan. The Tiger Belly Clan are the most honored. They fight to keep the western Enemy from crossing the narrows where the salt waters are less than five days' journey apart.''

"How many Mammoth People are there?" Singing Wolf asked, leaning forward, anxious to hear from her own lips.

"Many," she whispered. "So many. More than I've ever seen."

Raven Hunter cast a glance over his shoulder to the somber faces of his warriors who listened intently, fear glistening in their eyes. He laughed boisterously. "Well, they'll turn around now! Some escaped us. They'll run to tell the other clans of the bravery and fierceness of the People!"

The youngest members of the war party insolently lifted their chins, chests puffed out as they stood around the fire.

Singing Wolf pursed his lips and stared at the ground. The young imbeciles, couldn't they see what was happening? If Blueberry was right, the Others might be under as much pressure as the People. "What are these Glacier People like?" he asked tiredly.

"They're white-skinned, covered with hair. The Mammoth People fought them. The stories are that they came from the western edge of the world. They're fierce, fierce as Grandfather White Bear. Maybe they're his human children. I don't know. But they live by the salt water far to the southwest. Stories are told of how they float on the salt water in manmade hollow logs."

"Hah!" Raven Hunter laughed sharply. "No man floats on water. Trees don't grow big enough to—"

"Not here," Blueberry interrupted with trepidation. "But I've seen trees so tall they touch the sky. Big and dark—like dwarf spruce—but a person can climb a hundred feet high in them. I've been west of these mountains"—she pointed over her shoulder—"and seen the tall mountains that run out into the south salt water. The trees there are so tall they poke the sky."

"Fantasy," Raven Hunter growled. "This woman is spirit-touched. Living too long among the Others has done things to her mind."

She lowered her eyes, mouth hard. One by one, the warriors walked away, laughing at the stories she told. White-skinned men? Covered with hair? Grandfather White Bear's kin after all! A good story.

Singing Wolf waited, seeing the shame in her face, until the other men sauntered away to their own fires. "I believe you," he said.

"But they don't," she whispered. "Maybe I should go back to the Mammoth People. I don't know if I belong here."

"Forget about them. They're so puffed up from their battle successes they can't see straight."

"They'd better learn," she said ominously. "Because it's far worse than I told them."

A chill touched Singing Wolf's spine. "What do you mean?"

"There, to the far west, the ice is melting. The Glacier People are pushing the Others. But beyond the Glacier People, others still are pushing—people who look like us, and chase the Glacier People to the east and pin them against the sea—fierce and desperate men, who follow the animals to the north after the ice. So many hunt that mammoth there run at the slightest scent of man."

Singing Wolf frowned. "If all this fighting is going on, why did we beat the Others so easily?"

She met his eyes. "They didn't expect it, cousin. Always before, the People ran, left them the hunting grounds without a fight. These camps of Others became fat, lazy. All they had to do was kill a couple of the People and they could take what they wanted."

"Will they stay away then? Like Raven Hunter says?"

She shook her head. "No, they'll pass the message that you're no longer afraid and come hunting you."

"Can we stop them from passing the word?"

"No, cousin. Like us, they travel between camps. There are four large clans, each so big it has a gathering all its own. They pass a sacred mammoth hide from camp to camp to keep people informed. And the hide is guarded heavily."

"Maybe we could intercept the hide. Stop the—"

"Don't even think of doing such a thing! The hide is filled with Power. Just touching it would kill you."

Singing Wolf slammed a fist into the soft warm earth beside the fire pit. "There must be a way to stop them."

"Run. It's the only way," she insisted, a burning plea behind her eyes. "Don't you see? You've killed them. The way they believe, their dead will not go to the village of souls beneath the sea until each death has been paid for. It's honor to them, warrior's honor."

Singing Wolf filled his lungs. "You say there are many?"

"Like the stems of willow along the Big River." She shook her head. "And they have nowhere to go. Like the People, they are trapped. I've heard them. For the moment, they fear you. But what comes behind is even more terrible. The fear they have of you will melt like fat on hot coals. Those who follow are pushing the Glacier People south along the rocky coast of the southern salt water. Runners come to tell us this. The Glacier People would cut you to ribbons."

"So the Mammoth People have no other way but to take our lands?"

"Yes, and their warrior's honor requires that they hurt you in even more gruesome ways than you hurt them."

Singing Wolf's thoughts went to Laughing Sunshine and his child-to-be. Deep inside, a tremor shook his soul.

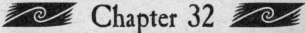 Chapter 32

Wolf Dreamer's keen eyes darted nervously back and forth between the old women. His cheeks had grown hollow, his hair hanging long on either side of his face, accenting his half-starved look. A trace of sorrow lined his young brow; pain was reflected in the set of his thin-lipped mouth. He rubbed his hands slowly back and forth while he waited, the muscles in his cheeks quivering as his jaw clenched.

"Tell me." Heron's voice came quietly across the crackle of the fire. The shelter glowed softly orange, highlighting Broken Branch's withered face.

"The People," he whispered imploringly. "My vision was hazy and wavering, but I thought I saw them dying."

Heron cradled her chin in her palms, eyelids lowered. To the side, Broken Branch listened intently. She prodded the fire with a split caribou bone.

"What else?" Heron prompted.

He shook his head. "There were women captives. Some . . . no, it just didn't come clearly."

"What did you feel?"

"I felt a presence. Like something was coming, something far over the horizon. Like the Long Dark . . . but different." He wet his lips, puzzled. "Like night coming from the west instead of the east."

Heron lifted an eyebrow. "You understand its meaning?"

"No."

"Didn't figure you did," she growled, leaning back in disappointment. "Well at least you've learned to walk. Now you have to learn some of the motions of the Dance."

"What?"

"You've got to learn some grace and stop stumbling around or you'll kill yourself."

He frowned, feeling that familiar pit of emptiness and inadequacy spread in his stomach. "I know some things. I call the caribou."

She shook her head. "No, that's not what I mean. Everything flails along in its own private dance, but beyond, there's only One Dance."

She's always spouting gibberish. The One this and One that. Why can't she just come out and tell me? "I still don't understand."

She lifted a hand, dark eyes drinking in his soul, drawing him on. She pulled back the wolf-hide mats. With a scapula spoon, she dug into the fire, spreading glowing coals over the rock. They sizzled wildly in the breeze that penetrated beneath the door hanging.

Never letting her gaze leave Wolf Dreamer's eyes, she wiggled her fingers, flexing them into fists as if toning the muscles. She settled herself on her knees over the coals, silver-shot black hair swaying.

Lacing her fingers together, she closed her eyes and breathed deeply, humming a haunting singsong chant. Serenity slackened her face, the lines softening as if she'd shed long years. Then she reached forward, placing both hands palms down on the coals, shifting, her weight full on them.

Wolf Dreamer gasped, glancing questioningly to Broken Branch. Frozen with fear, Wolf Dreamer stared as Heron scooped up the coals. The red eyes glowing between her fingers, she lifted them high over her head.

How long? He had to draw a breath. Then another, and another.

Still chanting, Heron placed the coals to her lips, her forehead. Finally she put them in her mouth, rolling them around before she spat them out. The coals landed on the hides before her. The pelt browned, blackened, and smoldered, a wisp of smoke rising as hair sizzled, shriveling and stinking. Eyes still closed, a translucent rapture spread across her face, the melody hummed to a stop. She drew a deep breath, letting it out slowly through her nose.

Wolf Dreamer reached out to touch her face, to feel the places the fiery coals had seared. The flesh was smooth and cool beneath his fingers.

She opened her eyes, unfocused at first, then blinked. Cocking her head, she turned to Wolf Dreamer where he sat, unnerved.

"'Your hands . . . your face . . .'" he whispered in disbelief, a feeling of dread coursing with his blood.

She lifted and opened first one hand, then the other. She turned her face, exposing each cheek to the light. Frightened, he reached forward to finger the hole burned in the hide, sucking his breath in and yanking his hand back as he seared his fingers. "How?"

"Not even a blister." She tossed her hair over her shoulder, watching, challenging.

"It can't be! You said there were laws!"

Unruffled, Heron scraped the remaining coals and charcoal back into the fire pit, hardly aware of Broken Branch, frozen, face a mask of awe.

"Close your mouth, old hag," Heron reprimanded. "You'll be catching flies pretty soon."

Broken Branch obeyed without thinking, scowling. "How'd you do that?"

"I danced with the coals."

Wolf Dreamer watched her, feeling some inkling of her truth pound inside. "With?"

"Instead of against."

"You mean you touched the coals' Dance . . . stepped into their tracks for a moment?"

"Not exactly. Beneath the coals' Dance is the One Dance. I stepped into the One's moccasins for a moment."

"How?"

"I found the stillness beneath the movement."

He squeezed the bridge of his nose. *The cursed silence beneath the noise, the cursed stillness beneath the movement.* The old witch was trying to drive him crazy. Through clenched teeth, he demanded, "How?"

"I quit my own Dancing."

"You quit your . . ." he uttered forlornly, shaking his head.

Broken Branch cackled, rocking forward to eye Heron severely. "I knew it. You're about as crazy as they come. You've got no mind left at all."

"I've been trying to tell you that for weeks." She glanced sideways at Wolf Dreamer, a sparkle of irony in her eyes.

He squeezed the hide of his long boots in a death grip. He was beginning to see what she meant, and it frightened him. "No-mind means no self to get in the way of just moving with the Dance."

"Sure. No-mind frees you to stop your own Dancing and move with the One Dance."

To steal time in which to think, he pointed at the coals. "You must have gotten burned a lot when you first started."

She smiled wryly, knowing what he was delaying and giving him the time he needed. "I had welts all the time."

"Can I . . ." He shook his head, not believing he was asking. "Can I do it?"

"I wouldn't have showed you if I thought you were too dumb to learn. But it's like crossing a mountain; the climb is hard. You can't understand anything about the whole world until you see the other side." She steepled her fingers. "This is another step on the way to ultimate Dreaming Power."

He shivered at the glow filling her eyes. "Another?"

"Oh, yes, one that you must be able to master, or all the

separate Dances going on around you will eventually trample you to death.''

Chapter 33

Against the pastel blaze of sunset, Wolf Dreamer ran, his actions repeated in vast amorphous shadows on the towering gray stone wall at his side. Down on the distant plain, he could see Heron's hot springs throwing steam high in the air. The mist glowed softly yellow in the evening light.

''Run. Run,'' he repeated over and over, trying to center his mind.

As his breath puffed white before him, his feet thudded into the thin crust of snow. His heels transmitted the shock, gravel crunching, as he vaulted smaller boulders and zigzagged around the bigger ones. A continuous cold wind blew off the ice to the south, chilling his face. Breath tore in and out of his heaving lungs, the dull pain in his chest barely masked by his burning legs.

Clear your mind. Run, Wolf Dreamer, run until your body is oblivious, until you are outside your mind, looking in. Dance . . . Dance.

He drifted in and out at first, tendrils of the feeling of freedom, of floating, barely perceptible. Then he was free, soaring beyond his flesh. In his joy at the accomplishment, the bubble burst and he was back, sensation crawling over his body like a swarm of insects.

He plodded to a stop, bending over, coughing, as his lungs bellowed for air. Sweat trickled down his face, steaming in the glacial breeze. Vaguely aware, he took one slow wobbly step after another, trying to still his lungs, rest the ache that knotted his legs. Like a bleached bone, the tongue in his mouth had gone dry. It stuck to the back of his throat.

He straightened, scooping the dusting of crystal snow from

a hummock of grass, letting the cool moisture seep through his mouth, trickle down his throat.

A line of white etched the eastern horizon. The Big Ice. He gasped, blowing hard as he walked, feeling the fire in his legs. Around him, glacial rubble piled high, the haunts of the frozen ghosts. The gravel underfoot insulated layers of ice. Water had pooled here and there, freezing into slick snow-covered traps. To the west the giant mountains shot up in icy splendor. To the east, the Big Ice had fractured, tilted, and crumpled, a jagged landscape of fissures and edges impossible to traverse. Only to the south did the ice flatten out. Overhead, the clouds streaked mauve, the coming of night imminent not just for this day—but for all of the Long Light as well.

The ice to the south drew him. Unlike the Dream, it didn't loom up like a massive wall, rather it had been broken, cracked and tumbled, sun-rotted and wind-buckled. Gray-white outcrops canted, angles rounded while weird shapes and spears of blue crystal jutted into sharp lances. Layers of sand and gravel streaked the mass, lining the white blue with black smears. Not so broken as the eastern ice, it still sent a chill down his spine.

"Can I cross it?"

He forced his weary muscles to climb a promontory. The lee side of the rock stretched out in a fan of ice, the cap rock polished, striated, and scoured.

To the south, the ice rose, white, sullen, to mix with the grayish clouds. His heart pounded in his breast. At the edges of his exhausted mind, a whispering of desire called, taunting, drawing. A high-pitched wail came faintly to his ears, drifting down over the southern ice. Ghosts? He strained to listen, but the blood rushing in his veins, the rasping breath in his windpipe, blotted the sound.

Below him, an undulating plain of snow-topped moraines and eskers mounded and rolled—tumbled waves of rock left by the retreating ice.

The stiffness out of his legs, he settled on a snow-encrusted rock, studying the gash cut by the Big River. Even now, when the Long Dark closed its freezing grip on the land, water roared and pitched, an incessant outpouring.

"So much."

The words died in his throat as something black and twisted rolled out, swirling in an eddy, catching on the rapids-washed rock. Curious, Wolf Dreamer worked his way down the polished top of the ridge, carefully moving along the piled boulders. Father Sun had dipped below the ragged mountain wall to the west by the time he picked his way through the treacherous rocks, some larger than a bull mammoth.

The dark spot swirled, battered, one horn broken off even with the skull. A leg had been violently ripped from the body. The reality remained.

"Buffalo! Did you come through underneath?" A giddy rush swept him as hopes taunted. "Somewhere, on the other side, there's a place where buffalo live." He swallowed hard, feeling tendrils of Wolf's promise twine through him.

Balancing, he leapt from rock to rock until he made it to the snagged buffalo. Grasping a torn hoof, he dragged the animal back, slipping and splashing in the frigid water.

"Maybe you didn't come underneath," he lamented, struggling to be realistic. "You could've been frozen here for hundreds of Long Darks."

While the cold water lapped his feet, he dragged the animal as far as he could toward shore, as far as the beast's dead weight could float. He wedged it against the current, snagging the gouged hide on a spike of wave-lapped rock.

Twilight glimmered brassy from the white crests of water rushing around his feet.

Heart beating, light failing, Wolf Dreamer used a chert flake from his pouch to cut open the gut cavity. Entrails bulged out in blue-gray ropes. He sliced open the paunch, green matter spilling into the water. A tapeworm twisted and wiggled before it disappeared in the sandy wash of icy water.

He dove for the worm, missing. "How long does a tapeworm live when it's frozen?" Fishing around in the paunch, he found a second, carefully catching it up. "Think," he gasped to himself, turning in the darkness. "Think how to find out."

He laid the parasite on the fresh dusting of snow, turning, dismembering the huge buffalo while his feet went numb in the cold water. Satisfied, he poked and prodded, finding none of the deep joints frozen. They numbed his fingers, but still weren't as cold as they should have been had they been trapped in the water under the ice. The gut, he thought, carried a slight trace of heat.

In the blackness, he turned back to the tapeworm. It had stuck to the snow, breaking in two as he lifted it. With some of the thin hide from the buffalo's groin, he bound up the parasite and turned his tracks for Heron's.

In his own mind, no doubt remained. In all their talks, Heron had never mentioned long-horned buffalo in the valley. No, this beast came from somewhere else . . . *beyond the ice.*

Sitting beside a crackling fire in Heron's shelter, Wolf Dreamer stared at the tapeworm he'd thawed. He prodded it. Dead. His eyes raised to stare absently at one of the drawings on the rock. Beneath the soot stains and dust, he could make out the effigy. A web drawn in a spiral. A fist knotted in his gut, a curious shimmering hazing the edges of his vision.

Why did Heron draw that in red all those years ago? What does it mean? Why a web? He shook his head vigorously, snapping his concentration back to the dead tapeworm.

Heron stretched out on her side across the fire, head propped on one hand, dark eyes watching him. Her long hair fell across her tan dress in silver and black strands that shimmered in the firelight. "What are you thinking?"

"That tapeworms don't live after they've been frozen."

"Then?"

"Then there's no way the buffalo could have been frozen."

"What else did you notice?"

He frowned at her, meeting and holding her probing eyes. Was this another test? "His paunch was full of green stuff, grass, plants, a couple of late-blooming flowers. His summer coat was just beginning to thicken. . . . and the tapeworms were alive."

"What do you think that means?"

"There's a place on the other side of the ice where buffalo live."

"You say he felt warm?"

"Maybe. My fingers were cold. I couldn't really tell, but the gut seemed to feel warmer. How long would a buffalo take to go cold? He had to have been under there for a while;

the body was all ripped up—like it had been caught and pulled
loose a dozen times.''

"Caught under there?'' She tapped her fingers, looking up
at the gray-mottled rock walls over their heads. "So he came
through a . . .''

". . . *hole,*" he breathed. In the firelight, the muscles of
his smooth jaw quivered.

Chapter 34

Poised on the balls of his feet, One Who Cries waited. The
big cow spun, wheeling, trunk high to scent Wind Woman,
little eyes hot and black in her shaggy head.

He could feel the tremors of her tramping feet through the
very rock he crouched behind. Like he always did when he
hunted mammoth, he wished he could let the runniness in
his bowels and bladder loose. The cow turned away again
and One Who Cries raised on his feet. Like lightning, his
arm rolled back, then snapped forward, his atlatl sending the
long dart arching to strike near the cow's anus where the skin
was thin, sensitive.

Once more, it worked. The dart Singing Wolf had so carefully crafted struck home, the shaft itself separating, the main
part falling back to earth, the lethal point and foreshaft deeply
embedded in the beast, continuing to slice tissue as the animal moved. The shaft clattered as it fell to earth.

The cow bellowed, whirling on her feet, trunk whipping
back and forth. Hot breath rasped from her mouth as she
sniffed for her tormentor.

One Who Cries scuttled through the rock, bent low.

It wasn't much of an outcrop to hide in. Just an angular
upthrust of black shale that created a sort of hogsback. Nevertheless, the mammoth couldn't traverse it. She could only
circle, and try to avoid the narrow-walled gully that erosion
had cut along the lower border of the rock. If she fell there,

the six-foot drop would kill her much quicker than One Who Cries' stone-tipped darts.

One Who Cries bent low, scurrying through a gap in the rock, panting and puffing, zigzagging between the walls of shale that thrust up around him. Seeing his chance, he scrambled for the long dart shaft, grabbing it up, sprinting for the safety of the rocks.

The cow caught a glimpse of him, screaming rage. She charged forward, accelerating her huge body in an amazing burst of speed. She stopped on the verge of bad footing, questing with her trunk. She'd almost caught him the first time he'd retrieved his dart shaft using the same tactic.

Heart pounding so hard he thought it would break his ribs, One Who Cries waited—safely out of reach. "Got to goad her, make her madder."

Laughing and dancing, he sailed a flat, hand-sized slab of rock to pelt her in the face. A shrill trumpet of fury smashed at him as he dodged away, yipping and whistling. He jumped a tilted gray slab, adrenaline pumping, and rolled to one side, crabbing through the narrow crevice as the berserk mammoth circled, gouging the resisting ground with her tusks, flinging ripped moss and grass to the air, broadcasting her frustration at his taunting.

The cow screamed again, brought up short by the angular black rocks. She shifted, one thick leg resting on the rock as her trunk sought him, picked up his scent, head extended forward, trunk reaching.

She staggered as the rock crumbled under her heavy foot, backing off, startled by what she'd almost done.

Heart hammering, One Who Cries waited where he'd crawled into a sheltering niche in the rock. As her trunk swung away, he scuttled farther. The cow squealed angrily, pounding around the outcrop, trying to circle his position. He fitted the last of his foreshafts into the dart body, twisting it into place, checking quickly to make sure it sat in the shaft straight. He puffed a final breath. The last shot.

"That's it!" he taunted. "Chase me! Come on! Lose all your sense! Be mad, Mother! Mad to the point of blood rage!"

He had room now. Circling his arms to keep her attention,

he shrieked and hollered. The cow stopped, tearing the frozen ground as she wheeled, snorting.

One Who Cries leapt, his last dart in hand, and lashed it forward, the atlatl providing two hundred times the power of his unaided hand.

The dart shot true, planting itself in the thinner hide behind the jaw—driving the foreshaft deep. The spent shaft separated to clatter noisily at her feet. The cow went crazy. Head up, trunk extended, she rushed forward.

One Who Cries screamed in fear, casting his atlatl to one side, running unencumbered for the edge of the rocks. The cow roared slathering wrath—the very earth shaking as she bore down on him. Not once did One Who Cries look back. His every thought centered on running, on picking his path through the uneven footing as he flew for the edge of the rock outcrop.

He made it, turning the corner, leaping nimbly along the path he'd cleared hours earlier. Legs pumping prodigiously, he bounded along the edge of the drop-off, one last jump taking him to firmer ground.

Heart thundering, he looked back, seeing the cow round the bend, seeing startled fear in her eyes as the gully appeared under her feet. She slid forward, legs locked.

Beneath her, the undercutting excavations One Who Cries and Singing Wolf had dug with such labor from the permafrost collapsed. The cow teetered, trunk whipping for balance. So much weight falls slowly at first. She had time to voice a final shriek as she toppled.

The ground slapped up at One Who Cries as her huge body slammed the earth. The sound of snapping bone seemed to stick in his ears. Then it was over. A rasping—like grinding ice—blasted from the cow's mighty lungs.

One Who Cries climbed up over the rocks, well out of harm's way, peering carefully over the drop-off. The red-haired trunk quivered, blood leaking from the mammoth's mouth. A frightened black eye stared up at him.

Wouldn't be long now. She couldn't breathe down there, the very weight of her body would smother her. She couldn't stand, her snapped limbs powerless. The top ear batted back and forth, her trunk questing, probing, determining the reality of her death. The ragged wisp of tail slapped behind her.

Singing Wolf called, "Thought she had you for a second there at the beginning."

One Who Cries closed his eyes, sighing. He looked down. "Yes, Mother, you almost did get me, huh? I'll relive that moment forever."

Singing Wolf stood on the hill, downwind, some three dart throws away, waving with his hands. Green Water, Laughing Sunshine, and the rest would come now. They would all begin the butchering process, rendering the huge cow for all they could take before beginning the long trek back to Heron's valley.

Puffing out his cheeks, One Who Cries shook his head at the huge beast, now still in death. "Another handsbreadth, Mother, and you'd have stomped me into red mush. Blessed Stars, there's got to be an easier way."

He sagged on the rock, remembering.

For a long time he looked at the dead mammoth, sadness and regret welling in his heart. Somberly, he went down to kneel by the mammoth's huge head and stroke it gently. From the sacred pouch hanging around his neck, he took the special amulets, breathed on them, and began the process of singing the cow's soul to the Blessed Star People.

The new darts had worked. Never had One Who Cries driven a point so deeply into animal flesh before. As they cut each of the foreshafts from the carcass, Singing Wolf nodded, muttering under his breath as he examined the depth of the wound.

"Still got a problem with the hafting. Can you make the point thinner at the base?"

One Who Cries rubbed his mashed nose with a bloody finger, frowning. "No, it'll break too easy on impact. I tried that, remember?"

"Maybe a longer point?" Singing Wolf asked. "Not quite as wide as this one?"

"Thought you said the People didn't make different styles of points."

Singing Wolf shrugged, sheepishly.

Long strips of meat covered the rocks. One Who Cries worked by Green Water, splitting long bones, helping pile the rich marrow on the greasy hide to be rendered for fat. Dancing Fox tended the hot rocks, carefully pouring liquid fat into intestines the way Green Water had taught her. It was such a tricky process; she couldn't let the gut bag burn, but she had to get the fat hot enough to run.

"Hey!" Singing Wolf snapped where he slashed at the thick hide with a sharp bifacial tool, flaked on both sides to create an acute cutting edge. A cur ducked his backhanded blow and jumped lightly to the ground, panting with excitement. The other dogs ran, yipping and snarling at each other, despite bellies which practically dragged the ground.

"Maybe we were better off without 'em," Singing Wolf growled, threatening the beasts.

One Who Cries looked up and grinned. "You'd rather carry everything on your back, huh?"

Singing Wolf sighed and shrugged. "No, and this time the dogs can sniff out bears for us, too. Guess we won't have to worry so much about being eaten alive."

One Who Cries sucked his upper lip, nodding. Pensively he looked up at the thick clouds rolling in from the northwest. Already they'd had snow, but the grasses had grown this year, curing brown on the stem. The fat on the mammoth's back where Singing Wolf exposed it was a foot thick, the meat beneath rich with the white deposits. Bloody, fat globules sticking to his forearms, Singing Wolf bent to his task again.

Green Water shook her head, looking up at the hunter as she whispered to the women working beside her. "You know, I believe Blueberry's stories about the Mammoth People. Even if Raven Hunter says she's lying."

One Who Cries listened pensively, nodding slightly in agreement.

Dancing Fox changed the position of her bulging bag, air starting to expand with the heat. Deftly, she let off some of the pressure. "I told you he was crazy."

"Singing Wolf isn't convinced. He might be heartsick at the things Raven Hunter led the young men to do but he's not convinced Raven Hunter's wrong in fighting for these lands."

"He's going to get himself killed."

"He's going to get all of us killed," One Who Cries added furtively.

As silence descended, he turned his attention to Sunshine and Curlew Song, who sliced long strips of meat from the shoulder, laughing as they walked to lay them across the willow tops. There, the meat would freeze-dry for the next couple of weeks, the heavy water weight sucked away by the cold wind.

From the corner of his eye, One Who Cries watched Curlew Song. Young and pretty, she kept glancing up at Jumping Hare where he worked to peel the thick hide back from the mammoth's rib cage as Singing Wolf continued to cut at the stringy gray tissue that bound the hide to the body.

She kept the young man's spirits up, kept a new shine in his eye to make up for the loss of his mother, Gray Rock. He'd taken her for a wife upon his return from warring with the Others. She'd come from Buffalo Back's camp: a woman of the Seagull Clan. He'd wanted her as a first wife. Then he had married Moon Water, a captive he'd taken in a raided camp.

Moon Water bent to her burden, looking sullenly up at Jumping Hare, a smoldering fire in her eyes. She'd be trouble; One Who Cries could feel it. Nevertheless, her lithe body and the way she moved with undulating grace drew his eye. A brief fantasy of stripping her, running his hands over her high full breasts, parting her firm legs, played through his mind. He felt himself—

The vision popped as an elbow punched his ribs. Startled, he shot a quick glance at Green Water. She doubled her fist, eyes knowing.

"Just daydreaming," he muttered.

"Sure," Green Water growled under her breath; but she couldn't keep the twinkle from her eye.

One Who Cries grinned sheepishly and went to gather another armload of fat as Singing Wolf cut it loose.

Everywhere, camps of the People had taken in the new women captured from the Others. The elderly women worked hard to teach them the legends and myths, to make them one with the People—even though they would always be second-class wives. The captives learned. They remained for the most part sullen, angry, servicing their new husbands with resignation. Still, many continued to try to run away.

"How long?" Green Water wondered, looking at the

growing pile of fat as One Who Cries dropped the greasy slab.

He stood, easing the crick in his back, trying to wipe the gobs of fat from his thick fingers. "Another week? Maybe two? The freeze will be hard in the ground by then. Snow won't be that deep and we can walk into the deep cold. There'll be good travel then."

"The sooner the better. Singing Wolf is worried."

"And I'm worried," One Who Cries agreed. "They'll strike back. According to Blueberry, they have to."

Green Water tilted her head, soft eyes on her husband. "I think she's seen a lot more of the Others than Raven Hunter. I listen to her talk and I think the men should heed what she says. If half of what she says is true—"

"We're in deep trouble," One Who Cries agreed, watching Blueberry take time to nurse her child.

Green Water nudged him, humorous reproach in her eyes. "The child will grow up as one of us."

"Can you believe Raven Hunter wanted to kill it? You'd think he'd learn."

"He's crazy." Green Water lifted her chin, long shining lengths of hair falling around her firm throat. A wistfulness lay in the corners of her broad mouth.

"I hope he's not as crazy as Dancing Fox says."

Fox sighed heavily, shaking her head. "He is."

Green Water studied One Who Cries thoughtfully. "Incidentally, I noticed that you told most of the band leaders how to find Heron's valley."

A few yards away, Singing Wolf had taken his baton, striking flakes off the sinew-clogged biface he was using to butcher the mammoth. The clack-snap carried to One Who Cries on the cold breeze, reassuring, the familiar sound of meat-making. Why didn't it soothe him?

He filled his lungs, blowing out into the cool air to watch his breath condense. Around him, the hills rose, crumpled shale outcrops on the ridges as the folded topography rose to the high mountains to the west. The air cut cleanly through his lungs, bringing the scent of mammoth and trampled wormwood and sedge. To the north, a somber bank of clouds rolled down from the salt water—a nasty storm from the looks of it.

"If the Others come this winter . . . as many of them as Blueberry says, we've only got one way to go."

"And if there's no way out of Heron's valley?"

He gave her a cockeyed glance and chuckled. "Well, maybe Heron can Dream them away, huh?"

"People!" A faint cry came, borne on the wind.

Singing Wolf stood up, looking to the north, shading his eyes with a blood-caked hand. Jumping Hare let the hide slide loose, craning his neck back and forth to see.

"Looks like Three Falls," Singing Wolf called. "What's he doing here? Thought he'd gone off with Sheep Whistle to hunt up north."

"I see Mouse," Jumping Hare called. "I'd know her walk. Broke her leg that time. When Strikes Lightning's dart didn't kill that buffalo along the salt water. There's more, too. Lots of the People behind them."

Green Water made a clucking sound. "I don't think this is good. Go see."

One Who Cries picked up his darts and trotted around the rock outcrop where he'd taunted the mammoth cow. The dogs were already barking, growling as they ran to meet the hounds with Sheep Whistle's people, snarling and fighting.

Three Falls walked in the lead of the group, a huddle of women behind him bent under flat-looking packs hitched by tump lines. They paced wearily, followed by one or two more hunters to the rear. Then came others, more bundled figures topping the horizon, walking bent against the skyline. The ones in the rear didn't look well as they limped along. No one noticed the scrapping dogs as they growled and yipped, the packs tearing into each other.

One Who Cries pulled up, sensing the wrongness. "Three Falls!" he called. "Welcome. Come, we've killed mammoth. We can feast you in real style."

A ripple of relief seemed to run through the group. Mouse—hair cut short in mourning for Strikes Lightning—lifted her head, a bit more bounce in her walk. Her young infant peeked out from her hood, a tiny face beside hers. Behind her a little girl toddled. More came, some still straggling over the hilltop to the north.

"There goes our winter's supply of meat," he whispered to himself.

Three Falls lifted grateful hands in the gesture of relief. "We'll enjoy your feast, One Who Cries, and offer thanks to the Blessed Star People for your shelter."

"I don't see much in the way of packs. The dogs aren't loaded. Isn't that Big Mouth back there?" The short, stocky man limped miserably. "Is he hurt?"

"Dart wound." Three Falls looked away nervously, lips pinched. "We had a wonderful hunt. Caught a herd of dall sheep in a little valley. Perfect. We'd butchered most of the carcasses, built caches so the permafrost would keep the meat. Thought we'd stay there all winter with the Others driven off and all."

A tendril of anxiety touched his stomach. "What happened?"

"The Blessed Star People saved us, my friend. Just luck. One of the young men was running to tell Raven Hunter and Crow Caller that we'd made enough meat to feed many. He saw the Others first, ran back, and warned us. Let me tell you, they fight better now. Killed four of the hunters who went out to drive them off. There were so many of them, old friend. So many. So fierce. We could no more drive them off than stop Wind Woman. But our position in the hills was good, so we didn't get slaughtered."

"How'd you find us?"

"Sheep Whistle told us which way you'd gone. We hoped you'd give us help." Three Falls shuffled his feet awkwardly, eyes to the ground.

One Who Cries looked out across the figures still straggling over the far hill. "Is Sheep Whistle here? He taught me the old stories."

"He's gone, my friend. Maybe later, tonight or tomorrow, we'll gather to sing his soul to the Blessed Star People."

One Who Cries flinched. "How did it happen?"

"The Others . . . Well, the dart caught him low, just above his manhood. Bad wound, that. Gut juices got into him. He started to stink and swelled up. We carried him for as long as we could."

"And your camp?"

Three Falls slapped his darts meaningfully. "The Others moved into it. Me, some of the rest of Sheep Whistle's band, we came to make sure the women will be safe. Then we're going after the Others to pay them back.''

One Who Cries shook his head. "Last time you paid them back, they didn't stay paid. Give it up. Too many have died already." He lifted an arm toward the oncoming swell of people. "Look at the women with their hair all cut short. It's got to end someplace."

Three Falls smiled wistfully. "Feast me and my warriors tonight, One Who Cries. Feast us well. Then we'll avenge our lost relatives."

"Sounds like Raven Hunter talking through your mouth."

"He's a leader." Three Falls nodded admiringly.

"Maybe."

Three Falls' brows lowered. "We need warriors. You'll come? You and Singing Wolf and Jumping Hare?"

"No." He shook his head certainly.

"But we have to—"

"No."

"You don't care about the murders of people you loved."

"We care more about the living. Singing Wolf, Jumping Hare, and I have talked about it already. We were afraid this would happen. We're going south to follow the Wolf Dream. If you really want your women and children to be safe, come with us."

Three Falls hesitated, then shook his head. "We must go back. It's . . . honor."

"Honor?"

Three Falls straightened, eyes brightening fiercely. "Warrior's honor." He shook his darts in emphasis.

A wrenching feeling of foreboding lashed at One Who Cries. He bowed his head and nodded slowly. His People grew more like the Others every day.

Chapter 35

The People snaked along over the undulating hills, gazing across the dots of sparse dwarf birch dotting the land. Snow already hoared the northern slopes. Stubborn leaves clung in auburn patches to the limbs. Father Sun's path sank closer to the horizon every day; the brilliant yellow light of summer faded now to a dull straw color. The drainages they crossed were blanketed with frost-slick leaves that crackled beneath their feet.

Dancing Fox adjusted the tump line biting into her forehead and glared at Mouse's back. The woman grated on her nerves like weathered slate against flesh. Talon, who walked several paces ahead of Fox, turned and grinned as though reading her thoughts, then waved her forward. She trotted to catch up.

"Get away. Walk back there," Mouse ordered, pointing.

"I walk where I please," Dancing Fox challenged, seeing Talon stop, turning. The old woman's eyes gleamed darkly.

"Your soul is cursed. I don't want you around my baby. You walk behind. Give us decent people some peace."

Dancing Fox moved like lightning, work-tough fingers clamping around Mouse's windpipe. As the woman croaked and struggled, Dancing Fox leaned close, peering into her eyes.

"The man who cursed me is a false Dreamer; he has no Power. That means his curse was meaningless." She tightened her grip, making Mouse gasp frantically. The woman futilely batted at her face. *"Understand?"*

She shoved Mouse backward, hard. The woman's stagger made the infant under her hood start to bawl shrilly.

Mouse rubbed her throat, staring wide-eyed at Dancing Fox. "You . . . you're crazy," she coughed.

Dancing Fox smiled grimly. "Remember that. There's no telling what I might do if I'm crossed." Coolly, she turned on her heel and walked on, aware of Singing Wolf running back to see what the commotion was all about.

She had no more trouble with Mouse that night or any

other. But she noticed that when any of the other women were near, they kept their eyes lowered. Respect? Or fear? Only Talon looked at her, winking in silent endorsement. Dancing Fox walked straighter, weapons held proudly.

Wolf Dreamer floated in the hot spring, Heron's sweet chanting buoying him, enfolding him. The lapping of the waves caressed his naked flesh.

"Lose yourself in the song," Heron instructed. "Free yourself. Move with the sounds. Dream this world away. It doesn't exist. Nothing exists but the Dance."

"The Dance," he repeated.

He leaned back in the water until it stroked his ears. The sounds of the birds vanished, a soft hum of flowing water filling in. Faintly, he heard Heron take up the chant again, the song rhythmic and haunting, a string of nonsense words. Because they made no sense, he shifted his concentration to the wavering sounds, imagining himself dancing to the cadence.

He blinked, lost, the world out of focus. He sat in Heron's shelter. His senses whirled with familiar shapes and smells. The skulls glared sightlessly at him, observing his very soul. The effigies and the colorful shapes drawn on the walls seemed to pulse with a life of their own through the thin layer of soot. The acrid odor of the geyser clogged his nose.

"Not . . . not the pool?" He looked around, seeing Broken Branch where she huddled in the far corner muttering to herself, a bright spark in her eyes.

"Not the pool," Heron told him. "Look at your hand."

He stared, gasping. An angry red blister rose from the center of his palm, the flesh seared. As he looked, bright pain brought tears to his eyes. He cried out.

Heron kept her taloned grip on his wrist, unperturbed. She rubbed grease mixed with herbs on the burn, binding his hand carefully.

"I see the question in your eyes. What happened? I put a coal on your hand, Wolf Dreamer. You never knew when it burned you. You know what that means?"

Despite the pain he nodded. "I found my Dance."

"That you did."

"But the coal burned me."

"Yes, you only shifted your mind. You didn't Dance with the fire."

"Then why'd you put the coal in my hand?" he asked a little resentfully, the pain increasing to a throb.

She grinned impudently. "I wanted to see where you were."

"Why couldn't you wait and ask me?"

"It's not the same."

He lifted a disbelieving brow. "Uh-huh."

"You're not far enough along yet."

He flexed his searing palm. "I can see that."

She hesitated, her jaw grinding softly in the crimson glow of the fire. "You see, to truly Dance, you need to Dance with everything around you . . . not just yourself. Then you have to become the Dance to touch the One. Then stop the—"

"But I made another step."

"Yes," she agreed. "Another step, Wolf Dreamer. Another step, but I wonder, will we have time?"

"What do you mean?"

She blinked, eyes on a distance only she could see. "Things are happening too fast. I wanted another couple of years. We may not even have all of this one." She patted him on the shoulder. "Next summer may even be too late."

"For what?"

She frowned, the lines in her ancient forehead deepening. "A terrible Dream rolled over me last night. I couldn't really see the images, they were fuzzy, but I felt the truth beneath them."

"What truth?"

"They're coming," she said hoarsely, pinning his eyes. "They'll be here before we turn around."

"The Others?" he guessed, swallowing hard. *He'd meet his father.*

"Something worse than them . . . some terrible darkness. I couldn't see clearly."

"Like the darkness I saw?" He shuddered lightly. "How much time do we have?"

"I don't know."

"How can we find out? If I'm not far enough along—"

"I . . ." She swallowed with difficulty, fear in her eyes. "I wonder if I'm still strong enough."

Reluctantly, she got to her feet and reached toward a high niche in the stone wall. Her hands trembled suddenly and she retracted them, rubbing the sweaty palms on her dress as she stared wide-eyed at the crevice.

"What is it?" he asked, frightened. "Can I get it for you?"

"No," she whispered darkly. "Only I can touch them." Again, she lifted her hands, wetting her lips anxiously as she reached into the niche to take down a carefully folded fox-hide bundle.

Dread prickled up Wolf Dreamer's spine. He stood next to her as she carefully unwrapped each of the folds, exposing thin shriveled black things.

"What are those?"

"Mushrooms. Remember? I showed you last summer, the ones growing where I dump the gut piles. Powerful things, they live off death, grow out of rot and corruption. Rebirth, Wolf Dreamer. Treat them with respect—Power grows in them."

He squinted at her, heart beginning to thunder in his chest. "Birth? You said they'd kill me."

She turned. A sharpness lay in her old black eyes. "They will. You're not ready for them."

"Why not?"

"You haven't seen the *Dancer* yet."

His eyes darted over the shelter, Broken Branch, and Heron, studying, thinking. What could that have to do with eating mushrooms?

"You understand?" she asked, cocking her head in desperate seriousness.

"No."

"Can the mushroom kill you if you're the mushroom? Can you kill the mushroom if the mushroom is you?"

His breathing stilled. "The One."

"Yes. The most powerful Dreaming of all must be shared with this little plant. Father Sun's joke, the mushroom. Colorless, it grows from death—in the dark; it brings life and Light. Rebirth. These . . ." She fingered the shriveled black slices. "These will let your soul go beyond the Dance to the—"

"But what if I come out of the Dream?"

Birdlike, she cocked her head. "And find yourself nowhere?"

"Something like that."

She laughed, throwing her back. "Then you'll know you're *there*."

"Where?"

"Nowhere."

Rather than demonstrating his stupidity, he decided to ask, "And what will that do for my Dreaming?"

"If you can find nowhere—the hole inside you—then you'll be able to juggle fire without being burned . . . and handle the poison." She nodded. "Yes, I see it in your eyes, you understand."

He swallowed. "In the 'hole,' the mushroom and I will be One?"

She gritted her remaining teeth and assented. "That's right. The ultimate Dreaming. Dreaming while you hover over death. And through it all, your body rebels. There's pain, sickness, vile sickness, and you have to go deep . . . deep into your very blood and Dream beyond the union of you and the mushroom. Be both and neither."

He clenched his fists unconsciously. "When can I try?"

"Maybe never, for all I know. And time's so much shorter than I thought. Raven Hunter defies the Dream. Your brother has an extraordinary Power in his own way. Different."

"He doesn't Dream."

"Not like you. But something . . . He has a Power all his own, an innate ability to Dream his will into other men's minds. To glimpse the way things might become. He's dangerous."

"Can I stop him?"

"I don't know. The two of you and the Other, your father, are the future of the People. Unless something is done, Raven Hunter will destroy the People from within while your father destroys them from without. And you?" She turned dark haunted eyes on him. "You have to find the hole inside— before you'll be able to find the one in the Big Ice to save them."

"What about this darkness you saw in your Dream? Is it—"

"It's something else, worse. It'll swallow all of us: the Others, the People—"

"Then . . ." He spread his arms wide, imploring. "We have to find out what it is before we can fight it. When will I . . . ?" He swallowed the rest, indicating the ominous mushrooms.

In a quick violent motion, she rewrapped them and clutched them to her breast. "Don't even touch them. A taste, a lick of the tainted fingers, and you'll die horribly. The life-sucking spirits of the Long Dark would be a pleasure next to this. I can't risk your life."

But the bundle drew his eyes, holding them like an eagle draws the stare of a hare.

Chapter 36

Raven Hunter motioned the old man in, indicating a seat.

Crow Caller settled himself with the care of the elderly, arranging his hides, smoothing the folds of his outer parka. His good eye took in the surroundings, the smoke-stained poles supporting the hide walls and roof, the carefully placed weapons, the bundled wolf hides and caribou robes. Several brown bundles lay stacked to the side. Firelight flickered yellow, casting the shadows of the two men over the tent walls.

"Here, old teacher," Raven Hunter said, offering a cup of tea in a carefully crafted horn made from the forward boss of a dall sheep.

Crow Caller drank it down and pointed to the stew boiling in the paunch bag over the fire. "I haven't eaten tonight."

"Please, fill your cup."

The old shaman smiled and scooped up some stew. He slurped noisily.

Dinner out of the way, Crow Caller burped and looked at Raven Hunter. "What did you want to see me about?"

"Three Falls has arrived," Raven Hunter began. "Sheep

Whistle's band has been attacked by the Others. I want your blessing to take the young men and hit them in their camps. They won't expect a fight in the deep of the Long Dark.''

Crow Caller fingered his chin, the white eye dead in his head. ''The young men shouldn't risk dying in the Long Dark. What of their souls, hmm?''

Raven Hunter spread his hands wide. ''Souls, Crow Caller? What of their future? *Our* future. Where does it all end? The Others will kill us, or absorb us. Three Falls sent a youth to watch the Others who took Sheep Whistle's camp. They, too, keep the young women they capture. Is that the future, Crow Caller? Our women bearing their young . . . more like Blueberry?''

''You have too much ambition for such a young man. Aren't an elder's words enough for you?'' He gruffly started to stand.

Raven Hunter gently pushed him back to the ground. ''Of course, I'm ambitious. I'm the salvation of the People. Do you Dream anything else?''

Indignantly, the old man said, ''I Dream many things.''

''Let's be honest, you and I. I've been keeping track of your 'Dreams.' Remember the prophesy at Mammoth Camp? Eh? All the hunters sinking darts into the calves? Hasn't happened yet. You Dreamed the birth of Strikes Lightning's first son. Remember? All that wondrous talk of him cradling the boy in his arms. It was another girl. Strikes Lightning is dead. Mouse is gone to One Who Cries' camp. And then there was the Dream about the—''

''Sometimes Dreams change.''

''And sometimes the important thing is that people believe . . . whether Dreams are true or not.''

Crow Caller shouted, ''Are you accusing me of lying?''

Raven Hunter toyed with a dart foreshaft, avoiding the shaman's eyes. ''I wouldn't want you and me to be enemies, old teacher. It wouldn't be good for the People.''

Crow Caller digested that, hard lines forming around his mouth. Finally he said, ''What are you after?''

''You've never really backed my raids against the Others.''

''I've never spoken out against them, either.''

''True, and I respect a man who waits to see where his best interests lie.'' He met the old man's gaze. ''But the time has come for you to decide." He leaned close, holding Crow Caller's good eye. The old man glared back defiantly. But after a few moments his stare wavered and fell.

"What do you want?"

"Are you with me . . . or against me?"

"Why do you need my backing?"

"Enthusiasm for war during the Long Dark will be . . . how do I say it? Lacking? No one wants to fight when the spirits might suck a man's soul away."

Crow Caller flashed his good eye to Raven Hunter's. "And a shaman's approval might make the difference?"

"Approval and promises of protection."

"And if I don't support this?"

Raven Hunter spewed a disappointed exhale. "A complete recounting of the times your Dreams were wrong could become the center of the People's gossip. Some might begin to openly mock you. Derision is the Dreamer's worst—"

"You're *threatening* me?" Crow Caller said, mouth open.

"No. I'm trying to give you enough information so you can decide quickly that your best interests are in supporting me."

Crow Caller's face puckered in rage. "My Powers reach far and wide. I have ways, uses for bits of hair, nail clippings, scraps of clothing. I know how to draw a man's soul out of his body and send it scurrying into the Long Dark. I can—"

"Shall we publicly test that?"

"What do you mean?"

Raven Hunter reached for his personal spirit bundle. "I'll give you this tomorrow where everyone can see. Then we'll all wait—the entire camp—to see what's stronger: your curses on me or my soul." His eyes glistened darkly. "Do you want to see that happen?"

Crow Caller squirmed, eyes darting nervously. "It would serve no purpose."

"Come, let's be honest, old teacher. Friend. We, who have so much to offer each other, shouldn't be adversaries."

Crow Caller sucked his lower lip, a pained expression heavy on his features. "You want to split the People? Make more disharmony when the Others are raiding and killing us?"

"No." Raven Hunter pursed his lips distastefully. "I want

unity. But that won't happen until you and I are on the same side."

A long silence passed as Crow Caller's face lined with uneasy thought. Raven Hunter waited patiently; the old man's shoulders slowly slumped. Before him, the Dreamer of the People appeared to wilt from the inside.

The words drawn out, anguished, Crow Caller finally whispered, "I . . . I'll help you."

"I knew you would. Have more stew, my friend. You and I, we shall remold the People."

Crow Caller shook his head, reaching the horn cup into the broth. "So young, yet so powerful. Where does this come from when I, with all my wisdom, must work so hard for Dreams I cannot trust?"

Raven Hunter blinked thoughtfully, listening to the difficult admission. "Your Power will return, old friend, now that you've decided to fight to save the People. I'm sure Father Sun doubted your devotion before and that's why it fled. It'll be back."

Crow Caller cast a skeptical glance heavenward. "Maybe."

"I'm sure of it."

"And you think this war against the Others will succeed? You think you can drive them back, once and for all?"

Raven Hunter twirled his dart point. "Truthfully, I don't know, but we'll make them think twice. Convince them there are easier fates than facing the People. Suppose Blueberry is right? If there are more people pushing the Others—and we make them bleed enough—maybe they'll go back and retake the lands they've been pushed out of."

"Blueberry also said there were many many Others. More than we could kill . . . more than we could scare."

"Then we'll die anyway. At least waging war will buy us time."

"Time for what?"

"Who knows, maybe for my silly brother to find the hole in the Big Ice. Maybe for the Star People to curse—"

"There's no hole!" Crow Caller growled.

Raven Hunter looked up to meet his hot black eye. "Then we'd better be able to push the Others back."

"How can I help?" The question came low and resentful.

"The People have grown slothful. We have to harden them,

make them tough and resilient so they have the heart to fight. *With your Dreams of our success to buoy spirits,* we'll raid and win, living off the bounty of the Others' hunt, begetting more young men from their women.''

"You upset the ways of the People." Crow Caller shook his head. "Killing and—''

"We don't have a choice.'' Raven Hunter exhaled on his dart point, breathing spirit into the stone, wood, and binding. "Until your Power returns and you can Dream another way out for us.''

"I don't think—''

Raven Hunter slammed a fist into the hides he sat on, a crazed look welling in his eyes. He leaned close to Crow Caller, twisting his head curiously. "What if I *do* turn the People's way upside down? It'll be much worse if we give up and let the Others kill us. How will one of our women feel when some sweaty Other is parting her legs and making her *his* second wife?''

"I still don't like it.''

"You know of another way? Tell me, I'll listen.''

Crow Caller frowned, jaw propped on a fist. "We've no place to go but into the Big Ice. And Runs In Light? Well, I'll die of an Other's dart before I lend anything to him.'' He shook his head. "I'll tell the young men to go with you. I'll make Power for them. Make it so they know they'll go to the Blessed Star People if they die.''

Raven Hunter nodded, a knowing glint in his eye. "I thought you would. We'll do well together, you and I. Indeed, we'll do well. And your Power will return, old friend. Just wait.''

Crow Caller resettled himself, fingering his beak nose. "You've got an interest in Dancing Fox.''

Raven Hunter shrugged and shifted his gaze to stare at his spirit bundle, tracing the magical lines drawn on the hide with his eyes while he contemplated his answer. The old man's tone hadn't been hostile, only curious and maybe a little jealous. Their current alliance was fragile. Could he risk the truth? Softly, he said, "Does that bother you? You threw her out.''

"You argued for her life.''

Raven Hunter looked up sharply. "One day she'll be my

wife. I've seen it. I've also seen a child—a powerful child—springing from her womb. I'm sure . . .'' His voice faded, eyes going blank for a few moments. ''I'm sure it's mine.''

''You've Dreamed?''

Raven Hunter ignored the question. ''Besides, she amuses me. And despite her shame, there is no other woman who draws me so.''

''Dreams? But you're nothing but a boy, just like that brother of yours!''

Raven Hunter clenched the dart shaft, muscles bunching on his forearm. ''Beware, Crow Caller. There are worse things than the spirits of the Long Dark. The time when you could call me boy are long gone.''

''I meant no harm,'' Crow Caller clarified quickly, a weak smile on his lips. ''Friends shouldn't snap at each other. Not when so much is at stake for the People, eh?''

''And Dancing Fox?''

He opened his arms, shrugging. ''What do I care? She would have left me to go with Runs In Light eventually, anyway.''

Raven Hunter nodded, looking half-lidded at Crow Caller. ''Then we understand each other.''

 Chapter 37

Sitting cross-legged in her shelter, a small crackling fire before her, Heron wearily rubbed the back of her neck. Wavering shadows crept over her collection of skulls, accenting the hollow eye sockets and glistening fangs of wolves and bears. The human skull studied her soberly, a macabre understanding in its empty orbits.

Yes, you know. The dead see so clearly. Only we who live constantly blind ourselves with trivialities. Tell me, noble dead, will I . . . will I be strong enough? Can I make the

*transition to the Dancer? Or will I fail again? Tell me, kind
dead, what vision fills your—*

Broken Branch ducked under the hangings, head cocked as
she looked at Heron. "He's gone. I walked him down the
trail to that big boulder."

She nodded, fumbling nervously with the hem of her caribou skirt as she looked away from the skull. Broken Branch
followed the path of her gaze, jaw working uneasily as her
eyes slitted. The old woman stiffened, hands going to her
hips.

"I couldn't have him here. Not now. This is too important.
I wouldn't want him to see."

Broken Branch shifted uncomfortably on her swollen feet.
"You scare me when you talk like that."

"I scare myself."

A long silence passed while Heron studied her old neme-
sis, smiling at the dart-sharp nose and sagging flesh. "You
know, I've almost forgiven you."

"Well, don't waste your time. I've never needed it."

Heron cackled, eyes gleaming. "You didn't, maybe, but I
did. I've had a wound inside me for a lot of years. I feel
better now that I sort of like you."

Broken Branch waved it away, waddling over to kneel by
the fire, hands extended. "Save your breath. I loved Bear
Hunter. If we could turn back time . . . Dream ourselves
back there again, I'd do it all over. Had a lot of good years
with him until he was killed."

"Why did you come back? You could be relaxing in some
young hunter's lodge now. It wouldn't be a bad life. They'd
feed you for the stories and for the raising of their young.
Elders are respected—well cared for among the People."
Heron rubbed her forearms, trying to loosen the muscles
cramping with the increasing tension in her breast. "You've
been quiet, gathering wood, cooking, preparing food for stor-
age. Such things aren't like you, Broken Branch."

"Hah-heeee! What do *you* know of me? Not like me, you
say? Hah!" She waggled a bent finger. "I saw his eyes,
Heron. You understand? The Dream . . . the Wolf Dream
was there, powerful. It touched my soul. Wound me up and
sent me falling into a Dream of my own." She shook her

head. "It's for the People that I came back, *for him*. So you could teach him."

"Why me? You don't even like—"

"Hush, you old hag. No matter what's behind us, you're still the best. The only Dreamer the People have left who can teach."

Heron massaged her forehead. The time was nearing and fear tingled in her belly. "He'll be powerful. Better than me one day . . . if he lives."

Broken Branch's joints cracked as she pulled another section of willow from the pile she'd laboriously hauled in over the long weeks of summer. "If? That got anything to do with that Dream you had last night?"

Heron stared sightlessly at the fire. "Sights. Sounds. Something bad's happening with the People . . . beyond the People. I . . . don't know. But many are coming. Stragglers walking up over the hills by the Big River. In front comes One Who Cries, Singing Wolf, and women I don't know. Behind them, a dozen bands are following. All fleeing to us."

"Trouble?"

"Deep fear." Heron shook her head. "It hangs over them as they walk. In the Dream I saw something growing in the dark. Like Grandfather Brown Bear, it filled the clouds, hidden there in the blackness, reaching down, huge paws hovering in the air, waiting."

"The same thing Wolf Dreamer saw?"

"I think so."

"Can you drive it off?"

Heron lifted her shoulder. "There's more. Raven Hunter walks north, skirting around a huge pool of blood; many young men follow on his heels. As the Long Dark grows, so does his power over them. Even some of the young women go with him, their darts on their backs, singing chants while Crow Caller blesses them, filling them with his claims of Power and protection from the spirits of the Long Dark. And beyond, on the other side of the blood pool, lie the camps of the Others, lit by shafts of glowing light, bars of color like that shed by the Monster Children fighting in the sky."

"I don't understand."

Heron puffed out her cheeks and spewed an exhale. "I

don't either. That's why I woke Wolf Dreamer up last night. I had to talk to him.''

''You told him more than just about the Dream. The yellow rock from the geyser. The white crystals from under the mammoth dung. The herbs for medicine.''

''They might come in handy. He'll have to know one of these days. He's learned a lot, more than he can even imagine. I just hope he knows enough.''

Broken Branch shifted, watching cautiously from the corner of her eyes. ''You act like you're not going to be around to finish teaching him?''

''Maybe not.''

''What are you talking about!''

Slowly Heron shook her head. ''All my life, from the time I left Bear Hunter, I've been in control of things—even if it was just observation. But the world is changing, people are dying and I don't understand it.''

''You can't understand everything in the world, Heron. Father Sun made—''

''Ah, but I can see the patterns, old woman.'' She squeezed her eyelids tightly closed before heaving a tired sigh. ''At least I used to be able to, but they're all jumbled up now. Broken and scattered like caribou bones in the spring. The old Dream paths are blocked, the new ones terrifying. Something's coming. I won't sit here and wait for it. No, old woman, I'm a seeker. I'll *know* what it is before it comes to swallow me!''

''Spirit knowledge took the place of Bear Hunter, eh?''

Their eyes held, Heron's going soft and watery. ''Yes.''

''That's why you sent the boy away? You're going to fight this . . . thing?''

Heron paused, biting her lip, brow furrowed. ''He'd distract me. Maybe see something he's not ready for yet. Canny, that one, sees things too clearly for his years sometimes. No, he might be hurt by all this.''

''What are you going to do?''

''Hush! *I need to see*, don't you understand?''

Firelight flickered over Broken Branch's taut face, her eyes fearful. ''You need to see. What of it?''

''You, you're of it.'' Heron arched her back, filling her lungs deeply, beginning the preparation.

"I'm of it?"

"Unfortunately."

"What do you—"

"Go stay below the pool. I don't know. . . ." She stopped when a quaver touched her voice. Gathering herself, she finished strongly. "I don't know how long it'll take, but don't come back until I call you. Understand? If you were to interrupt, break my concentration . . . I don't know what might happen."

Broken Branch got slowly to her feet, shaking her head. "You're a crazy old curlew, Heron. I'm going. Do your Dreaming, you old—"

"Broken Branch?"

"What?"

"About Bear Hunter . . ."

Broken Branch pursed her lips, dropping her eyes. "I was young then, the juices of life ran hot in my body. My heart ached for him. What I did—"

"Did you make him happy?"

"He never bedded another. When he went hunting, he ran all the way home to be with me and our children. We talked . . . laughed. Our children all lived to have families of their own. He used to love to rock the grandchildren on his knees at night."

"How did he die?"

"It was quick. Mammoth swung his trunk, Bear Hunter lost his footing and couldn't get out of the way."

Heron nodded in the long silence. "I could never have given him the things you did. Dreamers can never really love, Broken Branch. It's . . . it's a curse, you see. Dreamers who love destroy themselves or those they love. It's a fatal flaw. I tried to tell Wolf Dreamer. I hope he understands."

"Either he did or he didn't. You tried."

Heron nodded, smiling wistfully. "Get out of here. Whatever you hear, whatever you see, leave me alone! Understand? Alone . . . or you'll kill me."

Broken Branch's wrinkled mouth worked. "I'll not meddle in your Dreams, Heron." She lifted the hide flaps and disappeared into the bright midday sun.

Heron watched the flap wave slowly back and forth. She hesitated, dread making her hands tremble. "Get up, you old fool," she cursed herself for delaying. "There's no other way."

Jaw thrust forward, she stood, reaching for the mushrooms. Gently, she laid them near the fire, then grasped her bundle of willow stems, rich and red, and threw a handful into the gut bag hanging from the tripod near the fire. As they absorbed the water, their pungent scent filled the shelter.

She sucked in a shuddering breath and stared at the mushrooms, speaking intimately. "How long has it been? It was the night Wolf Dreamer called to me from the mists. You remember, don't you?"

The bag of mushrooms glowed darkly in the flames.

"We wrestled like two bears. . . ." She swallowed hard, feeling the fear in her gut widen. Her voice came barely audible, "You almost killed me. . . . Remember?"

She jerked her eyes from the bag and poked at the fire, getting the coals to even out. At the fringes of her consciousness, she could feel the presence of Broken Branch out below the pool. A distraction, still a distraction.

"Concentrate!" she reprimanded harshly. "She won't disturb you. She said she wouldn't."

Behind her, she heard a soft murmuring of voices and turned to stare at the mushrooms; they were calling her, beckoning like a lover.

"I'm coming," she choked out. Tears welled powerfully.

With shaking hands, she reached for the soaked willow stems. Chanting the old song, she cast the first handful into the flames. They sizzled wildly, steam and sacred smoke twisting through the soot-thick vent above.

Dropping her face in her hands, she fought the terror writhing in her breast.

The mushrooms whispered, their eerie voices echoing from the cold stone walls.

Chapter 38

As darkness fell, the brilliant lights of the Monster Children's War stained the sky, bands of orange, red, blue, and green undulating across the heavens. The People stopped to set up camp. Babies wailed their hunger, dogs yapping as men and women dropped their packs and went about gathering wood for supper fires.

"Where's Talon?" Dancing Fox asked, looking around.

Singing Wolf straightened, his keen eyes cataloging faces. "I don't see her. I guess I'd better go back and look. Maybe she stopped."

"I'll go." Dancing Fox stared uneasily at the falling dark.

"Alone? There might be—"

"Don't worry." She smiled slyly at him. "I lived out there alone, for several turnings of Moon Woman. I'll be fine. Besides, Talon's my responsibility. You keep camp in order, I'll find her."

He looked uncertain, but nodded.

Dancing Fox took her darts, walking swiftly back down the trail they'd made, scuff marks of the People's long boots marking the way where the snow had drifted in the lee of the rocks.

How long since she'd seen her? An hour? Maybe two? She'd become involved in a conversation with Green Water, talking about the Others.

Shadows stretched as the evening darkened. An owl hooted out in the rocks. Three crows passed overhead, their wings rasping on the air while they clucked and cooed to each other. Stillness settled on the land, dropping with the mantle of night.

"Talon?" Her voice carried like a bleat in the evening.

She picked up her feet to trot, eyes searching the trail as she wound around glacial cobbles.

"Talon?"

"Here, girl," it came as a faint echo on the wavering breezes.

Weaving through a jagged scatter of boulders, she found her.

Talon rested on a smooth granite slab. Behind her, boulders had been piled by the retreating glacier to form a shelter from the wind. Silt and sand had blown in to stop the gaps in the gray rock. A few tendrils of exploring wormwood hung from the precarious dirt. Overhead, the sky darkened, scattered clouds drifting down from the north.

Talon looked up, meeting her eyes. She worked her wrinkled lips over toothless gums and shook her head wryly before smiling. A twinkle reflected from the ancient eyes as she braced herself.

"Found me, eh?"

"You get lost, or stop to—"

"Can't go on, girl."

Fox bent over the old woman where she sat, hands clutching up one bony knee. "What?"

"It's just that time, is all," Talon said easily, head cocked to look up at Fox. "I've been holding the rest back, always the last in line. I think I'll just find a nice spot and sit."

"No, Talon. We're making camp. You can—"

"No." A delicate hand reached up to pat her as understanding dawned and Fox's eyes widened. "Now, child, don't start that. I've been around long enough to know how these things work. I can feel death close. My soul's itching to go." She waved toward the few gleaming stars poking through the rainbow blanket flooding the sky.

A hollow expanse spread in Fox's stomach; she whispered, "What will I do without you?"

Talon laughed. "Oh, you'll get along, child. I'm proud of you. You've got spirit like women in the old days. Ah, that day you grabbed Mouse by the throat made my heart warm. And then do you remember that dart cast you made before Renewal? Knocked that snow goose right out of the air! Lot of men can't make the beat of that!"

"Come on, you've rested now. Let's go. The People aren't camped more than a dart's throw over that hill up there. I should have kept better watch. If I would have—"

"Would have nothing," Talon grunted. "Took me two days of hobbling on these worn-out legs to finally get a chance to sneak away. And Green Water was enjoying talking to you. Good woman, that Green Water.''

''But you can't—''

''Of course I can.'' She pushed Dancing Fox away. ''It's a matter of responsibility. Look at me. I can't work hides. I fall asleep when I'm supposed to be caring for the children while the women are out hunting, trapping, and picking plants. Besides, I know I'm going to die this Long Dark.''

''You don't know that.''

''I do. And Fox, knowing that, what's better for the People? Should I sit around and eat up the meat stores, take food out of a baby's mouth? No, you never can tell about Long Darks. Food's critical.''

''What if I want you to have mine?''

Talon grinned tenderly. ''You're a good girl, but I wouldn't eat it.''

''Why not?''

''I've drained myself dry, Fox, teaching stories and what I know about hunting and gathering. That's how it works among the People. We pass things on. You live like I showed you, and one of these years, you'll teach someone. That's what's important.''

Dancing Fox shook her head. ''I can't see how you know you're going to die.''

Talon laughed. ''The young never can.''

''Camp's just a little way up the trail. At least go that far. I'll help you with—''

''No, child.'' Talon shook her head. ''Go on, leave me. I appreciate what you're trying to do, but I know better. The best I can do, I've done. You go find your Dreamer, girl. Find your future.''

Dancing Fox closed her eyes, sinking down to hold the old woman's skeletal hand. ''I . . . I'll stay. Keep you company. Make a shelter for—''

''Go,'' Talon whispered gently. ''I might hang on here for days. You'd be late in finding your Dreamer.''

''I'll find him later. Let me—''

''Fox?''

''Hmmm?''

''About this Dreamer. You've never known a real Dreamer and I'm afraid—''

"I saw Runs In Light after the Wolf Dream. And I was married to Crow Caller."

"It's not the same."

"What?" she asked with trepidation, seeing the old woman's hesitation.

Talon sighed, lungs wheezing. "The old Dreamers, the real ones . . . Well, I've never seen one with a mate."

"I don't understand."

Talon clucked her lips. "I figured you didn't. I never said much about your Runs In Light and all, but, child, if he's been with Heron you may not know him when you meet him."

"That's silly, of course I will. I've known him since I was—"

"That's not what I mean." Talon leaned her head back, old eyes scanning the stars. "Fox, Dreams change people. Something happens inside their heads. They lose interest in things of this world. In friends—especially lovers."

"But a Dreamer's just like anyone else. I mean, Crow Caller wasn't any different than—"

"Bah!" Talon hissed. "Crow Caller? He's no Dreamer. Oh, he had glimpses, once, years ago. Then the status got to his head, muddled it all up. That's why he lost it, child."

Dancing Fox squeezed the woman's hand, steering the conversation back to Runs In Light. "What about Light, Grandmother?"

"Real Dreamers lose interest in everything but the Dream. Nobody knows why it happens, but it does. I remember hearing about lots of broken hearts when I was a girl."

Fox breathed in the chill night air, filling her lungs. A weight lay heavy on her chest. "You mean he may not want me anymore?"

"That's what I mean."

Fox swallowed and let her eyes dart anxiously over the patches of snow glistening in the wavering lights of the Twins' northern war. Stubbornly, she murmured, "He'll be there, waiting, I know it."

A white haze grew on the horizon as Moon Woman gathered herself to spring into the sky. "He didn't come to the Renewal. You know why?"

"He couldn't. He was busy."

"If he'd really wanted to see you he'd've been there. He stayed with Heron because the Dream was more important."

"Why didn't you tell me, then? I could have prepared."

"At the time, well, it didn't make sense to lay another burden on you. Not with Raven Hunter making trouble. And . . . I thought I'd be there when you finally saw Light again and I could make the landing softer for you. I didn't know I'd give out so quick."

"I just can't believe he'd . . . can't." She shook her head, hope and anticipation mixing with premonition. All those long months, the suffering, the loneliness. Only his promise of love had kept her going.

Talon swallowed, the sound loud in the night. "This is the girl who worked so hard to make herself independent? You're stronger than this. Get your head back to earth. Only crows fly up there." She pointed a gnarled finger at the crystal night sky. "You're worth more than that."

Fox's heart throbbed as though it would burst. "He won't have me and you're leaving. I don't want to be alone. I need—"

"You don't need anybody, you've just been fooling yourself into believing that because it's the way of the People. A woman's supposed to depend on others."

"People need each other."

"Do they?"

"Of course."

Talon pointed a thin bony finger. "There's only one reason people are afraid to be alone. It's because they fear themselves deep down, child. They're scared to death there's not enough in them to survive without help."

"I don't fear myself," Fox insisted.

Talon smiled faintly, pride in her eyes. "Good. Because of all the women I've ever known, there's only two I thought could make it on their own."

"Who?"

"You and Heron." Talon sighed weakly and gazed out across the moonlit jumbles of rock. "I didn't know her so well. I was only ten when she left camp. But even then, I remember admiring her for going."

"What if it's not Heron who's keeping Runs In Light

away?'' Fox asked shakily, her mind seeking other possibilities.

"You mean what if you walk into his camp and find him with three wives?"

"Yes."

"You going to throw yourself off a cliff?"

Fox bowed her head, blinking at a long-abandoned bird nest tucked in the rocks no more than a foot off the ground. The sticks were crusted with frost. A broken speckled shell nestled inside, gleaming in the night. "No."

"Ah, it's easier to think about him belonging to another woman, is it?"

"I can fight another woman. I can't fight the whole spirit world."

"No, you can't. But he won't be the first person you ever lose in your life. There's worse things."

"Like what?" she scoffed miserably.

Talon eyed her seriously. "Like the death of the People. If he's sacrificing himself to the Dream, it's for the People. You understand that? It's not because he hates you."

Dancing Fox stared at the dark figure of the old woman, heart in her throat. "I'll learn to understand it."

Talon's voice warmed as she looked longingly up at the dim stars. "I know you will."

Long minutes passed while they listened to the rasping of Wind Woman over the rocky plains and watched the flickering northern lights.

"You're not coming back to camp . . . really?"

"No, I'm going to wait here and talk to the Star People." Talon squinted upward a little fearfully.

"I'm staying with you. It's not right that you die by yourself."

Talon shooed her away. "Dying's a private thing. I don't want you here."

A sob welled in Dancing Fox's throat. She forcibly choked it back. "Are you sure?"

Talon scrutinized her tormented expression. "You really need to be close to me to the end?"

"I can't stand the thought of you getting weak . . . and the wolves . . ."

"Well, I can't much either. You going to keep them off?"

"If you'll let me."

"You think you can face it? It'll mean that much longer before you find out what's happened to Runs In Light."

Dancing Fox's eyes locked with the wrinkled old woman's and some silent communication passed between them, tender and intimate. "I can face it."

She lifted the broken shell from the nest, tender fingers caressing the sharp edges.

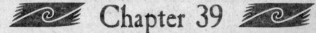

Chapter 39

The lodge stretched twenty feet across the base, rising six feet over Ice Fire's graying head. Caribou and mammoth robes were stacked neatly in the far corner, their hair glittering in the light of the fire burning in the rock-lined fire pit. Multicolored medicine bundles dotted the walls, each carefully placed to correspond to the direction that gave it Spirit Power.

He looked up, frowning at the bundle on the southern wall, the sea bundle. For days it had taunted him, its sweet voice disturbing his sleep. "I haven't closed my ears," he assured it softly, reaching out to stroke the bundle. "Keep talking. Eventually, I'll understand your message."

"Ice Fire?"

He dropped his hand, seeing Broken Shaft's face peeking through the door flap. He motioned the young warrior in, getting to his feet to hug him. Twenty Long Lights old, Broken Shaft stood tall and heavily muscled with a button nose and round face. His full lips were sensual as he smiled and pushed back a little, eyes drifting over the elder. "Thank the Great Mystery that you're all right. With all the attacks from the Enemy, I feared for your life."

Ice Fire smiled. "Don't worry. I know the time of my death, and it isn't for a while yet."

Broken Shaft cocked his head skeptically. "On occasion, I've known your visions to be wrong."

Ice Fire laughed. "But only on occasion."

"True, but it worries me nonetheless."

They exchanged a warm smile.

"You made excellent time." Ice Fire changed the subject. "I hope that means it was an easy trip with no troubles."

"Smoke proved difficult."

Ice Fire frowned. "Why? He's a good—"

"He met a girl from the Round Hoof Clan and lost his head. He brought her bouquets of autumn leaves for days before she reluctantly gave in and agreed to spend time with him. But the rest of the trip was uneventful."

Ice Fire's eyes crinkled in amusement. "Smoke stayed, I take it?"

"Indeed, he did."

Putting an arm around Broken Shaft's broad shoulders, Ice Fire guided the warrior to the fire, where they both settled on the sandy soil. "You look tired. Can I offer you a hot meal?"

"That sounds wonderful. I could eat an entire mammoth." The young man placed his darts to his lips a moment, apologizing for letting them out of his hands, before he carefully laid them to the side.

Ice Fire scooped up a horn full of the thick musk-ox stew, handing it to the grateful warrior.

"Thank you, Elder. I've much to tell you."

"Ice Fire?" Red Flint appeared in the doorway.

"Thank you for coming, old friend. Come in."

The middle-aged man ducked beneath the flap and ambled tiredly to settle on his knees across the fire. His eyes looked down, the lines around his mouth remained tightly drawn— as they had since the Enemy carried off his daughter, Moon Water.

Ice Fire's thoughts drifted, mind leaping space and time to imagine the pretty girl doing chores in the camps of the Enemy. The thought of her there left a burning resentment in his stomach. They'd have raped her by now. For all he knew, she already carried a child in her young womb. Pray to the Great Mystery they hadn't hurt her.

He'd become so lost in his thoughts, it took Broken Shaft

clearing his throat to bring him back. He looked up, somewhat startled to see the stew depleted by several horns, the haggard Broken Shaft looking respectfully his way.

"You have been to the Round Hoof Clan? And to the Tiger Belly Clan, too?"

Broken Shaft nodded, slipping into formal tones. "Yes, Most Respected Elder. The tidings are mostly good. Some of the pressure is easing to the west. Something happened out there. The Glacier People are moving south along the coast. Some of the other tribes are moving north still, others are slowing as our clans hunt out the game. The Great Mystery also punishes those who seek to drive us. Some terrible disease, a sickness of the soul, wastes their warriors. Oozing sores cover their bodies. For the moment, they aren't fighting as fiercely as before."

Ice Fire digested that, lost in thought. "Then our clans didn't lose so much land this year?"

"No. In fact, we gained some back." Broken Shaft grimaced and shook his head, glancing briefly at Red Flint.

Ice Fire followed his gaze, noting the older man's absent prodding of the fire with a willow branch. He turned back to Broken Shaft. "What's bothering you?"

The warrior raised his eyebrows expressively. "The salt water, Most Respected Elder."

"The salt water?"

Broken Shaft gazed nervously at the fire for a moment. "The land between the Round Hoof and Tiger Bellies." He shook his head. "Smoke and I passed at the beginning of the Long Light and traveled through Buffalo Clan to the Tiger Bellies. On the way back, not more than two moons ago, I tried to follow the same trail with Caribou Foot of the Buffalo Clan. The water had covered the old route. We had to go several days' journey to the north. It's eerie, plants sticking up as the water covers them. The land is narrower through there now. The northern salt water moves south, too. The seas are trying to meet. Not only that, but Caribou Foot tells me the rivers have never been so full. Half his clan were cut off from the dancing this year by the great western river. You know, the one that runs out of the other side of these mountains to the west. Not even the strongest and bravest would try to cross the swollen flood."

"So soon . . ." Ice Fire reflected to himself, a tendril of anxiety winding through him. A sweet child's voice penetrated his mind. His gaze drifted slowly to the sea bundle. "Is that it?" he whispered, eyes narrowing. "It's happening sooner than I'd thought?"

Broken Shaft swallowed uneasily. "What is, Elder?"

Ice Fire continued staring at the green and blue bundle, but it had hushed again. Blinking, he looked back to the warrior. "The seas are going to cut us off from the Glacier People."

"How?"

"By flooding the land."

Broken Shaft sat still and somber. "What if the water cuts us off from the Tiger Bellies? They're pushing back into land abandoned by the Glacier People."

Ice Fire lifted his shoulders in a shrug. "Then they'll have to face the Glacier People alone—as well as this horrible disease."

Broken Shaft swallowed and shifted, eyes turning to his darts. "If the water is going to drown the world, are we safe?"

"Don't worry about it. You'll be long dead by the time it follows us this far." He smiled, glancing at the bundle from the corner of his eye. *Won't he?*

Red Flint licked his lips and straightened. "Are the other clans sending warriors to help us fight the Enemy? We have to get our families back!" Viciously, he slammed a fist into the dirt floor.

Broken Shaft lowered his eyes as Ice Fire reached a comforting hand across to squeeze his friend's shoulder. "We'll get her back," he softly affirmed.

Red Flint relaxed a little, nodding tensely. "I . . . I know, Elder."

Ice Fire released his grip reluctantly, asking, "How many are coming?"

"Many," Broken Shaft said certainly. "With the Glacier People going south to take the land of the sick tribes, there is no one brave to fight. Warriors from all the clans are on their way here, to find honor fighting the Enemy with us."

Red Flint nodded again, a fist clenched. "This year, our warriors will win the Sacred White Hide back for our clan."

Broken Shaft grinned. *"I plan on it."*

Ice Fire smiled proudly. The hide was the sacred center of the tribe, the heart of the people, the promise of survival. Without the supreme Power of the hide, the Mammoth People would cease to exist. Each Long Light, it passed to the clan that had shown the most valor, gained the most honor for the tribe.

He bowed his head and nodded. "I've no doubts that you'll win it back for us."

Sleep did not come for Ice Fire that night. Like a dying salmon after the spawn, he twirled and twisted in his robes. The sea bundle called repeatedly, but he couldn't quite make out its words; it disturbed him deeply.

Wind tousled the door flap, revealing stars glistening in the dark bowl of the sky. He inhaled a deep tired breath and concentrated on the feel of the cold breeze washing over his face.

"Man of the Others," a voice called hauntingly.

He tensed, heart pounding. Holding his breath, he waited, knowing the Watcher's *touch*.

"I see you there," she said. "You can't hide." Her scratchy voice echoed around him like the pounding of the surf.

Rubbing hands over his eyes, he blinked anxiously around the lodge, finally rasping, "Who are you?"

"Heron. I've known you for years, man of the Others—since that day you raped—"

"I remember." He winced, memories stirring. Then, like now, the feeling had been that of a Dream. A feeling so strong, it had fooled him that day. Now it washed around him, a tangible presence that brought him bolt upright.

"Such a powerful Dreaming," he whispered.

"Are you ready to talk to me?"

"Yes." He pushed his hides back, feeling the presence wrap around his soul. Locking his mind on the essence, he stirred the fire—now gone to dull red embers—looking deeply into the coals.

"I'm here. . . ." she called, guiding his attempt to *see*. *"Here."*

A face formed in the crimson glow. She was old; silver-shot hair lay in waves over her shoulders. Even in her age, she remained a striking beauty.

"I see you," he whispered, voice low so as not to disturb the other sleepers. "Such Power . . . is it you who stands before us, drives your warriors against us?"

Heron shook her head, image shimmering in the rising heat of the fire. "Your son is responsible. You know him, don't you? The one born of blood?"

"No, I don't know him."

"Too bad. I'd hoped you'd seen him in your visions. He's a man of partial Dreams, glimmerings of greatness. He's un-schooled, impetuous. Like a caribou bull driven mad by flies, he charges ahead, heedless of the consequences."

"What does he have to do with—"

"He'll be the death of your people."

Cold fear constricted around his heart. "How? Your people are too few to stand against us. He can't—"

"Not alone. Why don't you ask about your other son?"

A tickle of icy sweat threaded down the side of his face. *"The boy with the rainbow. You . . . know him?"*

"Wolf Dreamer," she whispered, a curious awe in her tone. "He's powerful, man of the Others. Powerful like I could only wish."

"He'll join with his brother to destroy us?" Ice Fire shook his head wearily. "They can't. Not even with the help of your potent magic. We'll trample them—and you—into the snow." But he knew his fear showed on his taut face.

She cocked her head curiously. "Did you know that once, long ago, your people and mine were one tribe? We can be again."

"The same people?" He studied her serious expression. "If we were . . . why did we split?"

"Over the Dreaming. Your clans drove us out because they feared us as magicians. Thought we could witch a person's soul and pitch it into the void. That's why you're the only Dreamer among the Mammoth People—you killed the blood-line. Fools . . ."

"We didn't kill it," he said, heart thundering at mention of his sons. "We gave it to you."

"A very great gift, but it'll destroy you."

Anger and dread mixed into a terrible brew inside him. He raised both fists to the sky and screamed, "How! Tell me!"

"Your sons are coming for you. Coming from different directions, but coming."

The coals flickered and shifted as if they were underwater, and the Dream vanished.

Folding his arms over his chest, he hung his head and hugged himself, shivering violently in the cold. "My sons . . . ."

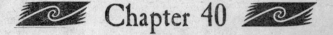

Chapter 40

Wolf Dreamer stood on the cloud-capped ridge, watching the People wind toward him. Tender emotions of warmth caressed his breast. They'd returned, safe and sound. His eyes searched for old friends.

A gray curtain of snow slashed at the undulating plain, roaring up behind One Who Cries as he led his band around the twisted glacial rocks. Wind Woman battered at them, breath like a knife in the chill of oncoming evening.

Wavering voices came to him on the gale.

"Thought we wouldn't make it!" Singing Wolf called, a smile on his lips as he pointed to the puffing billows of Heron's geyser where the steam blew away in torn clouds. "Looked like the storm would get us first."

"It's Wolf Dreamer!" One Who Cries shouted back, lifting a hand to wave.

He waved back, a smile lighting his deeply tanned face. The band trudged up to meet him.

"Well," Singing Wolf said, puffing out his cheeks. "We're here. I can't say how much I dreamed of this little valley in the last year." He turned, smiling. "It's good to see you, Wolf Dreamer."

"And you, cousin," he said, clapping the man gently on the shoulder. "Seeing you kindles a warmth in my breast. How was the Renewal?"

Singing Wolf exchanged a glance with One Who Cries before lowering his eyes to frown at the icy ground.

Wolf Dreamer tensed, gaze roving the People. *So many new women.* He studied them, sullen, bent under heavy burdens, eyes filled with hatred. The dogs were packed, even the puppies. So much baggage? For only a seasonal migration? He spied Mouse; she'd remarried to Three Falls. Her hair was cut short. Quickly he looked over the group. *So many widows.*

"What's happened?"

One Who Cries said through a long exhale, "The People are in trouble."

"What kind?"

"Raven Hunter raided the camps of the Others all summer." Singing Wolf looked away. "I went with him, once. I saw things that sickened me."

"Have they returned the attacks? Is that why so many of the women—"

"Yes, many times. All the clans are suffering. Our own young men are running off to defend their villages or avenge deaths even as we speak."

An ache touched Wolf Dreamer's stomach. He whispered, "During the Long Dark? That's crazy. No one can survive."

"Crow Caller," One Who Cries said reluctantly, "is promising the warriors spirit protection from the Soul Eaters."

His gut twisted at the name. He clenched his fists tightly to still the rising tide of emotion. "Don't they know by now he's a false Dreamer?"

Singing Wolf lightly kicked an ice-encrusted rock rooted to the ridge top. "Your brother has convinced most otherwise."

"Blessed Star People!" He squeezed his eyes shut, concentrating on the chill breath of Wind Woman flooding his face and flapping his hood. "Heron will know what to do. Come, let's seek her counsel."

"Are you sure she won't mind us being around?" Singing Wolf moaned. "We don't want her mad at us."

"She sent me to find you. She won't mind—at least not for a while."

In relief, Singing Wolf and One Who Cries laughed and

nodded, heading up the trail. People straggled behind them, the Other women casting hard looks at him as they labored past. Green Water herded several small children.

She smiled as she climbed to stand beside him. "You're looking well, Runs In . . . Wolf Dreamer."

He returned her smile feebly, wanting desperately to ask about Dancing Fox, but frightened of the answer. "You too, Green Water," he said lamely.

She laid a tender hand on his sleeve, a pained look in her soft brown eyes. "She's not here."

"She stayed with—"

"No. It's a long story."

"Tell me."

"She followed you, ran away."

"What . . ." The air went out of his lungs. *She tried to come to me.* "What stopped her?"

"Your brother found her before she escaped and dragged her back to Crow Caller."

Hatred welled hotly. His brother . . . always trying to hurt him. "What happened then?"

"Crow Caller accused her of adultery and cast her out. Raven Hunter . . . took 'care' of her." She tilted her head awkwardly, face downcast.

"Are you trying to tell me he . . ."

She lifted her eyes to probe his apologetically. "He kept her alive."

No! His own brother had raped the woman he loved? He rubbed hands roughly over his face, hiding his shock and disgust. "Raven Hunter. Everything comes back to Raven Hunter."

Green Water chewed her lip for a moment, looking at him from reserved, pool-like eyes. "She is coming."

His gaze shot to the trail and he took a halting step forward. She caught his arm.

"It won't be for a while."

"Why? Where is she?"

"Talon befriended her after Crow Caller cursed her soul. Together they left the camps, lived for a while in exile. Now she comes here, fleeing Raven Hunter's robes. Talon left the band to go off and die. Fox went looking for her and found us the next morning, saying she would stay with her friend until the end.''

"The storms are coming!"

Green Water pulled him back by the sleeve as he started up the trail. "She'll be fine. She's . . . well, not the girl you once knew. The last year has hardened her, like a good dart shaft in fire. She's fine out there. The girl you knew is gone . . . as is the young man she once smiled at."

He swallowed, searching her honest face.

"Trust me. She'll be here in. her own time."

"But she's coming."

His eyes fixed on the distant horizon where snow-heavy clouds twisted across the heavens and his heart pounded in anticipation, hope like a dull blade in his gut.

"She's well," Green Water comforted. "For an expelled woman. Just don't expect her to—"

"I'll punish him." He knotted a fist inside his thick mittens. "I swear, I'll pay him back."

"Shhh!" She placed mittened fingers to his lips. "Don't, Wolf Dreamer. Don't say it aloud. Not now. We need someone strong and wise to lead us. The People are already shredded like a mouse skin in a weasel's mouth."

He stood stiffly, not breathing. People straggled by, figures black in the night, battered by Wind Woman's merciless breath. So many? How would they feed them all? Diffidently, he forced himself to turn and blend with the flow of bodies. He had to talk to Heron.

As they rounded the corner, he could see Heron's shelter and the People gathering in awe on the banks of the hot springs. Murmurs of amazement filtered through the crowd. He searched but didn't see the old Dreamer. *Curious. She usually greets people before they get this close.*

Gazing through the eddying bodies, he looked to her shelter. The flap hung motionless. Somewhere in the back of his mind, dread built, a feeling as terrible as if the end of the world had come. He picked up his feet to run, panic increasing with each pounding step. Stopping before the flap, he shouted, "Heron!"

No answer came.

Breathlessly, he called again, "Heron?" He felt as though

his heart were breaking and he didn't know why. He stepped forward cautiously in the dark.

"Wolf Dreamer?"

He turned at Broken Branch's voice. "Where's Heron?"

The old woman waddled out of the dark, features illuminated by a burning knot of willow root. "In there . . . When you left to find the People, she did something. Said I should leave her alone."

From her ancient fingers, he took the root and clamped it hard in his trembling fingers. Then, bending low, he stepped inside, the fire flickering and jumping yellowly off the walls.

On the floor, Heron glared up at him, glassy eyes shining eerily in the light of the torch. Beside her lay gatherings of willow stems and . . . mushrooms. Their flat black shapes loomed dangerous, deadly, where they lay exposed in the folds of the fox hide.

Horror twisted his soul. He cried pitiably, "No . . . no, what did you do?"

"Dream . . . Dream, boy." The words shuddered from her mouth.

He crouched and touched her arm tenderly. "You're so cold."

Frantic, he plucked wood from the pile, applying the burning roots, thankful as flames licked up around the dry sticks.

"Here, sit up. Let me—"

"C-can't, boy. Poison. Can't move. Can't . . . feel. Dreaming, boy. Drifting. Not . . . not here."

He dropped to his knees, heart bursting, tears streaming down his cheeks. "Fight them," he whispered. "You can do it. Don't let their spirits beat you!"

He wrapped her in her robes, keeping her warm where she lay beside the crackling coals. "Please, Heron. Come back. I need you. I'm not finished learning."

"Dream, boy!" she croaked, saliva dribbling down her chin, eyes unfocused. "See? Look . . . there!" She cried:

"Built a big mountain out of dirt.
Raised on sweat and hurt.
Rose so high over the river.
Eating plants! Bah! No spirit in that.
Not like blood-filled liver.

"Father of Waters flows so rich,
Trickles water into the ditch.
Grow a plant, so tall and green,
Fruit is yellow. I have seen.
Feathers colored, the dead are laid.
Logs across and dirt is made.
Lazy sloth, in baskets carried—
Sun, man, and woman high are married."

"She's raving," Broken Branch murmured from behind him, voice shaky. "I don't know what to do for her."

"Nothing," Wolf Dreamer said in a pained voice. "We talked about this possibility months ago. I think I understand what's happening to her. She'll live so long as she follows the Dream. If she hesitates, loses herself for an instant—she's dead."

"Sun God!" Heron exploded, body jerking.

"Born of Light!
Spiral, you god of gaudy feathers!
Carry the plant upon your back.
Parch the seeds upon the rack.
Rocks like sky are passing by."

A black look crossed her face.

"Sun children . . . kill each other.
Long way south for the death of a brother.
Hot, dry, war is nigh.
Sing, Sun God, blood rises . . . stingers in the sky.

"And among the People?
Come the brothers!
Born of Sun. One is slayed.
Here, by the long trail, his corpse is laid.
Blood is spread, from the head.
Black one goes . . . aye, he's dead.
He who loves is lost and gone.
Render of the fair heart's song.
Woman weep, for not you know.
Lose forever—or live in snow!"

"That's it," he whispered, rocking her gently back and forth in his arms. "Follow the Dream through."

"You, boy," she whispered.

"You. Born of Father Sun.
Laid in the light next to night.
Choose, my people.
Dance the Father you don't know.
South, ever south we go . . .
Find an end to the blowing snow."

She blinked spastically.

"Death in the high plains.
Others come.
Our old path they follow from.
Shelters they dig in the ground.
Made like holes in the round.
Farther . . . farther south they go.
Shelters.
Rock piled high. Raise the infants to the god in the sky.
Earth, hey Earth, from it spread.
Raise the underworld of the dead.

"Flight of the bird, so big, so loud.
Calls the lightning from the cloud."

"What's she talking about?" Broken Branch asked.
Wolf Dreamer shook his head. "I don't—"

"Monster creatures on bellies crawl.
Bite a man's foot. Watch him fall.
Legless, armless, hair of scale.
Shakes a rattle on his tail.
Teeth of poison, hollow flail,
Makes blood black and frail."

Wolf Dreamer closed his eyes, her hand bound in his.

"East, aye, east.
Then south the trail.

Born of ice . . . the mother's womb.
Oh, black brother, there lies your doom.
Taken by sea, their father came,
Born of Sun, of Sun the same.
One must live and one must die.
See the souls rise to the sky.

"The sky? Aye, always the sky.
Blazing hot, and white the land,
Scorched by burning brand.
Dream the big beasts to the stars, away.
Their corpses bleach on dusty clay.
Change the land the People tread.
Find a new way . . . or we'll all be dead.
Learn the grass, the root, the berry.
Time is short, life not merry.
Pound and grind, grind and pound,
While the hot wind blows around."

"How do we know," Broken Branch muttered hoarsely, "what she means?"

"Who . . . who called?" Heron's head twisted. *"A voice out of time . . . Under it all, lies old pain."*

"It's me, you old hag," Broken Branch said in a strained voice.

"Hush!" Wolf Dreamer ordered in terror. Broken Branch's hand flew to her quivering mouth. Wolf Dreamer pulled Heron close, whispering in her ear, "Hold the Dream. Don't let go of it!"

"Broken Branch," Heron muttered, shaking her head violently. *"Death to the west! Bear Hunter? Bear Hunter! Come back to . . . to . . ."*

She stiffened, gasping, mouth open, eyes wide. *"Back to . . . the Dream. Gone . . . with Bear Hunter. Gone . . ."*

She stiffened, tongue protruding, images of horror reflected in her eyes. *"Can't . . . love . . ."*

The old woman went limp in his arms.

Stunned, he waited, rubbing his thumb across the back of her hand. "Heron? *Dream.* Follow it through!"

Her eyes emptied in the flickers of the fire. No expression changed her slack face.

"No . . ." he whispered in agony, shaking her gently. "No, don't leave me."

Broken Branch wailed, "She's gone! No, I didn't know what I was doing!"

"It wasn't you, Grandmother," he comforted. "It was Bear Hunter that killed her."

Broken Branch swallowed. "No, can't be. Dead. The man's been dead for years . . . years."

"She loved him." He fought the growing pit of cold expanding in his stomach. "She told me once. Can't Dream . . . and love."

The pain caught him unawares, wrapping around him, stinging his eyes, burning his heart. He barely heard himself start sobbing in anguish.

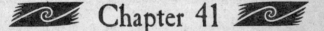 Chapter 41

Back bowed to the blowing snow, she walked. Her heart thudded hollowly against her rib cage.

She turned, looking back at the blowing gray-white swirls of snow. The high point where she'd laid Talon's lifeless body was wrapped in haze. Wind Woman, in a mirroring of her soul, picked that moment to whip the ground blizzard into a frenzy, blasting her with stinging snow and gravel.

Dancing Fox flinched from the gale, turning her steps again to the trail left by Singing Wolf and One Who Cries, seeing their marks, rocks piled atop one another. Step by miserable step, she walked, Wind Woman's harsh breath flapping her pack about on her back, sawing the tump line viciously into her forehead.

A deep emptiness loomed in her soul; another piece of her life lay frozen behind her, obscured by the endless spirals of snow. Spirals, like the rest of her life. An endless line going nowhere, a way of marking the turns of a circle. Always she returned to the place she'd begun, her soul naked and alone.

Jaw muscles clamped, a crying knot of hunger in her stomach, she walked, step after step, placing her feet just so on the rocks, using a three-point stance to cross sections where the snow made footing treacherous.

As the Long Dark grew, she stopped and camped by a pile of rocks marking the trail. Curling on her side wrapped in her double parkas and robes, she touched the jumbled rock.

"A link with the People," she whispered, blinking tiredly. "Proof that there's a future, if I can just keep following."

She glanced fearfully at the swirling snow, then pulled the robes over her head and closed her eyes. Her dreams revolved around Runs In Light, the softness of his eyes, the gentleness of his touch. Maybe Talon had been wrong? Maybe he'd still want her?

The next day, she ate the last of the dried mammoth meat—rationed into ever-scanter meals—and squinted out over the vast plains of gusting white. Would the storm never let up?

"I'm coming, Runs In Light."

She staggered along, placing one foot ahead of the other.

Around midday, she lost the trail. Somewhere, somehow, the piles of rock vanished. She backtracked, following her steps as far as possible, nothing looking the same. At the last vestige of her trail, she looked around, circling, seeking the marking cairns. Nothing.

Panic tightened at the base of her heart. Almost frantic, she ran, slipping, stumbling, barking her shins on angular outcrops of glacial rock. Struggling to the top of a ridge, she put a hand to her eyes and searched the land: nothing, no trail.

"No," she gritted through clenched teeth. "I can't be lost. I can't!"

Only the howl of Wind Woman's coarse breath answered. The arms of doom twined around her.

Stark branches of willow squatted on inverted images in the hot pool, rippling with the gusting wind. Singing Wolf stared at them, concentrating on the feel of the warm mist. A deep fear clutched at him. Something was wrong in the world, terribly wrong. It was as though a malignancy lurked out in the shadows, waiting with frightening patience for the People to grow comfortable and fat before it pounced.

Shoving his hands deep in his pockets, he fought the eerie sense of impending disaster. He'd never known this type of gnawing disquiet. It seemed as though the very ground beneath his feet might open and swallow him at any instant.

"You're worried?"

She came up behind him, placing hands on his shoulders.

"He's been gone two turnings of the moon." Singing Wolf filled his lungs, puffing out condensed breath.

"Green Water says he has to deal with himself. Understand Heron's death, and make peace with his conscience."

"You saw him when he left us." Singing Wolf shook his head slowly. "I've seen that look in the eyes of the old ones. It's there when they go out to die. Just empty, you know?" He turned halfway around to probe her sensitive eyes. "Like nothing's left in the soul."

"He'll heal."

"Maybe. If he lives. Only a fool goes out on the ice like that. Death is everywhere. All the cracks, the blocks broken and jumbled. No one can cross that. No one."

"He thought he could. You heard him talk about the buffalo." Laughing Sunshine tilted her face up to the warm fog, letting it drench her skin.

"I heard. When it comes to the buffalo and tapeworm, I believe him, too. But across the ice? No, we can't do that. That hole Wolf told him about must be the way."

"What if he can't find the hole?"

A tremor of anxiety touched him. "You think the children could walk across the shifting ice blocks? *I* wouldn't walk across them!" He lowered his eyes to stare at the wavering reflections of the winter-stark willows again. "If he can't find it we'll have to go back north—try and sneak past the Others."

Her hands tightened on his shoulder. "Buffalo Back is coming. Did you hear?"

He puffed out a weary exhale. "I did. It worries me sick. They run to us in the middle of the Long Dark? How will we feed them all? This valley doesn't have that much game."

Shamefacedly, she murmured, "That herd of mammoth are up in the foothills. One Who Cries wants to go hunt them.

In the deep snow, you'll do all right. Mammoth can't move in the drifts so well.''

"The old bull, he was Heron's. I wouldn't want to. I know Heron's dead, but her soul clings here. Hangs in the air. Waiting, watching. I feel it.''

She nodded, tugging the strings of her hood tight against the worrying of Wind Woman. A long silence stretched between them.

They stared at the western mountains, the glaciers rouged with pink fingers as the southern sun angled through the biting air. Clouds scudded out of the north, threatening even more snow. The puckered nipples of piled rock gleamed eerily as long drifts of snow tapered away from the knobby tops. Over the bitter land, the Long Dark dropped, each day shorter than the last. Wind Woman's harsh breath scoured the earth.

"Wolf Dreamer will be back.''

"You seem so sure.''

"I've always believed his Dream . . . even when you didn't.''

"I was younger then. Foolish. Broken Branch made me take another look.''

"Then you went back to see what was right—whose Dream to believe. You've seen.''

"Yes.'' Singing Wolf lifted a muscular shoulder. "But never in all the memory of the People have so many fled to such a small place. What if there's no way out? What if Raven Hunter doesn't drive the Others away? What if there's no way across the ice?'' He turned, looking down at her in the gray light of day. "We could die. I want you and my child to live.''

Chapter 42

Slick, so slick. Wind Woman tried to tear his fragile grip loose from the ice as he climbed. Around Wolf Dreamer, snow blew in wreaths, chattering softly across the ice. In the perpetual gray of the Long Dark, he proceeded, step-by-step, grip-by-grip.

Heron's soul had been prayed to the Blessed Star People.

Who am I? Where am I going? Heron, why have you left me here all alone? What did your Dream mean? I've tried, but I can't unravel the symbols: man-made mountains? A winding river? Sun Gods? Thunderbirds? A desiccated land and a scaled animal with no legs? What is this tall grass with yellow seeds? What are these rock shelters? Fantasy?

An aching numbness left his thoughts spinning without direction.

"Lonely. I'm so lonely." Around him, hour by hour, the Long Dark spun out its cold fury, ice cracking, the glacier ever active.

"Ghosts," he whispered. "Let them come. Them, and the spirits of the Long Dark." To the cloud-streaked blackness, he raised his hands. "Here I am! *Come and get me! I defy you!*"

Silence thundered at him.

His food had dwindled to one small sack of fat-filled pemmican. And around him, canted slabs of ice beckoned death. The wrong step, an inadvertent advance across a cornice, and he'd fall to be trapped forever in the hidden crevasses within the ice. Compressed, fractured, twisted and tortured, the gritty ice jutted and sloped. He'd entered a world of jumbled angles—no surface level, cold, murky shadows inhabited by the chill breath of the ice. Slabs towered above him, snow sifting down from the edges so high overhead. Gaps and holes fell away to shaded depths below—a trap of eternal frigid darkness.

Step-by-step, he probed, using his dart shaft to check the footing, moving with constant hesitation.

"Dancing Fox?" Her face filled his restless sleep.

"Thrown out? Disgraced? Why? Because you would love me? Because you would have followed the Wolf Dream?"

Love killed Heron. She told you . . . told you that day in the pool. A human who Dreams can't have the distraction, can't join his life with another's. If he does, he can't lose himself to the One. Can't forget who he is—and must be.

He gasped, fighting the hollow hurt inside. "Is nothing left for me? Am I to be alone forever? Hear me, Father Sun! *Am I to be alone forever?"*

His pain mingled with the gusting sigh of Wind Woman.

"Numb. Life is numb, black, like the Long Dark. That way we live. Step-by-step. Pain by pain." He looked up into the scudding smoke-shaded clouds. "Can't I be like everyone else? Can't I . . . love?"

Wind Woman worried his parka, howling her mad rebuttal across the cornices and spears of ice. She moaned and wailed, a haunting reflection of his misery.

"I don't want to be alone!"

Two weeks onto the ice, he could find no route. Only the wind at his back provided the direction.

From his memory, voices mocked.

"You're crazy to go out there now," One Who Cries had moaned, arms lifted. "Wait. Wait until spring. Then go. You can't go out and kill yourself just because—"

"I'll be back. I've got the Dream. Got the proof. Now I need the way."

They'd gone as far as the ice with him. Two of the dogs that had followed him were gone—lost in hidden crevasses in the ice. But he'd learned from their mistakes. The ice terrified him . . . worse than the reflection of anguish in Heron's dead eyes.

The pemmican lasted two more days.

Stillness. It woke him out of a deep sleep. Wary, cautious, he resettled himself, blinking in the grayness as he snugged his robes around his throat.

"Mad," he whispered. "I've gone mad. Hear the silence?" He laughed at himself. "I finally hear the silence."

He stood, cupping ice-encrusted mittens around his mouth, hollering, "I'm mad! Crazy! Hear me, Father Sun? Hear me,

Star People? See me! Crazy, huh?'' Turning to stare at the endless sculpted ice around him, he dropped his voice to a quiet whisper. "Crazy."

Silence. No wind. He chuckled, shaking his head. The growling of his empty belly echoed in the night. Behind him a steep-sloped drift rose. To either side, sheltering slabs of gritty ice thrust toward the sky.

Which way? He yawned, staring over the twisted vastness. A wonderland of—

The call wavered in the crystal clarity of the still air. Distant, it quavered and died, winding through the shattered world of snow-capped ice.

"Wolf . . . ?"

The eerie yips drifted across the waste again, faint, so far away.

There. That way. Noting the landmarks in his mind, he set out. The polished shaft of his dart served as a staff, seeking, ever seeking in the snow. He barely caught himself before he stepped over nothingness, the crevasse bridged by a thin drift of snow.

Backtrack, check the reference points. Pick a potential route around the crevasse, go. Step-by-step, grip by perilous grip.

Everything is lost to me now. I have nothing. Heron, you let love kill you. Dancing Fox? I need you. But can I let myself love you?

The ice shifted. He froze, barely breathing. A grinding came from beneath. For long moments he stood painfully still, arms outspread, fingers knotting in the side of the slab he traversed. The minute rumblings diminished.

"Ghosts . . ." He sighed. Relief warm in his veins, he extended a careful hand. Took another step, slowly working his way off the tilted block and onto another precarious slab of ice jutting up at an impossible angle.

Step-by-step, he continued, seeing where snow had crumbled and fallen into blue-black cracks in the ice. He slipped, rolled, caught himself at the last moment, and scrambled across a declivity. Below, his darts clattered on hard ice from where he'd dropped them in the mad bid for life.

"Close, ghosts. You hear? Close that time. Come on! *Come get me!*"

Panting fear, heart pounding in his chest, he reeled in the gut line he'd tied to the shafts of his darts. One by one, he checked the stone points, assuring himself they hadn't been damaged. Once more, he began the journey, going by feel, seeking that long low cry he'd heard earlier.

Father Sun worked his way across the southern borders of the sky, casting long black shadows across the ice wall. By night, Wind Woman had renewed her fury.

Crouched in a hollow excavated in the lee of a drift, he lulled himself to sleep with, "I heard it. I heard Wolf. He called. I know it."

As he drifted off to sleep, the Dream came again.

He trotted with Wolf along the Big River. Again he passed through the darkness and climbed the glacial walls to stare out over the green valley.

Dancing Fox waited there. Like a seal, she rose from a hot pool, water coursing down her brown body in silver streams. Her wet black hair—shining in the brilliant light—clung to her glistening body. She spread her arms as she walked toward him, drops like dew on her skin. He reached for her, feeling his desire build. She smiled, sunlight warm on the curve of her breasts, nipples erect in the cool air. Under the water, her legs began to part, ready to enfold his manhood.

As his fingertips traced hers, Heron's voice grated from someplace above. Dancing Fox stiffened, fear glazing her gentle eyes. As he watched, she changed, face wrinkling, shrinking, becoming Heron in death—terror etched forever in her eyes.

He jerked awake, shuddering wildly. "No, no, I . . ."

In the distance, an animal's soft haunting cries called to him. He pushed up, cold stabbing at his flesh, and gripped his darts.

"I'm coming, Wolf."

When morning came, his stomach cramped with hunger. A ground blizzard obscured everything within a hand's length of his face. Travel? When he couldn't see his very feet below him?

He dug another snow shelter and wearily closed his eyes and leaned back, an image of the green valley burning in his mind. The Wolf Dream lay just beyond his nightmares, beckoning, eternally over the horizon, veiled by blowing white.

Bleary-eyed, he set out after the wind dropped. Foot by foot, hand by hand, he continued, the gale to his back.

"I don't want to die out here." He shook his head dizzily, harshly reprimanding, "You're a coward! A crazy coward. You led the People to their deaths!" Then in a pathetic tone: "Nothing's working anymore. Can't live like a man . . . love. Heron's gone."

He laughed softly, derisively, weaving on his feet. "Dreamer? Me?" He looked up to the graying in the west. "Did you betray me, Wolf? Huh? Father Sun, did you let him betray me *and the People*?"

He caught himself teetering on the verge of a crevasse and stumbled backward, gasping, as he stared owlishly down into the darkness.

"I could just step off. Finish it. Become one with the ice. So easy. No more hunger. No more hurt."

The sound barely registered at first. A crunching of snow.

Blinking, he looked around, seeing nothing in the ever-present whiteness.

Again the sound pierced his concentration. This time, he crouched, staring. A shadow moved and hope welled like a tidal wave.

"Wolf?" He stepped forward. "Please, Wolf."

He tensed, heart slamming against his ribs. He licked his lips and swallowed. A black mote moved in the darkness. A mote that could have been a beast's nose.

The huge animal lumbered from behind the drift.

"Grandfather White Bear," he whispered in terror.

Chapter 43

Ice Fire stepped over the body of an Enemy. He hesitated, looking down into the young man's face. Barely more than a child, he'd died in the fighting, the side of his head bashed in.

"So young."

"Most Respected Elder?"

Ice Fire turned, looking toward Walrus where he picked his way through the ravaged camp. Mammoth-hide shelters lay smoldering. Smoke darkened the skies, ash swirling like snow. The dead lay in mutilated humps around the perimeter.

"Yes?"

Walrus grinned triumphantly. "We taught them this time, eh?"

Ice Fire filled his lungs, exhaling slowly, watching the condensation of breath before him. "Did we?"

A scream from behind them pierced the crystal air, grating on Ice Fire's nerves. He didn't turn, knowing without seeing what transpired with the woman.

"If we didn't," Walrus confided, "that will." He jerked a mittened thumb over his shoulder. "Men quickly lose their fire for fighting when they worry about their wives and mothers giving birth to their foe's sons."

He cocked his head grimly. "Don't forget, we've lost nearly as many women as they have."

Walrus waved it off. "We're stronger than they are. Their fighting spirit will die long before ours."

"Maybe."

"Ha! They thought we wouldn't fight back in the depths of the Long Dark. The fools."

Ice Fire's lips twitched. Not even his counsel could hold the warriors back. Too many atrocities had passed. Too many horrible deaths discovered in the wake of the Enemy's retaliation. His own warriors wanted blood—pain for pain.

"They are us," Ice Fire whispered, the wind gusting down from the north batting the long silver braids about his chest where they hung out of his hood. "We are them."

Walrus frowned uneasily. "What did you say?"

Ice Fire looked into the warrior's confused face. "Cousins. At least, that's what the old woman said." He lifted a shoulder. "I can believe it, upon reflection. They speak our language. No other Enemy do that. Our beliefs are not so different. Like us, they—"

"Then they've lost something in the past," Walrus asserted arrogantly. "I see no honor in them. I found my sister and her child, the infant's brains mashed out on a rock and crawling with maggots! That's honor? No, Most Respected Elder, these are less than beasts we deal with. I, for one, shall sing praises to the Great Mystery when I finally slay the last of them."

Ice Fire stared at him, trying to see through, into his mind. Walrus looked back for a moment before dropping his eyes and nodding, striding purposefully back toward where they burned the Enemy warrior with glowing coals. The women and children had been rounded up and were being forced to watch the display, lest they consider trying to escape.

He picked his way up the side of the valley, crusted snow crunching underfoot. A wrenching scream tore the very air; his steps faltered.

Looking back, he saw his own warriors bent over the bound prisoner. The man lay writhing, spread-eagled, naked on the icy ground. Despite the distance, Ice Fire could make out the action. While the warriors whooped and screamed insults, Red Flint scooped glowing coals from the fire pit, pouring them over the man's crotch. The shrieks intensified.

Ice Fire turned, features like graven stone as he looked up to see the lights of the Monster Children's War struggling across the sky. The Monster Children? Not the tears of the Great Mystery? Already the slave women's colorful cosmology intruded, softening the dogma of the White Tusk Clan.

A blast of ice-laden wind staggered him. "Great Mystery? How can I undo this? What is your purpose here? Can such hatred ever be untangled?"

The sound of the wind through the rocks echoed like mocking laughter.

Green Water saw the woman's shape as the ever-present mists shredded and blew away as the wind picked up.

Straightening and arching her back, she stared at the hobbling figure out in the flats.

"Someone there," she said, pointing.

Laughing Sunshine and Curlew followed her finger, nodding. "One of the People."

"Dancing Fox!" Green Water whispered. "One of you go, make sure we've got a warm fire and lots of stew. She looks hurt."

Green Water unlaced her snowshoes from her pack, tying them on to her long boots. Taking a bearing on the sun, she started out, making her way down the long slope to the flats below. As the mists whirled away, the glare increased, forcing her to slip snow goggles over her eyes. Staring through the slits, she continued.

By the time she made the bottoms, stringers of snow began angling diagonally across before her. The dot that marked the struggling figure vanished in the streamers of white.

"This is foolish," she grumbled under her breath. "Should have waited for the others."

Still, she plodded, swinging her broad snowshoes wide in the waddling walk necessary to keep from barking shins and tripping over herself.

How far? Green Water kept going, aware of the added mass in her belly. The baby slowed her, made her awkward.

She stopped, searching this way and that. Could she have turned? Checking the position of Father Sun against the time she'd spent, she looked again at the angle of the blowing snow before backsighting on Heron's ridge.

"Must be farther." She sighed and caught her breath before trudging on.

"Fox?" she hollered into the snow glaze. "Are you there?"

Nothing came but the whisper of snow blowing over the rippling sastrugi.

Green Water checked the slant of Father Sun in the sky. The baby shifted inside. Her legs had begun to ache. How long to get back? An hour and a half? Two? She hesitated, torn.

"Did you really see anyone out here?" she wondered aloud.

Racked by indecision, she found it easier to continue, fear

eating at her for every step she took beyond the relative safety of the camp.

"And what if it was one of the Others·you saw? What if Dancing Fox is long dead and you're walking right into a thrown dart point? What then?" she growled to herself, striding on, wishing she'd waited for One Who Cries. Wind Woman blew harder, the landmarks on the horizon obscured in the shifting curtain of wind-driven snow.

"Fox? Anyone?" She cupped her hands, calling again and again. "Who's there?"

Nervously, she ran her tongue around her mouth, shaking her head. Father Sun cast angling shadows through the ground blizzard, Wind Woman's temperamental gusts coming ever stronger.

Green Water stared over her backtrail, seeing her tracks filled in as she walked. Hunger tightened. Pregnancy did that. It chafed at the belly constantly, drained her of energy.

She called again into the wind and looked around. "No way I'll make it back before dark," she mumbled. The tiny irritation of fear fed on her hopelessness.

She turned, circling.

Faint, a slight mew caught her ear. She cocked her head. "Dancing Fox?"

Nothing. She started back, the ache of overstressed leg muscles leaving a trembling in her hips. She stopped, turning again into the north, walking back over her tracks. Indecision tormented her. She *had* heard that faint sound.

"You're killing your baby—and yourself," she spat hoarsely. "Go home."

But she shouted into the wind again. *"Fox?"*

"Here."

Faint, ever so faint. Green Water shuffled forward hurriedly, heart leaping. *"Where?"*

"Here." The voice came from upwind.

A faint brown form emerged from the restless snow only to be obscured by another gust. Green Water hurried· forward, panting, awkward with her distended belly.

"Fox?"

"Green Water?" Dancing Fox blinked up at her from sunken features. Snow crusted around her hood. She shook her head weakly. "Are you real? Not part of . . . of a Dream, or something?"

Green Water smiled and dropped to her knees, taking Fox's hand, squeezing it hard. "There, you feel that? Would a Dream squeeze you like that?"

Dancing Fox's forehead lined with confusion as she looked at her snow-caked mittens. "I . . . I don't know. I don't understand much anymore. Can't think too good. Get confused. Just go south, that's all. Lost the trail."

Green Water patted her on the shoulder. "Well, I saw you. You're almost there. Come on, One Who Cries will have everyone out looking. It's almost dark and I'm not home. He's a worrier when I'm in trouble."

Dancing Fox nodded loosely, head bobbing. "You have any food? Can't hardly walk anymore."

Green Water helped her up only to have Fox crumble in a heap, crying in pain.

"What's wrong?" She bent down, staring into Dancing Fox's lined face.

"Forgot for a moment." She stared up stupidly. "Hurt my ankle. Slipped on a rock a week ago. Hurts. Hurts worse than anything I've ever done to myself. Aches when I try and sleep. Like lances of fire when I walk."

"A week ago? And you're still traveling?"

For a moment, a sharp look filled Fox's face. "Cursed right, I am. You see a lot of choice out here?" Then her eyes lost focus.

"How long since you've eaten?"

Fox's brow lined again as she stared into the snow, thinking hard. "I don't know. Found a dead caribou. Nothing but bones . . . about two weeks ago, maybe. Ate the marrow. Then there was nothing . . . but snow . . . and wind. You know how Wind Woman is . . . mad, blowing . . . always . . . blowing. . . ." Her voice drifted away.

"Come on, lean on me. Another couple of hours won't kill you if you've made it this far."

"Ought to rest, sleep."

Green Water pulled her mitten off, reaching down the front of Dancing Fox's parka, feeling the skin of her chest, reaching around to an armpit.

"No, you're walking, girl. You rest now, you won't get up. You're too cold. Lost too much heat. Come on, up."

Green Water grunted, struggling with Fox's weight.

"Where's your other snowshoe? Why's this one tied to your pack?"

"Other one broke. When I fell. Tough to walk on one snowshoe. Other ankle hurts like a rock-smashed thumb."

"Here, hold on to me. I'll tie this on your good foot. You lean on me. Three feet is better than one, huh?"

Together, they turned, the last of the gray twilight fading in the southwest.

Teeth gritted, Green Water took the woman's weight. "You'll make it. You can do it."

Dancing Fox mumbled under her breath, "Nothing left. Only me."

"That's right. Keep going."

"Blessed Star People, that ankle hurts!" Fox groaned. "Why do we do this? Huh? Why do we suffer so? What's the reason? What's in living but hurt and pain and misery. People shouldn't have to . . . to live . . . in this kind of—"

"Hush," Green Water chided. "Save your energy for walking. That's it, one step at a time."

Even as she spoke, the breath grated in and out of her throat. Fire burned up her trembling legs, but they continued, Green Water reading the way from the stars.

How long? How many lifetimes did she spend out there?

Vaguely, she remembered One Who Cries calling. A dismembered recollection of him emerging out of the darkness, grabbing her up, hugging her gently and bending over Dancing Fox before bellowing into the storm. Then came hands, more walking, and finally the rocky descent to their shelter in the bottom of the valley.

As she huddled next to the fire, they brought Dancing Fox in, removing her ice-caked parka, rubbing her limbs and trunk, massaging her in the warm heat of the shelter before Singing Wolf cut the long boot from her left leg.

Green Water caught her breath at the size of Dancing Fox's ankle. Mottled and swollen; it hurt just to look at it.

"And she walked a week on that?" One Who Cries was astonished.

"Tough woman." Green Water sighed. "I don't know anyone else who could have done it."

Dancing Fox groaned and turned her head. "I didn't have any choice. There was only me out there . . . only me." And she closed her eyes tightly.

Chapter 44

Raven Hunter watched Three Falls as he looked away. The older hunters always looked away, even Three Falls, who had lost so many of his kin. The younger men, however, watched eagerly as the newest of the warriors of the People bent over the captive Other, leaning down as the man struggled, the skin of his chest gleaming in the firelight.

Crow Caller stroked a bone wand up and down a grooved caribou antler, singing his Dream of Power into the gathering. He chanted to the hollow zizzing of the bone. The warriors swayed back and forth, carried away by the Power of the moment, feeling the strength of their souls.

Raven Hunter smiled to himself, then leaned over the naked man, glaring into the captive's eyes.

"Kill me!" the Other demanded. "You hear? *Kill me!*"

"You'll die, but not just yet." Raven Hunter nodded his approval to an eager young warrior who'd shown exceptional bravery on the war trail, Crow Foot. The youth trotted forward.

"He's yours," Raven Hunter cooed in praise.

Crow Foot smiled suddenly, gazing hungrily at the captive. "Take him."

Bending down, the boy traced an obsidian blade along the Other's chest, watching him writhe as blood streamed hotly. Stifled whimpers escaped the man's clamped teeth. A tear crept past the Other's eyes to trickle down his cheek as Crow Foot moved the sharp edge lower, tracing it around the man's genitals.

"No Other should breed children to fight against us," the boy blurted violently.

Muscles knotting and sliding under sweat-shiny skin, the warrior thrashed and shrieked as the glass edge cut his manhood from his body. A roar of approval erupted from the watching warriors. The youth held the garish prize high, heedless of the blood that trickled down his arm.

Three Falls backed away in disgust, elbowing through the press, ducking through the door flap and into the darkness.

Raven Hunter followed patiently, ducking under behind Three Falls.

"I hate this!" the old warrior gritted through clenched teeth.

"It gives our young men heart." Raven Hunter walked to stand before him, wishing the light was better so he could see Three Falls' eyes. "Such rituals bind us more tightly than if we'd used mammoth sinew. It's a sharing of honor in there."

Three Falls stuck his chin forward, face masked in shadow, breath a white cloud before him. "A sharing of horror, you mean."

The Other screamed shrilly, as if to make the point. Three Falls winced.

"To bind a people together when they've been weak and fragmented is never easy," Raven Hunter reminded. "Think back at how the Others harried us, chased us like caribou. We weren't men to them, no more than I want Others to be men in the eyes of my warriors. Think back, remember those first raids we fought? Hmm? Remember how poorly we did? Look now, outnumbered, we kill many more of them than they kill of us. Why? Because of the courage, the spirit. Just like I'm building in there. You think that young boy won't fight? After I gave him the honor of cutting that Other apart, he'll fight until his heart bursts." Raven Hunter smacked his fist into a palm.

Three Falls lifted a shoulder. "Yes, we fight better. We're meaner—like a dog that's been baited, tortured, and abused with a bear hide. Is that what we're to become, Raven Hunter? Bear dogs? Creatures made berserk at the sight of an Other? A bear dog is less than a dog . . . less than . . . than—"

"Does a bear dog have any choice?" Raven Hunter asked.

"Do we? By becoming meaner, berserk, as you say, we keep our land. So I ask you, what's better? Living as a berserk bear dog? Or dying at the hands of the Others?"

"I . . . I chose to live." He glared nervously as he pushed past Raven Hunter, stalking across the camp, hide-bound feet crunching in the snow.

Raven Hunter shivered, following him with his eyes, stroking his chin thoughtfully as the sharp wind chilled his skin. A deep-seated unease stirring in his chest, he wavered as a particularly fierce gust of wind battered the camp. Eyes slitted against the knives of cold, he ducked back through the flap to the warmth within.

Young warriors cackled joyously before a row of captive Others, eyes gleaming in hatred. The Others, faces like masks, awaited their turn, sweat beading on tight faces. Their eyes reflected the horror.

"So many have left, fleeing south to Runs In Light," he whispered to himself. "But I have the youth bound to me. And with the youth, a man can take a people anywhere."

He pushed into the crowd, enjoying the pride and awe in the warriors' eyes as they looked at him.

The Other had become a bloody whimpering pile of meat. Crow Foot pranced around, stepping high, exhibiting a long section of thigh muscle he'd just stripped from the man's leg. Flinging it into the crowd, he dropped on the man's abdomen, slicing it open to reach within, drawing out a ropy handful of blue-gray intestines.

The warriors whooped and shrilled. Raven Hunter smiled, observing the raptorial faces around him. Indeed, here were warriors—his warriors. The hope of survival.

The next morning, Three Falls was gone.

Bowed under loads of frozen meat, the People struggled up the last rise, the trail familiar now. Breath puffing in the dark, coating the chests of their parkas in frosty white, they shuffled across the crest of the ridge.

"Careful," One Who Cries panted. "Trail's solid ice. Got to go down the side."

Singing Wolf grunted agreement, too tired to do anything else, following on trembling legs as his friend picked his path through the rocks. Behind, Jumping Hare, Curlew Song, and others staggered under their burdens while a long line of dogs shuffled in their trail, backs bent under packs of frozen meat.

Step-by-step they worked down into the valley, the snow melting as if by magic as they walked onto the ground-warmed rock.

"Wonderful thing, these geysers." One Who Cries sighed.

A dog barked, then another, before all the curs in the camp exploded in howls and yips, dashing out to confront the intruders.

Jumping Hare laid into the camp dogs with his dart shafts, keeping them from jumping the pack animals.

"Hello!" Singing Wolf called. "Hey, people. We're here!" He swung the heavy pack from his shoulders, dropping wearily on a rock, head hanging as he fumbled with cold-stiff fingers to undo his webbed snowshoes. Beside him, One Who Cries sighed as he deposited his burden. People emerged from the shelters to come scrambling across the dark rock. ·

"Singing Wolf?"

"Here." He stood to hug his wife, delighted at the feel of her bulging belly against his. Wouldn't be long now and they'd have a family again. The thought warmed him deep inside.

"We got a mammoth cow. Meat enough for everyone here. Some will have to move up there, though. Too much carrying. Not only that, but we saw sign of musk ox," One Who Cries said.

Green Water picked her way through the darkness, hugging her husband. "He's just come back."

One Who Cries frowned, kicking a dog away from the meat. "Who?"

"Wolf Dreamer."

Singing Wolf stopped at the anxious tone in her voice. "Where? What's happened?"

In the darkness, he could see the familiar shrug of her shoulder. "There. In Heron's shelter."

He could feel One Who Cries' eyes on him, waiting. "Jumping Hare. Keep the dogs out of the meat and see that it gets distributed." He started quickly for the shelter, One Who Cries on his heels as he walked the winding path along the pool.

"Wolf Dreamer? You there?" he called at the door.

"Come."

He anxiously licked his lips before lifting the flap. Heron's shelter always prickled his scalp. A Power place to begin with; something about the eyeless skulls, the intricate colorful drawings on the rock, the fetishes in niches, all left a man's gut rotating.

Singing Wolf blinked in the dim light of a fading fire, seeing Wolf Dreamer sitting up, hood thrown back. Then he stopped, One Who Cries pushing alongside, his flat face forward, peering.

But who was this man? His face, once smooth and young, looked pinched. A curious, knowing light burned in his black eyes. As if Runs In Light's features were possessed by someone else—someone different, strange.

"I . . . We were . . ." Words stuck in his throat. "You're back."

Singing Wolf shifted uneasily, waiting for One Who Cries to speak.

Wolf Dreamer smiled wistfully, sensing their disquiet. "I crossed the Big Ice."

Stunned, Singing Wolf dropped to his knees. "You . . ."

Wolf Dreamer nodded serenely. "But the People won't be able to follow in my tracks. It's too dangerous. Lost both the dogs. To cross is, well, a nightmare worse than Crow Caller's threats."

Singing Wolf slumped, weariness flowing back through his exhausted body. "Blessed Star People, that means things are bad."

"Bad?" Wolf Dreamer reached for one of the old sticks from the willow-wood pile and dropped it on the fire to a rising of sparks.

"Very bad," One Who Cries agreed. "In the three turnings of the moon that you've been gone, four camps of people have come over the hills to winter here. Beyond, down where the Big River flows out into the plains, the People find nothing but war. Our young men and the Others, they raid back and forth, moving constantly, striking each other. The old, the children, they can't travel constantly. Not in the Long Dark. So they come here to find peace."

"All but the young men and women?"

Singing Wolf nodded uneasily. "Yes, how did you know? The youth find this new life exciting."

Wolf Dreamer's eyes watered. "But who tells them the winter stories? How is the lore of the People passed on if all they do is run and fight? Who hunts for the old, the young?"

"Only our camp," Singing Wolf said softly.

One Who Cries sighed. "And the Others aren't leaving as Raven Hunter promised. The raids continue endlessly, back and forth. They're fighting through the Long Dark. Can you imagine that? What about the Soul Eaters?"

Singing Wolf added, "And our supplies are dwindling fast."

"What of the Others' supplies? Are they suffering—"

"They trade to different camps to the north and west along the salt water. They have plenty of food and new hides. They move their sick and old to camps farther up where meat has been taken and frozen. Then they send their young men to follow the Big River south, all carrying their weapons over their shoulders."

Wolf Dreamer's jaw muscles bunched under his cheeks. "And my brother?"

Singing Wolf lifted his hands. "He claims he's keeping the Others at bay. The People, at least the ones here—who don't count in the end—wonder. They see only disaster."

Wolf Dreamer nodded.

One Who Cries lowered his eyes. "We had hoped the Wolf Dream . . . That there was a way across the Big Ice."

Wolf Dreamer looked up at them, eyes oddly lit. "Across the Big Ice? No, not for the People. Too many would die, slip, fall, be lost in crevasses. There's no food up there. Only snow, and ice, and gravels melting out. I crossed the Big Ice in a month. Most of it without food."

One Who Cries looked nervously at Singing Wolf. "Then it looks like we'll have to take up Raven Hunter's way. Fight until—"

"No . . ." Wolf Dreamer whispered eerily. "My Dream is right."

"Right?"

Wolf Dreamer nodded. "I crossed the ice. Had to kill Grandfather White Bear up there. But I lived on his flesh." He extended a pouch.

With trembling fingers, One Who Cries undid the binding, spilling out a wealth of claws. Singing Wolf swallowed and looked up.

"Grandfather White Bear? So far south? He eats seals, hunts the ice." One Who Cries shook his head. "I don't understand."

"Bear Power," Singing Wolf added under his breath.

"No matter how he got there, he came, following my scent." Wolf Dreamer smiled at the memory. "I tried to run at first. Then I called him, like I did the caribou. Remember?"

They both nodded nervously.

"I Dreamed him over the slabs of ice. The trail circled a slab thrust up by the ghosts below. There I waited, Dreaming him past, his nose to the snow. As he came, I rose on my toes, Dreaming my dart point to the place behind the shoulder, driving it with all my strength."

"Ahhhh!" One Who Cries sighed, eyes glowing.

"And the dart point you made went true." Wolf Dreamer patted One Who Cries' sleeve. "Grandfather White Bear whirled and twisted and snapped the shaft, but in doing so, sliced his heart in two."

"You did this alone?" Singing Wolf asked, mouth dry.

"Alone." He nodded wearily. "And Grandfather White Bear's blood, heart, and liver gave me strength. His flesh made me strong. His hide gave me warmth beyond my parka and long boots. I lived."

One Who Cries shook his head.

"Then I killed long-horned buffalo that ran free across the vast plains on the other side of the Big Ice. The game is tame. I walked up to animals. They simply looked at me, wary, walking off slowly, or coming close to smell. You see, they've never been hunted by men before."

Singing Wolf straightened slowly, holding his breath. Could it really be true? "No sign of men?"

"None."

"Only the Big Ice lies between us and this . . . wondrous place?"

Wolf Dreamer nodded.

"But you crossed twice!" Singing Wolf cried. "Maybe

just a few of us could build a trail? Find a way for the elders and the children?''

"Impossible," Wolf Dreamer told them, eyes seeing someplace far away. "The ice shifts, blocks slide and crack. Any trail changes as it's made. What was safe the first time will be death the second. Every step must be felt out. That I lived is a miracle. And no, I didn't cross twice. Only once."

Singing Wolf shook his head. "You crossed twice, Wolf Dreamer. Or are you a spirit?" As soon as he said it, he regretted the words. This place of Heron's gave him fear nerves anyway. And if Wolf Dreamer were an apparition, his soul was already mostly sucked away.

Wolf Dreamer chuckled softly. "No, I'm no spirit, old friends. I only crossed the ice once. The way back"—he paused—"is much more frightening."

The hair on the back of Singing Wolf's neck prickled. He looked sideways at One Who Cries, who looked back, mouth open, hesitation in his brown eyes.

Wolf Dreamer steepled his fingers. "The way is only open until the Long Light advances. When the warm breezes blow, it will close. We can only cross in the Long Dark."

"Cross? But you said—"

"A poor choice of words." He raised his hands. "Better had I said *come through*."

"Through?" One Who Cries looked his mystification at Singing Wolf.

"Underneath, actually." Wolf Dreamer's eyes glowed again. "The way is dark."

"The way?" Singing Wolf held his breath.

Wolf Dreamer nodded. "The way is alongside the Big River."

"Like Wolf showed you."

"Yes. When the water builds up in the Long Light, it flows through a second channel. For two days, a man must walk in total blackness, feeling his way."

"The hole."

One Who Cries started. "You walked into that? Under that? You're *crazy*!"

"Hush!" Singing Wolf chastised harshly. "What else, Wolf Dreamer?"

Wolf Dreamer spread his hands again. "That's not the

worst. The ghosts are there, watching a man move in the darkness below.''

One Who Cries propped his chin in his hands. ''Under the Big Ice? After all the stories Crow Caller told? And you can hear the ghosts?''

Singing Wolf frowned at his cousin. ''Would you rather have the ghosts or the Others?''

''Give me the Others!''

Singing Wolf dismissed him with the wave of a hand, forehead lining in concentration. ''We could make a fire to carry. Render a lot of fat. Maybe make lines that people could hold.''

One Who Cries shook his head. ''But if we get lost in there, our souls will be trapped forever in darkness!''

Wolf Dreamer's eyes glazed, his mouth slackening as though on the verge of a Dream. His cousins hushed, studying the faraway gaze.

''The ice is melting,'' the Dreamer whispered hoarsely. ''Someday it will all melt off and people will cross on land, in the light of Father Sun.''

''Can we wait—''

''No.'' Wolf Dreamer smiled. ''It won't happen in this lifetime. We must go now, through the hole, before it's too late.''

''Too late?''

''Yes, before the salt water rushes down from the north to flood all the land and the hole closes up again.''

Chapter 45

Dancing Fox grimaced as she hobbled along the pool, thick streamers of white steam rising into the gray mist overhead. A dull pain still grated in her ankle. That she'd broken the thin bone along the outside of the calf was apparent, but it seemed to be healing all right—even if it left a lump. Too long Green Water had made her lie on her back.

She'd put off this meeting. Put it off in the hopes he'd come to her. In the long days since he'd returned, she hadn't parted Green Water's shelter flap, waiting in an agony of indecision.

As if by magic, Green Water appeared at her side. "Going to see him?"

Dancing Fox swallowed and nodded, perhaps too curtly. "What should I say to him? Start out with, 'My heart is glad to see you again'? Or how about, 'Your cursed Wolf Dream ruined my life. What're you going to do about it?' "

Green Water's kind eyes chided. "I don't think the last will help the situation any."

Fox shook her head. "I know. I'm confused. I've been scared to death ever since he returned. One minute I was afraid he'd show up and crawl into my robes. I'd close my eyes and hope, imagining how it would be. The next, I hated the very thought of seeing his face." She shifted off her healing foot, wincing in the process. "Everyone's in awe of him. It's a scary thing. Do I even know him now?"

Green Water crossed her arms, staring thoughtfully at the gravel underfoot. "I don't know, but you've changed as much as he has. No one knows either of you anymore. Perhaps you've both taken the responsibilities of leaders."

"They'd never let a cursed woman be a leader," she scoffed.

"A lot of people respect what you did out there, the way you handled Raven Hunter. They talk of the honor you showed by staying with Talon and how you traveled so far with a broken ankle. Some are even whispering that you have Power. That you can hunt on your own, maybe even Dream in animals the way Heron did."

"That's because they didn't see me eating rancid bone marrow, or shivering in my parkas, drenched with fear sweat that Grandfather Brown Bear would find me."

"You were scared when you stayed with Talon?" Green Water's benign eyes didn't waver.

Dancing Fox looked away, memories of the old woman's death too tender to deal with. "Terrified. She was my friend—

my teacher. I'll always be frightened to tackle life without her.''

''But you will.''

''Of course.'' She glanced apprehensively at Heron's shelter.

''You've heard enough from me. Go and see Wolf Dreamer. He'll help you find out what you want next.'' Green Water nodded encouragingly and walked off about her business, humming under her breath.

Dancing Fox sucked in a deep and anxious breath, then strode hurriedly, stopping before the door flap. Clearing her throat, she called, ''Runs In Light? You in there?''

''I've been expecting you.''

The familiar voice touched her, while some subtle quality set her on guard. She ducked through the caribou-hide hanging, looking around, seeing him on folded wolf skins, a white bear hide pillowed behind him.

Their eyes met. All the carefully prepared words vanished like mist in the morning sun. Her heart beat powerfully, a tingle in her limbs.

''I hear you tried to follow.'' He spoke softly, as if burying a deep hurt.

She smiled, oddly shy, looking away, seeing the skulls, the drawings, the holes in the rock filled with bundles of tied grasses and stuffed fox hides. A Dreamer's place. A place she could never share.

''Wolf didn't take very good care of me.'' She smiled uneasily. ''It turned out to be a difficult trip.''

He nodded, gesturing to the hides beside him. Hesitantly, she complied, sitting cross-legged on the soft caribou furs.

''You've changed. You're stronger.''

''Your brother saw to that. But then, you've changed, too. More confident, possessed. Being a Dreamer suits you.''

He looked away, face paling. ''It also costs a great deal.''

''Most things do.''

They sat in silence. Her heart roiled in her chest. She wanted to throw her arms around him, declare her love—but found herself afraid.

''Why is this so difficult?'' she asked. ''I came, Runs In Light. I followed you. Why weren't you at Renewal? I waited there, keeping myself for you. All those things you told me, about marriage and love, they kept me going all through this miserably long year.''

He swallowed hard, pain glittering in his eyes.

''Won't you speak to me?'' she pleaded, sensing a wrongness between them.

He closed his eyes, his entire body trembling.

She reached across, grabbing him by the parka and tugging gently at first, then harder, until he opened his eyes and met her gaze.

''Tell me what's wrong?''

''I love you.'' His voice cracked.

Joy and relief swelled inside her. ''And I love you.'' She let him go, sliding closer to him, so close she smelled his masculine scent. She searched his handsome face. ''Is that wrong?''

The muscles in his jaw leapt and quivered. ''You're the only thing between me and the Dream.''

She blinked. ''Between?''

''Back in Mammoth Camp, I didn't know what the Wolf Dream meant. How it would change me . . . or the People. Now I've seen. I've learned to Dream.''

She lifted a hand to stroke his smooth cheek. He flinched, closing his eyes. ''And you'll save the People.''

''Maybe.''

''But I've heard you found the hole in the ice?''

''It won't be enough.''

''What?'' She crossed her arms, trying to still the turmoil inside. Hurt, confusion, love, pain, hope; it all mixed, unsorted, leaving her heart hammering, blood pumping hot in her veins. From the contorted expression on Light's face he wasn't doing much better.

''I . . . can't let myself, my personal wants, get in the way of Dreaming the People to safety far in the south.'' A gleam lit his dark eyes as he stared at her. ''There's a beautiful land there.''

''What are you saying?''

''The only way to Dream—to really Dream—is to lose yourself in the One. To go beyond the motions of the Dance.''

''You're babbling nonsense. What does this have to do with our love for each other?''

He deflated like a punctured walrus-bladder float, puffing

his cheeks out as he blew a futile breath. "Nonsense? That's what I told Heron once. I didn't understand. How can I expect you to?"

"Tell me, do we have a future together?" Her voice trembled suddenly. "Or has some other woman taken your heart?"

"No one has taken my heart but you."

"Then—"

"I've *had* to choose!" he shouted, then lowered his voice to a wretched whisper. "I've seen the end of the People. Without a Dreamer, we have no chance. Raven Hunter has swayed the People one way. I must sway them another."

A pounding desire built to hug him, hold him, soothe his unrest. "I'll help you."

"No."

"But Dreaming isn't like some curse. Use your gifts to save the People, but—"

"It *is* a curse. It's like . . . like being born with a clubfoot or with a long nose. It's just the way things are. Because of that, I can't love."

"Why not? Didn't Heron ever love? I know the old stories about Bear Hunter."

"She . . ." He turned away, squeezing his eyes tightly closed.

Conflicting emotions warred. Exploit this hurt? Or cuddle him close, ease his pain, apologize. Frozen, she simply sat, paralyzed by the rending within.

"The man she loved killed her. Ask Broken Branch. She saw. Heron let herself love him for just a moment. But it made her lose the One and the mushrooms killed her."

Dancing Fox sat back, stunned by the haunted seriousness on his face. "You believe that my love will destroy you?"

"Yes." He shook his head as though trying to clear some deadly mental fog. "I've seen it happen to a woman with far greater Power than mine. I've chosen my . . . No, I've been chosen by the way. The People *must have a Dreamer.*"

Heart in her throat, she nodded slowly, that eternal emptiness yawning inside. "So, it's over? All this way, all this suffering . . . and you *don't* want me?"

At the pain in her words, his face twisted, a dull ache in his eyes. He whispered a dusty, "I'm sorry."

She nodded, standing, looking down while her soul screamed.

"Light?"

He looked up.

"Touch me, one last time." She reached for him.

He extended a hand, sympathy in his eyes. Only as their fingertips touched, something flickered across his face, as if a memory came unbidden from the recesses of his mind. He stiffened, staring at her in horror, face stricken, body going rigid.

"What?" she asked, pulling her hand back. "What's wrong?"

He turned away, burying his head in the white bear's hide. The sobs chilled her soul.

"Leave me!" he shouted.

Turning, she ripped through the hanging hide, running, heedless of her tender ankle. She almost bowled One Who Cries over, sprinting up the path, struggling to escape that last terrible memory of the horror reflected in his eyes.

Moon Water stretched her taut back muscles, wincing at the pain. From behind the veil of her hair, she watched her captors as they congregated around the young Dreamer. He was powerful for such a young man. The sight of the caribou coming to his calling had awed her. Despite the number of carcasses stretched out on the snow—and the work they entailed—the memory still brought a chill to her spine.

He may be as powerful as Ice Fire. As powerful as our greatest shaman! The thought brought a bitter sneer to her lips. Unthinkable! Unthinkable that these pitiful remnants of a people could have so powerful a Dreamer.

Seeing Jumping Hare looking in her direction, she quickly bent to the task of stripping the hide from a caribou.

Despicable! She, Moon Water, eldest daughter of the White Tusk Clan's Singer, must process a kill like an old hag! Rage and anger burned. The heat of it fueled her muscles, giving her strength to continue.

Her fingers cramped around the flat biface she used to cut the hide and dismember the carcass, the warm odor of caribou streaming up around her head. She stropped the tool on her long boot, cleaning the edge of resistant tissue before attacking the carcass again.

And this Dreamer was taking them under the Big Ice? It was insanity. No human could walk under ice!

But he had Dreamed in the caribou. She'd seen that. She'd seen him cure the infant born to that woman Green Water. She'd seen him suck the fluid from its nose and breathe life into the tiny blue fetus who'd been born so early. Powerful, yes; powerful, indeed.

"But not so powerful as Ice Fire," she whispered confidently.

She sank teeth into her lip, feeling her fingers strain as the gray quartzite biface severed the caribou's tissues. With a section of antler beam, she quickly knapped off a new edge, the long flakes driven off by her expert hand. The new edge sharp, she resumed skinning.

"But they can't keep me." From behind her swinging wealth of black hair, she glared hatred at Jumping Hare where he carried thick quarters from the butchering area. "And you'll soon have to forgo your pleasure on my body, bott-fly maggot! Stick to your skinny woman of the People. The daughter of the White Tusk Clan is too good for you!"

Soberly, she reached down, pushing hard on her belly as if to drive his seed out of her. Anxiously, she waited this turning of the moon, knowing her bleeding was overdue.

Soon, soon she would make her break, now that the Long Dark had begun to ebb. Before the People walked under the ice? She continued to chew her lip, her perfect brow furrowed in thought. The stories were that Wolf Dreamer had found huge herds of animals on the other side. If a woman of the Mammoth People were to find this magic hole, could not Ice Fire, with his greater Power, take all the Mammoth Clans through?

"I will wait." She smiled sourly. "Then we'll see how safe your hole in the ice is!"

Chapter 46

"I'm still not sure about this." One Who Cries shook his head, bending to stare into the inky blackness. A frigid breeze blew out of the slit in the grimy cobble-encrusted ice that spread in dirty heaps to either side: an awesome world sundered. Before them, the Big Ice lay in mounds and ribbed masses like piled scales. Snow gleamed softly in contrast to the dirty ice. Faint echoes of the tormented ghosts reached their ears even here.

A trail of rock—the washout from the runoff channel—led into the ice, an undercut pathway winding between walls of forbidding cold.

Muscles—like bands—tightened in One Who Cries' chest. As he swallowed, it seemed to stick in his throat—midway, like a crossed fish bone. Unease prickled the base of his scalp.

"So immense . . ." Singing Wolf gasped, arms spread as he looked at the ice rising high against the gray day.

One Who Cries nodded nervously. *Gray. The world has turned gray for all of us. Color is gone. Only desperation remains. Ice and rock ahead of us, around us. Behind comes painful death at the hands of the Others. Is this the way? Truly? Isn't there life and joy and happiness anymore? I don't want to go in there. Not into the darkness with the ghosts.*

Wolf Dreamer stood to one side, a brooding look on his face. He wore the tailored hide he'd skinned from Grandfather White Bear. The hem swung slowly in the breath issuing from the yawning crack before them, the long white hairs rippling.

One Who Cries looked back, seeing the stiff set of Dancing Fox's face. Studiously, she and Wolf Dreamer avoided each other. What had happened in Heron's shelter that day? What did it mean for the rest of them? More than the chill wind shivered in One Who Cries' thoughts.

"See how the boulders have been rolled out?" Wolf Dreamer called, leading them up on a pile of rock. "That's from the summer melt. This whole thing fills with water—a regular river.''

''Why's the ice only here? Why not all the way to the end of the world?'' Singing Wolf asked.

''Mountains. They come together here from the east and west, restricting the Big River. The ice forms higher and runs down here to block this one place.'' Wolf Dreamer pointed as he explained.

Behind, the People came, packs bundled high on their backs, rope made from braided lengths of caribou and mammoth hide—laboriously split—clutched in their hands. The dogs nosed about, sniffing with lowered heads at the dank exhalation.

Green Water stopped, hands on hips, her child peeking out from under her hood, like two heads perched on one body. The infant's dark eyes blinked in awe. One Who Cries caught his wife's gaze, smiling an encouragement he didn't feel.

Wolf Dreamer took the lead, placing each step carefully on the piled rock, keeping slightly to one side where the current had lessened, the sorted deposits providing more level footing there.

''This worries me,'' One Who Cries growled.

Singing Wolf shot a quick look at him and smiled weakly. ''Spirits are always getting mixed up in your life now, eh?''

He gave Singing Wolf his best scowl. ''I had to listen to *you*. 'Come on,' you said. 'We'll go first. Prove to everyone that it can be done!' And I listened. *I* listened to *you*! I'm out of my head! How do you talk me into these crazy things?''

''You were the one who agreed! You were the one talking about what the Others were going to do, about what would happen if the People stayed north of the Big Ice.''

''But that doesn't mean I ought to listen to your stone-brained—''

''Hush,'' Green Water commanded anxiously, eyes on the hole. ''Wolf Dreamer will lead us.''

One Who Cries filled his lungs with the musty air and sighed. ''Uh-huh.''

''We haven't died yet,'' Singing Wolf reminded through clenched teeth, following in Wolf Dreamer's tracks. His head bobbed this way and that as he cast uneasy glances overhead, eyes darting as he studied black shadows and niches that wormed away into the ice. Laughing Sunshine followed close behind, a knot of tension in her back.

"Haven't died yet—haven't died yet," One Who Cries repeated under his breath, glancing up at the cloud-shredded sky visible through the narrow crack above.

He swallowed, faint tricklings of sound barely audible from the ice to either side. Bands tightened on his heart.

"You coming? Or do I have to carry you?" Singing Wolf called from ahead.

Goaded, One Who Cries trotted forward, hair crawling—like being on a ridge just before Sun Father threw a lightning strike down. A curious wobble had unhinged his legs.

Fingers reached for him. He started, blinking in the gloom, seeing nothing. Fingers, soft, brushing, stroking death across his warm flesh—he could feel them. Ghost fingers, they flicked around him, leaving his skin to shrink against itself.

Fear! I'm more afraid than I've ever been in my life! It's not death. No, I can die. It's the darkness . . . the ghosts. A man shouldn't die in the darkness. His soul is trapped. Dark. Forever dark.

He stopped, panicked, on the verge of bolting back the way he'd come.

Behind him, he heard gravel and rock grinding under Green Water's feet. And more followed—all silent, scared numb by this insanity they were attempting.

From some deep depths, the courage came. Unwilling to let so many see his cowardice, he walked on, terror possessing his body.

The breeze carried strange scents to his sensitive nose: musty, cold, smelling sharp and tangy of rock and earth and darkness. One Who Cries clamped his teeth tight and fingered his darts as the slit of light overhead narrowed. Walls of grayness angled up from the sides, pockets scoured by abrasive water.

"And what good are darts against the ghosts of the dark?" he wondered. Some warning in his mind sent him scuttling to the side, the cool brush of the fingers tracing invisibly across his cheek.

In the lee of a turn in the channel, Wolf Dreamer uncovered an ember he'd carried in a shaped slate bowl, nudging it to touch a moss wick. A tiny light came to life.

One Who Cries shivered as they proceeded, the crack overhead vanishing at a bend in the rocky route. He took his turn, following Singing Wolf, Green Water grabbing the line behind him. He could hear his little son gurgling happily where he rode his mother's shoulders.

With all his courage quivering, he followed Wolf Dreamer into the black.

"Got to keep to the side here," Wolf Dreamer told them, voice echoing eerily, mixing with the creaking ghost voices of the black. "The water undercuts, eats its way back and forth under the ice. There are a couple of places where the roof is a little low, but enough water has run through to carve this out. There's lots of holes, too, where the water swirls, so watch your step."

Somewhere ahead in the pitch blackness a grating sounded, gritty, unclean.

"Ghosts," someone whispered.

"Don't fear." Wolf Dreamer's voice came from ahead. "I challenged them before. They're all around. Last time I had no light. Last time they let me pass in the darkness. Just be worthy. Show them honor and pride and courage and they will let you pass unharmed."

"No wonder they growled at Crow Caller's grandfather," One Who Cries grunted, trying to fortify himself.

Singing Wolf laughed too sharply. A brittle sound, it shattered in the dark.

The line tugged in his hand. Mouth dry, heart hammering, One Who Cries started forward, walking toward the fingers. *I'm racing toward a black soul trap.* Crackles of dread coursed along every nerve.

"Keep talking," Wolf Dreamer called back. "Where there are holes and places a person could stumble, tell the one behind you."

A sputter of voices broke the silence.

"Just show them honor and courage," One Who Cries mumbled to himself. He blinked in the darkness, shivering again at the faint noises in the ice around him. Overhead, something groaned loudly, horribly. *I have no courage . . . or pride . . . or honor! I just want light!*

Step-by-step, they moved, Wolf Dreamer's calm voice

keeping them together, his very Power hanging about them like a protective shroud in the blackness.

The grasping fingers of the dead dangled, waiting. His skin seemed alive with the feet of tiny things of the black.

One Who Cries kept his left hand knotted around the darts at his side while his right gripped the mammoth-hide line. As he felt with his feet, his eyes slowly adjusted to the darkness, faint images coming from the lamp in Wolf Dreamer's hands. Shadows flickered across the grimy walls, tall and long.

Behind, in the blackness, Broken Branch cackled, "Wolf Dream . . . Wolf Dream" over and over. The sound of human voices wove a frail shield against the horror of the squeaks and creaks of the ghosts hanging like bats in the black overhead.

Forever stretched. One Who Cries walked—fear like an animal in his breast, scurrying, eating at his heart. The gouged ice hung lower. His soul screamed, *Trapped, you're trapped!* Mouth dry, he forced himself onward. He fell over rounded polished cobbles, hide-wrapped feet sliding off the smooth surfaces. Behind him, Green Water hummed a spirit song to keep her courage, recradling the baby to nurse it as she walked.

They stopped every so often, shuffling forward to huddle around the sputtering grease-fed lamp Wolf Dreamer carried. Each time, the rest and food rejuvenated, a camaraderie of the dark binding them together, giving flagging spirits relief from the cold and the black, and the horrifying mewing of the dead.

By the time they'd made the fifth stop, a resignation had set in. They talked, laughed nervously, and One Who Cries actually looked up to where the tiny flickers of Wolf Dreamer's light played on the shining surface overhead. To his relief, no hollow eyes stared back.

The memory of sunlight became a dream. In rough places, One Who Cries pitched in to build a trail over the piles of rock, making it easy for the elderly and children who still stared wide-eyed at the darkness.

A hideous shriek began far overhead, rumbling down

through the ice like a bolt of lightning. The ground shook, forcing people to stumble.

"Grandmother?" Red Star called in a frail terrified voice.

"I'm here, child," Broken Branch responded.

"Can you hold my hand? I'm scared."

"Don't worry about the ghosts, child. Wolf Dreamer's Power keeps them at bay. We're safe . . . safe."

The shaking stopped, the shriek dying away to nothingness.

One Who Cries nodded uncertainly, wanting to believe. As an added protection, he refused to breathe through his mouth, lest something fly inside—some ghost reach in and hook his soul to rip it away into the forever black.

An hour or two later, they rested again, huddling close to one another. One Who Cries caught himself staring at the young man who had once been Runs In Light. Could this be true? That they walked under the Big Ice? Walked from one world into another? The shimmering hide of Grandfather White Bear gleamed in the faint flicker of the tiny lamp as Wolf Dreamer refueled it at each rest with a frozen lump of fat.

In the feeble glow, One Who Cries caught a glimpse of Dancing Fox's face. Her chiseled features were as cool as the ice around them—and as unforgiving. At that moment, her dark brown eyes lay on Wolf Dreamer, her soul bared in longing and pain. One Who Cries swallowed and pulled Green Water close, hugging her, thankful for her love.

Only then did he realize that Dancing Fox walked last in line. The most vulnerable, the farthest from the light, who would know if she were sucked away by some monster? Seeing the smoldering of her eyes in the dim glow of the lamp, he looked away. Who was this Dancing Fox? What had she become? Once Crow Caller had hurt her, kept her from the man she loved. But now Wolf Dreamer stood only a short distance in front of her and he'd built a wall around himself she'd never be able to climb. Her haunted eyes said she knew it. One Who Cries shivered.

One step at a time, they continued, forever moving, forever clambering over battered boulders, traversing holes, progressing. Rock grated hollowly under hide-wrapped feet, the echoes mixing with those of the ghosts, challenging the spirits, making a new reality in this place of darkness and fear.

"Bend here." "Watch this step." "Be careful through here." Had it not been for his imagination, he might have forgotten where he was. Only the cadence of Broken Branch's continued mumbling became a subconscious reality. "Wolf Dream." Over and over it echoed in his head—one with darkness.

They slept finally.

Awake. Darkness. Hear the clattering and echoing resonance as the ghosts do something in the ice. The feeble flicker of Wolf Dreamer's lamp is life. Sleep again, One Who Cries. Wolf Dreamer keeps the ghosts at bay.

How long was it? One Who Cries couldn't really say. The light grew slowly until they stared about owlishly, uneasy at first.

"Light!" Singing Wolf exploded. *"It's light!"*

"No," One Who Cries called, turning, looking up. "It's stars. The Blessed Star People!" He pointed high overhead.

"Dawn," Wolf Dreamer called back. "Look, you can make out the edges of the crack above us." Then, in a quavering voice, he whispered, *"We're through."*

Relief washed so powerfully through One Who Cries, it left him trembling. Blinking tears, he sagged to his knees, drawing Green Water close, hugging her tight. "We're through."

"Of course, husband. I told you the Wolf Dream was true," she chided gently.

Around them, whoops of exultation split the air, dancing, cavorting people gyrating happily.

Morning grew in the slit of sky, the clouds graying.

Wolf Dreamer carefully snuffed the tiny flame that had meant so much to them.

"Uh!" Laughing Sunshine grunted, wincing.

Singing Wolf moved quickly, steadying her. "What?"

She swallowed hard. "My time, the child is coming!"

Broken Branch cackled and yipped. "Wolf Dream! Her baby comes! Born to a new world like all the People! Haheeee! Wolf Dream! New life! Born anew!"

One Who Cries smiled, feeling Green Water's arm go around him. He studied the beaming faces of his people, seeing Dancing Fox in the light of the new day. His smile froze on his face as she met his eyes, a haunted emptiness there.

Chapter 47

"I can't believe this!" Singing Wolf shook his head, staring across the snow flats at the herds of animals. A small group of long-horned buffalo stood no more than a dart's throw away, watching curiously, ears flapping, tails switching, a curious gleam in their black eyes.

To the south, the divide they camped on stretched away into a white maze of ridges and dendritic drainage channels. Around them, black spruce stood, their ratty branches shifting with the wind that scoured the ridge top.

Behind, the Big River made a bend to the west, a narrow defile leading into the rugged ice-capped mountains beyond. Like a series of teeth, the range rose ominously, gouging at the gray scudding clouds. To the east, several days' walk, the Big Ice stretched, the horizon foggy and obscure. Where they sat on the wind-blasted ridge, the freezing currents carried the interminable cold up from the ice, blowing ever northward.

Beyond them, the caribou that had stopped to study them earlier grazed slowly as they moved away, nubbins of antlers beginning to form.

"And there's fresh mammoth sign." One Who Cries smiled happily.

"Wolf Dream. No Others here." Singing Wolf sighed. "I'm going to hate to go back."

One Who Cries stiffened. "Go back? Wait a minute. I thought you said 'go back'?"

He eyed his cousin seriously. "Wolf Dreamer is going for

another group. I think Buffalo Back will bring his people through this time."

"Go back? Like, from where we just came from?"

"Yes. Though I'm leaving Laughing Sunshine and my child here. The Others will be pushing closer to the People on the other side of the Big Ice, corralling them like deer for the slaughter."

"And you want to go back? You're crazy. Touched by the Monster Children's light. Why should we—"

"Someone has to tell of it besides Wolf Dreamer. Too many would refuse to believe him after—"

"That's true."

The voice behind caught them both by surprise. "I need both of you."

One Who Cries whirled. Wolf Dreamer stood there, a far-away look in his eyes. The white bearskin covered him from head to toe, a stark reminder of his Power. Now the hair seemed to gleam with a life of its own, trapping the light of the distant sun, ruffling in the chill wind.

"Both?"

"Raven Hunter," Wolf Dreamer whispered absently. His eyes had lost their focus, lips slack. "I . . . I can sense that there'll be danger. The Renewal . . . I'll have to Dream. I don't know what Raven Hunter might do. But I . . . I feel trouble. Blood."

"I'm going," Singing Wolf said.

"I knew you would." Wolf Dreamer gave him a grateful smile. "Jumping Hare will stay and hunt. Green Water will help him as will some of the others. They can keep the bears off. Keep our people safe."

Wolf Dreamer's serene gaze lit on One Who Cries and he seemed to fold in upon himself. He looked out over the plain before them and stifled a cry. The land called to him, its song sweet, trilling, that of a young woman to a lover. In the distance, he could see a family group of mammoth, their huge bodies mere dots as they used their long tusks to sweep the snow free of the sedges, grasses, and bushes.

"When will you leave?"

"The sooner the better," Wolf Dreamer responded. "The Long Light is growing. We can't know when the water will begin running again."

"You mean—"

"I mean it could begin tomorrow and forever close that hole."

In the silence, the three men met each other's eyes in turn.

"Green Water will want you to go," Singing Wolf murmured, eyeing his cousin askance.

"Of course she will," One Who Cries lamented. "Why couldn't I have married one of the whimpery ones who'd demand I stay and tend to her. Instead I had to marry rock-steady Green Water, who will nod her acceptance, hug me tight, and shove me down the mouth of the monster." But in his mind, he imagined the knowing, loving look she'd give him as he bravely set off back through the horrible hole in the ice—and his heart warmed.

With an almost physical pang, he turned away from the vision of the vast game-filled meadows. "Well, let's hurry, then."

Moon Water waited, seeing no movement. Her eyes darted to the powerful Dreamer, fearful he might have had visions of her plans. But he slept so still he seemed dead. Heart in her throat, she carefully placed each foot, fear making her movements lissome. She bent over him, easing the hide covers aside to lift the ground-stone lamp. Not even daring to breathe, she plucked up the straps for the pack that carried the all-important fat. Step-by-step she backed away. Like smoke, she drifted across the camp and into the darkness.

Taking care to hide her tracks, she lifted a flat stone from an abandoned burrow she'd found earlier and hid the items, carefully resettling the stone in place.

Quietly, she returned to her robes on the other side of Jumping Hare's woman. Soon Wolf Dreamer would return to his people on the other side of the Big Ice. Then she would be free to go herself, to return to her own people. Desperate longing filled her breast as she closed her eyes. Oh, they'd search for the lamp—but who'd believe she'd stolen it? They would search all the bundles, all the possessions, but Moon Water planned well, as befitted the great Singer's daughter. When she went, no one would know the secret of the passage to this wondrous land went with her. No one would know she carried salvation to the Mammoth People.

Chapter 48

Dancing Fox applied pressure to the stone scraper, tearing the last bits of tissue from the fine golden caribou hide. Wan sunlight warmed her beautiful face, glinting blue from her fluttering hair. Overhead, fluffy clouds drifted lazily through the azure sky, their shadows roving the undulating hills like living creatures.

"Moon Water's gone."

She looked up to see Curlew Song. The young woman's round face had pinched with disgust. Dancing Fox shrugged. "She's been waiting her chance for weeks. I thought everyone knew that from the way she skulked around at night."

"You've seen her up when we were asleep?"

"Many times."

"Why didn't you say something? Maybe we could have—"

"Tied her to the nearest tree? That would have just made her worse. She's not meant to be one of the People."

Curlew Song gave her a harsh look. "New women make the People stronger. They bring new blood."

"Only if they learn to accept their fate. Some never do—like Moon Water."

"Well," Curlew Song sighed gruffly, "maybe if she'd stayed longer—"

"When did she leave? I didn't see her go." *And I was up half the night, just like every night, weighing my future, trying to decide my path.*

"Jumping Hare stayed out last night to watch his rabbit traps. Thought he'd try and get the wolf that's been raiding them. She was there when I went to sleep last night. When I got up, her robes were gone. She'd taken her pack, too. I just made a circle of camp. Thought maybe she'd gone out to pout somewhere."

Dancing Fox stood, wringing the cramps out of her fingers. "Well, I guess we know where the lamp went, don't we."

Curlew stared, wide-eyed. "You don't think she'd—"

"Of course. She's headed home. She'll need it."

"To cross through the hole? Alone?" Curlew shook her head with disbelief. "No. She's not that brave."

Fox laughed dryly. "Oh yes, she is. I've been in her boots. I know what it's like to be a virtual slave. You know she hated us. Thought we were beneath her dignity. You can imagine what it's like to have some Other crawling on you, parting your legs."

"Jumping Hare isn't some Other! He's my husband—and hers!"

Fox grinned into the fiery eyes that burned down at her. "Yes, but you love him. Makes a difference to be split by the man you love."

"She could have, if she'd only given him a chance."

Fox stiffened suddenly, realizing the horrifying implications. "Doesn't matter now. What does matter is that we're in trouble." Hurriedly, she cleaned the clinging tissues from her scraper, flinging the fatty pink stuff into the berry bushes.

"What do you mean?"

"She'll bring the Others through the ice."

"Blessed Star People." A hand went to Curlew Song's mouth. "If they find the hole, we'll never be safe. They'll follow us across the face of the world."

"Exactly."

Fox opened her pack, dropping the scraper, several biface blanks, and a pouch of jerky inside.

Curlew Song frowned, watching the packing process. "What are you doing?"

"Going after her."

"But you can't go through the hole! Alone? Without a light?"

"Wolf Dreamer did. Now Moon Water is doing it." She lifted a shoulder in a shrug. "Besides, I've got black spruce wood, tinder, I'll carry enough for a fire if I need it. Other than that, I practically went through it in the dark last time. I was at the end of the line." Her fingers flew as she tied wood to the hide.

"Fox." Curlew's eyes shifted uneasily. "Don't do this. You might lose your soul under there. Without Wolf Dreamer to protect—"

Caustically, Fox responded, "Crow Caller cursed me to be buried. Maybe the time is right."

She looked longingly to the Big Ice. It shimmered beneath the gentle touch of Father Sun. *And Runs In . . . Wolf Dreamer . . . is on the other side. Maybe if I can just talk to him again.*

"Crow Caller was an idiot," Curlew Song said cautiously, looking over her shoulder just to make certain his ugly spirit wasn't hovering there. "Don't chance it!"

Dancing Fox slung her pack over her back, adjusting the tump line across her forehead. Playfully she batted Curlew on the shoulder. "Keep the fires going here."

Then she was off, working slowly to a ground-eating pace, feeling the stitch in her ankle.

"Going to tell the Mammoth People about our hole, huh? We'll see," she growled.

Wolf Dreamer would be facing Raven Hunter and Crow Caller. Against them, for all intents and purposes, he'd be alone. She'd been chafing about that ever since he'd left to make the return trip.

As she approached the worn channel the next morning, she could see a trickle of water running out of the snowbanks. The way in seemed to suck at her.

"So, it's begun to flow again." Her brow furrowed as she took a deep breath. "How long do we have before the hole is gone?"

Gritting her teeth, she entered the channel, seeing a woman's footprints in the soft sand. No doubt of it, Moon Water had gone this way. Heart thumping, Dancing Fox entered the shadowed chasm.

The ghosts shrieked at her to go back.

The changing of the seasons, opposites crossed. The Long Light grew out of the south as Father Sun's rays pushed the spirits of the Long Dark into the far north beyond the northern salt water and its floating mountains of ice.

With the melt came rumors. Carried over the trails by fur-wrapped hunters, the stories passed from lip to lip. Stories of a Dreamer—a powerful Dreamer. The youth, Runs In Light—once scorned—had Dreamed a way to the south.

Not only that, but he'd walked beneath the world! Walked under the Big Ice and the People were reborn! Reborn in a land where no Others walked. A land where the animals were truly brothers: unafraid. This Wolf Dreamer, they said he was born of Father Sun. Sent to lead the People to a new home.

Raven Hunter sat and squinted into the morning sun, ignoring the men who sat uneasily in a circle around him, waiting for his counsel. Their eyes on him made him consider. Over the last year, he'd hardened, handsome features tightening at the constant travel and the endless raids. His muscles had toughened, shoulders thickening while his belly tightened despite the better food. Now he walked like a young wolf, powerful, tall—a man without peers.

Fingering his darts, he contemplated the raids they'd made during the Long Dark. The Others remained, held at bay. Now the Renewal would be upon them. The spring hunt had begun. Piecemeal, they waited on the game trails to see what would move south with the melt, migrating into the Long Light feeding grounds. Only this year so many Others sat on the migratory trails they might get no food at all.

Would Buffalo guide his children through the ranks of Other hunters? Would Caribou? Or would they have to chase the occasional sheep in the high rocks, pray they could kill enough of the sparse mammoths to keep the People hale and hearty. How would the game react to the increased pressure of the Others? And how would the Others react? What if they didn't relent? Didn't take time for the spring hunt? What sort of Renewal could the People provide if their bellies were gaunted by hunger?

Raven Hunter shoved himself gruffly to his feet to pace. He pulled his new parka tight and smiled. A prize taken from the Others, the parka served as a symbol of his war prowess. Now, looking around, he realized how much they'd come to be like the enemy, stealing their clothing, eating food they'd hunted, bedding their women. Curious, he ran his fingers down the finely stitched sleeve of the parka.

And, of all things, this year the elders had decided to break tradition and hold the Renewal far to the south—in Heron's valley. In the very home of his addled brother!

Worse, worse by far, how could he hold territory when his young men had to retreat so far south to Dance? The Others would flood to fill any spaces they vacated.

"Do the old fools think the Others care for our Renewal?" he'd raged, stamping back and forth. "How long to get there?

Weeks? And the Others are supposed to obligingly wait in their camps?''

Eagle Cries had lifted a shoulder. "But we must Dance. Remember what happened two Long Darks ago when we didn't? The Soul Eaters of the Long Dark punished us. Besides, don't forget the Others have their own clan gatherings. They, too, must Dance, trade, take care of their—''

"Then we should strike!" Raven Hunter smacked a knotted fist into a palm. "They'll be vulnerable at their Dances—just as we are at ours. It's the right time to sting them, push them back before they—''

"But the Renewal is—''

"I've heard enough!" Raven Hunter glowered about him. "Who'll stay? Who'll fight for our lands?''

Around the circle, a few hands shot up. Some wavered hesitantly. The majority remained down.

A coldness worked along his spine. *Careful. I can push them only so far. While they'll follow me, they won't forget their precious Renewal. Is there an advantage in this? Some way I can discredit the elders through their shortsightedness at holding Renewal so far to the south?*

He filled his lungs, spreading his arms as he exhaled wearily. "I know, I know. Without our Dancing, the souls of the animals may desert us." He chuckled dryly. "Quite a situation we're in, eh? If we don't pray and Dance the Renewal, the animals won't let us kill them. On the other hand, if we leave our territory and go south, we'll hand those very hunting grounds over to the Others.''

He paused, searching their tight faces, seeing the blazing eyes, the grim mouths. Yes, these were warriors! His people! "So be it. We'll go south." He shook his head sadly. "And remember this next fall . . . remember who held Renewal so far from our lands. Some of you will die retaking what we will give up tomorrow. I hope those old men sing your souls well, my brothers and sisters, for they'll bear the responsibility.''

And besides, this way I can find out the truth of the nonsense that's circulating about my idiot brother.

With the courage and stamina of her people, Moon Water trotted out into the plains, the horrors of the hole below the ice lending speed to her tired feet. She would never forget that passage. The first time had been bad enough, buried there under the ice, only the faint bit of light ahead to guide her. The way back, alone with only the tremors of the ghosts as they groaned and wailed in the endless black, had been horror. No human word, no gesture had comforted her. When she stopped to sleep, it had been with fear, the whisperings in the dark growing louder around her as she cuddled the tiny fire to her bosom and prayed that the wretched ghosts would leave her be.

Now she ran, betting her speed and skill against the growing Long Light that she could reach the Mammoth People before the season of flies and mushy muskeg began.

Maybe the White Tusk Clan would be holding the White Mammoth Hide this year. Their war with the People certainly would have earned them honors among the clans. If they held the precious hide, clan leaders from the north and west would be flocking to Ice Fire's camp. A tingle of anticipation taunted her. If they were there . . . they'd hear what she told the Most Respected Elder about the hole, and the Dreamer, and the way to the south with its wonderful valleys filled to bursting with game.

All she needed to do was find a village of the Mammoth People. From then on, she would be safe and greatly revered.

She trotted and ran and trotted again, eating the last of the fat from the fuel bag, the lamp she'd carefully hidden where she could find it again. A wry smile crossed her lips. Oh, they'd looked hard and long for that. But she'd foxed them all.

Where could Ice Fire be? Where would she find a camp of the Mammoth People?

Chapter 49

Dancing Fox felt her way through the pitch blackness, her breathing echoing loudly from the icy walls. Water splashed around her feet, making the footing more precarious. Carefully, she placed her foot on a slanted rock and leaned forward. In a flash, her foot slipped off and she tumbled face-first to the ground, groaning softly at the sharp pain in her ankle. The joint raged, but the bone hadn't broken this time. Would she forever be favoring that four-times-cursed ankle?

The holes had filled with waist-deep water now. The passage not only creaked because of the ghosts, but it echoed with dripping water. Her soaked feet had gone so cold they'd become totally numb. The only dry places to sit were on the larger boulders that she blundered into in the eternal dark. Of course her kindling and fire sticks were soaked; she had no way to dry them.

The light came faintly at first. Icy water leaving her legs awkward and fumble-footed, she splashed on, jaw muscles clenched.

"You'll never reach your people, Moon Water," she promised fervently. "I'll find you."

The journey seemed to take forever. More than once she thought her end had come, that there had been a branching of the channel—a dead end leading her into the eternal bowels of the very earth.

Still, the light grew, the only sound her splashing feet and the gurgle of the increasing current. Sky appeared in the jagged cracks overhead.

She flailed and splashed her way around the end of the opening, dripping water as she limped up on the rocks to blink out at a gray overcast day.

"I'd have never thought it was true!" a strange voice said from the rocks above her.

She whirled, fumbling for her darts with cold-stiffened fingers. Three Falls shook his head at her. He was dressed in a frayed parka, and his middle-aged face shone like burnished copper from long days in the sun.

"Dancing Fox? What are you doing coming back? I thought only—"

"Chasing an enemy." She shivered, cold eating into her flesh as the wind sucked the last of her body heat away.

"An enemy?"

"Yes," she said, trying to relax, too cold to do much else. "But first, I've got to warm up."

"That a proposition?" Three Falls raised an eyebrow, smiling as he saw her expression. "I've got some dry stuff. Not much, just a little dry dung and a bundle of willow sticks. Strip out of those wet things."

She shucked off her pack, teeth chattering as he led her to a sheltered place in the boulders, unslinging his pack, building a fire as she peeled her sopping hides from her body. She wrung out the leather while he bent, spinning his fire sticks with practiced hands. Smoke rose from the charred tinder. Three Falls bent down, blowing softly, coaxing the flame to life. He backed away, motioning her forward.

She twisted her hair into a braid, couching gratefully over the smoking dung.

Three Falls sighed, letting his eyes trace the curves of her naked body. "The other way would have been more fun."

Dancing Fox looked up at him. "I've seen you naked before. No thanks, I'm not up to you. I like my innards arranged as they are." She frowned. "Besides, I thought you were one of Raven Hunter's admirers. He'd object, I'm sure, to your association with me."

"No," Three Falls grunted, working on her clothing, propping it to air out as much as possible. "His ways and mine are different."

"Are they?"

He tilted his head, brow lined with thought. "I'll kill Others. I'll fight for our land. But he's done things I think are crazy. He's taught the young men to torture the Others, cut them apart and eat the captives' hearts. There's something wrong with that. He's . . . I don't know, kind of crazy. You can't tell what he'll do between one minute and the next."

"I know." She nodded, shifting her weight, placing one foot above the fire, gasping ecstatically as warmth caressed her flesh.

"How long have you been keeping watch here?"

He filled his cheeks with air and exhaled furiously. "I'm not keeping watch . . . exactly."

"Then what?"

"I heard talk of Heron's valley and came here to look myself. I left Raven Hunter's camp in the middle of the Long Dark." His eyes were downcast. "I've kind of drifted here and there, hunting, trying to figure out what to do in my head."

"You deserted him?"

He gave her a sharp look. "I believed the tales of Runs In Light's hole in the ice. I came to join him."

A soft flutter of pride filled her chest. The People's faith had grown? Perhaps everything would be all right. If . . . "Did you see a woman come through before me? Moon Water? Jumping Hare's Other woman? Maybe two, three days ago?"

"No. I've only been here since yesterday."

"Well, maybe we can catch her."

"Let her go," Three Falls said softly, looking out over the piled rocks of the valley. "I've seen enough dead women."

"She knows about the hole in the ice. She's seen the other side."

Three Falls' eyes sought hers earnestly. "What's it like?"

"Go see for yourself." She pointed to the hole.

He shifted uncomfortably. "Is it just more rock, more scrubby wormwood and sedge, more of these sloppy rocky lakes? Flies and mosquitoes? Starvation around every esker and moraine? Fog? Blowing snow?"

She smiled and shook her head. "Trees taller than you can imagine. Game that's tame. A divide that looks like it leads down into another Big River—this one leading south. Maybe to another salt water where we can fish without Others attacking us. And there's no sign of men."

"I'm going!" Three Falls cried.

"No, you're not."

"But you just told me—"

"I've changed my mind. You've got to help me catch Moon Water first, or you'll end up sharing everything I told you with the Others."

"I won't kill her."

"I think her husband, Jumping Hare, will thank you for that."

He cocked his head skeptically. "Agreed?"

Reluctantly, she nodded. "I just want to stop her before she reveals the path to the other side."

"Let's go."

"Can I dry my clothing first? This is the first time I've been warm in days."

"Of course." He sighed, crossing his arms. "I like looking at your body. Makes me think of things."

"Then look the other way. My body doesn't think of yours."

"Unfortunate."

"Too bad you're a man with a caring soul. If you were a maggot like Raven Hunter, you'd—"

"I wish you hadn't put it that way."

"Uh-huh."

"It'll be a long hunt for Moon Water."

"Indeed."

The small fire of birch and willow had burned down to hissing, popping coals in the fire pit. Singing Wolf leaned forward, awed by these men who had dominated the ways of the People for so long. Beside him, One Who Cries sat, amiable face drawn with an unusually serious expression.

His white hair in two long braids, Buffalo Back carried the aura of age and power. He listened, nodding occasionally, the once-sharp eyes having gone softly brown over the years. His wizened face—like a dried puffball—betrayed no amazement.

Four Teeth—bags sagging under his old fleshy eyes—worked his gums absently, sucking where his cheek teeth had once been. Age spots dotted his broad face, accenting the deeply graven lines of his patriarchal features. With stubby brown fingers, he pulled at the hairy corners of his faded parka.

"You can't believe it. Buffalo, mammoth, caribou. The tundra there is shorter, but the animals are just fearless."

Buffalo Back shook his head. "Doesn't seem possible."

"But it is," Singing Wolf insisted. He gestured with his

hands, palms up. "Myself, I wouldn't have believed it. But it's there."

"I don't know." Four Teeth shook his head. "Going *under* the ice? Down in all that blackness? What if something happened? Huh? What then? Our souls—"

"And how much game is there?" Buffalo Back insisted. "How do we know we wouldn't hunt the place out? Then what? Come back here? Back under the ice?"

"Wolf Dreamer will know." One Who Cries crossed his arms.

"So we hear." Four Teeth grunted. "Where is he? Huh? He shows up and disappears into that hole in the rocks. You know what the People say about holes in the rocks? It's not right that souls go underground."

Singing Wolf stared wearily across the fire, thinking about Heron's shelter. His memories fixed on the firelit skulls and he shivered slightly. "I don't know what he's doing. Maybe I don't want to know. Dreaming, real Dreaming, makes a person nervous."

"Is he *really* a Dreamer?" A note of doubt lurked in Four Teeth's voice.

One Who Cries nodded soberly. "Heron told Broken Branch that he'd be better than she was."

"We'll see when Crow Caller gets here." Four Teeth squinted, tilting his old head. The light of the fire made a curious shadow behind his hooked fleshy nose. "Crow Caller, now, there's a man with Spirit Power."

Singing Wolf averted his eyes to keep from offending an elder. "I don't mean disrespect, Grandfathers, but many starved following Crow Caller's . . . 'dreams.' Broken Branch says his Dreaming is false."

"She's old."

"She's seen Dreamers," Singing Wolf countered gently, knowing this conversation was crucial. If he offended the dignity of the old ones, the clans would never follow them through the hole. "She saw the Dream in Wolf Dreamer's eyes."

Four Teeth scowled at him, obviously disgusted by his challenge. "You think you know more than I do? Huh? I'm twice your age."

Singing Wolf clamped his jaw a moment, then replied softly, "No, Grandfather. I was just—"

"Crow Caller will tell us the truth of this young Runs In Light," Four Teeth insisted stubbornly.

Singing Wolf leaned his head back, choosing his words carefully. "I have no doubts of the sincerity of your beliefs, Grandfathers. But we've seen them face off before, watched them stand in each other's Power. One Who Cries was there. I was there. Others can verify our words, though I speak with an open heart. Crow Caller cursed Wolf Dreamer, cursed him to have his stomach eat itself. Prophesied death for everyone who followed the trail south. Called down all kinds of trouble from the Long Dark. We all lived but one little girl. And Crow Caller said the Big Ice was death. We live—and our families are on the other side living in a beautiful land of plenty as we speak."

One Who Cries averted his eyes. "I was part of Crow Caller's band for years. But I'd never seen a real Dreamer until I saw Wolf Dreamer, and then Heron. I've watched these Dreamers call game. I've seen the Power in the dead eyes of a Dreamer. Crow Caller had nothing like it."

Four Teeth muttered under his breath. "Always thought Heron was a legend. You both know bad things are said about her. That she could suck a man's soul from his body . . . blow it out in the Long Dark."

"She fed us. Kept us warm," One Who Cried added uncomfortably. "For myself, I received nothing but kindness from her." He waved absently. "Sure, she scared me. Anyone with sense is scared around Dreaming like that. But she wasn't bad like the stories make her out."

"Then what was she doing out all alone like she had no relations, no people?" Four Teeth demanded. "You tell me, huh? What? That's not right! Good people don't run off like that."

"The Dreaming was better, she said. I heard her explain. She could keep her mind clear. Uh, uncluttered, she said." Singing Wolf shot a quick glance at One Who Cries. It wasn't going as he'd hoped.

"My mother knew her," Buffalo Back added. "I'll wait. I'll see what happens during Renewal. Maybe Heron gave

Runs In Light *bad* powers." His voice dropped to a hoarse whisper. "To hurt us."

"Why would—"

"For revenge. You know the stories of how the People scorned her Dreaming. It was strange and people feared it."

"Let's hear Crow Caller's words," Four Teeth interrupted. "Let's see what he Dreams."

In the uneasy silence that followed, Singing Wolf stared emptily at the fire. Would they never listen?

"Besides . . ." Four Teeth shook his head. "I can't believe it's right for us to leave the place Father Sun gave us for a hole in the ice. My father's father lived here. I sang my wife's soul to the Blessed Star People here. I know this land. *I can feel this land in my soul.*" He paused, letting his words sink in. "Raven Hunter's right. We have to—"

"The Others are coming." Singing Wolf rubbed the back of his neck. "We have to do a lot of thinking this Renewal. Things are changing. No disrespect, Grandfather, but this isn't really our land. Here? At Heron's? Five days' walk from the Big Ice? How much farther south are we than in the past?"

"We're not that far."

"I remember as many Long Lights ago as I have fingers on one hand." Singing Wolf held them up, wiggling his digits. "Remember that place we had Renewal five Long Lights ago? Out on the flats where the Big River flows into the salt water? It's how far north of the camps of the Others now? We've already had to move because of the Others. We can't hunt clams and shellfish and seals along the salt water anymore. For that matter, the salt water is more than three moons' journey to the north. The Others are there. Let's face it. We can't keep the Others back. There aren't enough of us!"

Four Teeth shook his head. "We'll drive them out, push them back. Father Sun gave us that land. He'll keep us safe. You'll see."

"I *did* see," Singing Wolf said passionately, keeping his eyes lowered so as not to irritate the elders. "I went to raid with Raven Hunter last Long Light. I saw. I killed a handful of Others in the fighting. I acted with honor. But I watched our young men rape women like they were rutting animals. I watched babies smashed and kicked and gutted. I watched men left to die of gut-juice poisoning. I fought for the People, and I saw what the chances really are.''

''You've lost faith! We'll win by next—''

''I *won't* wait! I've taken my family beyond the Big Ice. I won't watch my family and people slowly worn away like sandstone on a grinding slab. It's not dishonorable for a man to—''

Four Teeth sighed wearily. ''I know you have honor, Singing Wolf.''

''And he has something else,'' One Who Cries added. ''He has seen both sides for himself.''

Four Teeth frowned at him, lifting his chin ominously. ''You didn't fight, what right do you have to talk?''

''No, I . . . I . . .'' He stumbled over the words, shame rising crimson in his cheeks. ''I hate war.''

Buffalo Back smiled grimly, accusingly. ''So we've heard.''

''Coward!''

''I'm *not* a coward!'' One Who Cries defended bravely, lifting his eyes to meet his elders. The fire-stained pallor of the old men frightened him. Their cheeks caught the fire flickers hollowly, mouths pursed tightly. ''I just want to be left alone in life—to hunt. That's all. And I'm a fine hunter. No one can run mammoth like I can.'' He dropped his eyes again, fumbling with the hem of his shirt. ''But I don't want my Green Water taken by some Other while I die with a dart in my gut. Singing Wolf has been my eyes and ears. I've listened to him and spent many long nights in thought, trying to decide what to do, who to follow.''

Four Teeth relented, sucking his cracked incisors—the only teeth left in his head. ''A man has to do what he thinks is best.''

''That is the way of the People—the way I was taught. And the best I could see was to take my wife and my child to safety on the other side of the Big Ice. I've seen it—and it's as glorious as Singing Wolf says. I only came back to tell the People.''

Buffalo Back shifted uncomfortably. ''I'm here because the Others raided my camp. Drove me out. Many of my young men are dead.''

One Who Cries jerked forward, spreading his arms, pleading. "There's a place beyond the ice where there's no war! Come with us."

"I don't want to go under the ice. Souls get lost in darkness. Trapped, you know? I just want to keep my people safe while Raven Hunter chases the Others away."

Singing Wolf exhaled tiredly. "Think about this. We're holding Renewal here this year, as far south as men can go before being stopped by the Big Ice. The Others are pushing. Where will we go next year?"

"Father Sun gave this land to us. *Gave it to us!*"

"Why should we let the Others have it?" Buffalo Back growled.

"Because we may not be able to stop them." Singing Wolf said it coolly. "You've heard Blueberry? We've had captive women for a year. They talk about the journeys the Others take over great stretches of land. Walking for a whole Long Light and never leaving their territory. Can we, who are so few, stop so many?"

"The People won't run away through a black hole in the Big Ice!" Four Teeth thumped a fist on a bony knee in finality.

Buffalo Back nodded. "Let's wait and hear what Crow Caller and Raven Hunter say. Maybe even now they've driven the Others from the north and we can go back."

"Grandfathers," Singing Wolf murmured. "I know your respect for Crow Caller, but a new Dreamer has come to the People. Please, do not blind yourselves to his powers just because he is young. The People are at stake here. Our way is balanced between a rebirth and death."

"A new Dreamer?" Four Teeth scoffed, spitting into the sand beside him. "Runs In Light won't even face his own people. He hides in a witch's hole to avoid the shame he deserves."

Singing Wolf closed his eyes painfully. *Is this how it will end? What can I do to make them see? What?*

Chapter 50

Raven Hunter looked back at the rocky hills they'd traversed. Runs In Light's Dream had brought him here? Around him, the wormwood and sedge tussocks looked ratty, hugging the ground. Nevertheless, old dung proved game had been here. Down by the Big River, willow, dwarf birch, and berry bushes thickened and made a wall around the lusher wetlands there. To the west, magnificent mountains shot white-glazed peaks to spear Blue Sky Man's belly. Behind him to the north, a low line of hills ran in an arc to the Big Ice, visible in the distance where it curved around to the south, meeting the mountain ice. And his foolish brother had crossed that?

"Impossible!" he muttered under his breath.

"Runs In Light?" Crow Caller asked.

"Are my thoughts that apparent, Dreamer?"

"No one sane could believe he crossed."

"But the rumors are spreading like wildfire." Raven Hunter's frown deepened. Could they be true?

Heron's valley spread out before them, the hot springs sending plumes of steam into the coppery sky.

"Maybe we can put this Wolf Dream nonsense to rest, eh?"

Raven Hunter nodded soberly. "Oh, I intend to. One way or another."

"That's it!" Three Falls exploded with a disgusted snort.

"Curse her!"

Dancing Fox lay beside him, belly down, staring out over the marshy muskeg to where Moon Water ran to meet the men. No doubt about it, the way the camp had been laid out, it belonged to the Others.

"We still came pretty close. We made up at least three days on her." Three Falls rubbed his nose, making a clicking sound with his tongue.

"A half day. That's all we needed to catch her." Wearily,

Dancing Fox rolled over, face to the cloudy skies as she massaged her throbbing ankle.

"You've been in pain the whole time, huh?"

She nodded. "Seems like I always am. I suppose it'll get me in the end."

He crawled back off the skyline, watching as she wormed her way after him. "You're not like most women, are you?"

With thin fingers, she pulled her long black hair to one side and looked at him seriously. "If you mean like your wife Mouse, no."

He nodded. "I could come to like you a lot. You'd make a man a good wife. Bear strong sons."

She smiled. "Not interested."

"Am I that bad?"

She propped her chin in her palms, frowning. "No. You're a good man. I haven't had to drive a dart through you for jumping on me in the middle of the night."

"We've walked all through the middle of the night. It's tough to jump on you while we're working out a trail."

"Don't try. Men have a habit of sleeping after they finish. You might never wake up."

Three Falls chuckled. "I like my sleep too much. Come on. Let's go break the news to Wolf Dreamer that his Dream is now enemy knowledge."

Dancing Fox turned to take one last look at the band of warriors who ran to surround Moon Water, clapping her on the back.

"It's still a race," she whispered. "Them or us."

"If we hurry and get the rest of the People through, maybe we can cover the hole from the other side."

"How?"

"I don't know for certain. Maybe somebody"—he swallowed hard—"could stay behind and roll boulders across the entrance?"

She turned mocking eyes on him. "You've seen the size of the hole. A raging river makes it bigger every Long Light. You really think we could block it?"

He lowered his eyes, gesturing futilely. "No."

The shelters of the People had spread far and wide. The young warriors split off from the main party, seeking the tents of their relatives and wives near the clan standards that waved in the light puff of Wind Woman's breath. Crow Caller, joints no longer spry, barely kept his pace at Raven Hunter's side as they climbed the ridge.

"Four Teeth is there. I see Buffalo Back's totem, too. Seagull Clan is here. I wonder who leads now?" Raven Hunter crested the ridge, looking down on the lush valley, at the cauldron of the geyser and the curiously aqua blue water it spewed into the yellow-lined stream. Willow and birch—now depleted from many camps—lined the narrow valley. A worn path led to the bottom. Brown-skinned people floated in a large pool, laughing and splashing, sunlight gleaming from their naked bodies.

As he stared down, he added, "But we haven't seen much game on the way in. From the look of the tundra plants, I doubt there's much here. If nothing else, I've seen everything I ever want to about this south. Too dry here. Not enough water to keep the game in good graze."

"Perhaps," Crow Caller grumbled, breath coming in hard gasps. "But then, the Others have the best of that now, don't they?"

Raven Hunter blew softly. "For the moment, Dreamer. For the moment. You can't say they have as much as they would have without our efforts."

"No . . ." Then. "Smell that! How could humans live here? That geyser stinks! Smells like fat rotting in salt water."

Raven Hunter stopped for a moment and chuckled softly. "Maybe, but notice? No flies, no mosquitoes here. The smell must drive off the bugs."

Crow Caller snorted.

At the bottom, Four Teeth stood in front of his shelter, shading his ancient eyes, waving as they approached. He hobbled forward to hug Crow Caller, toothless grin exposing a pink tongue behind brown lips.

"And where is my imaginative brother?" Raven Hunter asked the elder after he'd paid respect.

Four Teeth scowled. "There. See that crack in the rock up by where the water runs down? Spends his time in there doing something. Singing Wolf and One Who Cries take him food every so often. They say he's preparing a Dream."

Raven Hunter chuckled and slapped his knee. "My brother? A Dream?" Winking at Crow Caller as the old man cast a gleaming black eye on the rock shelter, Raven Hunter turned away.

At the entrance, he stooped, ducking past a worn caribou hide, seeing nothing in the dark at first. "Runs In Light?"

"Drop the flap, Raven Hunter."

He did, seeing a dull red eye of fire.

"Your eyes will adjust. Come. Take two steps forward, then seat yourself."

Wary, Raven Hunter did, feeling carefully before he lowered himself on soft pelts. A dim outline began to form before his grayed vision. "Very creative. A special act to leave me awed by your claimed Powers?"

"No. I am keeping myself in peace, brother. Keeping my mind clear. Attempting to learn to do what I must."

"And what, pray tell, might that be? Conjure mammoth from clouds? Grow a lush grassy tundra here in this waste you've attempted to lure the People to? Come, Runs In Light, forget this—"

"Runs In Light is no more."

"Very well, *Wolf Dreamer*. Quite a name that. You know, Crow Caller is with me. He's looking forward to a . . . shall we say, test of your Powers? Hum? Should be a most interesting Renewal."

"And why are you here?"

"You're my brother. What would the People say if I just let you go on with this foolishness?"

"I'm deeply touched that you take your responsibilities for your relatives so seriously."

Raven Hunter laughed. "Oh, put your fears to rest, brother. I couldn't care less what you do to yourself. I, however, must at least claim to have made the attempt, you know? A brother has to show some compassion and try to bring his kin back to the true way of the People. I have a reputation to maintain. A certain status. People will think well of me when I tell them I tried to talk you back to your senses."

"Don't cross me, Raven Hunter. I see more than you can."

Raven Hunter laughed softly. "I suppose you'll Dream me away otherwise?"

In the darkness, he could make out Runs In Light's features

now. His brother reached, placing more willow sticks on the fire. In the increasing glow, he looked into Runs In Light's eyes; a thread of fear wound through him. A strength glowed there.

"I offer no threat, Raven Hunter. If you challenge me, I *must* break you. Discredit you. Throw you out. Pain and death stain your future."

A shiver traced Raven Hunter's spine. How serious Runs In Light was. And he truly seemed to believe it. For a brief instant, a flicker of premonition edged at him. A premonition he summarily dismissed. He had to get the initiative back, take control of the conversation. A thought came.

"Jealous over Dancing Fox?"

His brother flinched, looking up with wide vulnerable eyes. A nerve struck! In the dim firelight, Raven Hunter saw Runs In Light wet his lips anxiously. He laughed softly, repeating, "Jealous?"

"No. She's of no importance."

"But surely you know how much she loves you." Raven Hunter twisted the barb of his words. "Why her every waking thought is for you, brother. Surely after what she's suffered for you, you can't—"

"No!" He gripped his hand into a fist, eyes closed.

"No? And after her sacrifices?"

"I . . . Impossible, Raven Hunter. That life is closed to me now." He shook his head sadly.

"You really believe this Dreamer idiocy, don't you?"

A slight smile crossed his brother's thin face. "Yes, I suppose so, brother."

"Then your delusion can't be swayed? There's no way I can bring you to my side. We'd make a good—"

"*Your* way is that of the darkness, brother."

"I'd not be making claims like that considering how the People feel about holes like this." He gestured around, seeing some of the eerie drawings and effigies placed around. The white lumps had re-formed themselves into various skulls. "You really are absorbed by this delusion. If I believed in such silliness, I might worry."

"Will you stand in my way, Raven Hunter?"

He cocked his head. That voice was so precise, so . . .

convinced. "I must, idiot brother. This time your delusions stand in the way of the People's survival."

"You know you're half-Other?"

Raven Hunter stiffened, glaring. "I'm half—"

"Other." Runs In Light nodded slowly, assured. "Our mother was taken on the salt water. She died giving birth to us."

Raven Hunter caught himself. "Of course, more of your fantasy, hmm? Save it, Runs In Light. Save it for Singing Wolf and that gullible One Who Cries. Tell them of your imaginative phantoms. *They'll* believe your insane claims."

"Ask Crow Caller. Ask Buffalo Back. Ask Four Teeth. They know the rumors."

Raven Hunter shook himself. It couldn't be. No, this was another of Runs In Light's crazy notions.

"Ask!" he ordered. "It's *our* destiny, brother."

"I'll crush you before I—"

"Listen to me. I have no desire to take your life—but it's in the Dream, brother. *Don't stand in my way!"*

Silenced by the outburst, he fingered his chin, skeptical eyes on Runs In Light. "You never cease to amaze me. *It is* the future of the People we're dealing with. I'll not see them led off into the wastes by your quaint delusions."

Runs In Light seemed to sag. He took a deep breath and let it out slowly. "I'm sorry."

"So am I. Listen, there's still time. We'll get Crow Caller to sing a healing for you, claim you're—"

"And make your status that much higher? Allow you to demonstrate your compassion for your poor foolish brother?" He shook his head, smiling wistfully. "I'm afraid not . . . as if Crow Caller could be persuaded to such in the first place."

"Oh, he can. I have him firmly under my control. He's no fool. He sees where his best interests lie."

"No wonder you see Dreaming as a sham."

"Of course it is. Like all the other charades of healing, Dreaming, and magic. The purpose is to make people feel better. Lay the silly superstitions in their minds to rest. Like ice on a burn. The rest is simple. Drain pus, set broken bones, change diet so the right things get into a person's blood. I've learned a lot since I started mending hurt warriors."

And there are the visions which haunt me. Those I'll believe, addled brother. I've seen Dancing Fox—and her child. But nowhere do my visions show rosy futures.

"Heron said you were unschooled. But there's still time. Let me help you learn. I'll teach you everything she taught—"

"Don't be ridiculous." Raven Hunter got to his feet, looking around. So many fascinating things. He'd have to come back here sometime. Perhaps some of this might be useful in keeping his warriors motivated. "Yes, unschooled. Well, I'll leave you now and let you turn your thoughts to how you'll discredit Crow Caller when he unmasks your games."

"Tell him . . ." he whispered desperately. "Tell him I don't wish to destroy him."

"I'm sure he'll find your warning most entertaining."

He stopped at the flap. "Sure you don't want me to send Dancing Fox to you? She'd willingly fall into your arms, you know. I can tell you honestly, she's most ardent on a man's staff. Tight, passionate, worth your—"

Runs In Light jerked up clenched fists, shouting, *"Get out!"*

Raven Hunter smiled, not moving.

"Get out before you force me to do something I don't want to!"

"Really? Show me!"

Runs In Light trembled, crossing his arms tightly across his breast. He murmured, barely audible, "Please . . . don't make me, brother. I don't want to hurt you."

Beneath the azure vault of the sky, the huge straight mammoth tusk jutted up from the center of the cairn the White Tusk Clan had built to support their totem. From the top, mammoth tails hung down in each of the cardinal directions, swaying in the breezes. Bright feathers in turn decorated the tails, flicking color about the polished white-brown ivory.

Large tents of cured mammoth hide sprawled across the grassy flats. Supported by split mammoth bone and propped by anchored tusks, the tents provided relief from the constant sun. Long hours of labor had scraped the once-thick hide thin to allow a translucent yellow light to filter into the interiors. Before the doorways, a shimmering cloud hovered. The gentle breezes couldn't keep the flies from collecting in tall pillars, their myriad wings humming in a dirge fit to drive man and beast to insanity.

"We need more smoke pots," Ice Fire muttered under his breath. Black flies and mosquitoes as well as occasional hideous beasts—the gaudy yellow and black bott flies—all seemed attracted to this clan council.

"Seems the farther south we go, the worse the flies. Should have stayed down by the Big Water," Red Flint agreed, batting arms in defense. "Something about that salt water. The flies aren't as bad there."

Ice Fire rubbed his face, shooing the swarm before ducking into a smoky cook tent where the old women gathered around long pits laboriously excavated with their digging sticks.

"Safety." Ice Fire sighed, glaring at the swirling winged beasts beyond the opening. He looked around at the four mammoth tusks propped to support the low shelter. The heat from the fires ate into his backside. "Out there we're eaten alive. In here we roast."

"Take your pick." Red Flint laughed dryly, crouching down on his heels to avoid the heat and still remain in the protection of the smoke.

Ice Fire hated the sound of his cracking joints as he lowered himself.

"You've done well, old friend. This year you've returned the White Hide to the White Tusk Clan. How long since the last time?"

Ice Fire shook his head, white-shot hair hanging free over his shoulders. "More years than I have fingers on two hands. Where did we find honor? Only this year did these Enemy finally raise a leader who would challenge us." He chewed his weathered lip. "Even then, I could almost pity them. They're so few, we'll sweep them aside soon." He waved a callused and battered hand. "Look, look south. See those rocky hills up there? That's where they've run. I've been up there. Seen what the land is like. It keeps climbing. This river, so big and full of water, runs out of the ice that blocks the valley. That's where they've gone."

"You could pity them? They stole my daughter! You've seen how they desecrate those they capture! They're beasts!"

"Not beasts," Ice Fire corrected. "They've grown desperate. And that's a message in its own right. This broad valley is the last of their hunting grounds. They fight, but in the end they'll lose.''

"Perhaps. It's the way, I guess. Like our cousins to the west.'' Red Flint pursed his lips, moving his fingers nervously. "You think we're going to be caught like that someday? Like these Enemy?''

Ice Fire spread his wide hands. "Once, I would have said we couldn't be crushed by anything. Now? I don't know.''

Red Flint rubbed his hands together uneasily. "Have you sought visions of our fate? Do the Glacier People—''

"I've had visions. It's not the Glacier People. They, too, are running. Fleeing the disease that comes from the west. They're moving southwest along the southern salt water. They'll end up leaving in their floating trees. Finding a land that rises from the salt water.''

"But what of us?''

Ice Fire shrugged. "Too many things can happen. The disease rises in the west. If we turn back? Well . . . I don't see it all. The Watcher—''

"The old woman? The one who watched when you raped that woman.'' He glanced away at the look in Ice Fire's eyes.

"I met the Watcher.''

"You . . .''

Ice Fire brushed his hair over his shoulder, staring into the smoky air. "She told me the world's changing, but we can save ourselves.''

"How, Elder?''

"My sons are part of it.''

"Sons? But you have no—''

"Two. Twins. Like the Enemy's story of the Monster Children—locked in constant battle. But someday soon, one will triumph.''

"Which one? What does it mean for us?''

He waved it away. "I don't know. It's worse in my head than the way I tell it.''

"Tell me what you've seen. Maybe I can help interpret the images.'' Red Flint edged closer, listening intently.

Hesitantly, Ice Fire explained, "There's a young man, tall, straight, bitter with anger. He leads our clan across the back of the world. Through rock and snow and ice into a different place. Leads us to a great Dreamer and healer, who is me. I see myself, the angry young man, and . . . a child . . . all bound by red lines—like a web. And . . . and above, in the sky, a spider of stars holds the tendrils of web. We're drawn south by the sky spider. Unable to escape the web.''

He shook his head. "I can't make it out. Sounds crazy. One vision shifting to another. Changing shape, changing existences in my head.''

Red Flint ripped up some of the tussock grass. "Do our people follow the Enemy to this different place?''

"I haven't seen.''

"It's a frightening thought.''

"Visions are always frightening,'' Ice Fire agreed solemnly. There were so many things he could never tell anyone. Even his closest friends would think him mad. "I wish I'd never made that wretched trip twenty years ago. It seemed like I tore the world loose, sent it spinning like children-fling dried buffalo-dung patties.''

"Look.'' Red Flint pointed to a figure who raced across the camp. "It's Sheep's Tail.''

Ice Fire stood, shuffling his leg to get the circulation back in it as he squinted into the bright light. Sheep's Tail's face twisted anxiously.

"So, young man, the Enemy have raided your village again and stolen another of your women?''

Sheep's Tail lowered his flashing eyes, jaw muscles jumping in embarrassment.

"What's happened?''

He looked up, a curious fire in his eyes as he addressed his words to Red Flint, the Singer. "Moon Water's back. Your daughter's safe. She just came in with Walrus's people. She escaped from the Enemy. She tells a strange story you should hear. The Enemy have a great new Dreamer. He's taken them underneath the world through a ghost hole to a land of riches beyond belief!''

Red Flint broke out of the group, running for where his daughter stood in the distance. She was being carried into his tent by a cheering crowd.

Ice Fire stiffened, bits of vision floating up from the depths of his mind so recently stirred by Red Flint.

"From under the world . . ." he mused. "I'd better hear this tale of Moon Water's."

He battled the flies that sought his warm blood on the way across the camp, seeing people huddled beneath the tents, swatting at the beasts with tail quirts, waving wormwood and sedge over their heads.

Moon Water looked young, gaunt, and flushed with pride as he ducked under the flap into the muggy interior of Red Flint's family tent. She glanced up, recognized him, and dropped her eyes before turning to embrace her father.

He strolled closer, and when Red Flint released his daughter, Ice Fire clapped the girl on the shoulder. "First, let me welcome you back to the people. You have shown courage and bravery worthy of our songs." Then he raised a silver-shot eyebrow. "But I also hear you know of a . . . a ghost hole?"

She flashed dark eyes at him and straightened, aware all eyes were upon her. "I not only have seen it," she began uncertainly. "I've been through it, Most Respected Elder."

He blinked, the import of her words sinking in. "Through it?" Slowly he settled himself to a rolled caribou hide, heedless of the flies that swarmed about. "Explain."

She nodded seriously, a shiver taking her at the memory. "It's a terrible place, Most Respected Elder. Things . . . ghosts, howl in the ice. The journey is long, days and days, and cold, and horrors hang in the dark waiting to grab the unwary."

"Yet you passed unharmed?"

"I . . . maybe I showed courage to the ghosts. And pride and honor. Ghosts value such things."

He smiled warmly at her. "I'm sure they do. I didn't mean to mock your courage, Moon Water. You are very brave, worthy of every honor our people can bestow upon you. But tell me, what's on the other side of this ghost-filled place?"

Her face lit. "A valley like you cannot imagine! The game stands still while the hunter walks up to dart it. Buffalo, caribou, mammoth, musk ox."

"Stands still?" Red Flint cried, disbelief glinting in his sharp eyes.

She nodded. "The Enemy Dreamer said no man had ever been there."

"No man?" Red Flint shook his head. "The Enemy is tricky. Maybe they wanted you to—"

"No." Ice Fire held up his hand, bits of vision flashing in his mind.

In the silence, he turned, studying her where she looked triumphantly at Red Flint. A strong woman, this. Where was her like twenty years ago after his beloved . . . ? No, leave it. The dead are dead.

Moon Water edged forward slowly, then dropped to her knees before Ice Fire. "Most Respected Elder. Please, we must take the people through the hole before—"

"Yes, we must."

She smiled in sudden surprise. "We'll need to clear the Enemy out of the way first. Then we can—"

"Describe the Enemy Dreamer?"

"He is very young. Maybe nineteen Long Darks, with long black hair and an oval face. His eyes are large and filled with . . . with a strange light." After a moment's hesitation, she added, "Like yours, Elder."

Ice Fire filled his lungs, nodding. Even as the girl gave the description, the boy's face appeared in his mind, rainbow in hand, and a tremor shook him. To no one in particular, he murmured, "Come to me. Let us decide the futures of our people. Come to me, Dreamer . . . son."

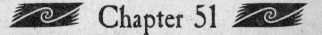 Chapter 51

Wolf Dreamer leaned back against the crusty rocks of the hot springs. He'd sought out a higher pool, hidden in the rocks above the falls. Small, it hid in dark shadows. Only a piece of Blue Sky Man shone over his head.

"Heron," he murmured painfully, "lead me. I must know what to do."

Fragments of his conversation with Raven Hunter echoed through his mind. He could see his brother's face—see the controlled anger, the darkness of his soul. Blood whimpered in Raven Hunter's tracks. Souls cried in the vastness—their way to the Blessed Star People unsung. Pain—pain followed Raven Hunter. It twisted in Wolf Dreamer's thoughts.

Everything had come unraveled. His mind, so carefully ordered, had lost the silence—the peace. The One eluded him in the roiling of emotions, remembered words, which—like Raven Hunter's face—he couldn't vanquish.

Confusion roiled in his stomach, stirring his mind and soul with the blackness of defeat. He felt so tired and so desperately, barrenly alone.

Why did he have to mention Dancing Fox? *"Sure you don't want me to send her to you? She'll willingly fall into your arms, you know. I can tell you honestly, she's most ardent on a man's staff. Most worth your . . ."*

Eyes squeezed tightly shut, he clamped his cupped hands over his ears, teeth gritted. Nothing stilled the voice repeating in his mind. A vicious thought speared him—a question of what it would feel like to love Dancing Fox. Flesh teased by the thoughts, he began responding, and cried out in horror.

I've seen the end of the People. . . .

"Heron? Help me!"

She appeared in his reeling thoughts, her face stiff, cold, blue in the light of the torch. Once again, he stared into her dying eyes, seeing the light of the soul fleeing the body.

"Bear Hunter?" her rasping voice called.

"Death," Wolf Dreamer whispered, Dancing Fox's image fading as Heron's haunting eyes became the total of his consciousness. "To love and Dream is to die." The beat of his heart pulsed through his body, as if pumping away the confusion.

"That's it, isn't it. Death is the end . . . no matter what."

An ominous feeling of wrongness swelled around him. He fought it, centering his soul on the concept of death, remembering every line in Heron's still face—in the glazing of her terrified eyes. Opening his mouth, he began chanting the nonsense song she'd taught him. He forced himself to concentrate on the sounds, clarifying his thoughts, forgetting the bustling world of people chattering in the main pool far below. They depended on him—those that believed. Yet he'd lost faith in himself. Would the rest of the clans ever follow? Or would he have to leave them to the death predicted in his Dreams? Sharp laughter drifted up to him, breaking his concentration. Then someone roughly scolded a child.

"Dance," he commanded himself. "Seek . . . seek beyond your self. Lose your mind. Become all—and none."

He shook his head hard, clearing the mental fog of self-pity, and continued chanting, chanting, chanting. . . .

Time stretched, the chant seeped into every corner of his mind until he no longer heard the lilting sounds of his own voice. Chant whirled into Dream. The One beckoned. Absorbed in the flow of his mental dance movements, he found he didn't need the song, that he couldn't stop the motions now; they possessed him, the fluid swaying like a balm on his wounded soul. Only the motions existed, blending with the caress of water around him, until finally he felt himself being lifted high into the air.

He Danced weightlessly in a sea of light. Time vanished, slipping into an eternal now where there never had been a Wolf Dream or a Dancing Fox—only a single moment of present awareness existed.

The Dance stopped.

He melted into the effulgence like a drop of water in the ocean. Nothing but light existed. Then in a massive and silent explosion, the light burst forth, washing through the universe in a gigantic tidal wave, spreading . . . spreading . . . conquering the darkness.

And he knew at that moment, knew at last what Heron's cryptic words had meant. "You've got to stop Dancing so you can get a good look at the Dancer."

Beneath the motions of the Dance was the Dancer. And beneath the Dancer was the essence of all that existed, the thing that tied the animals and plants to human beings: the One Voice, the One.

There was no Dancer. There never had been.

After an eternity, his body returned to him. He opened his eyes. The glare of the sun made him squint against the pain. Sound reached him as he floated. One by one, his senses tingled to life. With them, depression set in. He'd made another step, but why couldn't he stay in touch with the light?

Until he could hold the connection, he'd never be able to perceive the world around him as mirage. Fire handling and poison would be imposs—

Across the pool, from inside Heron's shelter, a babble of haunting voices called his name.

Cold fear touched his stomach. He turned to look toward them, seeing their black shriveled faces in his memory. An eerie wail rose, the mushroom's impassioned pleas pounding against him like fists.

He sank deeper into the pool, hiding . . . hiding.

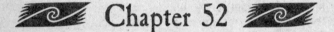

Chapter 52

His mouth had gone so dry. Fear did that, fear that he wasn't strong enough. Fear that he'd break down in the Dream. Fear that his denied love for Dancing Fox would rise to cleave him from the One, to leave him as horribly dead as Heron in her love for Bear Hunter.

"Go now, leave me."

He looked back and forth, seeing the nervous trepidation in One Who Cries and Singing Wolf's eyes. They sat silently, awkwardly, unwilling to abandon him in this most critical moment. His heart warmed to their loyalty and concern.

"The time has come for me to Dream for all the People. Don't you see?"

Singing Wolf frowned, stubby teeth sunk in his lower lip. "It killed Heron. And she was practiced."

He silenced him with an uplifted hand, smiling wistfully. "It's my time, Singing Wolf." Filling his lungs, he stilled his anxious heart. "Please, go now. I must prepare. See that no one disturbs me. No one! Not for any reason."

He closed his eyes, seeking to clear his mind, to prepare for what he had to do. Vaguely, he heard the rustle of their clothing as they left, the feeling of their unease heavy in the air.

Beyond Heron's rock shelter, he could feel the lifeblood of the People coursing through their bodies, their emotions roiling in the air around him. Their voices carried on the wind, calling out to Father Sun, to the spirits of the animals that had given them life this year.

With deliberate fingers, he plucked up the willow stems, dipping them in the water, sprinkling them over the fire. Leaning forward, he bathed his head and shoulders in the cleansing steam.

Beyond the flap, beyond the rock shelter, he could feel the beginnings of the Renewal Dance. The lilting melody of the old songs caressed the depths of his mind.

From beside him, he unwrapped the fox-hide bundle, letting his fingers play over the hard thin slices of the mushroom. Fear began to extend icy fingers into his thoughts; they curled and crept through his soul. Brutally, he forced them away, banishing the lingering remnants of the memory of Heron's eyes—horror-locked in death.

Four times, as Heron had taught him, he passed the willow through the fire, sprinkling the stems onto the glowing coals. Leaning forward, he bathed himself in the smoke, cleansing himself. Then, one by one, he lifted the thin slices of mushroom, passing them through the cleansing smoke before placing them on his tongue.

And the bitterness possessed him.

Dancing Fox struggled down the rocky path. Below her, the Renewal spread, the final dance lined out. Crow Caller—it had to be him—cavorted in the center near a smoking fire as the People watched, clapping their hands, bodies swaying to the familiar chants that called the souls of the animals.

"Just a little farther," Dancing Fox panted, feeling her breath burning in her lungs.

"Little farther," Three Falls whispered groggily, fighting against the exhaustion and pain and shock. "Just a . . . little . . ."

"That's right. We're saved. We're here." Dancing Fox collected herself and shouted, "Hey!" It came out as a garbled bark.

Someone turned. Young Moss, a tall straight youth, poked

Crow Foot, and together they raced up the path. Dancing Fox blinked her fatigue away, her smile a grimace as they took Three Falls from her shaking arms, supporting his weight. The bloody binding on his thigh told it all.

"Others," she whispered gruffly.

"How close?" Moss asked, lifting Three Falls' arm over his shoulder, taking the wounded man's weight.

Dancing Fox puffed, pushing her hair back. "Two days north."

Crow Foot grunted. "We'll have to get a war party together quickly."

"Not for those we met," Dancing Fox added hoarsely, coughing. "Dead. Killed them all. But more will come. More will always come."

Moss looked over Three Falls where his head wobbled unsteadily. "Nice work, warrior. I, for one, take back the things I said about your courage."

Glassy eyes met his. "Not . . . me." Three Falls smiled weakly. "First dart . . . got me . . . good. Fox . . . Fox killed all five. They didn't take her seriously. Bad . . . mistake."

Crow Foot looked over his shoulder to where Fox followed. "You? *You killed five?*"

She narrowed her eyes. "Quit gawking and see to this man. Where's Wolf Dreamer?"

Moss's expression soured, his voice derisive. "In the witch's hole."

"Hey?" Crow Foot called. "Looks like you stopped a dart, too. You're limping."

She glared at him. "If Three Falls dies, I'll get you next."

Something in the way she said it—in the hot anger reddening her face—stopped his surly reply. They nodded, bearing Three Falls away.

Dancing Fox stopped at the side of the hot pool, barely aware of the curious eyes as she wove through knots of people. In the center of the ring, she could hear Crow Caller's high-pitched voice exhorting.

False Dreams. She smiled wryly.

Bending to the warm water, she washed her face of grime and stale sweat. Heedless of the whispers hissing behind her, she shucked off her parkas, bathing her upper body. Sponging the water from her flesh, she flapped her skins over her shoulder and walked toward Heron's shelter. Life seeped into her with the chill of the breeze over her wet skin. The gooseflesh seemed to energize her.

One Who Cries stood there, arms crossed, talking nervously to Singing Wolf. He shot a quick glance her way and nodded as Singing Wolf continued talking. Then he started, head swiveling, mouth falling open.

"So I'm supposed to be on the other side of the ice," she grunted, already in foul humor.

They both rushed at her.

"What're you doing here?" Singing Wolf demanded frantically, trying to keep his voice down.

She glared at him from between slitted eyes, voice a low growl. "Trying to save the People. Something wrong with that?"

"Get her away," Singing Wolf pleaded. "Go, now, we may not have much time."

One Who Cries grabbed her arm, whirling her so fast she almost fell. "What the . . ."

"Hush!" One Who Cries appealed frantically. "He's Dreaming! Don't you understand? You know what that means?"

She snarled and ripped her arm away. "No, I don't."

"Heron," he gritted. "If he sees you . . . breaks the Dream . . . If he or the People mean anything to you, you've got to go. Anyplace. Just so he doesn't see you. You'll *kill* him!"

Through the haze of exhaustion and anger, it began to penetrate. "Where?" she asked listlessly.

"This way. Hurry." One Who Cries took her by the arm again, steering her through the crowd as the dancers took up the chant, circling.

"I thought my brother would have left his hole by now." Raven Hunter propped hands on his hips as he stopped before Singing Wolf. The man guarded the entrance as though his life depended on it.

"Renewal is almost over." Four Teeth met Raven Hunter's triumphant eyes. "Runs In Light won't leave the darkness?

He won't show himself to Father Sun? There are whisperings that he's a witch. When will he come out so we can see him?''

Singing Wolf cocked his head, studying Raven Hunter through narrowed eyes. "When he's finished Dreaming."

Raven Hunter chuckled to himself, looking around, watching the line of dancers circling the birch and willow fire. "One Who Cries went to stick himself into Dancing Fox? I have another rival?"

"Shut up."

Raven Hunter's face twitched. The time had long passed when a man could speak to him like that. He smiled threateningly. "I hear she killed five Others on the way here. Then she saved Three Falls' life. Practically carried him. Quite the woman, isn't she? And you hustle her away from my brother? Afraid he'll be diluted if his manhood throbs and erupts?"

"You don't understand," Singing Wolf said through clenched jaws. "I've seen him. I have some idea about what he's doing. There's a—"

"Quit stalling!" He gestured around. "You've heard the talk. The People think he's afraid—unwilling to meet Crow Caller face-to-face. Now here you stand, guarding his hole."

Singing Wolf shook his head slowly, a smoky haze of anger in his eyes. "You don't know what he's risking in there. You, you're his brother! And you don't understand what he's doing? He's Dreaming, even as we speak."

"He's hiding," Four Teeth grumbled. "His credibility's gone, Singing Wolf. Gone. Three days now since you told us he'd begun to Dream. Three days! And where is he? Huh? Where? I took your word."

"You don't understand the Power of the—"

"Bah!" Four Teeth spat to accent his disgust. "He's buried in those rocks there! Locked away. Under the ground. His soul's trapped. That's what he's done. Trapped himself."

Singing Wolf's face tightened, a pain in his eyes.

Raven Hunter took the opportunity. "Grandfather, don't chasten this hunter and warrior. He shouldn't suffer for my brother's delusions. Runs In Light is calculating, capable of twisting truths and men's loyalties. Singing Wolf isn't. . . ."

The hanging moved aside. He stood there, arms raised to

the sun, eyes closed as his lips moved in a wordless chant. He walked on unsteady legs, eyes opening.

Raven Hunter met those eyes—and unconsciously stepped backward, a cold chill tracing his backbone. His brother seemed someone else completely, eyes wide and gleaming. Wolf Dreamer passed him, passed him as if he didn't exist. Shooting a quick look at Singing Wolf, he caught the worship, the absorbing devotion.

A rustle disturbed the fringes of the spectators watching the dance. Mutters and whispers grew on the air as people shuffled, clearing an avenue. Those who met the Dreamer's eyes hushed, awed.

Raven Hunter heard Singing Wolf whisper, "Wolf Dreamer," and chafed at the adoration in his voice.

Raven Hunter flexed his muscles, calming himself. "There's still Crow Caller," he reminded as he followed in the wake of his tottering brother. "And if Crow Caller hesitates—I'll be there."

Chapter 53

Dancing Fox watched him from the cover of Singing Wolf's tent. Situated slightly above, she could see him as he stepped out, pushing past Raven Hunter and Four Teeth as if they didn't exist. Father Sun, at the peak of the Long Light, illuminated his face with a shaft of ocher light. Even over the distance, she could feel his vibrating presence. The People stepped back in fear.

Dancing Fox watched him, heart pounding. He'd drawn the wolf on his forehead, just as he had that day so long ago in Mammoth Camp. That day, he'd gone from her. And again, she saw the Dream in his eyes—a living ecstasy.

A dull ache filled her. A sense of premonition. This man, this Dreamer, she didn't know.

* * *

"I . . . am . . . alive!"

Like mist, he rose in the darkness, feeling the pulsing soul of the rock around him. Each of the tremors of the geyser surged through him, its waters like the blood in his veins. A shared reality—Oneness.

He walked in a Dream, passing the worn caribou flap into the light. Low now, hanging on the horizon, Father Sun blinded him with a painful brilliance despite his closed eyes. He lifted his arms, feeling the warmth—living in the Light.

"Born of you," he whispered, feeling the warmth on his skin. Before him, the Renewal pulsed, the souls of the People gleaming and glowing in their bodies. They shimmered and blazed like breakers in the moonlight. He saw them, knew them, felt them with his very soul.

The Light pervaded everything.

Like a spirit himself, he floated toward them, feeling them, their mutterings of awe sputtering disjointedly in his mind. Raven Hunter he recognized, curious at the Power of his brother's soul. As he approached, his brother retreated, surprised by the Power he projected. Already Raven Hunter had regrouped, strengthened himself. Then he passed, finding his way among the People.

"The earth is renewed," he explained, the rightness of their efforts heady within him. "You've shown Father Sun your gratitude. About you, the souls of the animals smile, warm, happy as they rise to the Blessed Star People."

A blackness, a foul corruption, stirred the silent crowd. Wolf Dreamer girded himself.

"Come forth, darkness! Our time is now. Our place is here. That which you've sought stands before you."

The black lesion among the People wavered, shimmering, changing shape as a space opened around it. The Dream spinning fire around the edges, Crow Caller's shape solidified.

Wolf Dreamer tensed, aware of those eyes, one black, one white. One of sight, one of darkness, opposites crossed. Each a lie.

"You have no purpose here, witch man," Crow Caller's ancient voice rolled in Wolf Dreamer's mind. "Go, boy. Leave us. You interrupt the Renewal. We've tired of your games and claims. We . . ."

Wolf Dreamer reached forward, grabbing the darkness with his hands, feeling the horror of the darkness, the confusion, the fear of such a corrupt soul. Like the sucking mouths of the Soul Eaters of the Long Dark, the blackness reached for him, trying to encircle his soul, to choke it away, drown it in the shadows of corruption. Wolf Dreamer weaved, darting this way and that, spearing the blackness with shafts of Light, driving it back, forcing the insidious feelers from his soul, his life.

The corrupted filth staggered away, seeking to flee, but he held it, surrounding the shapeless mass with Light, exposing it to Father Sun. The shadows shivered and writhed in the brilliance. He twisted it, and heard a cry of agony before he cast the thing down before him.

"Recognize yourself for what you are, Crow Caller!" he thundered. "Go! Cleanse yourself of the filth and rot which have possessed you. It is not too late to save your soul. Purify it for Father Sun."

The blackness shivered, backing away, crawling slowly to its feet.

"I curse you," came the voice. Hate battered at Wolf Dreamer's mind. A vile stench of wrongness tainted his nostrils. The blackness waved arms, tracing symbols for which Crow Caller had no understanding.

"I condemn your soul to be buried! I condemn it!" Crow Caller shrieked, frantic.

Around him, the People flooded back, as if washed by the waves of hatred.

"You have nothing within," said Wolf Dreamer's voice. "No strength, no Power of soul. Only blackness and rot power your words." As he spoke, the soul of Crow Caller split open before his eyes. "Ah . . . I see. Look within yourself, Crow Caller. See the lies? See the fear? Look what you have done to yourself. See what you would do to others! *Look inside yourself!*"

"No!" Crow Caller protested, the voice forced. "I condemn you! Hear me? Condemned to be buried—your soul lost in darkness! Trapped by the earth to . . . to . . ."

Wolf Dreamer closed, the Dream spinning out, showing him the way. Crow Caller danced back, the blackness quivering, fearing exposure.

"Look, within," he repeated. "You fear only yourself, Crow Caller. Your greatest death is ridicule. See the mockery you've made of yourself? Don't fear me, Crow Caller. Fear yourself. Fear what you've made your soul into. The lie you live is that of a coward—a man who's never faced himself!"

"No!" Crow Caller growled, his soul ripping at itself, growing angry. "I curse you, Runs In Light! *Curse you!*"

Wolf Dreamer straightened. "Runs In Light is no more."

Before him, Crow Caller produced a white bone, seemingly from out of thin air. The People gasped.

"With this, I curse you, Runs In Light!" His voice wavered, the cracks weakening it, causing it to tremble. "I blow your soul to the Long Dark!"

Crow Caller leaned forward, blowing hard through the hollow tube of bone.

Wolf Dreamer backed at the stench of the breath, hearing a horrified outcry from the People. He waved at the foul putrid air, fighting the sudden urge to vomit from the corruption.

From his pouch, he took a handful of the yellow crusted rock that formed along the banks of the geyser stream. Like Heron had showed him, he offered it to the four directions. At the top of his lungs, he shouted, "I clear the corruption from the air!"

He threw the yellow-caked stone into the fire, a stinking puff of yellow-green smoke arising. People backpedaled.

"And I blow it away!" Wolf Dreamer took the white crystals, laboriously gathered from under the dung piles, and poured them into the fire. They sparkled, hissed, and flared in an explosion like water on coals.

"You are darkness!" Crow Caller hissed. "Dark and bad. You are death for the People! Go back to darkness, *witch!*"

"Darkness?" Wolf Dreamer smiled. "I am Light. I am one with fire. You are illusion." So saying, he bent, driving his fingers deeply into the bed of coals, hearing the cries of the People as he lifted them high.

"I cleanse myself of your corruption, Crow Caller." The Dream spun coldly around him as he rubbed the blackness Crow Caller had blown on him away, willing it into the coals as he scrubbed his arms and face.

Around him, the souls of the People wavered in a rainbow of colors, shimmering in horror and doubt and awe.

"Cleanse yourself," he offered, handing the glowing coals to Crow Caller. "Dream yourself clean, man of the People! Drive the corruption from within. Here is Light." He spread his fingers to reveal the glowing coals. "I offer you a new way, reach out and take it!"

Crow Caller backed away, shaking his head, pathetically crying, "No! *No!*"

"Do it!"

"N-no!" he wailed, the blackness crumpling, folding in on itself, destroyed in the Light of the spitting smoking fire and its cleansing odor.

"A husk, like a maggot casing," Wolf Dreamer moaned, shaking his head. "That's what you've become, Crow Caller."

"No!"

Wolf Dreamer placed the coals reverently to his lips before dropping them in the fire. He turned, looking to the People. "Pity this creature for what it has done to itself. Forgive it for what it has done to you."

"Don't," Crow Caller muttered from where he crouched, looking up, blinking his one good eye. "Don't do this to . . . to . . ."

His mouth opened, pink tongue darting out between the stained pink gums as he grabbed at his chest.

Wolf Dreamer reached down, the Dream showing him the way. "His heart," he called. "His heart is jumping around, quivering. His soul is killing him. He dies . . . still a coward."

Crow Caller cried out, huddling there on the ground.

Wolf Dreamer straightened, feeling the corrupt soul writhing in agony. "One Who Cries." He recognized the soul as it parted from the crowd. "Take him, he'll be dead soon. Make him comfortable. He must deal with his soul now. Later all of us will sing him to the Blessed Star People."

The shimmering multicolored soul that was One Who Cries lifted the old man lightly from the ground, bearing him through the People.

Wolf Dreamer raised his hands and pointed northward. The souls around him shifted, fluttering and changing colors anxiously. He lowered his voice to a calming murmur. "There, the Others come. You must all make a choice. Our young men can die, kill their young men. Blood will stain the snow, leach into the rocks, trickle through the gravels. But nothing will stop them. See? Look out there! Beyond the hills, see them crouching? Hear the beat of their countless hearts as they close around to smother us? Look close, my people."

And he turned to look himself. A cry of fear rose in his throat at the vision that met his eyes. It came . . . the blackness rolling like waves toward them. "See?" he screamed. "The blackness there beyond the far horizon! Who can stand against that? Feel the Power coming, each step crushing our world?"

Someone cried out in anguish and a rumble of voices rose.

"But life can be ours. . . ."

"How?" someone called piteously. "Tell us!"

He pointed toward the Big Ice where it loomed darkly on the horizon. "Heron Dreamed. . . . She said we would find nothing here but pain, and death. She saw us ground away, bitter, angry, rotting within as we torture, and glut ourselves in an orgy of blood. Ground away! Like a sandstone cobble in a sea of flint! See us ground away? See us buried?"

He whirled at their gasp.

"Yes, buried! Covered by the Others! The ways of the People gone . . . forever!"

"Tell us how we can—"

"Wolf Dream!" Singing Wolf bellowed from somewhere far away. "Wolf will save the People."

"Wolf," he murmured. "Wolf . . . ."

One Who Cries struggled to keep himself from shivering as he laid the old man down in the thick robes of the shelter he'd borrowed. The low structure had been closest to the Dance, the easiest to carry the dying shaman to.

"There, rest easy," One Who Cries said, comforting.

"I was . . . powerful . . . once," Crow Caller whispered. "I led the People. Led them well. Tried to do the best. Tried, you understand?"

One Who Cries nodded somberly. "We remember."

"Did my best." Crow Caller swallowed hard. "But the

People, they always want so much. . . . So much . . . They
suck away your soul. Suck you up . . . like the Long Dark
. . . sucks up heat. They want . . . so much. Always . . .
hungry. Demanding . . . Can't . . . can't be wrong. Always
have to be . . . perfect. All the time. Had to . . . pretend.
Lie.'' He closed his ancient eyes. ''I tried . . . best I
could. . . .''

''We know,'' One Who Cries soothed. ''Rest now, Grandfather.''

''Pain,'' Crow Caller gasped. ''Deep. All along my left
side and arm. Pain.''

''Don't worry, you'll be . . .'' One Who Cries stopped
cold, staring at the place he'd left his darts.

''Dying,'' Crow Caller whispered hoarsely. ''Dying from
the inside.''

But One Who Cries was scuttling out from the caribou-
hide cover, staring about frantically as the crowd watched
Wolf Dreamer, hands raised, tell them of his Dreaming.

One Who Cries ran, skirting the crowd, searching. High.
Look high! He sprinted, leaping from boulder to boulder up
the ridge. He'd be up here, somewhere. The throng ignored
him, staring at Wolf Dreamer, enthralled by the haunting
tones as the Dreamer talked.

Must be high, nothing else would make sense.

He saw him as he scrambled over the rocks.

''No!'' The cry was torn from One Who Cries' throat as
he jumped, fingers outstretched. ''He's your brother!'' Too
far away. The man's arm had started forward, the familiar
dart beginning its journey.

A rock rolled underfoot as One Who Cries crashed into
Raven Hunter's legs, pitching the big hunter sideways. The
dart's path was disrupted, striking a child who stood at Wolf
Dreamer's feet. The tiny boy screamed in pain. The other
darts went clattering away in the rocks. Confusion swelled
as One Who Cries howled his rage.

Raven Hunter smashed him across the head with his atlatl,
ripping his cheek open. ''Let go of me! I'm saving the People!''

''You're *killing* us!'' One Who Cries bellowed.

He grappled with the hunter, rolling over and over. One

Who Cries grabbed up a hand-sized rock, swinging it, smashing it into Raven Hunter's ribs.

Again and again, the atlatl battered him on the head and across the face. Desperate, One Who Cries bent close to Raven Hunter's kicking legs and, with nothing better to do, sank his stubby worn teeth into the man's thigh. Raven Hunter roared.

He heard the blow that jarred his head; it sounded hollow, a sickly thump. Lights flashed behind One Who Cries' eyes and the world shivered and slipped under his loose fingers as he fell into gray.

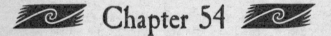

Chapter 54

Singing Wolf pulled One Who Cries' bloody head to his lap, calling softly, "Cousin?"

The People crowded around, staring. Singing Wolf swallowed hard. He sat before Heron's shelter, Raven Hunter standing haughtily before him, back straight, arms crossed, glaring around like a cornered eagle. Four Teeth rocked back and forth, sucking his gums, disbelief in his rheumy eyes. Puffs of clouds rolled down from the north, promising rain. The mountains—half-masked by the geyser steam—looked on, bored spectators.

The blood leaking out of One Who Cries' head had coated Singing Wolf's fingers—sticky, matting his hands.

"He'll live. Hardheaded that one." Four Teeth shook his head. The People stared, fleeting whispers of horror scurrying from lip to lip in the manner of running lemmings on the tundra.

The breeze whipped Wolf Dreamer's hair wildly about his head as he ducked beneath the door flap of an unknown lodge; the crowd parted, leaving a wide swath for him.

"Twisted Root is dead," Wolf Dreamer told them in a lilting voice. "I watched the boy's soul slip from the body.

A yellow-red soul, the wound left it blue . . . and green. Cold, you understand? Tonight I'll sing Twisted Root to the sky. The Star People will accept him.''

"Now what?" Raven Hunter lifted his chin, arrogant eyes seeking among the crowd, locking with the young men's.

Wolf Dreamer—lost in the layers of his soul—said slowly, "You killed one of the People, brother. A six-year-old boy. You broke the peace. The light is draining from your soul. You're losing yourself to the Power."

"He killed one of the People," Singing Wolf reminded. "The penalty is—"

"He's the best warrior we have!" Eagle Cries protested, elbowing in from the crowd. "He's shown honor in the fight against the Others."

Singing Wolf was on his feet, glaring into Eagle Cries' haughty black eyes. "He would have killed the Dreamer!"

"Runs In Light killed Crow Caller!" Raven Hunter's lip went up. "Witchery! That's how. He witched him!"

"Liar!" Singing Wolf gritted his teeth, fists clenched. In his breast, anger burned. "One more word, and I'll—"

"Wait." Wolf Dreamer placed a cool hand on Singing Wolf's shoulder, pulling him back. "I see your soul, old friend. You'd hate yourself if you followed your anger at Renewal."

Singing Wolf fought with his rage—barely winning despite the Dreamer's words.

"He's lied, murdered, raped. Why do I expect more from a coward who'd betray his people?" Singing Wolf looked down at the blood on his hands.

At the hushed explosion of breath from the People, Raven Hunter tensed, trying to take a step forward, restrained by Four Teeth, who stood behind him.

"You'll regret that," Raven Hunter promised.

"How have we come to this?" Four Teeth cried passionately.

"Witchery," Raven Hunter insisted. "I'll not see the People destroyed by my brother. When he killed Crow Caller—my friend—through dark Dreaming, I grabbed up my darts and—"

"Liar twice," a frail voice called.

They turned to see One Who Cries weakly prop himself on his elbows. Blood streaked his tanned cheeks in a web.

"What do you know, One Who Cries? Perhaps it's as Raven Hunter says." Four Teeth turned, uneasy eyes on Wolf Dreamer.

One Who Cries blinked, weaving before lying back down. He stuttered, "I—I . . ." in confusion, as if he'd lost his thoughts.

"It's as I say," Raven Hunter growled. "Dark Dreaming has no place among the People. My brother is a witch! He had all the People enchanted by his act. Fooled by his words and the way he stopped Crow Caller's heart. I would have freed them. I took the first opportunity, that's all."

"A man does things in passion," Buffalo Back agreed. "But the dart struck little Twisted Root. There must be punish—"

"It was an accident!" Raven Hunter protested. "What's wrong with us? Here, before us, is a witch! When I saw him perverting the People, I grabbed up my darts."

"Liar," One Who Cries whispered from where he lay. "You stole *my* darts. Then you went around to shoot from the side of the ridge where you had a clear shot. *My darts!* So no one would know who did it. My tent is across the fire, Raven Hunter. You planned it."

"Your darts?" Raven Hunter laughed. "Head wounds do that. Cause—"

"Who has the darts?" Singing Wolf cried out, looking around, arms spread. "Where is the dart that struck the boy?"

Twisted Root's father—tears streaking his face—came forward, a short length of bloody wood in his hands. "Wolf Dreamer pulled it from where it stuck out of my son's back. This is not one of the People's darts. It's too short."

Singing Wolf took the gruesome weapon, holding it up, displaying the broken point. "This belongs to One Who Cries. Look where the boy was darted. You'll find the detachable shaft with the fletching. Only One Who Cries makes a dart like this."

A woman cried as she pounced on the shaft, Twisted Root's blood marking the spot.

Singing Wolf turned to Raven Hunter, accusation in his hot

glare. "The penalty for breaking the peace—killing one of the People—is death."

Four Teeth closed his eyes, a look of misery on his face. He stiffened slowly.

Wolf Dreamer stepped to look into his brother's eyes and murmured, "I asked you not to try and stop me. I see loops and coils in the future—but not the whole length of the path you will travel. Go! Alone! Find your destiny."

Raven Hunter growled. "You're making me an outcast? Condemning me?"

Singing Wolf turned sharply. "He deserves dea—"

"Go! Even as we speak, the web is spinning out, brother. Seek your heritage, and return. So you can"—his voice faltered as he took a deep breath—"can force our final meeting. Opposites crossed. Final resolution."

"Your meaning is hidden, like a caribou fawn in spring." Raven Hunter's black eyes danced angrily.

"You must lose yourself to see, brother. Or remain in darkness. What do you choose?"

Raven Hunter turned, glaring out at the gathered crowd. "I call my brother a witch! I denounce him here, before you all. I, Raven Hunter, will follow no witch into the darkness! I, I alone, will stand before the Others and show you all what honor is!"

He searched their eyes, pinning each of his uneasy warriors in turn with his hot glare. "Who will come with me?"

No one spoke, no one moved.

After several heartbeats, Four Teeth said, "No one goes with you, Raven Hunter. I say you are outcast."

"But he *murdered*!" Singing Wolf exploded. "The penalty for murdering—"

"No. Raven Hunter will not die for killing Twisted Root." Wolf Dreamer shook his head. "More, he is not outcast."

Four Teeth spun on an ancient heel, face livid with rage. "You would *dare* argue with an elder who . . ." He stopped, seeing the Dream in the youth's eyes. Swallowing, he dropped his gaze, shoulders sagging. "No, Raven Hunter is not outcast."

"Raven Hunter must face the future alone."

"Cowards!" Raven Hunter exploded. "The Others will

crush us to dust! Salvation is out there! Warring with the Others! *There* is my honor, and I'll go take it!''

Breaking free of the hands that held him back, Raven Hunter stalked to his tent, a path clearing for him among the crowded ranks of the People. In silence, they watched as he picked up his weapons, robes, and pouch before running nimbly up the path. At the top, he stopped, turned back, an angry figure against a cloud-gray sky. He gestured once, futilely, and disappeared.

Singing Wolf sighed, looking back in time to see Wolf Dreamer turn, his face ghastly pale.

''Help me,'' he called softly.

Singing Wolf ran to grab his arm and lead him stumbling back to Heron's shelter.

''The end is coming,'' Wolf Dreamer murmured. ''See the spinning of the web? It spins around the darkness. It will . . . will . . .'' He broke into uncontrollable shivering.

A horrid fear was born in Singing Wolf's heart.

A low fire burned in the bottom of the pit. *Why must it fall to me? I'm not the one for this. Such leadership belongs to the elders. Why did Singing Wolf call me here?* Dancing Fox pulled her arctic fox hood over her head to block the icy breeze penetrating the shelter.

Singing Wolf peered into the fire, a frown lining his forehead. Four Teeth looked sick to the very root of his soul. Rain pattered on the hide roof overhead. The air itself hung heavy, damp, musty with the odors of the camp and the geyser. In the chill of the night, the fire did little to warm the small shelter.

''I think we should order everyone to go through the hole in the ice,'' Singing Wolf insisted to end the long silence.

''We really don't have much choice,'' Dancing Fox said as she stared into the black rain falling beyond the doorway. ''The Others know about the route south. Moon Water has told them everything by now.''

''Maybe they'll just let us go,'' Singing Wolf said in a monotone. Once more, he rubbed thumbs into his bloodshot eyes.

Four Teeth sat in the rear of the shelter, listening, eyes focused somewhere in the glowing coals as he rocked back and forth, lips moving silently. They were all awed, tired, drained clear to their souls.

Singing Wolf kept glancing uneasily toward Heron's shelter, where Wolf Dreamer lay delirious. Crow Caller's body had been carried to the high spot above the valley. Buffalo Back and a group of women sang there, urging the old shaman's soul to the Blessed Star People as Wolf Dreamer ordered. The People were in shock; silence—made heavier by the storm—hung over the camp.

Dancing Fox had walked among them, heart tearing at the confusion in their eyes, the uncertainty unraveling their souls. Had these truly been the laughing people of her youth? Now despair clung like a clammy film. Unable to bear any more, she'd gone to Singing Wolf, and he'd listened to what she said and brought her here to Four Teeth in hopes they might bring sanity out of chaos.

Singing Wolf shook his head. "Too much blood's been spilled. Raven Hunter's warriors tortured and mutilated the dead. To the Others' way of thinking, those souls will never go to the place of the dead under the sea. The families of those mutilated warriors won't rest until the souls have been appeased. It's honor."

"That true?" Four Teeth asked.

"Blueberry and I had long talks about it."

"The best bet is to get away. Go through the hole." Dancing Fox crossed her legs, wincing as she bent her ankle, and propped her chin on her palms.

Singing Wolf chewed absently on a leather thong as he spoke. "The People will go through the ice. There's no doubt of that now. Only the water's blocking the way. We have to hold on until the Long Dark. In the meantime, the Others aren't this far south . . . yet."

Dancing Fox worked her aching ankle as she looked at Blueberry. "Do you think we have that long?"

"Who knows? It'll depend on their clan ceremonies. It will depend on Ice Fire, too."

"Ice Fire?" Dancing Fox steepled fingers, frowning. "Their Dreamer?"

"Their equivalent to a Dreamer, I think. No one knows much about him. He's . . ." Singing Wolf looked perplexed. "Well, I hear he's a strange man."

"Anyone with Spirit Power is strange," Four Teeth muttered.

"We'll need to protect ourselves in the meantime." Dancing Fox met Singing Wolf's eyes across the fire. "We know the land down here better than they do. We can control some of the major trails through the hill country to the north. Maybe we can hold them back long enough to get our people through the ice."

Silence pressed on them, Four Teeth shifted. His stomach growled loudly in the quiet shelter.

"How's Wolf Dreamer?" Dancing Fox asked with trepidation.

"Bad." Singing Wolf's uneasy eyes met hers. "He's half in the Dream, half out. He can't keep anything down. Give him water and he spits it up. He lies there, singing, mumbling. Every time I'm in there, the look in his eyes scares me to death."

Silence stretched again as they stared soberly at nothing.

"We can't have more raiding then," Dancing Fox decided, forcing her mind away from Wolf Dreamer, stifling that longing to run to him and comfort him. "That only fuels anger among the Others."

"That's not how Raven Hunter trained his warriors," Four Teeth reminded.

"Already they're chafing at what happened to Raven Hunter." Singing Wolf steepled his fingers. "They were off balance, shocked at the Renewal. Everything was so incredible, they didn't know what to do. Now, they've had time to think. Some are wondering if it wouldn't have been better to go with Raven Hunter."

"But that's how the Dreamer's going to say it's to be done," Dancing Fox decided. "No more raiding."

"He will?" Four Teeth started, looking up from the coals.

She nodded. "He will. And if he doesn't—outside of the circle of us—who'll know?"

They shifted, throwing uneasy glances her way. Four Teeth straightened, about to speak. He stopped, closing his mouth, looking away.

"That's taking"—Singing Wolf winced—"a lot of . . ."

"Necessary precautions," Dancing Fox insisted. "That is,

if Wolf Dreamer doesn't come to his senses from the Dreaming and do it himself.''

"This could be dangerous," Four Teeth whispered. "We all saw what happened to Crow Caller. We saw.''

The silence grew heavy again.

They won't take the lead. It's the obvious answer. We've got to use the Power of Wolf Dreamer's name. If we don't, the cohesion of the People will leak away and we'll be broken again. Can't they see? It's now or never! Someone has to begin to undo what Raven Hunter created. The young men have to be stopped—now!

Dancing Fox steeled herself, choosing her words carefully. "I won't usurp Wolf Dreamer's responsibilities. I'm not interested in leading the People. But we don't know how long Wolf Dreamer's going to be locked in the Dream. We don't know if he'll ever come out of it. In the meantime, someone has to see to the People. This time it can't be Raven Hunter making his own way. It can't be the elders alone who do it. We all have to agree. Otherwise the People end up split apart like old caribou bone left in the sun. We can't have everyone following separate paths. We're not strong enough to do that with the Others closing—and nowhere to run. Are we agreed?'' Dancing Fox looked ardently from face to face.

One by one, they nodded.

"And how do you see us doing this, woman?'' Four Teeth asked, a labored quality to his voice. His old shoulders slumped in resignation.

Dancing Fox frowned. "Singing Wolf and Eagle Cries would be the best choices to direct the warriors. Together, they can lead the young men in a new direction.''

"But Eagle Cries worships Raven Hunter! He's—''

"He's respected by all the young men. We must join both sides of the People now or lose some forever.''

"Agreed.'' Singing Wolf sighed. "I'll talk to him. Oh, for the days when I could be a surly callous complainer. I owe Broken Branch for this.''

"For the days when we were all young . . . with no cares,'' Dancing Fox added softly. She turned to Four Teeth. "Grandfather, we need the elders to calm the People, remind them that food will be scarce until we're through the ice. We all look up to you and Buffalo Back and the others. You've got to reassure the People, inspire them. Remind them we are all one. Bolster their courage."

Four Teeth bobbed his shriveled head. "We can do that. For once, I'm pleased to hear a young woman talk with so much sense. Sense—among the young—seems to have blown away with Wind Woman's breath."

"I'll give some thought to preparing for the ice." She began cataloging resources. "We'll need to gather all the berries we can for winter food. We need to strip out the willows and dwarf birch. With game this scarce, there won't be much fat rendered. For light in the hole, maybe we can get by with willow roots dried in the sun. They burn fast, and they're heavy and awkward to carry and hard to keep lit. But they'll be light.

"In the meantime, we'll make a collection of all the fat we can find and store it someplace where the permafrost will keep it and the mice can't get it. What there is should be saved for emergency food—or in case the willows burn out under the ice. The children can organize drives, see if we can't trap mice and ground squirrels and dry them. All these young boys and girls can drive the shallows of the Big River for char and grayling."

"Starvation food," Singing Wolf said sourly. At Dancing Fox's hard look, he clarified. "But I gave up being proud a long time ago."

Four Teeth chuckled under his breath. "You really think the Others would walk into that hole?" he asked as he shook his head. "It just . . . well, you'd have to be crazy to walk into something like that. Crazy! People shouldn't be underground. You know, what if someone should die in there? How would their souls find the way to the Blessed Star People? They'd be stuck in the dark forever."

Dancing Fox shivered. "You don't know how frightening it really is. Wait until you walk through there."

Four Teeth coughed and spat into the fire, lips pursed sourly. "I've been a lot of places, seen a lot of things. I can't say I look forward to walking under the ice. This new land had better be all you say."

"It is," Singing Wolf asserted. "And who knows what we'll find in that valley running to the south?"

"Maybe a land without starvation?" the old man asked, a glow coming to his eyes.

"A place where the game is everywhere and we can raise our children without hunger," Singing Wolf whispered. "I remember Heron talking about a new plant that the People would eat. I can see myself growing fat in a new land. Yes, I can see that with little effort."

"Another Dreamer?" Four Teeth asked cynically, a haze of reserve in his eyes.

"No, I'm not brave enough," Singing Wolf added earnestly. "But we've got to do something. Look around. I see our people falling apart like an old parka when the gut thread rots. I don't like that hole in the ice. I can't see how Wolf Dreamer could have ever walked into it."

"Crazy! People with Spirit Power are all crazy," Four Teeth pronounced, pounding a fist against his knee.

"But he did. And found the path Wolf promised. Everything he said to us at Mammoth Camp has come true."

The rain increased, a gust of wind slapping the soaked hide overhead. Four Teeth reached behind him to drop another couple of twigs into the fire. The cheery crackle and additional light vanquished a bit of the storm.

Dancing Fox pulled her wealth of hair back where the breeze teased it. "We've got three choices. Stay and starve, push north and fight the Others, or go through the ice. I follow Wolf Dreamer."

"We all do," Singing Wolf agreed. "We have to if we want to survive."

She searched their eyes. "On the other side, it won't be easy either. All the People coming to Heron's valley have hunted out the game. Those hunters we don't need to scout the Others will have to search out every animal left up here to give us enough food for the trip."

"Not the old bull mammoth!" Singing Wolf insisted sternly. "He's Heron's. Dead or not, we don't need her wrath."

Dancing Fox scowled. "We don't have a meat supply to go into the Long Dark."

"Heron protected that old bull. I say save the old bull. More than that, Wolf Dreamer would save the old bull."

She threw her hands up. "All right! The old bull's saved!

He's life for the People, but I'll concede—which means that 'starvation food' is going to be very important. No time must be lost. Maybe the game will be as plentiful on the other side as it was this year. Maybe not. We all know animals move. We won't have as much to make do with. Like the horrible Long Dark, this could be a terrible year. Our clothes are worn, the insulating hair is falling out, the leather's abraded to holes. It'll be hard. One of the hardest things we've faced yet.''

"Our last chance,'' Singing Wolf whispered. "Do you agree, Grandfather?''

Four Teeth nodded, a sigh rasping in his throat. "I've heard Dancing Fox. If it will save the People, I'll do it. Let us hope the Others wait—and the game will favor us south of the ice, in this new land.''

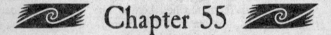

Chapter 55

The rolling hills were hazy, a green yellow that couldn't obscure the gray tones of rock. Wildflowers sprinkled the land in irregular patterns of yellow and blue, the blossoms already faded from the growing berry bushes. But no animals grazed within sight. Ice Fire sat cross-legged before a small fire, his gaze restless and flickering with disturbing thoughts. In the harsh white light, the muscles of his square jaw quivered.

Behind him, soft footfalls rustled in the grass; hide pants swished against the dew-covered blades.

"The farther south we go, the drier it gets, the higher it gets, the scrubbier the plants are.'' Red Flint shook his head nervously. "I don't like it.''

He took two more steps forward to gaze down at Ice Fire. "I've heard complaints. The hunting's not so good here. The elders are talking about moving north again to be where more game winters through the deep cold.''

"But the Enemy have found a way through the ice."

"Me? Travel days through some hole?" Red Flint exploded. "Do I look like a ground squirrel?"

Ice Fire cradled his chin as he looked out across the hills. Curlews chirruped on a nearby tumbled pile of boulders, beaks pointed to the drifting clouds.

"You heard what Smoke had to say? More hostile peoples are pushing east, filling the territory left by the Glacier People. It's the disease. Some horror is loose far to the west. I wonder how much time we'll have before they come to kill us. If the water keeps rising, the ghost hole might be our only hope."

Red Flint studied him through slitted eyes. "I think it's more than that, old friend. I think you're driven . . . obsessed by this vision of yours and that witch, the Watcher. Oh, yes, I saw you the other day. Your eyes went shiny, you didn't hear what was said to you. And then when you finally mumbled, you said, 'My son's coming.' What son? You have no son."

Ice Fire looked away, licking his lip. "I didn't know I spoke."

"You spoke. Many heard you."

"My son . . . doesn't matter. Our hope is to head south."

"You believe this ghost-hole story?"

"You call your own daughter a liar?"

Red Flint lowered his eyes, staring at the damp hem of his hide pants leg. "No . . . But I think she was taken in by that Dreamer of theirs and his delusions of a land of plenty."

"But she saw the game."

"She might have, but after people have been there for a year or two, it'll be gone—just like it is here. I say we head north. We left a perfectly good salt water full of seals and fish and clams and mussels."

"And already the Buffalo Clan is living there. They follow in our tracks while the Tiger Belly and Round Hoof Clans are restricted by the rising salt water along the western plains. True, it allows them to defend the west from the far Enemy and their disease, but people are worried."

"Let them worry. We know there's plenty of food along the coast. Meanwhile, let's destroy the Enemy here—make one concerted effort to wipe them out and live north—"

"Yes . . . but how long before the far Enemy and other tribes cross the water and—"

"Listen, old friend. I've had my ears open. I've listened to the representatives sent by the clans. Ice Stalker and the others say the White Tusk Clan is happy with what we've done. We've brought the White Hide home again. The old men think that's enough. But the hunters complain that the game isn't as plentiful here. The young women whisper among themselves, fearful of being captured by an Enemy. I see an erosion of will. A lack of commitment to the extermination of these Enemy. You must do something! Stir up their hatred! Remind them of the rapes . . . of the mutilated babies. Of captured warriors cut apart and left for the crows. You have that power! Make them hate! Or we'll lose the Hide next year."

Ice Fire looked up at him, smiling feebly. "And what are the other clan representatives saying? What do the Round Hoof and Buffalo think? Do they, too, argue for extermination?"

Red Flint's fanatic gaze fell. "Since being here, they have doubts about the honor gained warring with such a small remnant as the Enemy. They wonder whether we truly have courage." He looked away and rubbed his nose. "And many are clamoring for peace."

"The people tire of war?"

"Yes, but they don't understand that we have to—"

"What are they saying?"

Red Flint thundered, " 'Let the Enemy go!' they cry. 'We've killed enough to atone for the deaths of our own. Isn't that enough?' " He balled a fist. "Enough? *Enough?* Where's our honor? Already too many of our young girls carry their rotted seed!"

"Is this a personal battle? Have you stopped caring what the people want?"

Red Flint's lips twitched as he looked away, making a throwing-away motion with his arm. "Moon Water has told me over and over how the Enemy treated her. I want them wiped out. All of them. Pay them back for the mutilations of our young men. When the last of them is killed and buried, then I say we go back and live by the salt water."

Ice Fire lifted a shoulder, idly watching an eagle dive and

soar on the wind currents, a black dot swirling in endless blue.

"I walk around the camp and hear our children talking about the Blessed Star People. I like that. I hear them talk about the Monster Children. I like that story, too. Perhaps we shouldn't be warring with each other? We were one people once."

"Impossible! Relatives to an Enemy who cut my cousin's body apart when they captured him! *Cut him apart!* His soul's out there, wandering, crying for justice—and you'd befriend these Enemy? I say kill them for the vile corruption they are. Men, women, children! Brain them all. Erase every last trace of their seed from the earth."

"So, you will destroy your daughter's child when it comes?"

Red Flint jerked around, scowling. "Of course not! What sort of question is that?"

"The seed is this Jumping Hare's. Your daughter's child was planted on the other side of the ice by an Enemy. But then, you'll have to kill Wasp over there. Look at him." He pointed to the handsome boy who frolicked with a group, practicing throwing their darts at a mound of soil. Childish laughter lilted on the cool breeze.

"What are you—"

"He thinks he's going to be a warrior. Down Chest and Ten Feathers fawn over him. He was the child they couldn't have, remember? Black Claw picked him out of an Enemy camp years ago. Stole him away in the middle of the night. He's full-blooded Enemy. You'll break their hearts when you kill him."

"You're twisting my words," Red Flint grumbled, looking away.

"Am I? I don't think so."

"I don't like killing either," he muttered. "But we have to have a way of gaining honor or we'll lose the Hide again. And these Enemy and their disgusting ways are the best . . ." He stopped, shielding his eyes against the sun as he scrutinized the distant hills.

A muffled war cry rose on the breeze. The warriors in camp leapt to their feet, grabbing up their darts.

"I don't believe it," Red Flint murmured. "Look!"

Ice Fire turned, seeing the man trotting toward the camp. Even over the distance, he couldn't mistake the long parka of the Enemy. Shouts raised all around the camp.

The man continued to run as warriors boiled out of shelters, nocking darts.

"Careful!" Ice Fire called, quickly getting to his feet. "Keep watch! This could be a diversion, something to take our attention away from the rear."

Young men sprinted for the surrounding hilltops, heeding his orders.

No more than two dart throws away, the Enemy stopped, shucking off his parka, dropping his pack. Naked, he picked up his weapons and walked forward.

"Wait!" Ice Fire commanded as his young men raised their weapons, grinning as they moved to meet him, a blood glow in their eyes. At his words, they stopped, milling, uncertain at what the Most Respected Elder could want when prey presented itself so easily.

Ice Fire walked forward, snatches of the visions floating in his mind. *An angry young man. Defiant.* His heart began to pound.

"Respected Elder?" Walrus asked as he passed the foremost of the warriors. "No farther, he can hit you from there."

Ice Fire shook his head, absently aware of the looks they cast his way. His eyes remained locked with the Enemy warrior's. So close, yet so far away. As if they stared at each other through time as well as space. A tunnel darkened around him, hazy and fluttering. Ice Fire walked forward in a dream. His heart beat strongly, blood coursing in his veins as he went to stand before the young man, aware of his warriors closing around them, nervous, anxious for his safety—held back by respect for his Power.

The Enemy stood tall, straight, well muscled. The features of his face were finely formed, the chin strong, nose long and broad. High cheekbones cast shadows to either side of his firm lips. The forehead rose smoothly over emotionally charged black eyes. Like a bent willow, he stood, poised, chest rising and falling, belly tight, balanced for conflict. Not once did his eyes flicker from Ice Fire's.

"Who are you?" Ice Fire asked, standing no more than a body length from the Enemy.

"Raven Hunter," the man panted. "I've come to kill you."

Ice Fire flinched. "Why?"

Raven Hunter lifted his chin, the rolling tones of his voice clear in the still air. "I have come to take the heart and soul of the Others. By doing so, I'll destroy you—and save my people."

A stir came from the hawk-eyed warriors circling them.

Ice Fire nodded. "Wolf Dreamer has driven you out."

This time the Enemy flinched, jaw muscles leaping like mice on coals.

Ice Fire filled his lungs and blew it out. Turning, he raised his hands. "There will be no death here today." He looked harshly back at Raven Hunter. "Come to my shelter. We must talk, you and I."

"Why? What have you to say to me? I am here to kill you and die! My visions have betrayed me! My people have betrayed me. What's left?"

"I am," Ice Fire murmured.

"Then die!" Raven Hunter's hand whipped back, the dart nocked in his intricately carved atlatl.

With uncommon agility for his age, Ice Fire moved, leaping to grasp the stone tip of the dart as Raven Hunter threw his weight into the throw. Ice Fire's arm knotted, muscles cording and bulging. They stood for a second, face-to-face, struggling. Some wildness roiled in the warrior's eyes, terrified and angry. The wooden shaft bowed and split with a splintering crack.

As quickly, Walrus closed from behind, wiry arms clamping around Raven Hunter's chest. Other warriors rushed in, driving him to the ground, pummeling him with fists and elbows.

"I want him alive," Ice Fire ordered, gripping the dart meant for his heart in one knotted fist, a faint tracing of blood sliding down the meaty part of his palm where the keen edge had cut.

"Why?" Raven Hunter demanded, straining against his captors.

Ice Fire's eyes narrowed as an ache built in his chest. "I owe it to your brother."

Chapter 56

The mammoth-hide lodge stretched thirty feet long and twenty wide; a fire burned dimly in the center, crackling in the heavy silence. People crowded in, anxious to see what would happen to the crazy captive.

Yellow Leaf, a bent old woman with long gray braids, edged forward, eyes squinted. "I say we cut him apart just like he did our sons!" she cried, working her toothless mouth as she glared around the gathering. "Send his foul soul out to wander forever with my grandson's. That's justice! That's honor, to pay back in kind!"

Grunts of endorsement came from around the packed shelter, hard mouths set, jutted chins nodding approval.

Ice Fire bowed his head, clutching his arms tightly across his breast. Red Flint wanted a campaign of extermination. The angry warriors were with him, ready to crush the last of the Enemy before they could escape through the hole. The rest of the White Tusk Clan felt satisfied. They'd run the Enemy out of the good country. Now they wanted to enjoy their spoils before the Buffalo Clan moved into those grounds.

"You do know who this is, don't you?" Moon Water's voice cut through the throng as she elbowed her way forward. "This man is their war leader, Raven Hunter. He's the one who's led the raids against us. He's the one who told them to crush our infants and torture old women. He led them—made them do it. You want revenge? Here's the one to get it from."

She sought out the greatest warriors, chin high, challenging, her swollen belly reminding them of what the Enemy did to captives. "When you kill him, kill him slowly. Then, according to his beliefs, bury him in the ground."

Raven Hunter heaved against the thongs binding him, muscles straining under sweat-smooth skin. "No! Don't bury me! Don't leave my soul in the—"

Walrus kicked him in the side, doubling him over, leaving him grunting and shaking as his stomach heaved from nausea.

Ice Fire studied him.

hatred between our peoples? Has he rent us so far asunder I can never repair the rip?

Walrus stared down near the Enemy. After thinking for a moment, he said, "I heard that my nephew, Young Bird, screamed for three days while they piled coals on his body. I heard this Raven Hunter cooked his legs off his body. Cooked Young Bird's manhood and then made him eat it. I think we'll make this Raven Hunter die very slowly, very painfully. I, for one, will urinate into his empty eye sockets. Then we will bury him. Perhaps while a little spark of life remains in his body so we know we capture his soul underground."

Raven Hunter's jaws worked, black eyes sparkling with a soul-deep fear. Terror-sweat had begun to bead on his naked body.

Horror gripped Ice Fire's heart. *My fault . . . that you're here at all.* Tears stung his eyes. He blinked them back quickly, exhaling. "Tomorrow. As the sun rises, we'll begin. We'll torture him for four days. A holy number, four." He looked around. "In the meantime, go to your shelters. Rest well this night, for once we start, there will be little sleeping with this Enemy's screams in the night."

"Even the ghosts of the dead will cower in fear," Yellow Leaf hissed as she spat on Raven Hunter. The Enemy warrior twitched as if he'd been stung.

Walrus looked up. "I'll stay to watch him. It wouldn't do for him to get loose."

Ice Fire nodded, motioning the others to go on about their business. Raven Hunter stared up at him, hate glistening in his black eyes.

"So," Ice Fire whispered as he knelt down. "You'll see what it's like for your victims." He frowned, cocking his head. "Tell me, what do you feel?"

Raven Hunter's thinly pressed lips betrayed his fear. He said nothing, looking away.

Ice Fire nodded solemnly. "It's hard to believe such cruelty could come from me. . . ."

He saw the glint of comprehension in Raven Hunter's panicked face. Shock and disbelief flickered in the pools of his eyes.

"You know," Ice Fire whispered. "Did your brother, Wolf Dreamer, tell you? Perhaps the witch, Heron?"

Raven Hunter's eyes narrowed to slits.

Ice Fire watched him for a moment, pensive as he fingered his chin. He turned away and nodded to Walrus, clapping him on the back. "Nice capture out there. I suppose you'll be wrestling white bears next?"

Walrus chuckled, fingering his darts.

"It'll be a long night. I'll make us something to drink." Ice Fire bent over the fire, pulling herbs from his pack and mixing them in a horn spoon.

From the corner of his eye, he studied his son, knowing what had to be done, contemplating the terrible danger involved.

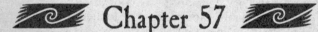

Chapter 57

"Stop! Who are you?" Dancing Fox demanded, darts held loosely in her hand.

She faced them on the narrow rocky trail, twilight falling as the lavender night grew out of the east. Three young men of the People, weapons clutched, crouched warily until they recognized her.

She stepped toward the tallest man, Red Moon. "You're going to raid the Others, aren't you?"

He clamped his jaw, saying nothing.

"You know the Dreamer ordered that no one raid them again. You defy him?"

Red Moon lifted a shoulder. "What business is it of yours, woman?" He lifted his chin, an angry glint in his steely eyes.

"If you raid, you'll split the People. Do you want to—"

"Perhaps I'd leave you with a little something on the way, eh?" He suggestively caressed his crotch.

The two youths who followed laughed out loud, eyes gleaming in anticipation.

Dancing Fox lifted a brow. "More of Raven Hunter's teachings?"

Red Moon took a step closer, leering. "He told us all about you. The way you—"

"Another step and I'll kill you," she replied easily.

Red Moon chuckled, laying his weapons to one side. "Kill me, woman? I've heard the stories that you killed five Others. *Five?* Not all liars died with Crow Caller."

"Five," the cool voice added behind them. They whirled, eyes wide. Three Falls hobbled out. "I was there. She has more courage than three children who would rape a woman. As if *you* could rape *her*."

They started at the scorn in his voice. Red Moon swallowed loudly in the dusk, eyes going uncertainly back and forth, realizing how boxed in they were. The two youths with him sidled into the night, feet scuffing softly on the rock as they backed away.

"What's your decision, Red Moon?" Dancing Fox toyed with a dart. "Will you betray the People? Disobey the Dreamer who destroyed Crow Caller and Raven Hunter with mere words? You'd give the Others reason to raid us when we're ragged and tired? You'd bring their revenge down on us when all we need is another full moon before we can leave this place forever? Is this what honor means to you?"

In the gray evening, she could see the other two boys leaving. The sound of their feet beating against rock turned to a run. Red Moon shifted, head down, swallowing hard. In a final decision, he threw his darts violently to clatter off the rocks before sprinting off in the direction of his fellows.

Dancing Fox closed her eyes, exhaling wearily as she sank down on the rock. "Close one, that time."

Three Falls grunted and shuffled his way over the rock. "But Red Moon was the worst. Stopping him stops the rest. Maybe that's time enough."

She lifted a shoulder. "Maybe. The young men chafe more every day." She shook her head. "How did Raven Hunter do it? Drive them all wild like that?"

Three Falls propped a foot on a boulder. "He gave them a taste of Power. Let them see how fear could dominate their victims." He paused. "But then Raven Hunter drove you into being who you are today, too."

She stiffened, meeting his gaze, finding tenderness there. "Relax, he's gone."

She shook her head. "For me, he'll never be gone." *And I can never forget his visions, what he promised so long ago.*

At the thought of being dropped in a hole, Raven Hunter's soul screamed within the cage of his exhausted body. His dreams raged unmercifully, his skin crawling at the imagined feel of the ground as it was thrown over his flesh. He could smell the dirt, damp, musty, clogging his nostrils and mouth, the taste of eternal death on his tongue, grit scratching on his teeth. He could feel the chill eating into his flesh, rocks gouging his skin. Cold, eternally black; his soul writhed and howled at the thought. Rot and blackness surrounding him, he could feel the fire in his lungs as they burned for air. Dirt choked in his convulsing throat, the spark of life draining away while his soul remained, trapped, unable to escape that cage of earth—locked in the roots and rot and cold—forever.

Raven Hunter filled his lungs, opening his eyes, enjoying the feel of the air as it rushed in and out of his body, soothing as it drifted across his skin. The fire glowed dimly red, faint flickers eerily etching the stretched hide of the shelter overhead.

The place had become familiar by this time. He knew the post supports that held up the roof. The bundles of hides, the hanging pouches full of meat, the curious fetishes hanging from the walls, all had been memorized. This silent, warm shelter would become a bedlam of his screams. The mute fixtures of the lodge would bear witness to his excruciating anguish. Now, in the red light, the shelter seemed harmless—peaceful.

How long until morning? Until they came to torture him? He swallowed hard, mouth dry and tight. Would he scream as loudly as the Others he'd burned and cut? Would he bellow as wretchedly when they smashed his bones? Would he shriek as vilely when they cut his penis and testicles off? What sound would he make as they placed sharp obsidian to his quivering belly? How would their hands feel, squirming inside his body as they ripped out his intestines? Could he keep his sanity when their rough fingers pulled his eyeballs from the sockets?

A wailing agony of horror whimpered through his mind.

"Life can be most precious, don't you think? Especially when the end is near."

Raven Hunter jerked his head around to see the tall Dreamer they called Ice Fire. This was his father? No! Impossible!

"Walrus is asleep. That drink I mixed for him contained a priceless root. Comes from the far west. Getting scarce now with all the different people moving."

"Why?" Raven Hunter croaked.

"Time to talk." Ice Fire moved to squat to one side. "I wanted to find out who you are. Why you do what you do." He cocked his head. "Heron told me you were born in blood."

"Heron." Raven Hunter closed his eyes. "The Dreamer." He sighed and shook his head. "I suppose Runs In Light let you know I was coming."

"Your brother?"

Raven Hunter nodded miserably.

"No."

"Then—"

"Why did you come? Just to kill me?"

Raven Hunter moved his tongue. "They'd have laughed. Joked about me. I . . . I had to show them. Let them see that Raven Hunter could die as he'd lived. Unbowed, a leader worthy of their respect."

"Doesn't look like it will be that way." Ice Fire casually twisted one of his long gray braids. "But then, why did you drive the People to fight us? What did you gain from that?"

Raven Hunter smiled grimly. "I made them warriors. Until Runs In Light stole them with his tricks, I was the man who led them. *I led the People!* You hear? And I would have remade them, strong, powerful. Then we would have come and faced you, and pushed you back. That's what I offered them. I gave them my strength, my visions."

Ice Fire nodded seriously. "Power."

"Of course," Raven Hunter rasped. "What else is there? Respect? Another word for Power. Wives? A powerful man has as many wives as he needs—and his children have more than any others. Power is life! It's control of that which is about you. And I saw! Understand? Unlike my weak brother's foolish Dreams of holes in the ice, I saw the People saved! Saved!"

"Why cut up our warriors when you caught them?"

Raven Hunter twisted against the bonds, lips tightly pressed. "Because I wanted your heart and soul to fear us. Fear me! That's why I came here. I came to kill you, their greatest Dreamer. Then, even in death, they'd fear me! I'd have them!"

Ice Fire leaned back, brow furrowed. "You know what the coming four days will be like? Do I have to tell you?"

Raven Hunter filled his lungs, battling for sanity as his imagination pulled up details of the tortures of his captives. "I . . . I could probably teach your people a thing or two about pain. Yes, I know what they will do."

Ice Fire nodded soberly. "All things considered, I guess you do." He paused. "But suppose there were another way?"

Raven Hunter stiffened, a frantic leaping of hope in his chest.

Ice Fire resettled himself. "What would it be worth to you if I gave you the 'heart and soul' of the Mammoth People?"

Raven Hunter narrowed his eyes, sensing a trap. "I . . . It doesn't make . . . Why? Why would you do such a thing?"

Ice Fire smiled. "You're cunning. You don't leap at the chance."

Raven Hunter chewed his lip as he considered. How long until morning? "You'd let me kill you?"

Ice Fire spread his hands wide. "I'm not the heart and soul of the Mammoth People. I'm only the healer for the White Tusk Clan. No, the heart and soul is the White Hide. A mammoth calf who came to us and gave us Power. Each year one clan or another earns the honor of holding the Hide. Without it, the Mammoth People would be less than nothing. Forsaken by the Great Mystery."

Raven Hunter shook his head slowly. "No, this is a trap. Some way to make me foolish, or to dishonor me. You wouldn't do this to your people."

Ice Fire studied him from slitted lids, chin propped on steepled fingers. "Wouldn't I? What if by the Mammoth People losing the Power of the White Hide . . . *my* Power became more? Hmm? What if I could fill that gap?"

Raven Hunter smiled as it came clear. "And of course, you'd get no blame." Raven Hunter nodded.

"And your visions?" Ice Fire lifted an eyebrow. "If you returned among your people bearing the White Hide, wouldn't it make you a man of status again? Wouldn't the young warriors look up to you? This Wolf Dreamer would be discredited. What's a Dream compared to deeds? What's a Dream compared to a warrior who has escaped the Others—with their sacred Hide?"

"And you gain what?"

"I become the most powerful man among the Mammoth People. All I need is for you to take the White Hide beyond the Big Ice. No, don't look at me that way. I know Wolf Dreamer found a way. But do you think *my* people would pass through such a hole?" He shook his head, a grim smile on his lips. "Like our Singer said, we're not ground squirrels. No, I want the White Hide gone. I don't want any party of warriors stealing it back again, returning triumphantly with it over their shoulders. That would be . . . well, a definite embarrassment."

"You've got this all thought out?"

Ice Fire nodded. "It works the best for all of us. Your people are beyond the ice. My young men don't die. I have peace and become the ultimate Power among the four clans. You have your status as the greatest of your warriors. You've broken the spirit of the Mammoth People, stolen their greatest totem, and left them behind." He spread his hands. "We both win."

Ideas raced in Raven Hunter's head. The bits of vision coming together in a whole. Wolf Dreamer destroyed, Dancing Fox would be his—forever. Her Power would be growing now, a fitting mate for him. A flush of excitement surged through him. *Perhaps the vision wasn't false after all!*

"She'll bear me a powerful child," he whispered, nodding to himself.

"Who?" Ice Fire asked. "You have a wife?"

Raven Hunter chuckled. "No, but I will."

"You sound excited by the prospect."

Raven Hunter squinted calculatingly. "I've seen her path, Other. I don't know what it means yet, but Dancing Fox's child will create a new future for the People. Some molding of something new . . . something great. She's a key figure—a Power among the People—and I intend that she be mine and mine alone!''

"You can bend this great woman to your will?''

Raven Hunter nodded. "Oh, I've done it in the past. I'll find a way in the future. It hurt me to let her go. Hurt like nothing else ever has. But I saw it, even then. She had to be tested—shaped by suffering. That deep essence of her soul had to be hardened, like a dart shaft over a dry fire. But it was worth it. Now, she's ready to help me change the destiny of the People.''

"And she's not for Wolf Dreamer?''

Raven Hunter barked a laugh. "He's locked in his Dreams. I've heard the story. He turned her down. Turned *her* down! The fool doesn't realize how important she is for the future!''

Ice Fire nodded, eyeing him curiously.

"Free me!'' Raven Hunter demanded, heart pounding. "I'll take your White Hide. I myself will lead the People through the ice hole. You have a bargain, Ice Fire. Your people for mine.''

Ice Fire rocked back on his heels, hard eyes veiled. "I must warn you, the rest is up to you. The Hide is in the small shelter in the middle of the camp. Four young men, one from each clan, sleep around the Hide. Are you skilled enough? Can you get in silently and get out again without waking them? No, you can't kill the guards. Do that and my warriors will hunt you to the end—no matter where you run. Kill the guards, and you also destroy the Power of the White Hide.''

Raven Hunter nodded, brow lined. "I am the best hunter among the People. I can do anything.''

Ice Fire's smile spread, crinkling the lines around his mouth. "I'll also warn you, the Hide is heavy. One man can carry it with difficulty. You'll be sore-pressed. Among my people, the young men train constantly, hoping they're worthy of the honor of bearing the Hide. Drop it, treat it roughly or without respect, and the Hide will suck up your soul, little by little, until you find yourself floundering like a beached whale. Are you strong enough to carry the Hide? The Power it holds will destroy a man who shirks his responsibilities to it.''

Raven Hunter glared his disdain. Who did this Ice Fire

think he was? "I'm ready to take the Power. I'm the greatest of my people. I fear no test. I'll be more than worthy."

Ice Fire nodded. "Yes, you're everything I'd feared you'd be." He reached down with a sharp chert flake and severed the bindings on Raven Hunter's arms.

Chapter 58

Dancing Fox stood uncomfortably at the edge of the hot pool, watching the bright water swirl and splash against the yellow-crusted rocks. Overhead, another gray day promised freezing rain. The billowing cloud of geyser steam rolled out, pushed toward the Big Ice by the cruel wind. Dismal weather; the misty air reflected her own emotions—damp, shadowed, without joy or light, or warmth.

Behind her, the camp of the People looked worn and frayed. As they scuttled back and forth, bundled figures worked at stuffing berries into bags before the humid air could spoil them. Drying racks were hurriedly stripped of the remaining meat. A reality of famine had reared its head as hunter after hunter returned empty-handed. So few caribou had been slain. Only the old bull mammoth paced the hills now, trumpeting his loneliness to the wind-blasted rocks. The musk ox had been hunted out long ago.

"It's the ice—or nothing," she told herself again, irritated by the growling of her stomach. She'd restricted her meals, setting an example of abstinence for her people. They watched soberly, rationing their intake.

A bitter gnawing ate inside her as she glanced at Heron's shelter, seeing One Who Cries emerge and head straight for her.

"He'd like to see you."

Dancing Fox nodded, a knot tying at the base of her throat. "I'd hoped to be back and gone again before he found out."

One Who Cries chuckled softly. "Not anymore. You've

become too important for your own good." He cocked his head, bland features bending into a puzzled expression. "You and Green Water related?"

She smiled at him and shook her head, turning down the path, winding through the shelters. Children ran around her legs, laughter reserved as they chased each other, dogs barking at their heels. One Who Cries followed her. To still the violent spasms in her heart she asked, "I take it that he's feeling better?"

"He's healthy as a musk ox in rut. I . . ." At her tightening expression he added, "Bad choice of words."

She waved it off, dread building.

"Anyway," One Who Cries added too briskly, "he came out of it fine. Just woke up and looked around and said he was hungry. Ate like a mammoth bull in spring. Then he got up and walked out into the light. He climbed up to a high spot and sat there for a day. Dreaming, I guess. But he said he was being One."

"Dreaming," she growled to cover her conflicting emotions.

At the flap, she stopped short, unsure. All the confidence fled as she stared at the stained and worn door hanging. A tremble made her heart light. He was there. Just beyond that cracked bit of leather. So close, yet an eternity away.

She closed her eyes, frozen with indecision. *I don't really have to see him. I could just say no and walk away.*

"Go on," One Who Cries urged gently.

It took all her nerve to lift the flap and step in. A bright fire crackled in the oxidized fire pit. He looked up, eyes meeting hers, melting her where she stood. The flames cast a reddish gleam over his handsome face, touching his tan leather shirt and turning it into a flickering ocher mantle. His waist-length hair hung loose over his broad chest, brushing the dirt floor.

"I hear you've practically been running the camp," he greeted, expression warm and concerned.

She shrugged, steering her thoughts away from him, back to the People, and finding refuge in the problems. "The worst part has been keeping Raven Hunter's warriors in line. The younger ones keep trying to sneak off to raid the Others."

"And the Others?"

"From what we can gather, they're involved in the fall hunt. Making meat for the winter."

"Will you sit?" he asked.

She settled herself hesitantly on a caribou hide, muscles tense, hands clasped to still the need to fidget, and looked across at him. His tall body had gained some perfection in the past months; a serenity and grace pervaded his every movement. And his eyes . . . even when he looked at her, he seemed to be staring into some distance in his mind.

"I approved all the suggestions you made. I know Four Teeth is your mouthpiece, but Singing Wolf and One Who Cries back you up. I didn't . . ." He smiled wistfully. "I didn't know what the Dreaming could do to a person. How it affected the mind and body and soul. Or I would have been here to help you."

"I know you would have," she whispered, heart thudding sickeningly. *If only I could reach out and touch you . . .*

"Thank you for taking care of the People for me."

"What's next?" she asked, keeping her voice steady, diverting him from personal subjects.

He frowned slightly, a fleeting change of expression. "We go south as soon as we can. Beyond that, I can't see, except that something cataclysmic looms on the horizon."

"Cataclysmic?"

"Yes . . ." He clamped his lip with his front teeth. "Opposites crossed. Balances equaling each other. Conjunction."

"What are you talking about?"

He spread his hands, leaning back. "Words aren't meant for Dreams."

She nodded, having no idea what he meant. "Are you finished with the mushrooms?"

He looked up at her, eyes haunted. "One more time. On the other side. At the conjunction. Then I'm through."

"And then what?"

He stared blankly. "What?"

"Can you ever . . ." She stopped, squeezing her eyes closed. "Will you ever be a normal man again?"

He cocked his head quizzically. "Normal?"

In the long pause, she could see him searching his mind.

"Will you ever be able to love again?" she asked bluntly, nerves strung as taut as a bowstring.

His smile grew slowly, making his face glow. "I love everyone, Dancing Fox. It's part of the Oneness, you see. I—"

"Ah . . ." A hollow ache built in her stomach.

He smiled, a kind expression on his young face. "You're asking more, aren't you? If I'll ever feel a *special* love—like I once felt." He shook his head slowly. "Those feelings are illusory. That's what killed Heron. She never really allowed herself to go all the way. That center of her soul wouldn't surrender. Wouldn't become nothing."

She waved a hand negligently. "It sounds like nonsense."

"Nonsense? That's a good expression. A place where sense isn't. No me or you. No black or white. The pulse of One— and None." He cocked his head sublimely, eyes going over her face tenderly. "Do you understand?"

"I understand," she croaked. But she didn't.

"I love you more now than I did before," he said softly, reaching out to touch her arm gently. "Because I don't . . . don't want you now."

"Don't want—"

"I know your soul for what it is. Pure and beautiful, and the same as mine." He spread his arms wide, taking a deep soothing breath. "The same as everything's. Humans only *want* what is different from themselves. You and I, we're one."

Defeated and confused, she sighed and stood. "I take it you'll agree to anything I say about moving the camp? About establishing chores for people?"

He nodded. "No one could do it better than you."

She walked to the hanging, staring back. "It snowed a little last night. The water that froze in the boiling paunches the other day never unthawed. I'm going to start the elders down to the hole. Will you lead them through?"

"I'll do anything you want me to."

A grim smile touched her lips, the ache intensifying to throb through her. "Hardly," she whispered, stepping through the flap.

A dead weight lay heavy on her soul as she started across camp.

* * *

The shelter stood dark, a musty smell wafting on the breeze filtering through the door flap. In the dim light of a dying fire, dozens of hostile, hurt faces shone sanguinely.

"I don't know what happened!" Walrus defended sullenly. Standing with hunched shoulders in the far corner, he slapped his pants hard. "I felt fine and then—"

"And then you fell asleep and let an Enemy steal the Hide!" Red Flint raged, pacing before the fire.

Ice Fire gritted his teeth and knotted futile fists at the door where it flapped in the wind. "Of all the . . ." He shook his head violently. "You were fine when I left. We talked about the hunting, about whether or not the Enemy would raid with their war leader dead and buried, and I asked if you'd be all right. 'Sure,' you said. 'He's going to be no trouble.' And you laughed. So I went back to Red Flint's shelter and went to sleep."

Walrus's face fell, his defiance shattering like a skim of ice under a hammerstone. For a brief instant, Ice Fire's chest tightened, regret filling him. This doughty warrior deserved better than the pain he was forced to give him.

"Walrus wasn't the only one," Yellow Calf reminded, glaring at the four young men who sat in the back of the shelter with their faces downcast in shame. Yellow Calf's arm shot out. "The finest of our young men? These . . . these . . ." He couldn't finish, he was shaking so hard. He turned his back to them.

Ice Fire paced up and down the narrow aisle in the packed shelter. "What happened isn't important anymore."

"Not important?" Horse Tracker thundered. "The White Hide's been stolen by an Enemy! You tell me what *is* important!"

"Getting it back!" Ice Fire roared. He looked around in the sudden silence. He shouted so rarely, it stunned people now. Every man, woman, and child in the clan stared openmouthed at him. They waited, hearts and souls wrenched by the greatest tragedy to have ever befallen the Mammoth People. He cringed, feeling their pain touch his heart. But there was no other way to force them south.

Horse Tracker raised his hands, dropping his head. "We'll get it back."

"Of course we will!" Ice Fire slammed a fist into his palm, then turned pensively to Yellow Calf. "You represent Buffalo Clan. Horse Tracker speaks for the Round Hoof Clan and Ice Stalker speaks for Tiger Belly. Does everyone agree that I shall speak for White Tusk?"

Heads nodded all around the shelter. "Very well, I say this. Send the fastest runners we have to Buffalo and Round Hoof Clans. Ask for their best warriors." He raised a hand. "I warn you, only the best, the bravest!"

Horse Tracker threw his shoulders back, saying tersely, "All our young men—"

"Will all your young men be willing to walk under the ice through the ghost hole in pursuit of the Enemy? Do they have the courage to fight and die under the ice. In the blackness?" Ice Fire cocked his head, waiting.

"You haven't mentioned Tiger Belly in all this," Ice Stalker pointed out, his thin face grim.

Ice Fire nodded. "I don't think we can afford to have the Tiger Belly Clan weakened when the diseased peoples to your west would try and force you back." He gestured. "If it does turn out that the water is rising to cover the world, it will meet between your lands and the far Enemy's. Do we want it to close behind them? Or in front?"

Ice Stalker considered that. "We'll hold the western borders of our land." He paused for a long eloquent moment, then stabbed out a finger. *"But you had better recover the White Hide!"*

Ice Fire held his eyes until the leader looked nervously away. "I understand Tiger Belly Clan's concern. You've honored the White Hide for many years. But that does *not* mean the rest of us value it less."

"Just get it back," Ice Stalker rasped before striding angrily from the shelter.

"Yellow Calf? Horse Tracker?" Ice Fire turned his cool eye on them. "Are you willing?"

"Send the runners." Horse Tracker sighed. "I am responsible for my clan. We'll go south—through the ice—and get our Sacred Hide back."

Yellow Calf nodded. "My clan is with you. And this Enemy will pay."

Chapter 59

Snow clung to the air, stinging Raven Hunter's face as he trudged toward the mountains forming a high ivory wall. The sky glowed dully with waving curtains of gray clouds. *Storm coming.*

He staggered under the weight. Rolled in a long tube, the heavy Hide bowed his shoulders where it bent over his back. Step by agonizing step, he climbed up the rocky slope.

He'd avoided the easy trails, pulling his exhausted body over the roughest paths he could find. They'd never follow him here. Never! Wind Woman's violent breath caught him, almost toppling him over under his burden. Gasping, he grinned into the evening. Wisps of snow twisted out of the mottled sky. He turned in the last light, staring back over the flat, seeing the snow where it blew in streamers along his backtrail.

"Made it! Made it this far." Puffing his exertion, he threw himself into the last ascent, legs trembling as he topped the ridge and froze. A woman waited, eyes on the trail to the west that he'd avoided.

"Dancing Fox," he gasped, chuckling. *"Dancing Fox!"*

She turned, catlike, darts ready to cast.

Hunching his back to redistribute the weight, he reeled forward.

"Raven Hunter?"

"It's . . . me," he wheezed, settling the heavy Hide as he dropped, panting, grinning up at her. In the back of his mind, Ice Fire's warning about the Hide sucking up his soul rang like a warning shriek, but he ignored it, unable to bear the weight any longer.

She stared at him, chin up, expression cold as the glacial snow blowing down from the cloud-black sky. Wind Woman whipped the thick flakes around, a sheet of snow obscuring the plain below.

He coughed, trying to catch his breath, and waved at the rolled Hide. "There! Look, see! The very soul of the Mammoth People is mine!"

She studied the thick roll of hide indifferently. "So."

He realized she remained wary, balanced, darts poised for thrusting.

He wiped the sweat from his clammy brow and blew a thick puff of breath into the falling night. "It's their totem, you see? I went down to die—to kill this Ice Fire of theirs. To show everyone that I was still the warrior of the People . . . despite Runs In Light's tricks. Only I stole their most sacred totem, the White Hide, the heart of their people. Now I'm taking it south, through the hole in the ice. With this Hide, I reclaim my place as leader of the People!" He shook his head, snorting condescension. "So much for my brother."

"You stole a mammoth hide from the Others?" She shook her head, watching him uncertainly.

"Their *Sacred* Hide," he corrected emphatically. "Don't you see? I've gutted them, just like that! They can't stand against us now. I've stolen their spirit, their will to resist. Now"—he grinned—"I've found you. The visions, you see, they're coming true. With this Hide, I destroy Runs In Light. I vanquish the Mammoth People. I reclaim leadership, taking us all to the other side of the ice. Then you're mine. No one else will stand against me."

She shook her head. "Never."

"Forever," he corrected, smiling victory. "I'll break Runs In Light. Disgrace him."

"Why? You don't need to—"

"Yes, I do. It's part of the Dream. We have to fight and I have to win. It came to me the night after I stole the Hide from Ice Fire. I saw it all clearly then. Yes"—he laughed softly—"clearly."

She crouched, darts ready, tangles of black hair fluttering before her as her thoughts jumped to Wolf Dreamer's words. "The cataclysmic . . ."

He laughed gleefully. "Remember those nights when we shared robes? Remember?"

He patted the shining White Hide. Thoughts of her warm body against his stirred his long-frustrated manhood. Chuckling again, he carefully unrolled the White Hide, the snowy hair gleaming in the faint light.

In a sultry voice, he called, "Come, Dancing Fox. I've missed you. It's been a long time since I parted your legs.

Now the visions are coming true. Come lie with me. My body cries for yours, and I've never loved any woman as I love you. You and me, we're the destiny of the People. Conceived on the White Hide, our child—''

"Will never exist," she hissed, backing up a step.

He ran his fingers through the long white hair of the Hide, stroking it lovingly. "Yes, it will. I've seen. Come. Let's hurry.''

She turned and ran, jumping lithely down the rocks.

"No!" he shouted, a flush of anger spurring his weary body as he leapt after her. She was outdistancing him, running with a slight limp. On trembling legs, he followed, his lungs barely recovered from the difficult climb. For long moments, the gap remained the same until he slowly drew ahead.

Heart pounding, lungs burning, he closed, forcing every last bit of his energy into the chase. She whirled, hearing him close, darts ready.

He slid to a stop, staring at the desperation in her eyes.

"I'll kill you, Raven Hunter!"

Slowly, he spread his arms, gasping for breath. "You'll be mine in the end; the visions say so. You think you can elude me? I'm the best tracker of the People.''

She shook damp hair from her eyes. "I've killed Others, Raven Hunter. I'll kill you. You've seen me. I don't miss what I cast at. Stay back.''

Breast heaving, he smiled. "Kill me. Come on. Do it!" he taunted. "Do it quickly, or I'll find you. Somewhere, you'll sleep. You can't outrun me. You can't escape me. You'll slip and I'll have you and the future. You'll bear *my* child.''

She backed away, a step at a time, jaw locked with determination. "Follow, and I'll kill you.''

"You don't understand. With the White Hide, no one can stand against me. It's proof of my destiny.''

"Oh?" She continued to back away. "And where's your Hide?''

He stiffened, remembering how the evening light had shone off the white hair where he'd unrolled it on the rocks. He shifted nervously. What if someone came along and . . . No, that was unthinkable!

Seeing his indecision, she added softly, "Sure, you can

chase me down. Finally corner me, catch me off guard, but you can't while you carry that Hide."

He considered it—too true. Ice Fire's words haunted him. *"Are you strong enough to carry the Hide? The Power it holds will destroy a man who shirks his responsibilities to it."* Annoyance ate at his resolve. The answer came.

He smiled. "For now, the Hide is enough. With it, all things will come . . . including you."

"To plant your seed in my belly, you'll have to keep me tied like a dog. But, remember, you, too, must sleep sometime—be less than alert. And when you do, I'll drive a dart through your cursed body. By the Soul Eaters of the Long Dark, I swear. You hear?"

He nodded, turning on his heel. What were the Soul Eaters of the Long Dark against the Power of the White Hide?

"You'll be mine," he called over his shoulder as he trotted down the slope toward the gleaming Hide, now partially covered with snow. *"I've seen it!"*

Chapter 60

On the other side of the Big Ice, the mountains rose, some of the peaks to the far north familiar. The range extending to the south, however, gleamed in unknown patterns. Here, in the broken foothills, patches of spruce mixed with open grassy meadows, amber now in fall color.

Overhead, the last flocks of geese winged southward in irregular V's, their voices haunting as they called among themselves.

Behind, the wind blew chill off the Big Ice. Storm clouds continued to pile up along the northern horizon while the valley of the Big River hooked below the uplands the People now hunted. Such a rich land, this. A feeling of freedom spread among them as they crafted new shelters, tailored new clothing, and awaited the coming of the Long Dark. The vast grassy valleys to the south beckoned, moving splotches of game visible from the heights.

The trap had been built along a game trail, hidden deep in the shadows of the trees. Broken Branch had picked the place, turning on her swollen ankles, mouth working as her eyes studied the spot. She'd poked at the soil with her digging stick and grinned.

Green Water climbed out of the pit, a bloody quarter of elk over her shoulder. Under the weight, her steps careened, the leg bone eating into her shoulder. She stumbled to drop the heavy weight onto a mat of spruce needles, then blew an exasperated breath. A strange animal, this. The antlers were a lot like those of the caribou, only the hooves were much smaller, the rump brown, and no white beard hung under the animal's neck. Other strange animals had fallen to her pits. Another deer, smaller, with forked antlers, abounded. Other than that, no sign of horse could be found. Musk ox and mammoth and long-horned buffalo were everywhere, though—and this interesting brown deer, which had a sweet and delicately flavored meat.

"I could almost wish this one had gotten away," Broken Branch muttered as she looked up from the bottom of the hole.

"He almost did," Green Water reminded her, images of the brown deer's incredible agility lingering. When it fell through the trap she'd carefully dug, the big animal had whirled despite a broken front leg and yelped as she approached. In a desperate leap, it had cleared the pit, landed on the broken leg and tumbled back in. By the time Green Water closed, the animal had leapt again, locking its good front leg along with one rear. While it teetered at the edge of the pit, clawing with the other back leg, she'd driven a dart deeply into its side, sending it crashing once more into the hole. This time the large span of shiny antlers had caught, breaking the animal's neck.

"So much bigger than caribou!" Broken Branch grinned up from the bottom. "Fat meat and good game! Ha-heeee! Wolf Dream did us good!"

Green Water's baby cooed and gurgled in agreement where it swayed in the breeze, dangling in a hide bag from a spruce limb.

Green Water smiled at the child, bending over to pluck up some of the snow and scrub the caked blood from her fingers.

"People'll be coming through the ice soon." Broken Branch's lips spread in a wide grin to expose her toothless gums, the wrinkles of her face rearranging into different patterns.

Green Water nodded. "Water's down in the Big River. Curlew Song was down there yesterday."

Broken Branch's ancient fingers gripped a heavy bifacial chopper. Despite the cramped space, she skillfully smashed the ribs loose from the spine and sternum, exposed now that they'd removed the front and rear quarters. With a flake from her pouch, she sliced through the diaphragm and grunted, lifting the heavy ribs up to Green Water.

"Lot of meat here. Not a mammoth, by any means . . . but enough to last a family a full turning of the moon." Green Water carried the flopping ribs to the pile, thankful the flies had frozen out.

"I wonder who Wolf Dreamer will bring. Buffalo Back's clan? All of them?" She shook her head. "Hard to think about what's happening on the other side of the ice when we've done so well here." She severed the heart sac, lifting the thick organ out, flicking bone slivers off the meat as she sucked the blood from the wide aorta, pumping the muscle to squirt the warm fluid into her mouth.

Smacking her lips, she handed it to Green Water, bending to cut out the lungs and liver.

"My One Who Cries will be coming home." Green Water sighed longingly, reaching down for the thick liver, taking time to bite a chunk from the rich organ, chewing and taking yet another bite, enjoying the taste of the new creature.

Broken Branch turned the stomach inside out, inspecting the rough surface. "It'll do for a boiling bag."

"When do you think they'll start through the hole?"

Broken Branch wiped a blood-encrusted hand across her wrinkled forehead, squinting up at the slant of sunlight. "Maybe a week. We'd better have lots of food stored—just in case all the clans come at once."

"You think they will?" Green Water asked, worried. They'd laid in a lot of food, but not *that* much.

Broken Branch turned her withered face up. Sunlight gilded

her wrinkles. "Depends on how bad the pressure from the Others is. And how many believe the Wolf Dream."

The band of the People gathered on the rocky hillside above Heron's hot pool, their bodies silhouetted against the wavering flames of the Monster Children's War. A few stars peeked out above the southern horizon, sparkling in the frigid night air.

"I know many of you fear the ice." Wolf Dreamer turned, hands raised. "Don't worry. I've Dreamed the ghosts away. Tomorrow you won't even hear a groan from them."

Who's he trying to kid! One Who Cries wondered to himself. He stared curiously at Wolf Dreamer, uncomfortable with the detached gleam in the young man's eyes. He'd lost weight, and more sooty smudges than usual lined his face. He'd gone to Dreaming constantly, only appearing for brief moments when he sensed it necessary to reassure his people. *And why'd Singing Wolf and Dancing Fox have to run off and leave me here to keep things going? Why is it always me? I hate messing around with spirit stuff!*

"There'll be no ghosts?" Four Teeth wondered aloud.

"The Big Ice is nothing more than illusion." Wolf Dreamer smiled serenely.

Four Teeth cocked his head, squinting uneasily at people around him. "What's he mean by that? Illusion?"

Wolf Dreamer ignored the question. "One Who Cries tells me the water has ceased to run. Gather your things."

"You will protect us?" Buffalo Back called.

"My soul is yours. We walk together in One." Wolf Dreamer smiled radiantly and walked back down the slope to Heron's shelter.

"Walk together in One?" Buffalo Back asked, perplexed. "What's he talking about?"

The People looked anxiously back and forth, eyes veiled.

One Who Cries had seen that look before—among a herd of caribou about to bolt as they sensed a hunter's keen eyes upon them.

One Who Cries—without thinking—called out, "Use your heads. The man's a Dreamer. He means we go through *one hole* together." *At least, I hope that's what he meant.* "I've been through there. Dancing Fox came through alone—with no light. Wolf Dreamer knows what he's doing. He's Dreamed us safely through already.''

"What's he going to do now?"

One Who Cries shrugged irritably. "Talk to the ghosts, maybe. Tell them we're coming and to leave us alone."

He looked around, suddenly aware he'd become the total center of attention. For a half second, he stood there, speechless, undone by their shining eyes. He could see the fear that lay hidden behind set mouths, worry grating at the bottoms of their hearts. They *wanted* to believe—desperately.

One Who Cries caught himself before he lowered his eyes. Instead he looked back, saying the first thing that came to his staggered mind. "I've been through to the new land. The animals are fat and unafraid! Not only that, but we've got a Dreamer to call them in. There won't be any Others there. We can live in peace, see what's to the south beyond the ice."

"But we have to walk under the ice for two days?" Four Teeth shook his head.

"It's not that bad! We've all had to walk in the depths of the Long Dark. There's not much difference. My beloved Green Water carried my little son through. Curlew Song walked with Jumping Hare. Even Old Broken Branch went through." He paused, frowning. In a wry voice he added, "Well, no wonder the ghosts didn't want to mess with us."

A chuckle of laughter broke the dam of reservations.

A warmth spread through his breast as he looked at them. His people, they looked back, a trace of the old humor in their eyes. "Sure, it's a scary place under the ice," he agreed honestly. "But we're safe. I've seen the truth of the Wolf Dream." He waved his hands. "Oh, I know, I've sat around the fires with you, heard the stories. What if this? What if that? Well, the time's come to go. There's nothing here for us anymore."

Several looked up at him with beaming hopeful faces, nodding, eyes alight. As suddenly, he swallowed hard, realizing what he'd done, what he'd given them of himself.

"One," he whispered under his breath, taken aback. *Like Wolf Dreamer says, I've given them something of my soul.* He tried to feel around, to see if any of him was missing, but he seemed whole, curiously satisfied—even if their staring eyes left him shy and embarrassed.

Four Teeth nodded agreement as he stepped over next to One Who Cries. "I've heard the Dreamer. I've heard One Who Cries, Singing Wolf, and Dancing Fox. If we have even a little bit of their courage and honor, no harm will come to us."

One Who Cries grinned sheepishly. "If a coward like me can make it through just think how well the rest of you will do!"

The next morning, they wound their way out of Heron's valley, leaving behind trampled snow, the refuse of a year's occupation, charred fire pits—and the bones of the dead. One Who Cries stood on the rim of the valley, looking back. The stinking geyser billowed toward the snow-gray sky in a puffy cloud. Around the spots where the shelters had been, rings of brown from discarded scraps and chipped stone flakes remained. The willows had been systematically trimmed out, their roots riding high where they'd been tied to packs, the sweet bark eaten while the outer material had been woven into rope and string. The People used all of the willow.

We are so few. Where once the People would have streamed by for hours, now we are this pitiful remnant. Look at us. Our clothing is worn, torn, polished thin from use. The children walk on legs like spindles. No face is without lines traced by pain and loss. Is this what we've become? He shook his head.

Tired, ragged, they walked southeast to the Big River, a line of bobbing forms. Together they followed the Dream. But what of the Dreamer? A gnawing misgiving ate at the base of his heart. Every time he thought he'd come to know the man Runs In Light had become, he changed, became someone different. Each time the sensation was more and more disquieting. *I feel like I lose more of my old friend every moment.*

He looked ahead, seeing that thin figure walking with a straight back, head held high. Though he couldn't see his eyes from where he stood, he knew what they looked like: distant, shining with an eerie illumination.

One Who Cries sighed. "Well, he's led us this far. The end is almost come." He shook his head, muttering softly under his breath. As the last of the women passed, he took one final look at Heron's valley before following in the steps of his tattered, weary people.

Everyone tried to pack in around the outskirts of the council. Ice Fire found mild amusement in their jostling. Beyond the bobbing heads and the whispers back and forth behind secretive hands, he could see the marshy lake they'd just skirted. The ice still couldn't be trusted to bear a man's weight—so they'd gone the long tedious way around through the rocks. Behind him, to the south, the hills of the Enemy rose. There, in the final holdings of the Enemy, the web would be drawn tight. There, it would all be played out.

A fitful burst of wind harried them as he tried to bring his thoughts back to the council at hand. Strange developments, these, but what did they mean? He looked up to see the confusion in Broken Shaft's face.

"We were dead. They caught us completely by surprise." Broken Shaft lifted his arms helplessly. "I was in the lead. The trail ran around this big boulder and they were standing there, up above us, with darts and big rocks to throw down. Like a mammoth in a gully, we couldn't do anything."

"For one, I was ready to die," Smoke continued. "I nocked a dart in my atlatl and glared up, trying to judge the angle, and someone yelled, 'Stop!' "

"It was a woman." Broken Shaft shifted nervously, looking around at the hard-faced men who stared back at him. "A beautiful woman." He scuffed the toe of his long boot in the snow. "She held up both hands and spoke. I suppose if it had been a man, I'd have darted him just like that. But a woman? A warrior doesn't expect a woman to stop a fight. Not when we were in such bad position."

"And what did she say?" Ice Fire frowned, feeling the pull of the south.

"She said to go back," Smoke told them, looking around. "She said that the People were tired of warring. That too much killing had gone on. She said that we should leave all but one dart on the ground and keep that one for protection from bears. We should take our lives which the People gave to us, and to come and tell our elders that our lives were given back for some of the ones they'd taken in war."

Whispers broke out among the listeners.

Ice Fire considered it, a flicker of hope born in his breast.

Broken Shaft shook his head uneasily. "It's a strange thing. I've never heard of an Enemy not killing. I don't understand this."

"They want peace."

"*Peace?*" roared Red Flint. "They've stolen the White Hide and they want peace? They've cut apart our young men, raped and carried off our young women? And *they* want peace?"

"The man, Raven Hunter, stole our White Hide," Ice Fire reminded. To Smoke he asked, "Did she say anything about the White Hide?"

He shook his head, looking nervously around.

"Cowards," Red Flint growled, spitting angrily at the smoldering fire. "You could have killed them, wiped them out for—"

"We'd have died!" Broken Shaft protested, hearing surly mutterings among the watching warriors. "Dead, we do no good to the people."

"Cowards do no honor to the clan!" Red Flint sneered.

"Enough." Ice Fire turned, meeting the hot eyes of the warriors. Behind him, Broken Shaft, Smoke, and Black Claw stood defiantly, glaring back.

"Singer?" Broken Shaft challenged in a strained voice, his handsome face twisted. "Don't call us—"

"For my own part," Ice Fire softly interrupted, "I can't remember ever mistaking wisdom for cowardice." One of the warriors behind him grunted affirmation while the accusers shifted their glances.

Red Flint hissed something under his breath, violence in his eyes as he stared at the warriors.

A wound opened in Ice Fire's heart as he watched his old friend's face contort in rage. The other warriors shifted, some looking nervously at Red Flint, some chewing their lips as they glanced anxiously at Ice Fire.

Broken Shaft blinked and lowered his eyes, exhaling heavily. "I'm sorry, Elder. I didn't know our actions would—"

"It's the theft of the White Hide," Ice Fire decided in a voice loud enough to be heard by all. "We're losing our tempers, not thinking clearly."

Broken Shaft and his friends fidgeted nervously—unsure of

themselves. Across the lake, a lone goose fluttered her wings as she struggled to walk on the thin ice.

"I think . . ." Ice Fire hesitated, a deep frown incising his brow. Then he looked up at Broken Shaft. The young warrior searched his face, silently seeking guidance.

"Most Respected Elder, tell me what's right? I'll do whatever—"

"You already know," he comforted, coming to a decision, patting the man's shoulder affectionately. "You left when the Enemy woman gave you your life. You speak correctly when you say you're worth more to the clan alive than dead."

"Yes, Elder," the warrior muttered gratefully.

"I don't like dealing with the Enemy," Red Flint insisted. "Taking anything from them—even a life—makes me feel shamed!"

"Remember that we've hunted them, pushed them, driven them from the last of their lands over the years. Hmm? Put yourselves in their place. Would you have spared the lives of Smoke, Broken Shaft, and Black Claw?"

"But they're not human beings!" Red Flint cried. "They don't have the Great Mystery! They don't have the clans! Their dead don't go to the Camp of Souls beneath the sea! They aren't like us! They're animals! Less than animals!"

Ice Fire paced slowly back and forth. He searched each of the faces in the silence following Red Flint's outburst. "Blueberry was one of your wives, Sheep's Tail. Was she an animal?"

The young warrior looked quickly around, seeing all eyes on him, and swallowed, lips moving. "Well, she wasn't a very good wife. I had to beat her all the time to keep her civil."

"But she did bear you a strong son." Ice Fire cocked his head, eyes throwing the challenge to Red Flint.

The Singer walked to stand directly in front of him, jaw clamped tightly. "I won't stand more of this Enemy diluting our ways!" he shouted finally. "I won't! We're losing ourselves!"

"Do you want the robe of Most Respected Elder?" He gently unslung the snow white fox hide from his shoulders, caressing it lovingly for a moment before handing it to his old friend. He waited, seeing unease replace anger on Red

Flint's face. "I'm waiting, Singer. If you want the robe, I'll surrender it willingly."

A hush draped over the spectators.

Red Flint's eyes dropped and he licked his lips. "Things have changed, is all," he added lamely, ignoring the fox hide before him.

"The whole world's changing," Ice Fire murmured understandingly, withdrawing the white cloak and swirling it around his shoulders again. "We're changing, too. Many things are different. That's why it's time for careful thought instead of brash action."

"And what are you going to do about the Enemy? How are you going to get the White Hide back?" Red Flint asked.

Ice Fire turned to Broken Shaft. "This woman, did she have a name?"

"Dancing Fox."

"Dancing Fox." He nodded, Raven Hunter's words fresh in his memory. "A very powerful woman," he added as if to himself.

"You know of this woman?" Red Flint asked skeptically, off balance from the recent confrontation.

"I know of her. She may be the key to getting the White Hide back."

"An Enemy woman?" Red Flint exploded scornfully. "A . . . *a woman*?"

"She trapped us," Black Claw added soberly. "And she commanded the men in her war party. They listened and they obeyed."

"So she has some foolish young men whose rods she's sliding up and down, that doesn't—"

"One of the 'foolish young men' was Eagle Cries. Remember him? I do. I remember him leading raids through our camps not so long ago at Raven Hunter's side. He's no foolish young man." Broken Shaft waited for rebuttal. None came.

Ice Fire fingered his chin, brow furrowed.

"Then what do we do?" Walrus asked uncertainly, still hurting from the stigma of being the man who lost the White Hide. "All this talk isn't getting us closer to the White Hide."

Ice Fire turned on his heel, keen eyes on Broken Shaft. "You can find this ambush place again?"

"Of course."

"I've been trying to forget it," Smoke growled.

Ice Fire smiled faintly, eyeing the man askance. "I want you to take the whole camp there."

"The whole camp?" Red Flint cried, shocked. "Are you crazy?"

"No, and I'm wagering Dancing Fox isn't either. When we march up the trail, we march with our women and children first."

Red Flint gasped. "You're out of your mind! They'll ambush—"

"Either trust me, Singer," Ice Fire whispered painfully, "or take my robe and outcast me from the clan."

Red Flint's jaw trembled as he met Ice Fire's hard eyes.

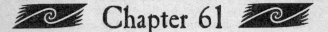 Chapter 61

Raven Hunter beat his way up the slope, hunger tormenting his belly. At the top of the ridge, he looked down, crestfallen to see the empty valley below. Not even the obscuring steam of Heron's geyser could hide the reality of an empty camp. From where he stood, he could see the rings where the shelters had been.

He puffed a heavy sigh and lowered the weight of the Hide from his shoulders. He looked out over the plain he'd crossed. From his pack, he took the last of the berries he'd found clinging to a snow-packed bush. One by one, he ate them, legs trembling.

Snow whipped out of the heavy sky, flakes drifting past, borne on Wind Woman's chilling breath. A thin brown line marked the Big River to the east. Where would . . . The hole in the ice. They'd left for the south, following his foolish brother.

Drained, he could barely fuel his anger. So, Runs In Light would have the honor of taking the People through the ice.

He'd gain status by that. Raven Hunter slitted his eyes in the cold breeze, looking to the south, the white mass of the ice hidden by curling mists and low clouds. To have missed the opportunity to lead them with the White Hide hurt—but not terribly. Its Power would bear him through, would wrest Runs In Light's authority away on the other side.

He blinked somberly at the Hide, knowing what it meant to the future. He stroked it with loving fingers, tracing the texture of the carefully tanned leather. So soft. Whoever had worked it had been a master. Even through the tips of his half-frozen fingers, he could feel the Power, charging—like the static found in rubbed fox fur.

"With you," he promised the Hide, "I shall become the greatest man among the People. No one will have more wives than Raven Hunter. No one will be stronger. No one will disagree when I speak. You will give me all this—and more."

The wind picked up, and he pulled himself to his weary feet. His stomach pulled tight around the berries, gurgling in the cold wind. From where it drifted around the rocks, Raven Hunter scooped a handful of snow, chewing and swallowing the cold lump. He shivered as it traced down his throat, chilling his hunger-haunted belly.

Grunting, he lifted the heavy Hide. Did a man weigh less? Turning his steps toward the river, he staggered off along the rim of the valley. The muscles in his thighs and calves strained and knotted, sapped by the eternal weight of the Hide. Couldn't the four-times-cursed Mammoth People have found a lighter totem? He barely cast a sideways glance as he passed Crow Caller's bones, scattered across the rocks now, half-hidden in snow. The skull lay on its side, empty orbits reflecting weirdly from the skift of snow that had blown in. Rodents had chewed the arches of the cheekbones. Maggot casings lay in the nasal passage. A bit of scalp had desiccated and curled up around the vault of the skull, gray-shot hair blowing across the snow in brittle strands.

Raven Hunter shuddered, curiously riveted by the hollow-eyed stare. In a dark corner of his mind, he could hear a dry laughter: Crow Caller's laughter, haunting, mocking.

He stumbled away.

Their tracks were partially drifted over, but that many people left a trail even a blind man could follow. Raven Hunter chuckled to himself, panting under the weight. Was it his imagination, or did the White Hide grow heavier and heavier? Where he'd rested only three or four times a day after leaving Ice Fire's camp, now he could stumble along for an hour before sagging wearily to the snow, lungs heaving, belly wailing. His reserves had gone, leaving him famished, thirsty.

"But the Power's mine," he reminded himself, feeling the flush of energy surge through him as he stroked the White Hide. "My Power!"

A deep dusty laugh erupted as he thought of how Runs In Light's expression would change as he strode into camp with this magnificent prize. With fumbling fingers, he pulled a core from the pouch, striking a sharp flake from it with a hammerstone. Using the flake, he cut a strip from around his pouch. Dropping the flake and core inside, he began chewing the resistant leather. Food. It would keep him going. All he had to do was make the camp of the People. From there, his destiny would be evident. They'd feast him with the best cuts of meat, lay warm liver at his feet. For him, they'd share fat-soaked berries, hand him horns full of strong black-moss tea to wash it all down.

Chewing the rubbery stuff, he stood, shouldering his burden, and followed in the tracks of the People. The breeze stiffened as Wind Woman's breath rolled across the land from the far north. Raven Hunter paused, sniffing. Caribou! He laid the Hide to the side, settling it carefully on clean snow. His stomach growled and twisted at the thought of fresh meat, his mouth flooding with anticipation.

Without weapons, he'd have to be canny, careful. Sniffing the wind, he circled, a snow-blown moraine to his side, the land dropping away to the broad braided channels of the Big River to the east. Behind him, the White Hide rested on the drift, oddly white against the dirty snow.

On silent feet, Raven Hunter ghosted along the rock to peer over the top of a boulder. An old bull stood below, one eye white with blindness. The animal's head hung and it walked with a limp, the left front quarter lamed.

Raven Hunter's belly cried out.

The old caribou, exiled by the younger bulls, had been pursuing its path alone, missed by the People's hunters in its solitude. Now, it only waited for the wolves . . . and Raven Hunter.

He slipped around the rock, eyes on the animal. He'd have to act judiciously. Even an old caribou like this one could kick a man's ribs to jelly.

Raven Hunter crawled up over the rock, trying to get above the animal, keeping downwind on the blind side.

The caribou grunted softly, a puff of condensed breath twisted and blown away in Wind Woman's growing fury. The animal shifted, back to the wind, looking around with its good eye. Raven Hunter froze, noting for the first time that the blind eye, like Crow Caller's, was on the left side of the head. He started, carelessly knocking a rock loose to rattle and tumble down.

The old bull's head snapped up, ears swiveling. Nervously, the animal trotted off, nose to the wind, sniffing anxiously.

Cursing himself under his breath for such superstition, Raven Hunter followed, sneaking through the falling light. The old caribou hobbled ahead, always just out of reach. Still, it drifted into rougher country, the glacial rubble piled ever higher, a perfect place for a man to ambush the old beast, bash it to death with a dropped rock.

Raven Hunter licked his lips, the lure of the hunt driving him. With a full belly, the White Hide wouldn't be so . . . *The White Hide!* Raven Hunter looked over his shoulder, back at the way he'd come.

The old caribou hobbled along on its lame leg, pausing every so often to scent the breeze and stare around with its one good eye. An animal near death, its ribs stuck out, pelvic bones visible through the thin hide.

Food. Easily had for a short stalk, the right ambush. Food that a man without weapons couldn't have hoped for.

Behind, the lure of the White Hide tugged at him. *And what if I'm not worthy?* Raven Hunter wondered. *What if some wolf comes along and chews it? Or a mouse strips the hair to make a nest? What if the White Hide thinks I've left it?*

Frantic, he looked at the old caribou where it followed a rocky drainage up into the boulder piles. Raven Hunter worked his cold fingers together, knowing the chances were excellent that he could circle, drop a heavy rock, and the old deer would be trapped. Generally, the washouts led to dead ends, blocked by huge boulders undercut and tumbled by the melt.

And if the White Hide were damaged by his negligence? The Power would evaporate—leave him. Dancing Fox would never be his. The People would never be his. They'd laugh that he'd let his stomach stand in the way of leadership!

For a long moment, he watched the old caribou walk into the certain trap. A wrenching agony possessed him. He imagined the thick steaks, the warm liver and heart blood.

Worry over the White Hide grew. What if—as he stood here thinking of food—a wolf was already ravaging the soft leather of the White Hide? What if some bear had found it— was rending the Sacred Hide to shreds? He winced, looking longingly back at the old caribou as its rump disappeared in a bend in the washout.

Raven Hunter turned heavy steps back down his trail.

"The Hide will keep me," he whispered. "The White Hide is my Power. The White Hide won't let anything happen to me. It's Power—it's my destiny!"

He ran on wobbly legs, frantic to assure himself that the Hide remained safe. On uneven footing, he tripped, falling, pain lancing up his arm as he bruised his elbow. For a moment, he lay half-stunned.

"The White Hide . . ." He gritted his teeth, staggering to his feet despite the thrumming agony in his arm. The feeling came back as he bulled along, anxious eyes seeking his tracks. He practically fell over the trail left by the People, turning, running on rickety legs.

He cried out as he found the Hide, resting where he'd left it on the stained snow. Whispering to himself, he caressed it, heedless of the numbness in his arm. A surge of relief washed through him with the power of sexual release.

"You're safe," he repeated in an undertone. "Safe. See? I'm worthy of you."

His arm wouldn't work to lift the burden. Pain flashed white in his mind, leaving him dizzy, disoriented. His empty stomach rebelled, causing him to retch. Breathing deeply, he controlled his spinning senses, backing under the Hide. With his good arm, he managed to roll it over one shoulder. He grunted, lifting, almost falling under the burden.

"Power," he whispered, cheek against the soft leather. "The heart and soul of the Mammoth People. My destiny. The greatest warrior of the People. The leader. No one is stronger than Raven Hunter—the half-Other! No one!"

The next morning, haggard, tripping, eyes glazed, he located the entrance to the Big Ice. The chill wind caressed his face as snow drifted down around him. His hurt arm had swollen, the joint throbbing violently. His stomach churned. He chewed stoically on another strip of leather from his battered clothing.

"Close now," he grunted to the Hide. "So close. Just through the ice . . . through the ice." Wearily, he hefted the White Hide again and wandered into the blackness.

One Who Cries joked in the dark, patting shoulders, telling stories on himself. Occasionally a knotty willow root would smolder and die, causing mild confusion until it was rekindled. For the most part, they conserved the fuel, eyes adjusted to the blackness.

Time stretched. So many people moved so slowly. "I thought you said *two* days?" Four Teeth muttered nervously under his breath.

"With a small party, that's all. With this many people?" One Who Cries lifted his shoulder. "We're in good shape. We haven't used half the fire yet. The People are growing used to it. Now that the first fear is gone, it's not so bad."

And the ghosts had been mysteriously, forebodingly quiet— just as Wolf Dreamer promised.

"For you maybe. You've been through before. But the rest of us—"

"Don't worry. We're protected."

As they continued on, he noticed people veering to the side to step around some obstacle; he eased forward.

Wolf Dreamer sat silently before an oil lamp, the moss wick fed by a preciously hoarded lump of fat. He stared at nothing, unseeing despite the activity around him. One Who Cries patted Four Teeth on the shoulder and went to crouch by Wolf Dreamer.

"Wolf Dreamer? Can you come back from the One and talk to me?"

The youth's eyes flickered slightly and slowly cleared. The Dreamer looked over, questioning. "Wh . . . what?"

"It's going pretty well. Everyone's happy. But we're moving a lot slower than I thought. Might take four days to get everyone out."

"It doesn't matter." He smiled. "Look at them, you can see their souls are healthy. I feel sorry for Four Teeth, though, he's dying."

One Who Cries squinted, seeing the old man talking in low tones to Buffalo Back. "Dying? He looks all right to me."

"A black spot is on his soul."

"A black spot?" One Who Cries shifted uneasily.

Wolf Dreamer smiled benignly. "The soul is a reflection of the body it inhabits. Four Teeth will feel fine. Then the life will ebb as his body fails. He won't feel much pain."

One Who Cries scratched under his chin. Maybe coming to talk to Wolf Dreamer hadn't been such a good idea. Half-hesitant, he asked, "Uh, my soul look all right?"

Wolf Dreamer chuckled softly. "Yes, One Who Cries, your soul looks fine. See that you keep it that way."

"Uh . . . yes, I—I will." He shifted his feet, feeling the gravel crunch through the holes in the soles of his long boots. "Um, do you know how things are on the other side of the ice? I mean, well, Green Water and the baby. I haven't seen them in half a year. I've been worried."

"You didn't say anything. I could have told you."

"You could? I mean, well, everyone else had their own problems." He asked with trepidation, "How are they? Healthy?"

Wolf Dreamer's smile beamed like rays of light. "Very. Green Water misses you and the baby is growing, becoming stronger every day."

One Who Cries stifled the ecstatic abandon that filled his heart before he chewed his lip and looked over. "Uh, why haven't the ghosts been groaning at us?"

Wolf Dreamer cocked his head as if listening and then spread his hands. "I Danced with the ice, told it to be silent. The ghosts did as I Danced them."

"Uh . . . well . . ." One Who Cries nodded uneasily.

Wolf Dreamer reached down by the lamp, drawing a spiral

in the gravel. "Look at this, One Who Cries. See what I draw. The ice is melting. The world is changing. Look at the spiral. See the way it's a circle on top of a circle? Like the Dance of the seasons, the years, and the lifetimes of a man, a mountain, and a world. Everything is One. It all goes around and around. An eternal Dance."

One Who Cries studied the spiral and realized the Power it held.

"Use it," Wolf Dreamer remarked. "Remember, it's the sign of the One. So is a cross, opposites crossed, like the Directions. Each symbol like that is a reflection of life. It's a drawing for what can't be expressed in words."

"Singing Wolf ought to be here."

"You'll tell him after I'm gone."

His heart stopped, breath stilled in his lungs. He stared hollowly into the Dreamer's serene eyes. "Gone?"

"Life and death; it's all the same."

As One Who Cries searched his mind for the right words, he watched Wolf Dreamer's eyes glassing over as he drifted away again.

"Wolf Dreamer?" Then more softly, "Wolf . . . Dreamer? Where are you going? Don't leave us."

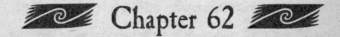

Chapter 62

"Their women come first." Eagle Cries looked up from the rock he lay on, perplexed as he stared into the blowing snow.

"Looks like an entire clan on the move. Coming right for us. But I've never heard of the Others coming with the women first. And look, there's children with them."

"This will be a slaughter," Eagle Cries added with a grin. "Kill their women, and they'll never come so arrogantly to our land again."

Singing Wolf's hard face tightened, eyes far away, as if

envisioning his own wife and child facing darts. Dancing Fox squinted into the growing storm.

"There's one man walking in the front," Big Mouth called softly from the side. "See? The one with the white cloak slung about his parka. That's a man. Why only one?"

"Ice Fire." Dancing Fox sat up. "Not only that, but see, he comes to the place where we turned back their advance scouts. No, I think this is more than an attempt at taking our land. If it was war they sought, the young men would come first—alone."

"You're not going to trust Others?" Eagle Cries looked up.

Crow Foot and Full Moon grumbled to each other on the other side of the defile. Dancing Fox shot a hot glance in their direction. "Eagle Cries, if any of the young men start something, your first cast is into them."

"Into our own . . ." His mouth dropped open.

Dancing Fox tilted her head, knowing all eyes had gone to her.

"That's what she said," Singing Wolf supported. "I heard the Dreamer put her in charge of the warriors. He came out from a Dreaming and told me. Act against Dancing Fox, and you act against the Dreamer and the People."

Eagle Cries dropped his eyes, a sullen expression on his face.

"You can always follow in the footsteps of Crow Caller," Dancing Fox reminded casually. "No one forces you to obey the Dreamer."

The warriors stared uneasily back and forth as she crawled back from the edge.

"What are you doing?" Singing Wolf cried, trying to keep his voice down.

"I'm going to see what Ice Fire—if that's who that is— wants. I'm going to see why he's come like this, leading women and children."

"It's a trap," Eagle Cries sputtered angrily. "These are Others, woman. The ones who drove us from our lands. You'd talk with such maggots?"

She stared at him, a cool control asserted in her crossed arms. "It's time to see what can be done about all this. The Others know the way to the hole in the Big Ice. What do we do? Try and stop them? Just the handful of us who remain on this side of the ice? If we try and stand up to them, we'll die. You, me, our families. Moon Water knows the way. Our old people can't outrun their young warriors. We can't close the hole through the ice. So, what will we do? Here, at least, we have an opportunity to talk.''

''Go.'' Singing Wolf motioned, eyes on Eagle Cries. ''It's time for sense instead of anger. Perhaps words will do what darts have failed to.''

''Cover me from above. If they didn't come to talk, I'll try to kill Ice Fire and escape up the trail. Our position is strong enough you should be able to keep them off.'' She hesitated. ''Assuming a dart from above doesn't skewer me.''

Eagle Cries' jaw ground loudly, muscles knotting in his cheeks as he lowered his eyes. ''You'll be safe from above,'' he mumbled. ''I swear by the spirits of the Long Dark.'' He looked meaningfully at the rest of the warriors where they crouched in the rocks, watching.

Nodding sharply, she took the trail.

Her ankle pained her, sending stitches up her leg. But then, it always did now when a storm was blowing down.

She stepped down the rocks into the narrow defile, winding around the bend where they'd ambushed the Other warriors. That event, too, had strained her authority. Perhaps, however, it now paid off. Perhaps the lives of those warriors had brought Ice Fire.

She stepped around the corner, seeing the Others climbing up from below. Snow had begun to fall from the darkening sky, big fluffy flakes landing on her shoulders, sticking to the fur at the side of her hood, melting coldly on her bare hand where she gripped her darts.

The man in the front looked up, stopping. A young man ran up from behind, pointing to the cleft where she waited, chattering excitedly to the leader before running nimbly back down through the gathering Others. A visible tension rippled through the group as they shaded eyes against the snow, staring up at her from under the flats of their hands.

She stepped forward, anxiously bracing her feet apart. The man continued his walk up the trail, now less than a dart's throw away.

As he closed, she studied him. Tall, lean, he wore a doubled parka, hood thrown back to expose his long graying hair. A white fox-skin cloak lay over his shoulders. His feet moved surely on the trail, each step light.

Her heart began to pound again as she looked into his knowing eyes. A Power lay there, a Power like the one she'd seen in a young Runs In Light's face. A longing restricted the base of her throat. She'd loved the man who'd once looked at her out of those eyes.

"Ice Fire?" she asked when he finally stopped, no more than a body length away.

He nodded, studying her. His handsome face hardened. "Dancing Fox."

She stared intently, going over his every feature. *He looks so much like Runs In Light.*

"Tell me what you're seeing?" he asked softly.

"Nothing . . . I . . . you look like someone I know."

"And you look like someone I knew once. She was part of a Dream. Had the Spirit Powers and Heron not been interfering, and had I been in possession of my senses . . . things might have happened differently that day on the beach."

His voice touched something deep within. A shiver finger traced up her back. "Spirit Power makes people do strange things."

He nodded, heedless of the rapidly falling snow that swirled on the whimpering wind. "You sent my warriors back."

"The time for killing is over. You came with women and children in the lead. What do you want here? This last refuge you've left us is almost devoid of game. We haven't much left but our lives and our honor. Still, we'll keep what's ours if you've come to take it."

His nostrils flared as he filled his lungs. A curious smile bent his lips. "Perhaps the time for taking from one another is over, too."

A tracing of humor animated his eyes. A part of her instinctively sought to trust him. She waited, knowing the bargain was yet to come. He watched her, as if knowing her very thoughts. A quizzical expression vied with a deep regret in his sensitive eyes.

"Is it?" she riposted.

"We've taken your land. You've taken our soul. Haven't we hurt each other enough?"

"We've heard your people live to kill, that the warrior way is where you find honor. Have you changed so much since I sent your warriors back?"

He dropped his eyes to stare at the snow gathering on her long boots. "Perhaps it's not a change so much as a return to the old ways."

"I don't understand."

"We come from the same people. Didn't Heron tell you? Had my grandfathers not feared yours, our loins would have interlocked. Our clans would share meat over a warm fire today." He paused, eyes softening. "Had Spirit Power not intervened, perhaps these years of war and rape would have been avoided."

She watched him warily. "You seem at home with Spirit Power."

The lines around his mouth tightened. "Spirit Power is just that. Power. How it's used—what it becomes—depends on the emotions of people involved. Some will use it for only good. Some for only evil. I've reason to regret some uses and to hope for others."

She nodded, respecting the earnest way he spoke, attracted to his humility. "You and your people climbed so far to tell us that?"

He shook his head. "We came for something of ours that you have."

"The White Hide?"

"Yes."

She slitted her eyes, tensing. "One of our people has that hide. His name is Raven Hunter. He has been disgraced by our Dreamer."

"We know him. We'd planned on torturing him to death for the horrors he committed on our relatives. He escaped, taking our most sacred White Hide with him. Now we must get it back. Perhaps we can come to an agreement which will accomplish several aims. Will you and your warriors accept a truce? Will you be willing to listen as we listen to you?"

She considered, studying him, looking for the trap. "A lot of pain has been inflicted. Many of the People cry for the blood of Others. They cry for revenge."

A grunt of assertion came from above despite the orders to remain quiet. Ice Fire must have heard, but he betrayed nothing, gaze steadily locked with hers. "It won't be easy," he admitted frankly. "Among the White Tusk Clan, many have suffered at your hands. Even my Singer wishes death for all of you." A wry smile crossed his lips. "Is that not yet another thing which binds us to each other?"

She chuckled before she caught herself.

A twinkle of appreciation sparkled in his knowing eyes. "Leaders with a sense of humor can get along."

She nodded. "Maybe. Tell me where we shall talk?"

He gestured over his shoulder. "A storm comes. I see from your clothing that times have been hard. There has been little game in your camps recently. If you will allow us to camp on your land, we will supply you with shelters and food. Our hunters had a good year. Perhaps we can begin a mending of the rift between our peoples. Out of all this trouble, perhaps we can bring good. Do you think Father Sun would mind our offering a truce for peace in his name?"

Her eyes narrowed. He wanted to make an offering to the People's gods? Where was the flaw? Could she trust this man she instinctively liked? He did offer food and shelter. Too many nights they'd been freezing in their worn-out parkas, huddled together for shared warmth.

"I'll need to talk to my warriors."

He nodded, arms spread wide. "You might want to argue with some haste; this looks to be a bad storm. If you could fight it out in a hurry, we could be pitching camp and cooking food for all before it gets really bad."

She laughed and nodded, holding his warm eyes. "I'll argue fast, Ice Fire." She wheeled and trotted up the trail.

Eagle Cries and the rest watched from outside the camp, huddling close in the growing cold, fingering darts as they stared through the haze of blowing snow at the Others staring back, fingering their darts in return.

Inside the main lodge, the leaders of both tribes sat together around a large fire, the flames flickering golden across their wary faces. Rich aromas of caribou steak and sweet boiled roots filled the smoky air.

Singing Wolf tilted his head to stare through the partially open door flap at the evil night. "They'll freeze out there."

Dancing Fox took another bite of the roasted caribou, chewing it thoughtfully. "Maybe it'll cool some of their anger."

"Anger cools slowly," Ice Fire admitted unhappily as he wiped greasy fingers on his long boots. He shot a quick glance at Red Flint, who glowered around the lodge.

The old Singer grunted, casting surly eyes on Singing Wolf. "Some of us bear too many scars."

"We all bear scars," Singing Wolf remarked mildly. He wiped the grease from his mouth. "I, for one, took the heart of a warrior of your people and placed it in the Big River so it would go to the Camp of Souls under the sea."

"You . . ." Red Flint swallowed hard. His eyes shifted away and he got to his feet, walking to the flap, crawling out into the snow beyond.

Singing Wolf closed his eyes and sighed. "I fear peace will not come easily." He shook his head. "It's been a long time since I was warm. If you'll excuse me, I'm taking this opportunity to sleep without my teeth chattering like gulls' beaks."

"Sleep without fear, *friend*," Ice Fire assured.

For long moments after Singing Wolf rolled in his robes, Dancing Fox sat staring into the fire, a prickling awareness of the Others' Most Respected Elder obsessing her.

"You surprise me."

She looked over at him, experiencing that same tingle when their gazes touched that she had all evening. "Why?"

"I don't expect such poise and intelligence from a woman so young."

"I'm not young anymore." She rubbed her eyes, feeling the incredible mantle of responsibility weighing on her shoulder. "I was young once, three years ago—an eternity."

He paused, fingers tapping lightly on the hides the women had laid over the floor. "I'm surprised a man hasn't made a wife of you. Your beauty takes a man's breath away. When I look into your eyes, I see strength and soul." He paused, unsure for the first time since she'd met him. "You have a lover?"

She smiled wryly, curiously unperturbed by his forward

question. "I loved once. It seems a Dream has stolen his soul more completely than I ever could have."

Ice Fire smiled wistfully. "Wolf Dreamer. Heron must have led him to that."

She studied him speculatively. "What do you know of Heron? Of Wolf Dreamer?"

He leaned back, face going serious. "I . . . met him in a Dream. You see he's . . . my son."

She straightened. "You're his father?"

The edges of his lips twitched. "Yes, his and Raven Hunter's. That's why I couldn't let him die—despite what he'd become." His eyes flickered to hers. "Is that a terrible weakness? That I couldn't kill my son?"

She thought about it, a tenderness in her breast that he would confide in her. "No, I don't think so." She shifted, reclining, pulling her hair to the side. "All of us, all people, have to cherish our children. They're the future."

He played with a frayed corner of the white fox cloak. A corner—she noted—that had become smudged from fingering, the hair mostly gone, worn away. More than anything else, the action made him less powerful—a frail human like herself.

"The future," he repeated. "Yes. That's why I couldn't watch Raven Hunter die—no matter that he'd earned it."

She inspected him, the wariness back. "For the mutilations and retaliation?"

At her cooling tone, he looked up. For a moment, he searched her eyes, then shook his head slightly. "For being what he is." He paused. "Let's see, how do I explain." His hands molded the air before him. "A man, or woman for that matter, is body and soul; agreed?"

She nodded, waiting.

"The body can be flawed. Maybe born without fingers, maybe it's not strong enough to stand the cold, or it coughs and dies, or it's stillborn." He shifted again, straining for the right words. "It's the same with the soul. In Raven Hunter's case, something is missing. He's preoccupied with himself . . . with this obsession for Power. And the problem is that he has glimpses, visions of what could be. Only he doesn't have the ability to extend that part of soul and share the identity. Understand?"

"Share the identity," she mused, bracing her chin on her palm.

"Yes," he whispered, handsome lines of his face puckering. "A healthy soul can extend itself, put itself in the place of another creature's experiences. From that comes wisdom. I learned it long ago." He stared at the fire, a sadness deep in his eyes. "Raven Hunter, however, has none of that compassion, that extension of the soul."

She reached over, touching his shoulder, meeting his eyes as he looked up. "But you saved him anyway?"

For a long moment, they stared into each other's eyes. He lifted an eyebrow. "I'm not all that compassionate." He looked around, seeing Singing Wolf's slack face in the back where he slept soundly. "Perhaps I'm as much a monster as Raven Hunter. I provided him with the opportunity to steal the White Hide."

She started. "You let him steal the . . ."

Ice Fire lifted a shoulder. "It's a means to an end which needs to be met." He gestured, mouth working, a conspiratorial light in his eye. He lowered his voice and she bent closer. "You must tell no one. Not your people, and especially none of mine. I've seen where my son Wolf Dreamer is going. I know the future of the People is in the south. And I know we were one, once, long ago. I don't know why, but somehow, I was set up. My wife died. My life changed. I loved her with all my heart. And when she'd been taken, I left. Just like that. Men who've been hurt terribly, they do strange things sometimes. We were camped along the salt water at the time, down where the land bends south, where the southern sea is only a month's journey away. That camp's under the water now, long buried, but something drove me east along the coast."

"*Something* drove you?"

"At night, Dreams haunted me. My wife filled them, and I felt the presence of another woman. Like me, her soul cried out over the loss of a loved one." He studied her. "I don't know if you can understand, but I thought it was a Spirit Woman—to take the place of my wife." He swallowed. "Then, one day, I awoke, and the Dream was powerful. I walked in a daze, hearing a calling—a powerful calling. It stirred me and I felt desire for the first time since my wife had died. And then I saw her. Beautiful.'' He reached up, gently touching Fox's long hair, a reverence in his eyes as he ran his fingers along her face.

"I knew it was the Dream woman. I . . . I stalked her, afraid she'd disappear into the mists, back into the sea. That fear drove me to a madness, and when she saw me, and ran, I chased her down.'' His hands knotted and he closed his eyes. "I took her there on the sand, the Dream pounding in my ears. With each movement of my body, the Power built until my soul sang and seemed to explode with the glory of it.

"And I came to, lying there on her, totally spent. And I looked down into her eyes and saw pain and hurt and disbelief all rush up at me.''

He frowned at the fire. "And I realized what I'd done. The edges of the Dream were there, the Spirit Woman watching from someplace else through a Dream. And I knew it wasn't that girl, so beautiful, so vulnerable. When I looked into those shattered eyes, I knew I could have loved her. That she could have loved me. Only Heron's Dream changed it. It wasn't supposed to have happened like that. And the children that rape bore were different, changed by the violence of their conception. Circles within circles, everything changed and no reason why. Like a spiral, which is the outside and which the in?''

She stared at him, soul drifting in his soft eyes. "And you think it would have all been different without Heron?''

He nodded miserably. "The woman on the beach and I, we were to love, to unite the People. Instead, so many died. Raiding began because I wasn't the one to return with a wife of the People—to link our clans which had been split so long ago.''

"Perhaps Heron had her reasons. I hear she was driven by things beyond her, too.''

He nodded contemplatively. "Maybe.''

"Didn't you tell your—''

"I've told no one the whole truth. Oh, Red Flint knows some of the story. But not the Power of the symbolism. He doesn't know how important it is for us to go south. If he did, he'd probably kill me on the spot and assume the Most

Respected Elder robe, despite the fact that visions scare him to death."

Dancing Fox touched his hand, feeling his fingers twine strongly with hers. "Why did you tell me?"

"I don't know." He focused on the fire a moment, then asked, "Tell me about you? What drives you?"

"The survival of my people."

Ice Fire's eyes deepened and she seemed to fall into them. "And what would you give for that survival?"

"Anything."

"I know a way."

She probed his gentle expression cautiously. "Tell me about it."

"Will you trust me? Take me and a handful of my young men to your camp beyond the Big Ice to get the White Hide back? If your people were to return it as a gesture of goodwill, and my clan were to offer gifts of clothing, food, and new shelters, we might be able to forge a new people."

"Or reforge an old one?"

He smiled, squeezing her hand. "Yes. Then you think we could share the south together?"

"Together." The word rested easily on the tip of her tongue. "I've been alone for so long, I'm not sure what that means anymore."

His warm smile caressed her heart. "Nor do I, but it's part of the Dream. A chance to reunite that which should have never been sundered."

She peered into the fire, watching the rose-amber flames lick at the rocks lining the pit. Slowly, her eyes shifted to rest on their entwined fingers. Noting her gaze, he hesitantly brought his other hand over to turn up her chin and meet her eyes.

Do I trust him? She looked hard into his eyes, trying to read his soul. *How many times have men made promises to me? He has a new land to gain. And the People? Can we stand against them in the end? His warriors look healthy, strong, eager for war. Can our young men stop them?*

A grim reality blocked her thoughts. *What choice do I have? And yes . . . despite my fears, I trust him.* Her heart raced. *Fool!*

"It won't be easy," he warned, seeing her caution. "I think we both know that."

She nodded. "I'll take you—and only a handful of your young men—to the People. Call it a test of your resolve. But Raven Hunter will be there."

"Yes." He nodded soberly. "I've been preparing for that final confrontation."

"It will be . . . cataclysmic." She stilled, tensing.

He nodded soberly, meeting her eyes. "You know what's coming, then?"

Her teeth ground hollowly as she nodded. "Not completely."

He began to say something and hesitated, seeing her stiffen. "I wish I knew which of them is stronger."

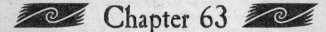 Chapter 63

Wolf Dreamer resettled his legs, easing the cramp. His mind continued to replay the scenes of joy and release as he'd led the People from the cleft in the ice. Little Moss had danced out of joy—an expression of the One not even the young boy understood. Shouts and cries had carried sharply on the cold air, people hugging each other, laughing, some with tears tracing down wrinkled brown faces long etched by sorrow and hardship.

He'd led them, climbing up out of the valley, the first to see Jumping Hare as he came streaking down the slope, his arms waving wildly, face radiant.

So much joy after so much suffering. A spiral, a circle within a circle having no distinction between the levels. All things came around, changing, moving down the spiral of life. Despair's time had passed for this cycle. Only challenge remained—until the next curve of the spiral.

And how could anyone forget the shining relief in One Who Cries' face as he ran to his wife that day, stopping, holding her at arm's length as they both looked into each other's eyes with worship. They'd embraced then, violently, holding each other until ribs cracked.

Wolf Dreamer lowered his head, feeling air and life filling his chest. With a sigh, he stood, plucking his hide from the ground, a lingering remorse over the loss of Heron's shelter nibbled at his peace. Ah, for the darkness, the faint moist odor of the purifying steam. He looked around, seeing Broken Branch dropping boiling stones into a buffalo-gut bag. Steam.

Wolf Dreamer considered, hearing the commotion around the camp. Distraction, no way to clear his mind. They wanted him to Dream the animals in tomorrow.

Walking to the fire, he bent and picked up a burning chunk of spruce. He couldn't help but feel their eyes on him as he studied the glowing end of the thick branch, bluish smoke twirling in the cold air. Grunting to himself, he turned, walking up the slope toward the trees, blowing on the branch to keep it burning. The People parted before him, conversation evaporating.

In the trees, he snapped more dead branches from the snags and threw them into the fire over his glowing embers. As they crackled to life, he kicked some of the hand-sized cobbles—like Broken Branch's boiling stones—from the snow and piled them in the fire, letting them heat.

He could feel them. On all sides, faces peeked from around rocks, from over drifts, through the trees, as the People came to peer at him. They followed him everywhere, watching, ever curious at what he might be about.

Distraction.

Dreaming was becoming impossible.

"You told me, Heron. But I didn't believe it could ever be so difficult."

He walked along, scooping up snow, cradling it in the hem of the robe he'd taken from Grandfather White Bear's steaming body that day so long ago on the ice. Hunching over, he rolled the hot rocks from the fire, using them in the same manner as a mother might warm her child's robes. The robe over his head, he reached for the snow pile, sprinkling the white crystals over the rocks.

Sizzling explosions of steam rose warm, circling about his

head. Perhaps it wasn't Heron's shelter, but it cleared his mind, eased his thoughts with that feeling of Oneness. As the steam dissipated, he sprinkled more snow on the rocks, breathing deeply, feeling the tensions, the distractions, fading. He could carry his geyser anywhere now. He could cleanse his mind—Dream.

Stretching his consciousness, he sensed a dark presence moving somewhere nearby. His heart pounded suddenly. As he'd known for months, the conflict approached, drawing down from the north.

He pulled his white bear robe over his head, letting the steam fill the canopy and caress his face. In the moist darkness, painful images swirled.

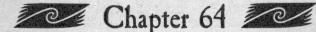

Chapter 64

In the eternal blackness, Raven Hunter stumbled over a waist-high boulder, banging his head as he fell. Pain blasted up his hurt arm, leaving him nauseated and sick, lights whirling through the blackness before his eyes. He lay there, the weight of the White Hide pinning him on his injured arm. Air rasped in and out of his laboring lungs. A new pain stung his head where he'd cracked it on the rock.

"Got to keep going," he choked. "Power's in the Hide. Power's mine. Got to keep going."

With his good hand, he felt out the position of the boulder, dragging the heavy Hide over it, maneuvering with his good arm, straightening and pulling the Hide over his shoulders. He locked his knees to brace his trembling legs. One step at a time, he felt his way along, the ghosts creaking and moaning in the ice overhead. Gravel crunched under his worn long boots, the chill eating through the holes where the leather bunched and chafed against the blistered soles of his feet.

Step-by-step, he continued, feeling the way by keeping to

the gravel, bent low to keep from banging his head on the overhanging ice. Around him, the forbidding black stretched.

He rubbed his cheek against the White Hide, feeling the Power it held, letting it soak into his very skin. He'd cut away his pouch, eating it strip by strip for the little strength it held.

Onward he plodded, driven by the future, goaded by the Power that would be his when the People saw the White Hide. They waited for him—and the White Hide—somewhere ahead. Beyond the blackness.

The mountains shaded lavender in the silence of dawn, stars twinkling low on the southern horizon. Before them, the Big Ice loomed—a vast white wall, ghostly in the soft light. Wind Woman whipped snow from the ridge tops, sending them stretching like long fingers into the sky. Guards hunched over a small fire, clutching their robes as they looked out across the crystalline wastes.

Singing Wolf stood apart, a foot propped on one of the boulders that tumbled down the slope around them. He'd been up most of the night, thinking, worrying—but it was none of his business. Still, he winced as his gaze drifted to Ice Fire's shelter. Nestled in the center of the camp, the hide roof glistened with frost. Every night for the past week, Dancing Fox had gone in to share dinner with the Most Respected Elder and not come out until dawn. Her warriors, especially those from Raven Hunter's old band, bristled, stamping around threateningly, charging treason.

Singing Wolf heaved a tired sigh and contemplatively smoothed the snow from the rock beside him, whispering to himself, "No, she's no traitor."

He'd seen the tender looks Fox and Ice Fire had started to share, the guarded way they touched each other—and he understood their newfound togetherness. The elder reminded them all of Wolf Dreamer. How could Dancing Fox not feel longing for the man? She'd loved the Dreamer with all her heart.

And maybe the fact that Fox and Ice Fire shared robes would strengthen both peoples. Yes, maybe. He gripped a handful of snow and crushed it into a ball, then tossed it silently into the lavender rays of dawn.

"This is crazy!" Eagle Cries whispered viciously from down the slope.

Singing Wolf turned to see the youth's fist lifted toward the Others' camp. In the dim rose-amber light of the fire, Eagle Cries' face twisted with anger.

"Tomorrow, we take these Others into the hole under the ice? I can't believe it!"

"I can't either," Crow Foot remarked. His round face glowed boyishly smooth in the dim light. "We lead men who raped our women and killed our brothers into the heart of the People's camp? It's madness."

Singing Wolf massaged his forehead and tiredly headed for their fire. They started, surprised, as he appeared out of the darkness. "Don't forget the oaths you swore to uphold the peace."

Crow Foot turned, catlike on his heels. "You've always been weakhearted, Singing Wolf. I remember the day you ran out on Raven Hunter and the rest of us. Oaths didn't matter so much then, eh?"

Singing Wolf's breath fogged around his face. "What Raven Hunter did was wrong for the People. Wolf Dreamer is doing right for us."

"Right for us," Crow Foot mocked. "Is it right that I clutch to my bosom the beast who killed my sister?"

Singing Wolf blinked and lowered his gaze. "I know it's hard, but we all have to—"

"*I saw him in Ice Fire's lodge!*" Crow Foot shouted, the echo running through the camp and down the valley.

"What's more important? Your dead sister? Or the survival of the People?"

Crow Foot took a step forward, nose inches from Singing Wolf's as he stared into his eyes. "How can leading these animals to our women and children save us?"

"I believe the Dreamer."

"You believe." Crow Foot sneered, spitting his disgust.

By sheer force of will, Singing Wolf stifled the rage that exploded in his heart. "I'll wait," he managed to say, biting off the words. "I think, *boy*, that more than you or I can know is at stake here. I think this is a matter for Dreamers and Elders."

Crow Foot tensed as if stung. "And I think we should kill

them all.'' With the speed of a mouse, he darted away into the darkness.

Singing Wolf glared after him, seeing the youth's shadow flicker across the ice.

''Raven Hunter would know what to do,'' Eagle Cries defended. ''He'd never have made a pact with the butchers.''

I've changed so much, thought Singing Wolf. *Once, it would have been me clamoring for the blood of the Others. Now, I can't afford my temper. A childish outburst would kill the hopes of the People. Is this constant futility what leadership means?* Singing Wolf studied the angry youth beside him. *How much smarter is One Who Cries, who avoids such dangers.*

In a neutral voice, he murmured, ''You promised on the spirits of the Long Dark to wait, to see if some way could be found to make peace. Is your word good?''

Eagle Cries turned, the glow of the fire, reflected from the snow, shone on his strained face. ''Yes, man with no courage, I'll wait. But once we're there—once we're at the camp of the People—my word will be done.''

A soft scritching of boots on gravel came from around the boulder, as though someone stood listening. Singing Wolf and Eagle Cries halted, tensing a moment. When no more sounds came, Singing Wolf continued tiredly, ''And the rest of your warriors?''

''They'll keep their word. Unlike you, we place a value on honor. Raven Hunter taught us that.''

''And what else did he teach you?'' Dancing Fox asked as she came around the side of the huge dark boulder. She was dressed in a worn caribou parka, her black hair glistening against the background of white fox fur in her hood.

Eagle Cries jerked, asking maliciously, ''Has Ice Fire tired of you already? Go back to his—''

''Answer my question, warrior!'' Dancing Fox's voice cut as coldly as the crystals of snow blowing in Wind Woman's breath. ''Is hatred all that Raven Hunter taught? Did he forget that wisdom and the ability to think are important too? Did he teach you all to disregard the ways of our elders? To forget that the People have struggled for hundreds of Long Darks to live in peace as Father Sun wished?''

"Raven Hunter *is* the son of the Father Sun!" Eagle Cries shouted. "He was born to lead us to a new way."

"Then why didn't you follow him after the Dreaming?"

Eagle Cries clamped his jaw and crossed his arms brusquely over his chest.

As the silence stretched, Singing Wolf repeated, "Why didn't you?"

"That may have been a mistake."

"I don't think so."

"Look, don't you see? What if there is peace? Eh? What then? How do we keep who we are separate from the Others? Does Father Sun get replaced by the Great Mystery? Does Dreaming get replaced by their visions in high places?"

Dancing Fox asked, "Isn't that what Raven Hunter wanted? To destroy Wolf Dreamer? Kill him with a dart in the middle of a Dreaming—*during the Renewal, of all things*?"

Eagle Cries sputtered a sigh. "That was wrong. It was a crazy thing done in anger. He'd just seen his friend killed by witchery. He—"

"It's witchery now?" Singing Wolf lifted a brow. "Not Dreaming?"

"I . . . I don't know anymore. Maybe it is."

"Fine children of Father Sun we are." Dancing Fox exhaled gruffly. "In our camp, the warriors can't wait to drive darts through the Others, watch their blood run out, and laugh while they die. In Ice Fire's camp, they can't wait to get their White Hide back and drive darts into our bodies." She shook her head. "And we'll all die if we don't change."

"What do you mean? Die?"

"You've heard the Dreamer. The world's changing. The ice is melting and the seas are rising. Perhaps the doom callers are right. Perhaps everyone in the world is crazy."

"Perhaps," Eagle Cries agreed sullenly.

"Will you keep your oaths until we meet with the People?" she implored.

"We'll keep them. But after that, we're free men."

"And what will you do with this freedom?"

He shrugged irritably. "Maybe no Others will make it back to tell their warriors how to find the hole in the ice."

"Moon Water stayed with the rest of the White Tusk Clan. She still knows where the hole is."

Eagle Cries laughed harshly. "Then she'll have to die, too."

"And Jumping Hare's child?" Singing Wolf asked coldly.

"It's half Other." Eagle Cries grinned malevolently.

"So's your hero, Raven Hunter," Dancing Fox muttered. "Maybe true strength comes from a mixing of our blood with theirs, eh?" She turned and strolled away toward the rising sun and Ice Fire's camp. A tendril of smoke twisted from the elder's lodge, the soft glow of fire penetrating through the door flap.

Clouds drifting on the horizon glowed pink and orange now from the sliver of gold peeking above the distant mountains.

Eagle Cries frowned and turned to Singing Wolf. "What's she talking about? Raven Hunter can't be . . ."

It hurt his eyes. Had the sun ever been so bright? Cloud Woman parted long enough that a shaft of light practically blinded him. Raven Hunter looked away, tears coming to his eyes. On his shoulder, the White Hide beamed, the reflection illuminating the ice that parted to either side as he stumbled out, his back crying as if it had never been straight before.

His useless arm dangled, swollen, the fingers puffy, the lines of his hand disappeared in the bloated member.

Owlishly, he looked around, seeing the pockmarks where the feet of the People had passed over the gravels. Snow blew down from the icy ridge overhead.

"We made it." He nuzzled the White Hide with his cheek. "We're close now!"

Snow had blown across the trail, but as Raven Hunter looked around, he could see the route they'd taken, the streak of white where the way led up through the brush at a bend in the river.

Bowed under the weight of his burden, he stumbled off, panting in the light as Cloud Woman drew herself close about the sky, threatening, ominous in the still air.

A crow cawed from high overhead.

Their camp nestled at the edge of a grove of towering spruce. Buffalo-hide lodges sprouted in a rough semicircle around a central open space where children played and women and men labored at butchering the wealth of animals their Dreamer had called.

Wolf Dreamer sat on a fallen log, gazing at the carcasses. As they'd died, he'd suffered with them, feeling the stinging darts biting deep, invading the delicate tissues of their hearts, lungs, and livers. One with them, he'd choked on their blood, shared their terror as death's fingers stole through their minds and their eyes grew dim.

At the same time, he shared the joyous abandon of the People, now wading through dispatched animals: life for another year. Meat and new clothing would fill the lodges.

Yet . . . beneath the suffering and joy, a deeper reality called to him—but he knew he couldn't let himself drown in that truth until, like spider, he'd thrown out the first threads of the crimson web.

"Huh!" One Who Cries grunted, walking up to stand by Wolf Dreamer. "You know, we've butchered a lot of animals here, but I never noticed before. The lungs, none of them have worms in the lungs. Wonder why?"

Wolf Dreamer's eyes drifted to the looming blackness in the north that gained Power with every breath he took. "We're not the only life moving south."

"You mean the hole will widen and let animals through?"

He smiled faintly. "Soon the mammoth and caribou and buffalo will walk down this way of ours. Where they walk, the worms ride."

"Is that good?"

Wolf Dreamer gave him a wry grin and spread his arms, beginning to dance, spiraling around in a circle, never stepping on his tracks again. "See me dancing? How many times have I been around?"

"What?" One Who Cries asked, bewildered. "I don't—"

"Look!" Wolf Dreamer danced back to the beginning before jumping out of the center and lifting his brows questioningly. "Now, tell me which came first. Did I dance from the inside out, or the outside in?"

"Inside out first and then outside in second." He pointed. "Any hunter can tell by the tracks."

Wolf Dreamer sighed, disappointed. "What came first? The inside or the outside?"

One Who Cries pursed his lips. "What does that have to do with worms?"

Wolf Dreamer threw back his head and laughed until he had to hold his stomach. Feeling foolish, One Who Cries began laughing, too, nervously trying to decide what he'd done that was funny.

Wolf Dreamer settled on a log and patted it to indicate his friend should join him.

One Who Cries gave him a speculative look from the corner of his eye as he cautiously lowered himself. "I don't like it when you start talking in words I don't understand. You're always drifting off, leaving us alone, without your guidance."

"I know . . ." he said tiredly. He smiled shyly like the old Runs In Light would have. "In answer to your question, the worms will come south, too. They—like us—live off the animals. Many of the creatures that live south of us will die off. Partly because the world is changing, partly because of us—and the worms. Change is the breath of the One, a step in the Dance. You have to see the Dancer . . . but the Dancer is never there."

One Who Cries bit off what he was about to say concerning the worms, a look of mystification spreading over his flat features.

Here is a good man. Though One Who Cries doesn't know it, he Dances closer to the One than all the others. He is pure, unimpressed by his growing stature. A slight pain touched him. *I will miss this man more than any of the rest. And the end is coming so soon now, so very very soon.*

In the distance, a child raced through camp, carrying a stick high over her head. A dog leapt for it, barking at the girl's heels.

"I never know what you mean anymore."

"Another follows me who will explain."

"Who? Can we—"

The sensation burst upon him, leaving his senses reeling. He would have fallen from the log but for One Who Cries catching him, supporting his weight while the world shimmered around him.

"I have to go," Wolf Dreamer groaned, breathing deeply as he pushed to his feet, arms out for balance. He felt the red tendrils wrapping around him, the strands pulling tight. "The web is almost complete. The spiral of the spider is coming together."

One Who Cries narrowed his eyes, looking up at the young man who had once been his friend. "Go where? Can I come and—"

"No. I have to prepare myself, to ready the Dream."

He caught his balance, turning his steps upward, toward a high spruce-covered ridge that overlooked the camp. His feet had never seemed lighter, nor his heart heavier.

Chapter 65

Darkness swelled around them, heavy and damp. Above, the ghosts groaned and shrieked, their voices often so loud the People couldn't hear one another speaking. Ice Fire braced his back against the gritty ice wall, feeling along the rough surface with his hands as he cautiously placed each foot. Dancing Fox walked gracefully in front of him, silhouetted by the fat-fed lamp Moon Water had told him how to find. Such a little light, such a terrifying place. And she had passed through here in the darkness—while water ran? His respect and admiration grew.

They pushed onward, a bond forming despite the bristling hostility. Men and women alone with their fears, not even their intense hatred could separate them from the rumbling ice overhead.

"I'm more awed by Wolf Dreamer every day," Ice Fire admitted. "How could anyone trust themselves to this?"

Dancing Fox nodded soberly. "And I've been through it twice before. It never gets any easier."

A sudden grunt sounded; Red Flint fell with a sodden thud. Something snapped like a dart shaft. He groaned and caught his breath.

"What is it?" Singing Wolf called in the darkness, voice echoing eerily.

"My foot," Red Flint groaned, the sound of his hides rustling against the rocks and gravel.

"Here. I found you. Take my hand," Singing Wolf comforted. "I'm bending down to feel your ankle. Can you guide my hand?"

Dancing Fox turned, starting back with the lamp. Ice Fire followed.

In the dim light, they saw Singing Wolf bending over the Singer, running quick fingers down the elder's leg. A moment later, Red Flint gasped.

"I can feel it through your long boot. Broken."

Red Flint choked some whimpering sound. "Not in here," he whispered.

"We'll get you through," Singing Wolf reassured. Unslinging his pack, he laid out a long rawhide thong and two sticks. "Let me splint that. We can bear you on our shoulders."

"Wait," Broken Shaft called from further behind. "He's our Singer. We'll carry him."

Into the darkness, Ice Fire called firmly, "We'll take turns carrying him—and anyone else who hurts themselves. Or have you forgotten where we are?" He looked around, meeting worried eyes in the faint light cast by the lamp.

The ice shifted somewhere overhead, the rasping vibrations loud around them. For a second no one moved.

"We'll *all* take turns," Dancing Fox said crisply into the resulting deadly quiet. The subject closed, she bent down so Singing Wolf could see better as he bound willow artfully around Red Flint's leg.

Fires sparkled like amber jewels strewn across the camp. People stood silhouetted before the flames, roasting meat, fiddling with boiling bags. In the light of the fires, prosperous new shelters of freshly scraped hide rose. The odors of cooking meat, roasting liver, and fat filled the air along with the pungency of a strange smoke. For once, the raking breath of Wind Woman had stilled. Sounds carried on the quiet night, the stars glittering, the mists banished for this evening of celebration. Raven Hunter sighed in elation and relief as a pack of dogs yapped suddenly and raced out into the growing darkness toward him.

"Get away! You filthy . . .'' Raven Hunter cursed, kicking weakly at the darting beasts.

"Who comes?"

"Raven Hunter," he told the guard arrogantly, trying to stop wheezing. Legs trembling, he staggered past, hearing feet trotting behind him.

"You're hurt. Let me help you. Is that someone wounded over your shoulder? A body? What—"

"Get away!" he cried as the young man reached for the White Hide. As if his words had triggered it, Wind Woman gusted out of the north, a biting nip in her cold breath.

The man backed uncertainly in the dark.

Raven Hunter's eyes gleamed as he stepped into the light of the biggest fire, easing the White Hide down on Green Water's unoccupied robe. The People gaped, eyes wide as if one of the Monster Children had stepped magically from the sky and into their midst. Wolfishly, he peered around. Thick chunks of spruce popped and cracked, twisting spirals of sparks whirling up into the night sky.

"Raven Hunter!"

His name passed from mouth to mouth.

Yes. He laughed to himself, turning on his heels and pinning their eyes, delighted by the awe in their laughter. *I'm back, my people. I have returned . . . with a new way. A way you'll all follow. Now, none may question me. None may challenge MY leadership.*

"Look at him! He's different—changed." "Look at the light in his eyes. Like a Dreamer—he's seen something." "How did he dare to come back?" they murmured, backing away as he laughed.

"Raven Hunter?" Buffalo Back appeared from out of the dark, head tilted, rheumy old eyes faded and unsure. Firelight flickered across his wrinkled face.

"I have returned!" he called out. Straightening his back, he jammed his good thumb into his chest, ordering at the top of his lungs, *"Look at me!"*

They came from all around the camp, feet grating on snow. Anxiously they looked, hissing questions back and forth behind their hands.

"See me?" he called. "Look at a hero!" He knotted a fist and raised it high over his head. "I, Raven Hunter, the first warrior of the People, went to kill the Other shaman, Ice Fire! I, Raven Hunter, first warrior of the People, stole the White Hide instead! What is the life of a worthless Dreamer when the heart and soul of a people can be looted away?"

"You did what?" Buffalo Back asked, eyes going wide. "The White Hide? The White Mammoth Hide? The one their Power . . ." He gulped, unable to finish, and backed away a step. A hushed chattering picked up among the rings of spectators.

"I took it!" he asserted, the thrill of victory shooting up through him, lending strength to his weaving body. "I robbed them of their spirit—of their courage and will. Do you think they can stand against us now? Do you think the silly tricks of my witch brother can lead you? Here! Look at me and see a man of true Power! My father, Father Sun, is more powerful than their Great Mystery. Now their greatest totem has fallen to us . . . to me!"

"But they'll come after it!" Buffalo Back cried. He advanced, chin thrust out, hands imploring. "You can't take such a powerful—"

Raven Hunter lanced stiff fingers into Buffalo Back's old throat. It took all his strength, but he backheeled the man, his useless arm flapping and blasting pain. Nevertheless, as the old man dropped, choking and gagging, Raven Hunter centered himself, dropping his knee across the old man's throat, his total weight behind it.

The snap carried loud in the air, people staring, mouths opened in shock. For a brief second they stood, then rushed forward as a river when the spring ice breaks, reaching for him.

"*Stop!*" he shouted, slashing out with his good hand as he jumped backward to grip the White Hide.

People milled, losing momentum, some in the front stepping back as Raven Hunter lovingly stroked the Hide. He felt the Power, using it to push them back. "Yes, you feel it, don't you? The White Hide serves me. I am the Power of the People. As this Hide kept the Others—made them strong—so shall it now keep the People."

Broken Branch hobbled her way through the assembly, elbowing people to get them to move. She stopped, swinging her wizened head around the circle, then stared down at Buffalo Back, grunting under her breath. When she looked up, her eyes glittered.

"So," she accused. "You got Buffalo Back this time? Who's left? Four Teeth and me? Then you don't have any elders to stand before you."

"I have the Power, old woman." The surge filled his chest. "See the White Hide? It's mine. The gift of Father Sun to me, his child. You know the story, don't you, old woman? The story of my mother, taken by Father Sun as she walked by the salt water?"

"Yes, but it wasn't—"

"And two sons were born, taking my mother's life in the birth." He cackled the Power of it. "A woman can't bear Father Sun's children and live. The Power is too great. That's why I've always seen. I'm his new way for the People. Look, old hag, see the White Hide? We're here, south of the ice, and Father Sun has given me the strength to carry the White Hide away from the Others. Father Sun has tried me, molded me through hardship and suffering. He's shown me fear and cold and hunger and pain. And now, he's shown me the way to lead the People."

"You killed Buffalo Back!" Broken Branch cried feebly, pointing with a gnarled finger. "You've broken the People's peace. Last time, Wolf Dreamer kept us from casting you out. But this . . . this is too much!"

He closed his eyes to slits. "You'd try me, woman? One step closer, and I'll kill you. That's the Power of the White Hide. Unless you can feel the Power, you can't understand what it gives me." He reached, energized by the touch of the Hide, grabbing up her skinny arm. He closed his thick fingers around the wailing woman's wrist, feeling the brittle bones sliding across each other. Her hideous cry fueled him, goading, as the bone cracked and snapped and Broken Branch screamed agonizingly.

He released her, letting her collapse in a whimpering heap at his feet. The cold Power radiated through him, as his hot gaze cataloged their horrified faces. None could meet his eyes; they backed away, swallowing, shaking their heads.

He seated himself, careful of his swollen arm. "Is this how

you treat the bearer of the White Hide? Is this a hero's welcome? Bring me food. Hot roasted liver, thick steaks rich in fat. Now! Or the old woman dies.''

Green Water separated herself from the crowd, ignoring his attention as she gently bent over Broken Branch, attempting to lift her.

"I didn't say she could leave.'' Raven Hunter glared icily.

"I didn't ask you.'' Green Water met his eyes, a strength there he'd never seen before.

He moved quickly, tumbling Green Water aside with his foot.

Overbalanced, she rolled, catching herself on propped hands. Green Water's eyes sparked like flint off granite as she stood, jaw muscles jumping with anger.

I've never noticed how attractive she is. Perhaps she can warm the White Hide for me until Dancing Fox arrives? He chuckled to himself. How long since he'd had a good woman?

He reached down, dragging Broken Branch closer. The old woman huddled over her broken arm, clutching it as she moaned to herself. His eyes didn't leave Green Water's.

"Sit,'' he ordered, gesturing to the ground before him. She started to shake her head as he reached down, gripping the back of the old woman's neck. Green Water froze as Broken Branch stiffened.

"Sit,'' Raven Hunter repeated, voice soft.

"Don't do it!'' Brown Branch raged, slapping and kicking at Raven Hunter. "Your head's blowed up like a walrus bladder. What makes you think we'll obey your foolishness?''

He easily shoved her aside and leaned down to glare into her withered face. "You won't have a choice,'' he said, stroking the Hide. Then he turned back to Green Water. "I said sit!''

Eyes locked with his, Green Water lowered herself, lips twitching, missing no detail of his actions.

Two girls, almost to womanhood, set a hide boiling bag full of meat before him, then darted nervously into the night. After taking note of the silent people, Raven Hunter attacked it with abandon, eating heartily but slowly, knowing the risks of overeating on an empty stomach.

"Where is my brother?'' He looked up, saliva filling his mouth with the blissful taste of fresh meat. Strength, drawn for so long from the White Hide, was replaced in his stomach.

Jumping Hare's tight expression barely changed. "He's out there, in the dark. One Who Cries went to get him."

Raven Hunter cocked his head. "Out in the dark?" He burst out laughing. "My idiot brother's out in the dark when his better comes to lead the tribe into a new land?" He laughed again. "Oh, that's rich, isn't it? That's the man you trusted yourselves to?"

Some of the young men began looking back and forth. The demonstration of Power over Buffalo Back, Broken Branch, and Green Water had shown the White Hide's gift. Raven Hunter nodded, catching their eyes. "Yes, my friends, think of it. You turned your backs on me at Heron's. Thought you'd seen a greater strength than mine, eh?" They lowered their eyes, heads bowing to the validity of his words. "But who comes in out of the night, the White Hide of the Others over his shoulder? And where is Runs In Light? Oh, excuse me. *Wolf Dreamer*." He cocked his head. "What? No answer? It wouldn't be because he's out in the dark . . . *having false Dreams*?"

They all shifted as Raven Hunter continued to eat, rationing himself piece by piece, savoring the taste so as not to bolt the food and vomit.

Green Water's glittering eyes never left him. A defiant woman as well as an attractive one? He'd find a lot of satisfaction in driving himself between her legs. He'd have to kill One Who Cries—or perhaps the coward wouldn't challenge his authority.

"A new land, a new leadership." He wiped his mouth with his sleeve. "You see, from now on, the strong will dictate where the bands move. We've made a mistake all these years listening to the likes of Buffalo Back." He pushed the corpse with his toe. "As a result of their decisions, we're wasted, ground away by war and disease. That won't happen again, I promise. I'll rebuild the People. Make them strong so that no Others anywhere will ever wear us away again. Like the wolves, our strongest will lead."

He looked up, chewing, hearing the young men whispering back and forth. "Do you like that? Would you be wolves? Or like the musk ox, slow and stupid?"

A gleam had settled in the young men's eyes. Raven Hunter smiled. "Yes, you remember the honor I led you to. You remember the strength that was ours before Wolf Dreamer tricked us." He looked around. "What does one do with a witch?"

"You know nothing of Power, young idiot," Broken Branch spat from where she hunched before him. She started to scuttle away, but he hooked a toe under her arm and hauled her back, chewing thoughtfully as he looked down into her hate-filled eyes. Green Water started to her feet as he kicked the old woman to the ground and settled his worn-out long boots over her neck. Green Water froze, fear of him bright in her eyes. The corners of her wide lips trembled.

"A worthless woman, you know?" He chewed and swallowed. "She's borne all the children she'll ever bear for the People. Should have killed her clear back at Mammoth Camp. Remember the discussion we had? About how a woman was good only to grow a man's seed? Now she eats our food, drinks our tea. Without her, there's more for everyone."

"No!" Laughing Sunshine and Curlew rushed forward, stopping as Green Water thrust her hand out.

"That's right." Raven Hunter plucked up another small piece of meat, plopping it in his mouth, feeling life born again in his aching joints. "He who challenges, faces not only me, but the White Hide. You rush forward, the old hag dies. You kill me, the Power of the White Hide is unleashed against the People. I'm the future. I'm destiny. Bring me new long boots, a new parka. This is winter. A leader of the People shouldn't be dressed in rags."

"What of your wounded arm?" Salmon Bone asked.

"A man of Power needs no arm." Raven Hunter yawned, staring at them through slitted eyes. *And still no Runs In Light? Oh, this is good indeed! The Power of the White Hide must have gutted the poor fool, filled him with fear. Real Power has that ability.*

"You're sick," Green Water whispered. "Twisted. Filled by some wretched ghost."

He laughed. "I'd expect a statement like that from someone who doesn't understand—doesn't see with the clarity I do. It's in the Hide. My visions have been true all along."

He smiled at Green Water. "And beginning tonight, I shall plant my seed among the People."

She sucked in her breath. "You wouldn't . . ."

He pressed down slightly on Broken Branch's neck while the People shuffled nervously, the young men's eyes veiled. In the background, Raven Hunter saw One Who Cries start forward, hearing the last. Hard hands grabbed him back, people whispering tersely in his ear.

"People," Raven Hunter added reasonably, "have certain responsibilities to those with Power. I was born of Father Sun's seed! I am the gift of Father Sun—the way to the new life. What woman with sense wouldn't want to share my strength?"

"Me!" Broken Branch hissed from under his foot. Raven Hunter looked down.

"The old way must go." He smiled at her. "As I speak, I'll crush the life out of your thin neck, old hag. The Power of the White Hide—"

"—is nothing in *your* hands!" a strange and powerful voice commanded.

People turned, squinting into the blackness of the forest.

Raven Hunter balanced his foot, the breath wheezing in and out of Broken Branch's constricted throat.

They walked in from the side, ten people. Eagle Cries, Dancing Fox, Crow Foot, and . . . and Ice Fire? Red Flint? Raven Hunter's eyes narrowed, confused.

"No closer," he ordered. "The White Hide's mine! The Power's mine."

Ice Fire walked carefully forward, calmly parting a way through the People. Behind, the Others advanced, Red Flint supported between Singing Wolf and Broken Shaft.

Raven Hunter hunched, grabbing up a corner of the White Hide, kicking Broken Branch ahead of him. "Stop, Ice Fire. Another step, and I throw the White Hide into the fire." He balanced there, Ice Fire halting in his very tracks, a wary look on his handsome face.

"You don't know what that would do."

"Destroy the heart of the Mammoth People. I'd roast your soul!"

The Other warriors tensed, eyes darting back and forth,

fear replacing the haughty distrust in their eyes. Nervously they licked their lips, waiting for Ice Fire.

"And you'd bring the combined clans of the Mammoth People down on you." Ice Fire crossed his arms over his chest. "Oh, the runners are already on the way. So far, only the White Tusk Clan has fought with you. But behind us comes the Buffalo Clan, behind them, the Round Hoof Clan, and last but most deadly comes the Tiger Belly Clan." He shook his head. "The White Hide is very important to us. The man who destroyed it would never be safe. We'd hunt him to the ends of the world."

The frown tightened Raven Hunter's face. "But you said . . ."

Ice Fire smiled wistfully. "I lied."

Raven Hunter's cheek began to twitch. "Lied?" Then he laughed, feeling the Power of the White Hide. "But I fooled you. I was worthy of the Hide. I carried it here. By myself. Up over the rocks, through the ice."

Unminded, Broken Branch scuttled away into the darkness.

"And look at you." Ice Fire shook his head. "Wasted, thin, you look like a starving wolf pup."

Dancing Fox nodded soberly. "That's why you didn't follow me that day. It's destroyed you."

"It's sucked his soul away."

Raven Hunter flinched, heart pounding. No! What did the old man know? The Hide had kept him alive, not harmed him. "I'm—"

"And the caribou?" Ice Fire asked easily. "You turned your back on it. We read the story in the tracks, Raven Hunter. Obsessed with the Hide, you'd starve to serve it. Is that how you'd lead the People?"

Eagle Cries looked back and forth. "What's this about the clans? What about more of them coming?"

Like a wash of cold water, Raven Hunter understood. "You used me," he breathed. "You knew they'd follow! You *knew*!"

Ice Fire stood placidly, looking at him through narrowed eyes. "Of course. The clans of the Mammoth People needed a powerful excuse to follow you south through the ice. Only the White Hide would drive them to it."

Raven Hunter stiffened, weaving on his feet. A nauseated cramping gripped his stomach.

Eagle Cries and the rest shifted slowly away from the jittery Others. Dancing Fox stared about nervously, seeing the lines drawn, aware of the darts being fingered by both sides. Only Ice Fire seemed calm. He smiled serenely.

"There is still time," Eagle Cries added. "We kill the Others, take the White Hide back through the ice. If we left it there, maybe they'd leave us alone. Maybe—"

"No!" Red Flint cried out, ripping loose from Singing Wolf's arms and taking a step, only to crumple to the ground crying out as he reached for the White Hide. "It's not for Enemy hands. It's for the clans . . . the clans alone!"

"I say kill them." Eagle Cries had backed away, Crow Foot and the rest doing the same. The Others dropped into a defensive circle around Ice Fire, Dancing Fox pointedly outside their ring.

"Stop this!" she cried, stepping forward, arms uplifted.

"Our oath ends here," Eagle Cries reminded, a hard set to his lips. "We've brought them safely without raising weapons. But now they're here. My oath is dead!"

Mutters of agreement followed, darts clicking as eager fingers nocked them.

"Others." Raven Hunter sneered. "Brought to a camp of the People." He raised his fist over his head, shouting, *"Kill them!"*

Arms arched back, ready to cast their darts; the Others gripped their weapons for release. Raven Hunter laughed hysterically as he danced from foot to foot, the Power of the White Hide hazing the images of carnage in his mind.

"Wait!" Dancing Fox cried, hands up, standing between the sides. "Wait."

"Die!" Raven Hunter roared.

"He is here?" Wolf Dreamer asked softly as the hurried steps crunched on the snow.

One Who Cries lifted the black flap of the sweat lodge Wolf Dreamer had built of bowed willows and covered with hides. A white gout of steam rolled out.

"He's here," he assented. "You'd better come quick. Broken Branch sent me for you. She says there's going to be trouble. You've got to come.''

Wolf Dreamer cocked his head, seeing the worried patterns of One Who Cries' soul; yellow, red, and orange, they wove together through the man. The bitter taste of the mushrooms coursed in his veins as he watched in fascination.

''It doesn't matter,'' he pronounced seriously. ''Raven Hunter's trouble will pass.''

One Who Cries reeled back, stunned, the colors changing in his soul. ''Of course it matters! What of pain and hurt *now*? What of the People suffering? Curse you, Wolf Dreamer, don't you remember? You were one of us! You're our Dreamer! You've got responsibility. We *need* you!''

''Tell me why you need?''

One Who Cries gasped frustration. He shook his head suddenly. ''Are you so far from us? We're here because of the Dream. For all I know, we are the Dream! We—''

''Yes, now you see.''

''And—and if that's so, you've got to come Dream it all right again!''

''Illusion has no right.''

One Who Cries stifled an anxious cry. Futilely, he beat his fist into the ground. ''Look, I can't argue with you. I just want to hunt in peace, huh? That . . . that's *my* Dream. You must come drive Raven Hunter—''

''Then you should Dream for yourself. Hunt within the illusion to find—''

''Hunt within . . . Great Mammoth!'' One Who Cries exploded. ''Can't you understand we need your Power!''

''You don't need me.''

''Yes, we do! Raven Hunter's coming with some sort of Power . . . some White Hide. You have to go and—''

''It won't matter in the end.''

One Who Cries sputtered and stopped, a dot of blue growing in his soul. Fascinated, Wolf Dreamer watched the blue expand, seeing One Who Cries' desperation become all-encompassing.

Through a strangled voice, One Who Cries choked, ''For the spirals maybe. I don't know.'' And he was gone, steps pounding away across the snow.

''For the spirals,'' Wolf Dreamer repeated, seeing inside

the illusion, feeling Wolf's call. "The spirals of the web. Yes . . ."

He smiled into the blackness, gazing gratefully at the remaining withered black mushrooms resting on the hide in the corner. He got to his feet, walking as if he were a mist. Around him, he could see the colorful souls of the animals, of the trees, each reflecting their own existence in this realm.

Time slipped and bent around him, making each step a journey into a different world, like looking through sections of swirled ice. Images bled into each other, forms shifting, lines bubbling out of shape. Before him, the People stood like a wall of blue-green color. Fear there, anxiety, anger, it all mixed in splashes of vivid colors like the Monster Children battling in the sky, or sunlight through a haze of mist, breaking into bars of colors.

He wove around them, his soul touching theirs, feeling the straining anxiety. Color everywhere, even the fire rose red and yellow from the glowing bed of coals. Two groups separated, the Spirit Power they'd breathed into their darts clinging to the keen stone points. Their souls twisted in red-orange anger and greenish violet fear. Here were souls about to be severed from the body and they couldn't stand it.

There stood Raven Hunter, a weird black swirl lit by a red yellow within, streaked by the spring green of pleasure and ambition. Muscles moved along the warrior's arms, poised to release their darts.

"If you cast against each other, you'll break the spiral," he said softly, projecting his voice to their very souls. "We can't do that and survive."

They froze in their places, turning to stare at him. A white shimmering of curiosity softened their images, all uneasy except for anxious Dancing Fox and the man. The . . .

Wolf Dreamer stopped dead in his tracks.

"So," he greeted, noting the shimmering white fox hides on his shoulder. "We meet, you and I. I offer greetings, Father."

The man nodded, a Power within him, his soul tight and controlled, balanced between spirit and body. "Wolf Dreamer."

"Kill them!" Raven Hunter bellowed from the side. "I am the future of the People. Here lies destruction! Death at the hands of the Others! I have the Power of the White Hide. I'm born of Father Sun! Come to lead—''

"You're born of me," the man said, tone leaving no doubt.

Wolf Dreamer smiled, cocking his head to watch the whirls of white light dance in his father's chest.

"Why did you lie to me?" Raven Hunter insisted.

"To save you." Ice Fire sighed. "I let the White Hide pass judgment on you. You did what you did to yourself. Your soul is—''

"Powerful!" Raven Hunter hissed.

"Your soul is a darkness, brother," Wolf Dreamer said sadly. "You're not whole, Raven Hunter. You have no sharing of the soul."

"Shut up! What do you know of souls, of Dreams? I've seen, seen the future, me and Dancing Fox. My child taking the People south into—''

"You've seen no future of yours," Wolf Dreamer murmured. "You saw only a glimpse of your father's."

Ice Fire frowned, staring. "Mine? What—''

"No, it was mine!" Raven Hunter insisted, slamming a fist into the White Hide.

The Other warriors mumbled in fear and rage, easing forward on cat feet.

Wolf Dreamer bowed his head and watched the flames dance for what seemed an eternity. His thoughts drifted away, images of Heron's visions floating through his mind. Sights, sounds, rising mounds of dirt along a winding muddy river. Rock-walled shelters rising five stories high, the corners of the rooms sharp against the sky. Long shelters, built of bark, all centered around tended fields of long-eared grass, its yellow kernels spilling life upon the mats of the Peoples.

Hunters came, long-limbed men, bearing darts as they stalked the buffalo. As the plains dried, women slapped desert plants, knocking the seeds into woven containers. A long thin creature crawled on its belly, fangs in its head, tail hissing in a buzz. Far to the south, men built mountains of stone while Father Sun descended to earth, plumed in feathers and scales.

"It can be saved." Ice Fire's voice penetrated the Dream. *"Saved . . . saved . . . saved . . ."*

Wolf Dreamer nodded. "Yes. That which has been sundered must become One again."

"Let me help you," Ice Fire offered, striding slowly closer to Wolf Dreamer.

In a shimmering fog, he saw him stop. Wolf Dreamer gently reached out a hand and touched his father's chest, the place the white light flowed from. It warmed him, sending tendrils of harmony rushing through him. Before he realized what had happened, Ice Fire had enfolded him in strong arms and hugged him tightly to his breast.

"My son, you've done well for the People."

Wolf Dreamer's gazed at Dancing Fox. She stood rigidly, though her eyes lay warm on Ice Fire. He widened his eyes, seeing the tiny dot of white light growing in her belly.

"A son . . . for a son," Wolf Dreamer breathed, "now I understand, Heron."

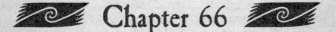 Chapter 66

Wolf Dreamer floated in the bliss of Oneness with his father, eyes blind to the world of illusion fluttering around him.

Through his haze he faintly heard Raven Hunter say, "So, the fawn has lain with the bear. Look, warriors! This will be the death of the People!"

A rumble of hostile voices pierced the stillness.

Reluctantly, Wolf Dreamer pushed Ice Fire away, breaking the embrace, and focused on his brother. Raven Hunter stood tall, chest thrown out arrogantly. His feet straddled the dead body of an old man.

"You killed Buffalo Back," he said softly.

Raven Hunter laughed. "And I'll kill you—as I should have years ago."

As Wolf Dreamer stepped forward, Dancing Fox reached to pull him back.

"Don't do this! He's not worth—"

He smiled at her, and tenderly reached down to lay his hand on the new life that sparkled in her belly. She started, but didn't pull away, gazing up questioningly. "You hold the strands of the web. Did you know? From you it will shoot forth, spiraling across the face of the world."

"What?" she asked feebly.

Tired, he felt suddenly very tired. From the corners of his mind, he heard the faint call, an eerie familiar howl. He turned slowly, looking over his shoulder to the south. From out of the forest, Wolf loped to stand at the edge of the gathering, one foot raised, nose up scenting the air. A tremor shook him. "Is it time?"

"You've shown them the way, man of the People. Come."

Wolf Dreamer swallowed hard and closed his eyes, nodding. Then he turned back to Ice Fire. "Let no one interfere."

"But you can't—" Dancing Fox cried.

Ice Fire's arm restrained her as she started forward. "No one will interfere."

"I call you witch, brother!" Raven Hunter roared, eyes gleaming in hatred. "I'll kill you before you destroy the People!"

Behind him, he heard Dancing Fox plead with Ice Fire, "Let me go, he's not strong enough! Raven Hunter has—"

"No."

Raven Hunter circled the fire cautiously, his good hand gripped into a tight fist. A surge of young warriors followed him, ready for the battle to break out.

"Stop them," One Who Cries shouted, running forward.

"No!" Ice Fire caught him by the shoulder, whirling him around.

"They're *your* sons! You can't let them—"

"It's the Dream!" Ice Fire whispered urgently. "Don't meddle in what you don't understand!"

"But your sons!"

Wolf Dreamer stood serenely, feeling the gaze of Wolf on him as Raven Hunter charged, roaring like a wounded bull, "I'll kill you, brother!"

Wolf Dreamer listened to the words, his soul still reeling from Wolf's presence. For a brief moment, he'd almost forgotten the Dance. Now he whispered with the mushrooms singing in his blood.

"Don't do this, brother," he implored, opening his arms as Raven Hunter stopped in front of him, glaring. "Come, come with me. Our time with the People is over. Come, follow me to the south. Let me cleanse you, let me teach you to Dream."

Around him, the souls of the People glowed, frightened, nervous. Some watched with anticipation, ready, drawn by the violence. Others reflected pain, anxiety filling them. They'd be free soon, these people of his.

Raven Hunter took a step to the side, moving easily. "Even wounded, brother, I'm still more than a match for you. You think your Dream is stronger than me? Stronger than the Power of the White Hide? Look at you, *lost in your head*! You'd lead the People? You? What do you know of *this* world, Wolf Dreamer?"

"He's right," Wolf murmured. The beast's voice echoed from the trees. *"Your time here is done."*

"But I . . . I have to save the People from him." He turned uncertainly, meeting Wolf's yellow eyes. "Don't I?"

"You've already saved them."

Raven Hunter guffawed and gazed around the crowd, pointing at his brother. "Look at him, talking to the air! He's mad. I told you all long ago! And you still followed him."

Wolf Dreamer looked back, seeing the deadly resolve in Raven Hunter's soul as it blackened. "You've chosen." And at that, he stepped around his brother and into the fire, Dancing with the flames as they licked at his flesh. The souls of the People flickered with fear as he bent and plucked the coals from the pit.

Raven Hunter watched nervously, the first signs of uncertainty reflected in the shadows of his soul. Carefully, Wolf Dreamer drew the effigy of Wolf on his face with a searing coal, the same effigy he'd drawn that long-ago day outside of Mammoth Camp. Then he reached for Raven Hunter.

Frightened for the first time, Raven Hunter stepped back, holding his broken arm protectively.

"Come, brother," Wolf Dreamer called, following, arms open. "Step into the Light. Embrace me, let my soul mingle with yours. Opposites crossed. Resolution."

"No!" Raven Hunter crouched and charged. He caught Wolf Dreamer with his one good arm, dragging him out of the fire and smashing him to the frozen earth. The air in his lungs exploded past his teeth. For a second, he Danced with the pain, shifting its illusion away as he gulped for breath.

Raven Hunter slammed his fist repeatedly into Wolf Dreamer's face, bellowing in rage, "You're a witch! I'll kill you, bury you so your soul . . ." Raven Hunter's fingers wrapped themselves around Wolf Dreamer's windpipe, choking off the air. Wolf Dreamer's lungs began to clamor. In the Dance, he watched them begin to turn blue.

"It doesn't matter," he mouthed silently. "Nothing—"

"Stop it! *Stop it!*" Dancing Fox screamed from somewhere far away.

Wolf Dreamer lay still, conscious of his body's struggle for life, feeling his brother's fingers go tighter, hearing Wolf call him again. *"Come . . . Come . . ."*

His soul shivered, longing to follow.

Raven Hunter's scream rippled like a physical thing as it tore through the People, changing the colors of their souls. He leapt up, releasing Wolf Dreamer and standing menacingly over him. "Get up!" he shouted. "Get up and fight!"

Wolf Dreamer gasped for air, lying weakly for a moment before stumbling to his feet. His throat rasped as he drew air into his lungs. A blinding flash caught him as Raven Hunter kicked him in the belly. Wolf Dreamer sat down hard, a warm rush spreading below his heart.

For a moment, he retreated into the nothingness beyond the Dance. With a curious detachment, he looked back at his suffering body. Raven Hunter had kicked him again, flopping his empty flesh sideways to heave and retch on the trampled snow.

Raven Hunter laughed, the black green of his soul sparkling as he bent down and settled his knee on Wolf Dreamer's throat. His body twitched, and Raven Hunter looked up at Dancing Fox, cackling his victory.

From the side, a bent shape scuttled out of the darkness. The soul shifted between red, green, and blue. A sparkling lance of orange-white pain shot up from one of the old woman's arms. Despite the agony it caused her, she crabbed forward, keeping to the shadows behind Raven Hunter as he bellowed victory to the People.

Wolf Dreamer shifted to look back at Wolf. The beast had trotted closer. He stood so close now, Wolf Dreamer could feel his warm breath on his face. *Do I have to go back? Is there a reason to leave the peace, the silence of the One? I don't want to go back. Not even for the brief moment it will take to bring this to a close.*

Wolf only stared, yellow eyes glimmering with the firelight.

Wolf Dreamer Danced back into his body as Broken Branch reached from the shadows. Despite the blinding pain from his crushed throat, despite his burning lungs, he felt the cool polished wood as the old woman thrust it in his grasping hand. The lingering essence of One Who Cries seeped from the worked wood of the foreshaft, caressing his fevered skin. Resolution. He lanced the stone-tipped dart up, following the vibrance of Raven Hunter's hard soul to the center of his brother's Dance.

Raven Hunter stiffened as Wolf Dreamer drove the dart deeply into his side. He knew—with the hunter's skill—where the tender organs of life were most vulnerable.

Somewhere in the shadows, Broken Branch cackled happily.

Raven Hunter whirled slowly in the light of the fire, mouth open, moving soundlessly as he stared around at the People. From the wound, blood coursed down his side and leg, dripping onto the snow in bright scarlet spots.

He blundered through the fire pit, traces of flame eating up the sides of his long boots. He shrieked loudly as the coals burned through the holes in his boot soles. Howling in agony and fear, Raven Hunter bolted into the night.

In the silence, the People watched, their souls wavering in a panoply of light.

The world spinning, Wolf Dreamer turned to his father. "Once you looked into the night sky and saw the Spider among the stars. And now his web has begun to spiral. A son . . . for a son."

"*Come . . .*" Wolf's haunting voice called, and he felt a familiar velvet nose nudge his hand.

He looked down and held the beast's eyes for a moment.

Then Wolf turned and trotted to the edge of the trees, waiting.

He followed on rubbery legs, staggering toward the darkness, the mushrooms whispering with anticipation.

"Wait," One Who Cries called, coming along behind. "Where are you going?"

Wolf Dreamer reached out a trembling hand, touching One Who Cries, feeling his warm soul. "Where you can't come, old friend. To a place Wolf calls me."

"Wolf?" One Who Cries stood, a lost look on his face as he shook his head, but he stayed, watching as Wolf Dreamer faded into the dark trees.

From the shadows behind him, Broken Branch's ancient voice whispered, "Wolf Dream!"

The camp had been placed on the edge of the timber. There, a shoulder of the hills provided protection from the north winds, while from the heights, the People could see for a day's march or more over the sprawling grasslands to the south. On the gentle slopes below the camp, thick fall grasses waved in the wind. Far to the south, a range fire sent a gray-brown plume of smoke to the cloud-puffed sky. A large herd of buffalo splotched the rolling lands to the east while several mammoth grouped together under the watchful eye of an old cow in the lush drainage below. Another of the marvelous new animals—the pronghorn—ghosted fleetly across the grasslands, following in the wake of the buffalo.

One Who Cries shifted and shot a look over his shoulder at the sienna-colored lodge. "You'd think it wouldn't take so long."

Singing Wolf lifted a shoulder. "It always takes so long." Practiced fingers whittled away at the dart foreshaft he crafted so carefully.

"Can't figure. You make the best foreshafts. They have to be fit just right. A little bend and *poof!* The dart doesn't work. Can't understand how come I can't make them like that."

"Same reason I can't make a point like yours."

"Binding's still too thick." One Who Cries frowned pensively at the point he pulled from his pouch.

They sat silently for a while, One Who Cries running his

eyes over the colorful chert, Singing Wolf shaving long slivers of wood from the foreshaft.

"Moon Water still mad at Jumping Hare?"

"Does the sun come up in the east?"

"What are they doing together? You'd think he'd kick her out. That woman's nothing but trouble."

"She could be trouble in my robes anytime." Singing Wolf chuckled. "You saw what happened. What's she going to do? Go back to Red Flint's lodge? After Jumping Hare came in and offered a stack of robes as tall as a man for her? Not only that, but Red Flint got three of our darts from him! No, she's not leaving. Besides, those twin kids of hers are still his."

One Who Cries sucked in his cheeks and chewed them. "And to think we used to war with White Tusk Clan?" He looked absently out to the south. "You think Wolf Dreamer knew it would be like this?"

"Yes."

Ice Fire came to squat next to them. "I think he saw it all—and more."

"You look nervous," Singing Wolf pointed out. "Don't be. I've been through it five times now. It's always the same."

Ice Fire smiled too quickly as he rubbed his palms back and forth. "Five times? For me . . . this is a first."

"Green Water will take good care of her. Not only that, Broken Branch is in there. No bad spirit will fool with Broken Branch. White Hide goes to Tiger Belly Clan again?"

"You've seen any Enemy here we could earn it from?" Ice Fire pulled his white-shot hair back. "No, I think Tiger Belly will have the White Hide for a long time now."

"Water's still rising. After a while, they'll have to find honor somewhere else."

Ice Fire laughed. "They'll think of something."

One Who Cries turned the point and shook his head. "Too much binding."

Ice Fire cocked his head, trying to take his thoughts off the activities in the lodge behind him. "How about driving two flakes off from the base forward? You know, like grooves."

One Who Cries studied the base of the point. A skeptical look on his weather-beaten face, he pulled his sandstone from his pouch and between grinding and some initial flaking, prepared two special platforms.

"Here goes." His tongue crept out the side of his mouth as he frowned in concentration. Like lightning, he tapped the baton across the platform, a long thinning flake snapping out of the point base.

Ice Fire beamed as One Who Cries turned the colorful stone over. He eyed the point again and grinned, driving the second flake from the other side.

"Hey!" Singing Wolf exploded. "Now, cut that out! Every time I sit down you're—"

"Oh, hush! 'Cut it out . . . Cut it out.' That's all I ever hear from you. Every time I start doing a little flint knapping, you're howling about the flakes being all over! When was the last time you got stuck with one of my—"

"How about the point?" Ice Fire asked from the side.

One Who Cries sheepishly mumbled, "Oh, yeah."

He lifted it. The length of a man's hand, it gleamed in the sun, flake scars rippling to catch the light. It was made from red-banded caramel-colored chert, its parallel sides ending in a keen point. The base was concave below the new flake scar. One Who Cries turned it over.

"It worked," One Who Cries said breathlessly. "Look!" He grabbed the foreshaft from Singing Wolf's hand, fitting the fluted point into the binding. "That's it!"

Ice Fire and Singing Wolf leaned close, sighs of admiration escaping their lips.

"You know," Ice Fire mused. "That's almost too pretty to throw into an animal."

One Who Cries glowed.

Behind them, the voices of the women grew louder. Ice Fire stiffened. Even Singing Wolf—old veteran that he was—cocked his head, eyes tense.

The squall of the child carried shrill in the still air.

Moments later, Broken Branch hobbled out of the tent, beaming a toothless smile through her wrinkles.

"A boy." She chuckled. "Ha-heeee! As if the Dreamer hadn't known!"

A curious feeling swelled in Ice Fire's chest. "A son for a son. Yes . . ." For a moment, he twisted his hands nervously in his lap, thinking about Wolf Dreamer. They'd searched for him that night after the fight, but had found no traces—not even tracks marred the snow.

But the wolves had howled triumphantly for days.

"And my wife? How's Dancing Fox?"

"Oh, fine. Just fine."

Broken Branch hobbled in front of Ice Fire, heading to the fire glowing a few feet away. She held the baby up to Father Sun, then passed him through the cleansing smoke of the fire four times.

"Listen, boy," Broken Branch ordered softly. "I'm going to tell you the greatest story of the People. You have to remember it so you can tell your sons and daughters and their sons and daughters. You're the center of the web, little one. Your brother, Wolf Dreamer, said so and he was the greatest Dreamer the People ever had. He knew. He *knew* . . .

"See? Do you?" Broken Branch lifted a withered arm and pointed out across the lush valley bursting with game. *"Look there:*

Built a big mountain of dirt.
Raised on sweat and hurt.
Rose so high over the river. Eating plants.
Bah! No spirit in that. Not like blood-filled liver.
Father of Waters, flows so rich . . ."

Singing Wolf laughed softly, waggling a finger at Ice Fire. "See. I told you it would go all right. Dancing Fox is too tough to . . . *OUCH!"*

"What's wrong now?" One Who Cries wondered, staring at his point.

"What's this?" Singing Wolf held out his hand. A red-banded yellow chert flake to match the one driven from One Who Cries' point stuck deeply into the meaty part of his palm.

Ice Fire started to laugh but a faint soft mewing came from the bundle in Broken Branch's arms and a strange feeling came over him. His chest tingled with hollowness.

He shook himself, but the feeling wouldn't let him go. Crossing his arms, he hugged himself tightly. His eyes were drawn to the valley in the distance. Thick green grasses waved beneath the gentle caress of Wind Woman. Mammoth lifted his shaggy head, startled suddenly, as though he too saw the silvered shadow that bounded through the grass, bushy tail catching the glittering gold of dawn as it ran to touch noses with musk ox and caribou, mouse and buffalo.

Almost like a whisper in his mind, Ice Fire heard a beautiful voice say: "This is the land of the People . . . I show you the way, man . . . I show you the way . . ."

HISTORICAL NOVELS
OF THE AMERICAN FRONTIERS

DON WRIGHT

☐ 58991-2 THE CAPTIVES $4.50
☐ 58992-0   Canada $5.50

☐ 58989-0 THE WOODSMAN $3.95
☐ 58990-4   Canada $4.95

DOUGLAS C. JONES

☐ 58459-7 THE BAREFOOT BRIGADE $4.50
☐ 58460-0   Canada $5.50

☐ 58457-0 ELKHORN TAVERN $4.50
☐ 58458-9   Canada $5.50

☐ 58453-8 GONE THE DREAMS AND DANCING $3.95
           (Winner of the Golden Spur Award)
☐ 58454-6   Canada $4.95

☐ 58450-3 SEASON OF YELLOW LEAF $3.95
☐ 58451-1   Canada $4.95

EARL MURRAY

☐ 58596-8 HIGH FREEDOM $4.95
☐ 58597-6   Canada 5.95

Buy them at your local bookstore or use this handy coupon:
Clip and mail this page with your order.

Publishers Book and Audio Mailing Service
P.O. Box 120159, Staten Island, NY 10312-0004

Please send me the book(s) I have checked above. I am enclosing $_____
(please add $1.25 for the first book, and $.25 for each additional book to
cover postage and handling. Send check or money order only—no CODs.)

Name _____

Address _____

City _____ State/Zip _____

Please allow six weeks for delivery. Prices subject to change without notice.

MORE
HISTORICAL NOVELS
OF THE AMERICAN FRONTIERS